BREATHING HERE IS INJURIOUS TO YOUR HEALTH

The Human Cost of Air Pollution and How You Can Be the Change

Jyoti Pande Lavakare

hachette INDIA

First published in 2020 by Hachette India
(Registered name: Hachette Book Publishing India Pvt. Ltd)
An Hachette UK company
www.hachetteindia.com

SRD

ISBN 978-93-89253-10-8

Hachette Book Publishing India Pvt. Ltd
4th & 5th Floors, Corporate Centre,
Plot No. 94, Sector 44, Gurugram 122003, India

Typeset in Perpetua Std 11/13.5
by R. Ajith Kumar, New Delhi

Printed and bound in India
by Manipal Technologies Limited, Manipal

FSC www.fsc.org
MIX
Paper from responsible sources
FSC™ C104740

BREATHING HERE IS INJURIOUS TO YOUR HEALTH

Jyoti Pande Lavakare is a financial journalist who has worked for both the national (*Economic Times*) and international press (Dow Jones Newswires) between 1990–2002, reporting from South Asia, and has also written regular columns on start-ups and the entrepreneurial ecosystem, for the *Business Standard*, *New York Times* blog (*India Ink*) and *Economic Times*. From 2013 she began working in the area of air pollution and co-founded Care For Air in 2015, first as a platform to build awareness and advocate for clean air, then as a registered non-profit.

PRAISE FOR THE BOOK

'As we are born into this wondrous planet, it is our first big gulp of air that teaches us how to survive outside of our mother's womb. Air, that invisible thing that we inhale and exhale every day of our lives. It is our breath that ensures we are alive. Our right to life is underlined by our ability to breathe clean air.

For the millions of children, elderly and people that breathe toxic polluted air each day of their lives, the full extent of [the] damage this causes their health is still to be fully understood. 14 of the 21 most polluted cities of the world are in India. Air pollution is a huge environmental risk to human health. Asthma, croup, COPD, cancer and other serious illnesses are caused by air pollution. The solutions exist to beat air pollution; what is missing is the personal and political will. This book can change this. Jyoti has written a deeply personal and powerful book that I believe will evoke our empathy and our action. A must read!'

– **Dia Mirza**, Actor, Producer, UN Environment Goodwill Ambassador and United Nations Secretary-General's Advocate for Sustainable Development Goals

BREATHING HERE IS INJURIOUS TO YOUR HEALTH

To my mother and Anjaneya

You that seek what life is in death,
Now find it air that once was breath.
New names unknown, old names gone:
Till time end bodies, but souls none.
Reader! then make time, while you be,
But steps to your eternity.

– Baron Brooke Fulke Greville, 'Caelica 83: You that seek what life is in death'

Contents

Prologue

Never

January 2018

I am on my way to drop my daughter at New Delhi's international airport for her flight back to university when my mother's heart stops beating. This time, she isn't going to revive, though I don't know that yet.

'How bad is it?' my husband asks, his voice carefully neutral as he peers through the grey miasma of Delhi air and expertly navigates the crush of vehicles. I hug my daughter tighter as I look out at the ubiquitous blue metal barriers installed by the Delhi Metro Railway Corporation, half-crushed scaffolding and construction debris that have narrowed our lane, slowing us down further.

Idling traffic growls and beeps around us – two-wheeler riders in their helmets and puffy jackets, autorickshaw drivers muffled up against the January cold so that I can only see visors and eyes. The scene looks eerie and dystopian in the smoggy light of a weak morning sun. I can smell the pollution. As an active clean-air campaigner for the past four years, I have become something of an expert at this. This morning's air feels particularly heavy with particulate matter (PM) and sulphur and nitrous oxides from the traffic. Heavy and cold. Toxic.

'Is *naani* worse?' asks my teenage son. I hear the concern in his voice, feel my daughter's body tense up, my husband's hands tighten on the steering wheel as they wait for my reply.

From the first light of that grey morning, the WhatsApp group I'm on with my siblings has been buzzing with updates about my mother, punctuating existing stress with additional sorrow. Another cardiac episode. But because there have been previous ones like this, beginning with a first, critical one 14 days go, on New Year's Eve, during which a visiting overseas relative, a physician, quickly and efficiently jump-started her heart with epinephrine, I'm unsure how serious this is. I don't know if her heart is resilient enough to withstand another bradycardia episode.

'I don't know. It always sounds bad. What shall I do?' I ask no one in particular. I look at my phone again, scanning for updates, a nervous tic that I've recently developed. My eyes have begun to water. I can sense the beginnings of the familiar, dull pollution-induced headache kicking in as vehicular fumes find their way into the car despite the tightly closed windows.

'Don't worry, Mom. She revived last time. She'll be okay.'

My daughter rests her head on my shoulder, her wayward curls spilling over. I stroke them absently, chewing my lip till it hurts. She is my eldest, our family's sweet glue, and I've spent the last year preparing myself to let her go. This will be her second term away, and I've had time to get used to her absence, of a family getting smaller, but it is still an unfamiliar feeling. I really want to see her off peacefully, spend a few calm moments of affection with her – the morning has been an anxious rush of last-minute instructions, packing, checklists and reminders, leaving no time to express love. But.

The tinny pings of WhatsApp notifications are creating a delicate mesh of invisible tension inside the car, as imperceptible as the toxic particles swirling in the air outside. I feel paralysed with indecision, torn between generations.

'Do you want to get off? Get an Uber and go to her?' my husband asks as the stalled traffic around us begins moving sluggishly, the sounds of revving and honking announcing a green light.

We are halfway to the airport when the messages increase in urgency and crescendo. So, I quickly book an Uber and get off at the next signal.

But in the short time it takes me to reach my mother, she is gone. Her body is still warm when I arrive, but her pulse is a flat line.

Her room smells of apples and disinfectant. The blue walls look down silently, sympathetic witnesses to the saga that began here exactly 42 days ago, when I brought my mother back from the hospital in an ambulance, exactly a week after a failed dose of chemotherapy had landed her in the intensive care unit (ICU). At that time, this room had resounded with a great bustle of activity, my older sisters standing by, ready to receive us, the newly acquired hospital bed angled just so, medical instruments, monitors, air purifiers whirring in place, everything disinfected, sparkling clean. Ambulance personnel had carried her stretcher up the narrow stairs, even as a nurse, an attendant and I flapped around, trying to screen her from the eyes of curious onlookers who had gathered amorphously around us.

Voices had echoed down the granite stairs, instructions shouted out, a nervous excitement in the air as the entire family worked in unison and hope. We learnt to read an oximeter, work the BiPAP, understand the medication and interpret the high-pitched squeaks and beeps of the different machines the home-nursing staff hooked her onto. Of all these, the BiPAP, the bi-level positive airway pressure machine, an almost-ventilator was the most critical, pushing air into her lungs, forcing her to breathe.

'Tight, like this,' the nurse had said as she taught us how to fit its round, silicon mask over my mother's delicate nose and generous mouth. I didn't know this then, but the machine is often used to treat chronic obstructive pulmonary disease (COPD) – an umbrella term for lung and respiratory diseases that make breathing difficult. It is lifelong smokers who usually end up with COPD. It was this BiPAP machine that my mother would slowly begin to depend on, her sweet voice slowly fading into a hoarse whisper as she chanted 'mask, mask' every time one of us removed it, to feed, brush or groom her – or just see her vanishing smile. Sometimes, it seemed to be the only thing keeping her alive.

Forty-two days ago, I didn't know it would come to this. At the time, all I understood was what the nurse told me – that the rhythmic beep and whirr of that machine signified that my mother was alive and breathing, even if not completely on her own.

Now, sitting in the quiet room by my mother's still body, stroking her almost unlined face – her suffering drained away, her expression peaceful at last – I suddenly realize what is different. The machines have fallen silent, their tinny periodic whistles hopelessly mute in a farewell that has only just begun. The only sound that burrows through is the low, relentless whirr of the air purifier in her room. Nothing else.

It is when I exhale that I realize I have been holding my breath.

It feels as if I have been holding my breath forever. From that first phone call on the night of Diwali in 2017, when I had rushed inside from lighting tiny terracotta diyas outside in the garden to answer the phone and heard my brother-in-law's voice in disoriented disbelief. Those words: *lung cancer. Stage four.* They didn't belong here, in my house, in my life. They could not be connected with my mother. *Malignancy.* Words that felt like a whip. *Metastasis. Adenocarcinoma.* Words that reverberated louder than the firecrackers going off outside. *Pleural mesothelioma.* My mother was a non-smoker, a Hindustani classical vocalist. There was no history of cancer in our family that I knew of. *Lymph node biopsy. PET scan.*

Of course, it is all a mistake, I told myself. A lie. But who would play such a cruel trick? She'd gone for a regular medical check-up. Well, maybe a little more than that. A check-up because she'd been feeling 'a little breathless' and that was annoying her.

That Diwali night, dimmed of all light, was less than three months ago, but it feels like a lifetime has gone by. It is no trick. Not a lie. One instant, I'm with my children, watching a lit-up Delhi sky, its sulphurous fumes overpowering the vanishing fragrance of frangipani and harsingar, explaining to them a Supreme Court judgement that has banned the sale of firecrackers to fight pollution, and in the next, I'm listening to a voice of doom sentencing my mother to death. *Terminal.* The realization settled around me like a shroud. My mother was going to die. Not eventually, in the nebulous future, but in the sharp, immediate finite. Within moments of becoming aware of that truth, I knew I would never be the same again. What I didn't know then was *how* I would change. As I caress the still-warm body of my mother – whose musical voice, the slow *alaaps* and rapid *taans*, the melodious gymnastics I will never hear again – I am about to find out.

Everything is still. I feel like I am floating. After the morning's hectic activity preceding our airport run, this feels surreal. I feel spent, empty. There is no emotion left. The silence around my mother has an entirely different quality, and I absorb it, soaking it into my skin, into my blood and bones, right into the centre of my soul. Inside that silence, my mother lies still on her bed, in her room with the blue walls – and I wonder where she really is.

'You just missed the rude doctor who came in and declared her dead.' I hear my nephew's voice before I feel his presence. He has entered silently and looks at me, dry-eyed, then opens his arms. I rise and hug him, his strong young body feeling so different from my mother's soft, fragile one. He has already ordered an icebox and called the crematorium on my father's instructions. He had all the numbers he needed on speed dial. We have been prepared. So well prepared. All that is left to do is to inform the relatives.

It is only later that I will realize how ill-prepared we really were, despite those early hours and days passing by in a series of well-orchestrated moves, from choosing an electric cremation over wood burning to locating a priest who knew how to conduct last rites specific to my family's cultural context.

Because how do you prepare for the loss of the one who gave birth to you, the keeper of your memories – even the unformed ones, the ones you don't remember, the ones you didn't know how to articulate into stories? How do you prepare to let go of the one who'd forgive all your faults, even the ones – especially the ones – they always complained to you about?

A rush of unhappy memories from the last three months begins to swirl. From that day in October when I got the news to a week later when my pathologist friend validated the biopsy, confirming the diagnosis, to my mother's birthday when, instead of celebrating, she packed for her hospital admission. Then, more tests, the hope in her eyes fading as she tried to understand what was happening, then tried not to.

The first line of treatment for her lung cancer failed in mid-November, the medicine targeted to limit the growth of the cancer cells having no effect on the fluid building up in her lungs. I could sense the optimism of her attending oncologist dimming. But he was too seasoned to let her see it. 'Well, it's too bad that the EGFR test hasn't given us the report we wanted,' he told my mother, holding her hands in his own, smiling into her anxious eyes, his jovial voice at variance with the shadow on his face. 'That would have helped the Erlotinib target the cancer cells effectively. Next step: chemotherapy.'

My mother shrank back, her hopeful smile fading as she looked around for my father, shaking her head at him. It took us a week to persuade her – after we had persuaded each other, because none of us was convinced about chemotherapy to begin with and spent hours arguing, googling, debating and prevailing upon each other, convincing ourselves that we had no real choice, that we must give it a chance.

'A baby dose,' the oncologist reassuringly called it.

And so, it seeped into her blood one Saturday in November, as the sky outside turned grey and grim with smog that was building up in the city. Farmers in neighbouring states had started burning crop stubble as usual, the seething smoke beginning to shroud Delhi in the uncomfortably familiar way that typified the city's winters. But we were too busy with our own darkening thoughts to notice that the air outside was closing in on us, like my mother's mortality.

Why? Why her? A non-smoker with no family history of cancer. No symptoms. This question consumed me in the initial days. However, other more action-oriented questions around her immediate care took precedence in the brief moments that the doctors spared for us – including, now that the Epidermal Growth Factor Receptor (EGFR) test had failed, could we afford the next-generation sequencing test as a last resort?

One day I found myself in the hospital elevator with her attending pulmonologist. 'Why?' I asked him. 'Why my mother?' He looked up from his phone, his private smile fading as he recognized me and said, almost indifferently, as if I should know the answer already, 'Aren't you the daughter who works in air pollution? And didn't you say she's lived in north India all her life? Then why are you asking this? There's really nothing else that explains "why her" except the foul air she has breathed all her life.'

I felt like he had punched me. Because, chillingly, I did know, I realized, at least in theory. Wasn't this in the fifth slide of the introductory PowerPoint that my clean-air non-profit Care For Air (CFA) presented, the one titled 'The Health Impact of Air Pollution'? My co-founders at CFA and I must have told thousands of listeners in schools, resident welfare associations (RWAs), hospitals, and even on the television panels that I'd started appearing in, how exposure to air pollution can trigger lung cancer, heart attacks, strokes, diabetes, obesity, autism and dementia, among a host of other non-communicable diseases.

How different it was, to know in your head and to know in your heart.

He stepped out of the elevator. I followed. A team of nurses and resident doctors were waiting for him to begin the morning rounds.

'But there were no symptoms, Doctor. She was perfectly fine,' I could hear my voice rising. Not even a cough. Just a little breathlessness...' But he was gone.

As I stood in the long hospital corridor, watching the disappearing trail of white-coated doctors and their nurse-attendants flow seamlessly from room to room, the words of another thoracic surgeon – with whom I had recently begun collaborating to spread awareness about pollution as a part of my clean-air evangelism – came back to haunt me.

Just months ago, Dr Arvind Kumar, who heads chest surgery at Delhi's Sir Ganga Ram Hospital's Centre for Chest Surgery, and I had been discussing the health hazards of breathing in polluted air and how it affected human lungs – something he had first-hand experience with, having treated thousands of lungs, healthy and diseased, in his surgical practice at the large private hospital.

'In Delhi today we are all smokers from our first breath, whether we've ever held a cigarette in our hands [or not]. We all have smokers' lungs,' Dr Kumar had said, corroborating what I'd learnt from reading public health research. 'This is why lung cancer cases are on the rise.'

Breathing, it seems, had become the new smoking.

I thought of how long it had taken me to start questioning the quality of the air I breathed after I moved back to Delhi from California in 2009. Four years. Four years before discovering, independently, and then together with other questioning minds, that the beautiful misty haze that made the Delhi horizon look ethereal to so many people was noxious and slowly, silently, killing us. Many of those friends had turned into environmental migrants, fleeing the city because of the pollution as they gradually discovered the evidence and science behind it. I wondered if I would have moved my young family to Delhi had I known how lethal the air was.

'But the paradox of lung cancer is that although it is increasing and killing more and more people, it is one of those cancers that is 100 per cent preventable', I had heard Dr Kumar repeat often. 'Hundred. Per cent. Preventable.'

He and I had frequently discussed on various pollution forums how lung cancer can reach its terminal stage silently and asymptomatically. He had told me how almost 80 per cent of lung cancer cases were usually diagnosed at a very late stage, leading to a high case fatality ratio.

'God has given us 70 per cent more lung capacity than we need, because lungs are crucial to life,' he had said once as we stood in the smoggy shadow of India Gate, waiting for a television crew to set up cameras. 'But what this also means is that by the time doctors find out the extent of damage to the lungs from any disease, it is usually too late.'

My mother was now living this 'too late' time warp. Too late. It seemed that my mother's only fault was that she was a long-time resident of Delhi.

Through the years of researching the science behind pollution, building awareness and advocating for clean air, I had never imagined that the horrific ill effects of pollution were sitting in my own backyard, coalescing in the lungs of my mother. Yet, here she was, struggling to breathe as doctors discussed over her head whether to insert another needle into her lung to drain out the fluid building up endlessly inside through what they called a 'pigtail' or to artificially obliterate the cavity between the lung linings by sticking the pleura together so that the resulting adhesion didn't allow any fluid pus or blood to build up between the layers. 'Pleurodesis?' they consulted with each other as my mother looked hopefully up at them from her hospital bed and I looked down at her, imagining this feisty woman as another statistic in a lung cancer roster.

Dr Kumar's observations were based on increasing cases of lung cancer in Delhi, which he began flagging as an 'epidemic' in 2017. His anecdotal observations fit neatly in with my own remembered evidence, data, facts and research. He told me that in his surgical practice, until recently, he used to see more men, mostly smokers. But now, he says, he increasingly sees more women – non-smokers, younger – whose lungs, instead of being a healthy pink, are a smoky black.

'I now see black lungs even in infants,' Dr Kumar says.

His words remind me of another CFA slide, an almost macabre image the air pollution awareness and advocacy platform has been sharing since 2015 to demonstrate how air pollution affects human lungs. These photographs – of the pulsating black lungs of a 52-year-old Delhi resident juxtaposed with the healthy pink lungs of a 55-year-old resident of Himachal Pradesh – were taken by Dr Naresh Trehan, a cardiothoracic surgeon of repute, during his surgeries. He had first shared these images publicly with *India Today* magazine in 2015, several months after we – a self-selected bunch of professionals, mostly concerned parents – created CFA. We had immediately incorporated these images in our presentation, using them to talk about the negative impact of toxic air on human health in an attempt to make the invisible harm visible.

If breathing is the new smoking and smoking kills, then breathing in Delhi kills.

I'd only recently begun to realize that it wasn't just Delhi. Most of India has poor air quality. Whether it is Mumbai, Kolkata, Chennai, with the sea and riverine breeze to blow it all away, or Bengaluru with its gusts of rain to wash away the toxins – all had poor air quality all year round. The difference was just in degrees.

Meanwhile, I felt a slow-burning anger grow inside me when pulmonologists and other doctors attending to my mother mentioned that it was air pollution that had most likely triggered her lung disease. How could they be so casual? And if this was such common knowledge, why weren't there more warnings and alerts as with other public health emergencies? Why weren't more doctors and hospitals calling out this invisible killer? Especially since, as Dr Kumar said, lung cancer was 'hundred per cent preventable'.

At the time, I didn't have the mind-space to get deeper into these issues, didn't want to think about how pollution had seeped into my mother's lungs – and was probably seeping into mine and into the lungs of others I loved. All I wanted to know was if there was any chance that chemotherapy, radiation, *anything,* would give her a few more years. Good years.

We found out soon enough. The 'baby' dose of chemotherapy was more than my mother could handle. Calling it a cute name didn't change the toxicity of the cocktail of chemicals that should have killed the cancer cells and left my mother unharmed. Four days after it dripped into her body, she took an unexpected turn for the worse and was rushed into the ICU at 2 a.m. Groggy with sleep, exhausted from just looking at her suffering, I half ran, half walked with the green-uniformed attendants as they wheeled her down the corridor into an elevator, then through another maze of corridors and past two sets of double doors beyond which I couldn't accompany her. She looked at me, her eyes dazed, her face swollen, her hair damp with sweat and other body fluids and asked for my father. That was the last time I saw her without a BiPAP mask.

My mother's stay in the ICU affected her deeply. In there, she became just another body, to be monitored, fed, changed and tolerated by young nurses whose eyes gave away nothing, who had seen too many deaths, too close, too often. There was too much death coiled inside those plastic-curtained alcoves, cocooned inside hearts and lungs and kidneys and pancreas, waiting to uncoil and strike, too many sights, sounds and smells of decay.

Something else happened inside the ICU, a medical issue that none of us ever fully understood, and doctors shied away from explaining. Something that caused my mother's heart to weaken, her will to fade.

Since then, I've learnt about ICU psychosis, in which patients experience anxiety, hear voices or suffer paranoia. But even without this knowledge then, as a family, we vowed never to make her endure this again if we could help it. Her oncologist supported my mother's desperate attempt to get out of the ICU. In fact, he seemed to suggest we could even take her home.

'Are you telling us there is nothing more you can do?' I asked him incredulously the day after she was moved from the ICU to the regular ward. His normally optimistic facade had suddenly slipped, his boyish face suddenly unhappy.

Then he seemed to pull himself together. His eyes through his stylish spectacles looked back at me steadily. 'I'm saying that you have a window, a very short window of time, to move her home, if that's what you all want. The hospital and I personally fully support palliative care,' he replied, his measured voice devoid of all emotion.

I felt breathless with anger and frustration.

'But won't she get better care here? Won't we be reducing her chances of a longer life if we take her home?' I persisted, refusing to understand what his eyes were telling me.

'Hospitals have protocols and policies, especially for emergency situations like what happened on Wednesday,' he said in his clipped voice. 'As a doctor, I won't be able to intervene in established protocols if she is critical and needs to be hooked up to a ventilator, conscious or unconscious.' The words tripped off his tongue smoothly, making me wonder how often he must have had to say the same thing. For a moment, we looked at each other wordlessly. Then, suddenly, urgently, lowering his voice to almost a whisper, he said, 'You have a tiny window. Just take her home. Go.' He had a weary compassion in his eyes.

But I couldn't let go.

'You said she was very well preserved for her age! That all her organs are untouched by the disease! That she would come out of this, if she fought it!' I could hear my voice rising. I didn't want compassion. I wanted the look I had seen last week, when he was thinking of next steps, his voice sparkling with optimism, his smile genuinely upbeat.

But when his eyes slid past me to the next patient's relative, I knew he was done.

Maybe he was just saving us from the final indignities of begging for more time while she remained captive in the ICU and wasn't going to sacrifice us to the hospital's commercial, churning machinery. I'd heard enough horror stories of large Indian hospitals keeping dead people hooked up to life support machines for days to make more money.

Already, our family had been riven by arguments over whether to go ahead with chemotherapy. Now, after its colossal failure, and my mother's rapid decline into dependence on a half ventilator and multiple machines, our options were severely limited. She was also getting weaker at a rapid pace.

Even though I wasn't my mother's beloved firstborn, nor her second, nor even the son she had so desired, she and I shared a unique bond. Towards the end of her life, that bond, steeped in music, coloured with art and home aesthetics, tightly woven with every ephemeral *alaap* and *taan* she ever taught me, mutated into one of trust and dependence as she asked me difficult questions about her illness and leant on me for medical advice. I had become the de facto coordinator of her medical treatment – all queries related to doctors, diagnoses, treatment, devices were filtered through my knowledge parameters and networks. In turn, I leant on my nephew, young, strong and preternaturally wise. Too afraid of what I might find, I didn't google tests, treatments, prognosis. Instead, I asked trusted friends who were physicians, diagnosticians, laboratory technicians or just survivors of similar experiences for help and advice.

Sometimes, our whole family pooled its resources, drawing strength from each other. At other times, we fought, angry that this was happening to us, frustrated with the system, the trust deficit we had with it sometimes transferring to each other, frittering away our meagre energies on bitter bickering and one-upmanship.

My father and I went over finances and budgets of how long he could afford to pay for high-end hospice-type home care. His insurance was generous and would take care of all hospital bills as long as my mother remained in hospital. It would be much easier to keep her at the hospital where the responsibility for her health and life belonged to professionals. But with the doctors suddenly seeming to give up on her after the second line of treatment failed, there seemed no point in keeping her there in limbo, vulnerable to hospital-acquired infections. We were going to take Mom home. That, we decided, was that.

But how do you remove someone from hospital who is struggling to breathe and is hooked up to a machine pushing oxygenated air into her airways, whose lungs are attached to a plastic bag via a fluid-draining catheter and whose every medical parameter needs to be constantly monitored? I was soon to discover the existence of the medical home-care industry. As I sat with my mother while the discharge and billing process began, outside her window, emerald-green trees beckoned invitingly, misty silhouettes swaying gently in the wind – at least her hospital room on the sixth floor had an unfettered view of the outdoors, I thought bitterly. If I didn't know how toxic that mushroom-cloud-like air was, I would have found the view beautiful. Somewhere below us, deep in the bowels of this shiny hospital, the machinery grinding the paperwork for my father's government-sponsored insurance churned slowly, and I waited for it to spit us out, as my mother struggled to breathe, the monitors beeping and purring. How could it have come to this so quickly?

But if I think about it now, it wasn't quick. My mother had been living in north India all her life. Her condition probably deteriorated in tandem with the decline in air quality. Perhaps that serious attack of pneumonia she had had 10 years ago when I was abroad had been the first sign of the disease, of her weakening lungs.

A thin needle had been draining out the endlessly forming pleural fluid in her left lung that made her breathless, collecting it into a plastic bag. Now, a new machine, BiPAP, pushed air into her lungs. I looked around the room. There were no air purifiers.

It was a difficult morning, sticky and thick like tar with unmade decisions. Against Medical Advice – an unfamiliar term that reminded me that the world would continue to exist, even as my mother would not.

The day we finally brought my mother home was muddy, dusty, the typical shadowy Delhi haze hanging low, held close to the earth by dropping temperatures, blurring outlines of buildings and trees.

I didn't know it then, but this was the last journey she would take with me alive.

Once we brought her home that final time, the family's position became clear and unexpectedly unanimous, given that we were all highly opinionated individuals – four siblings, their spouses and their children. My usually indecisive ex-bureaucrat father had taken the lead in deciding that prolonging the life of a terminally ill lung cancer patient, bedridden, immuno-compromised and unable to breathe on her own – whose dignity was being compromised diaper by ugly diaper, and who had almost no agency left except to look at us with those pleading, haunting eyes, begging to be put back on the BiPAP – would be an unforgivable betrayal of someone he had shared 63 active years of his life with.

And later, when it got worse and she stopped eating, it was he again who took the decision not to force-feed her via a tube. And, when her heart sank, it was he, white-haired and watery-eyed, who barred the home nurse from using adrenaline, reminding her to keep with the DNR covenant – 'Do Not Resuscitate'. So easy to say. So hard to do.

My mind travels back two days, to a bradycardia attack my mother suffered. Her third, or perhaps fourth. This time, I happen to be in the room when it happens, as the machines scream out their alarm to the rhythm of her sinking heart. I call out frantically to my sisters, my nephew. No epinephrine, we remind ourselves. No adrenaline. DNR.

But even if you're convinced about DNR, it is impossible to sit by while someone's heartbeat, respiratory functions, blood pressure and oxygen levels dip, and do nothing. I join the well-intentioned but ham-handed efforts to revive her. Such situations require us to provide deep, painful stimuli. We press down on her ribs, pinch her extremities, shout her name, including her maiden name, slap her wrists, pump her heart by pressing her ribcage rhythmically, urgently, to try to revive her, all eyes riveted on the monitors and machines surrounding her. After the first 20 minutes, I find I can't do it any more. Her hands and forearms are soft, her calves and feet, smooth, fair, unwrinkled, like a young girl's. Pinching and smacking feel like a violation. I back up to the far wall, confused, unable to hold back my tears as I watch the tableau by her bedside as if this isn't my family, it isn't my mother.

I see him then, my father, standing at the door. He is silent, watchful, though his eyes are wet. He doesn't come in, but his mouth moves in prayer, and at one point he squeezes his eyes shut as if he can't bear to witness this spectacle. When he opens them, our gazes lock briefly before I look away, my own vision blurred. I hear his voice echoing in my head, 'Let her go naturally' – words he has said repeatedly over the past two weeks.

Though there is no adrenaline shot this time, just panic and lots of activity, my mother's pulse revives, her heartbeat becomes stronger and, an hour later, she is stable again. All parameters normal. Stable. Breathing through her BiPAP, still there. Still present. But sleeping. Sleeping.

It is only the next day, yesterday, that we realize that something has changed this time. She is sleeping too much, responding too little, not eating, and her eyes, the last time I see her alive, are dull, their natural sparkle missing. When the stoic attending physician asks the family to come together to meet him, I suspect that it is going to be some sort of an end-of-life talk.

The plan this morning had been to drop my daughter at the airport and head straight to my mother's house for 'the talk'. But now there is no need for it. And it is no longer my mother's house, because she is gone.

Even as we deal with post-death formalities, the tectonic plates of affection that hold my parental family together shift to reflect a new normal, a life without this larger-than-life woman in our family who meant so many different things to different people.

'I'm so sorry for your loss.' 'So sorry.' 'Sorry. For. Your. Loss.' I hear the words through the morning of the following day, and I don't know if it is my ears that are numb or my heart, but I feel if there ever were words that were more inadequate than these, I don't know what they are.

I will hear many more such words, inadequate on a day that stretches out like a dark tunnel, thin-aired and never-ending, the day my mother will be cremated. But I'm not thinking of that as I drive through almost empty Delhi roads in the early-morning misty January chill to where she lies, un-breathing.

The family has taken turns to sit with her last night, her icebox shimmering in the middle of the room. She had hated being alone, especially in closed spaces – elevators, CT scan machines and metallic tubes for MRIs – and especially at night. Now, on the morning after, her home is where I am headed, to bathe her, dress her, get her ready to turn to dust. Ashes to ashes.

There is a hint of spring though it is January, *makar sankranti,* the first day of *uttarayan,* and it cuts through the air heavy with pollutants to give me a whiff of the 'other' Delhi, the one I once loved. I briefly glimpse that Delhi as I drive through wide, empty streets, the urban sprawl hiding some of the remaining beauty within. I pass a lane I know well. It leads to a magical place. Past a white temple and its surreal splendour, the temple where I got married. I wonder if there is time to turn in, to follow the ordinary road that leads to extraordinary old monuments, right up to the Hauz Khas tank, along a narrow, cobbled street, to the very end where an elegant arch stands, modest as a bride, its intricate work half hidden behind layers of dirt and pollution. Entering through an emerald garden opening up unexpectedly to an azure sky, to a space that makes you want to take a deep breath and shout out loud, your breath coming out as white ribbons against the cerulean sky. Cerulean, azure and all the shades in between. Colours I've forgotten the sensation of. The sky is only one colour now, in Delhi winters, and that is a dystopian grey.

I accelerate past the lane. I'm not going in to see more of my illusions shattered. This isn't the Delhi I grew up in, loved. The Delhi in which I discovered my identity, the Delhi whose grand buildings I floated through, studying, reporting, working. The city where I birthed my children. As if on cue, a shaft of sunlight aims itself at me, piercing through the smoky air, but before I can greet it and let it uplift me, I remember where I'm heading. I have to arrive before 8 a.m., the cremation is at 11. My mother always took time to get herself ready, and today, we, her daughters will be doing that for her.

There is a priest. We await instructions. We've just dressed her, sponged her body, now cold, hard from the ice overnight. We choose what sari she would have liked to wear. We squabble. Which one would *she* have chosen? What a strange and weird thought. But then my mother loved dressing up, matching her blouses, the 'arty' bindi that she would admire whenever I crafted it out for her with eyeliner, kajal, this and that.

For the last time I apply lipstick on the cold lips, choosing a colour carefully from a drawerful of different brands and shades. I wait for her to ask, '*Main kaisi lag rahi hoon*?' But all I hear are Vedic chants. The ceremonies have begun.

Women don't ride with a dead body, they say. Women don't go to cremation grounds. We don't know. We don't care. Her four daughters ride the hearse to the crematorium, because it's not a dead body, it's our mother. And even though I will have to breathe the pollution of a hundred wood-burning pyres, I don't want to miss inhaling the smoke that was my mother.

When the final moment arrives, I realize nothing has prepared me for it. The time when her beautiful, well-preserved, to me always 16-year-old body – because she never told us her age – is loaded onto the rails that will take her in to be incinerated by electricity. I will never hear her voice, touch her skin, paint her nails, make a bindi on that unlined forehead, colour her hair, sing with her, duck her dirty look, pretend not to see her gesturing me to sing, sing with her. Sing with her. I will never sing with my mother.

Her body is on the rail now. A man, a crematorium employee is touching her, feeling her ears, her hands, feeling through the cotton wool we were told to plug her ears, nostrils, mouth with, inside which we were told to hide some gold bits. He is looking for gold! But she was the gold. She was my mother. She *is* my mother.

The rail begins moving towards the mouth of the furnace. There is a loud sound and lots of shadows. The space we are standing in is dark, sooty. I feel the spirits of all those who have left their bodies here before. The rail is still moving. A loud clang and the mouth of the furnace opens, and her body enters it, relentless rails moving ahead, without giving us time for a final hug. I move towards her; someone restrains me. I take deep breaths. There is another clang, louder this time, the loudest vibration I've ever heard, and it pierces my whole being.

I cry out aloud, an involuntary sound. Someone is hugging me. Tight. It is a restraint. It is my husband. I feel the wet of my tears. I look back. Her body is disappearing into a dark, cavernous space. Alone. And just like that, she is gone. Forever. *Never* to return.

I guess I didn't know what *never* really meant. This is the day I understand.

1

Forget

January 2008

The time difference between New Delhi and Palo Alto in the San Francisco Bay Area is thirteen and a half hours. In the summer, it is twelve and a half hours – which makes it easier to calculate the best time to call family back home. When my phone rang early on that cool, dark January morning, I knew it was the call I had subconsciously been dreading every day and every night, ever since I moved to the United States.

'Hello?' I said into the phone, breathless, wide awake in an instant, my heart thudding in my ears.

It's these unexpected calls at odd times that we worry about, all of us who live time zones away in the land of our choice, away from the land of our birth. We never stop waiting for these calls, and after a few years, it becomes a habit, the waiting. And then, we stop holding our breaths, because we have become used to not breathing in that way any more.

My call, at 4 a.m. that pre dawn morning informed me that my mother was sick – sudden, acute pneumonia – and asking for me. The doctors were hopeful but, really, anything could happen.

She was older than she admitted to any of us, unlike my father, who delighted in telling the world how incredibly, hopelessly old he was. My father had diabetes, emphysema and hypertension. He had survived prostate cancer, a bacterially caused ulcer that bled into his gut until his haemoglobin fell to dangerous levels, and a wrongly implanted pacemaker. He was no stranger to hospitalizations. My mother, on the other hand, just got colds. As a teenager, she had injured her back after a dangerous fall from the terrace of her childhood home, but she'd never been admitted to a hospital for anything more serious than childbirth. I'd never seen her seriously ill.

My mother was a singer and had trained as a classical vocal musician, and in the long days of recovery from her fall, in a world with hardly any electronic entertainment, the girl my mother was, sang and sang. She told me that at first, she sang to dispel her fear of perhaps never being able to walk again, but that, as she got better, she sang in hope, in gratitude and, finally, in joy. And the song never left her voice – it only grew bigger, brighter, clearer, sweeter.

Suddenly, desperately, I wanted to hear that voice.

Music and my mother are so intertwined that my earliest memories of her are through song. She sang every single day of her life. For years, I awoke to the sound of her *riyaaz*. She sang for joy, at relatives' marriages, festivities, Holi, saawan, teej; she sang for moksha and nirvana, at memorials, funeral ceremonies. She sang because it made her happy, and she sang to overcome her loneliness and fears. Music helped her cope with the early death of her adoring and adored father, of her fragile, wistful mother, the deaths of some of the childhood family she held dear; uncles I never knew, aunts who fascinated me with their eccentricities, cousins I disliked but she loved.

She sang to help her through her destiny, to sublimate her ambition to sing professionally as her talent became compromised by domesticity. She sang to unwind the smoky ropes of attachment that bound her to her birth family and then to her married family, her children. Us. It had been her meditation and her life. I didn't want this phone call to be about her, but it was.

'Hello?' I whispered again. Or did I shout? I felt confused, unable to inhale or exhale.

'It's Mom,' my sister said baldly, no preamble, her voice burrowing through the time zones that separated us, echoing off the ivory walls of my cosy bedroom. I stumbled out of bed to move closer to the window, pulling aside the embroidered white cotton curtains to look out. My eyes focused on the ginkgo tree that swayed right outside my window, its yellow flowers visible in the milky moonlight. They looked serene, alive. The slight flaw in my glass pane made them look like they were encrusted with ice crystals. I tried to take deep breaths to calm my nerves and a racing heart.

'Is she okay? What happened?' I said, but I couldn't hear my words. Had I spoken them out loud? I cleared my throat.

'She's in hospital. Pneumonia. She wants to talk to you.' My sister's voice sounded tightly controlled, as though she was in a hurry to disconnect. She had clearly been instructed by my mother not to tell me more than she had. So it can't be that bad, I told myself. Mom was still in control, which meant that for now I could hold off on planning a 24-hour airplane journey. But I couldn't be sure.

For a family as dramatic, dysfunctional and boisterous as ours, the eerie calm in my sister's voice in that purple California pre dawn sent my imagination into overdrive. Before I let her hang up, I made her promise that she would make sure Mom called me as soon as she could, as soon as the doctors allowed her to.

Yet, unable to wait, I called back several hours later, to find my dad home alone, still awake despite the late hour in India, and in a ruminative mood. Both of us wanted to talk about her. I let him tell me again how 55 years ago he had pretended to need the washroom so that he could legitimately walk through my mother's childhood home to catch a glimpse of her, his would-be bride. Crossing the central red-brick courtyard of my grandfather's rambling haveli in energetic, small-town Meerut, he had opened a couple of wrong doors in his supposed search for the elusive washroom.

He had heard her before he spotted her. In one of the high-ceilinged rooms, sitting with her tanpura, her face turned towards the sun, practising a raga. He told me how her midnight hair had cascaded down to her waist and her jewel-like voice entwined a necklace of musical notes around his supple, young spine, drawing him involuntarily towards her. The patterned sunlight filtering through the latticed stone vents where the wall met the ceiling enhanced her beauty, entrancing his young heart. He forgot about the washroom, forgot the venerable family elders waiting patiently in the front room, cloistered in claustrophobic conversations finalizing the details of the forthcoming nuptials, matching horoscopes, discussing the delicate issues of an arranged marriage, until his older sister, who was sent to fetch him, found him standing outside the door to her room, bewitched and disoriented.

'Actually, our *rishta* had already been arranged by the elders in our families, though we hadn't met each other. But then, people, distant relatives, others, started whispering about her fall; some said that she limped. My family asked me if I wanted to see her. So I decided to show up with my elder sister – she was much older than me... We just dropped by, without warning.' I heard nostalgia in his voice, recognized the old-fashioned concern of a family who wanted to ensure their eligible newly minted bureaucrat son's potential bride wasn't lame. But such concerns came to naught as my father unexpectedly fell in love with his arranged-marriage bride, snared by her impossibly black, long hair and magical voice. Or maybe this is just something I wanted to believe, as today, for the first time, he elaborated on the story further.

She was singing Bageshwari, that queen of ragas, light-hearted and romantic, he said. She was probably more beautiful in his eyes that afternoon than she would be ever again; her music, enchanting, magnetic, the notes of the raga creating an almost visible aura of beauty and longing around her. It was that event that ultimately compelled him to choose her, really choose her to marry, he said softly, really choose her, regardless of whatever the elders had decided.

His voice, slow, thoughtful in the velvet darkness of his night, entered my home through the sky and the sun and the wind that connected our worlds and fell around my feet in little glittering heaps. The blue sky and dazzling golden-white Californian sunshine outside that I took for granted was making my eyes water, and suddenly, also making everything crystal clear. Everything about them, that is. My parents.

After we finished talking, I sat for a long time at my little square pinewood table that overlooked the garden blooming with camellias in shades of blood red and pink, and thought, probably for the first time, of my parents as people. Just a boy and a girl in the mid-1950s at the cusp of their life, of their dreams, hopes and desires. What defined them at their very core? For my mother, it was easy: music and melody are what defined her.

I thought of her, her music, her voice, of all the songs I still wanted to learn from her. I thought of the millions of fights we had had, three-quarters of which were about why I wouldn't practise my ragas. When she ultimately went back to her music, becoming a student once more (she earned her second master's in Hindustani classical music at 58) and stopped living her dreams through my singing, I didn't feel like I'd won any battles. Instead, I felt a burden I didn't fully understand lift slightly.

Her voice had been the constant in my life, peripatetic as it was with my father's transferable government job posting us to different cities and towns in India every few years. It had brought me stability, taught me unconsciously that music could transcend loneliness, fear, anxiety. Even as schools and teachers changed, new friends were made and old ones wept over, homes and related environments transformed; that was the one thing that remained constant. Wherever we were, I always woke up to the sound of my mother's riyaaz as she trained for Hindustani classical music. From early childhood, versions of the morning Raga Bhairav interspersed with Asavari or their derivatives wafted into our still-dark bedrooms, and by the time the slow, languorous *alaaps* gave way to vigorous *taans*, the clear, pink light of dawn would have touched our faces and I would know it was time to get out of bed. This gentle awakening with morning ragas stayed with me for years. This was also, I realized later, her 'me' time, the time she carved out for her first – and deepest – love.

Sunlight was slanting in through the patio door onto the hardwood floor. My cheeks felt wet by the time I roused myself from my thoughts, and I found myself singing, to ease my sorrow, to relieve my anxiety, come to terms with the vast miles that separated me from my family. I sang till I cried. And I cried until I could sing again. And I waited.

She called me two days later, in the early hours of our morning, before the children left for school, and I didn't know what to say to that soft voice that breathed gently across the ocean.

'Talk to me,' she whispered. 'Don't worry. It's just pneumonia, but I'm…' Her sigh trailed off. Old? Scared? Going to die?

Voices screamed in my head and I felt choked, full of remorse that I'd never really expressed to her how much she meant to me. But I couldn't speak. I stood still against the glass patio door, listening to her breathe 7,700 miles away, until, unexpectedly, I found myself singing into the phone. It was a *nirguna bhajana*, a prayer to the Almighty to help us get across the sea of life in a boat blessed with His spirit and strength; metaphors of surrender that made my voice quiver and my eyes grow moist.

It was a haunting tune, one that she hadn't taught me, and she was entranced, asking for an encore. I sang it again for her, in a stronger voice, less hopelessly now, and then again, until they took the phone away from her.

She called me again that evening, asking for more, trying to learn the tune from me, singing in a raspy, uneven whisper. She was a wonderful singer and teacher, but to my utter delight I found her to be an inept learner, and I threw my musical weight around. It was the only song I knew that she hadn't taught me, and I wasn't sure I could give that up. But she was a persistent student and called every day until her breath grew stronger and I was ready to give up my song to her.

She recovered then, but today, nine years after that incident, while I struggle to process her terminal diagnosis, I wonder whether that episode of pneumonia – what her doctors called 'walking pneumonia' – should have alerted me to the beginning of the cancer that would consume her.

Perhaps that's when I should have realized that her lungs were at risk. Or, perhaps, that's when they weakened, compromised further by the steadily worsening quality of the air in the city where she lived. I have often wondered whether her being a classical vocalist could have made things worse for her. A singer, like an athlete, breathes deeper and longer, and thus she would have been inhaling larger quantities of polluted air. Could that have compromised her lungs more than others? But then, more vocalists and athletes would have been dying of respiratory illnesses in India, where pollution has become endemic. Or could her being a classical vocalist have given her lungs *greater* endurance? Could all those years of riyaaz have strengthened her lungs, used to belting out intricate *taans* at top speed, punctuating them with lilting, slow, disciplined *alaaps*, her control over her breath complete? After her final diagnosis, these alternating thoughts tormented me, thoughts I wanted to forget.

After her bout of pneumonia, my mother was advised to be more careful in the winters. When I moved back to India a year after this episode, I would constantly keep an ear out for the sound of a persistent wheeze or a cough when speaking with her. There was none, though she did seem to have become more prone to winter coughs which could degenerate quickly into a wheeze. But back then I put it down to ageing, rather than what it really was: years of constant exposure to air pollution and second-hand cigarette smoke.

My father had been a smoker and it was his lungs that we had always worried about. He had tried and failed to quit – until one day, suddenly, he did. By then, it was clear his lungs weren't in great shape. When I bought air purifiers for their house in August 2014, they were for him, his emphysema, his lungs. My parents had laughed at my obsession with polluted air and called it 'nonsense'. We had focused so much on his COPD that my mother's regular 'winter coughs' and compromised lung function remained under the radar – until the unexpected diagnosis of terminal lung cancer.

In those days following that fateful Diwali night when air pollution stopped being just a dry, precise science to me that I understood in my head and took the shape, instead, of a killer of epidemiological proportions, affecting my life, I thought of my childhood and how my mother shaped it with her music, which I later made my own. Music became an important part of my life, comforting and calming in times of stress, uplifting during my lows and inspiring me at my highs. I used it to my teenage advantage, coincidentally most efficiently when one of my father's official transfers posted us back to Meerut, my mother's *maika* (parents' home). My grandfather's haveli still stood tall, forlornly majestic, rising high within the narrow lanes that criss-crossed around it. He had been a rare scholar of Prakrit and Sanskrit, two languages that remain alive, but barely so, in little crucibles of learning embedded in universities.

This was the 1980s, and I used the great foundation her classical musical teaching had given me to quickly learn all the popular ABBA and Boney M. numbers that I performed at school events, my popularity in my new school growing as theirs peaked. *'Hasta mañana, till we meet again, don't know where, don't know when,'* I'd croon into the mike from the high stage to a sea of girls in blue pinafores, in the process, both fitting in and standing out as the new girl yet again.

With the gift of her music, I suddenly found myself equally sought after by the most popular girls in the school, as well as the sharp-eyed, sharp-eared nuns who spotted in me a singer of hymns that accessorized our morning prayer assemblies. They quickly picked me for the school choir, looking benignly at me from under their wimples, eyes magnified by soda-bottle spectacles as I sang to the Lord in prayer in the mornings. But come school fêtes, festivals and functions I was up on stage, guitar in hand, belting away the latest pop numbers.

'So I say, thank you for the music, the songs I'm singing. Thanks for all the joy they're bringin'... So I say thank you for the music. For giving it to me.' ABBA said it best.

How I wish now that I'd sung this to my mother. Another thought I want to forget.

After my two older sisters had flown the nest, my mother and I developed a new understanding as I basked in a larger share of her maternal attention. She giggled with her new set of postgraduate musical 'classmates', and I with mine. That was the calm before our relationship turned stormy for a while, punctuated by acts of rebellion on my part and bursts of temper on hers, the way the relationships of teenage daughters and mothers are wont to be. My father's job had transferred us to New Delhi by now, and my rancour and adolescent angst soon burnt itself out, not like an explosive firecracker that zooms into a smoky night in a brief moment of glory, but like the embers of a campfire left to smoulder and die overnight. Now rebellion was replaced by a harmonious bond, which deepened further after the plaintive notes of the *shehnai* had ushered me out from under my parents' roof. By the time I became a mother – and understood her better, in a whole new way – this more mature bond had solidified into a steady attachment, like a heartbeat you don't notice until it goes missing. Or a breath. I noticed this only after I moved overseas, realizing the depth of my emotional dependence on her, an uncut umbilical cord.

Now, here it was again, the red-hot fury – not at her this time, but on her behalf. A despairing anger that festered and grew as the grey air outside seeped into my mother's body through her lungs and oozed out like pus into a plastic bag attached to her left lung via a needle she never complained about. Her left lung. The primary node from where the cancer spread.

The anger would flare up without warning, making my jaw clench, my teeth hurt, coagulating inside my head as I watched the trees below her window swaying angrily in a grey November breeze. Her cancer was a ticking time bomb around which we rearranged our lives, recalibrating to a new normal we hoped would last. But, despite us cajoling her with enticing little meals, my mother withered away in front of our eyes. I want to forget those images too, remember her as she was before the flesh fell off her bones.

After the chemotherapy, we were terrified of passing on any infections to my mother, and I wished the air purifier running in her room was able to filter out microbiological pollutants, too. When she developed an unexplained fever, and we had to get an X-ray, the hospital sent a portable machine home. Her attending pulmonologist shook his head sadly over the test results as he prescribed one more round of antibiotics. We had often discussed the ill effects of air pollution on human lungs. When I asked him – as I've asked many pulmonologists, thoracic surgeons, ENT specialists and paediatricians – whether he warns his patients or talks about the deadly effects of pollution with any of them, he shook his head. 'What's the point?' he said.

What's the point? What's the point? The words thrummed white-hot in my head. Actually, I wondered sometimes what was the point, especially when another friend, ENT surgeon Dr Rajesh Bharadwaj, explained to me how it would be a logistical nightmare to teach patient after individual patient the health harm caused by pollution.

'Especially, when we can offer no real solutions,' said Dr Bharadwaj. He sounded disheartened. 'Public health workers can touch hundreds of thousands of people at one go. In clinical health, we see one patient at a time,' he pointed out. Public health is the neglected stepsister of clinical medicine everywhere, but nowhere more than in India. Frustrated with the situation, he had recently begun making presentations wherever he could to spread the word about the impact of air pollution on respiratory health.

Dr Bharadwaj showed me his slides. They were very similar to the Care For Air slides. We were all using the same public health data and research available in the public domain. It is unfortunate that this science and evidence is tucked away in silos.

The doctor noted that people are getting sicker at younger ages. 'Twenty years ago, the reaction to an asthma diagnosis was disbelief,' he says. 'It was a social stigma. Now it is as prevalent as the common cold. The acceptance of nebulizers has increased. Mothers *ask* for them. One out of three children is asthmatic now, compared to one out of ten earlier.'

'But in the end, we doctors are limited even in the protective tips we can offer our patients,' he said, sounding defeated. 'What's the point?' There it was again. *What's the point?*

It wasn't until a year after my mother's cancer diagnosis that a credible institution accurately captured my confused, angry thoughts on how much longer I could have had her in my life had she never breathed polluted air. In November 2018, Dr Michael Greenstone, Milton Friedman Professor in Economics, and Claire Qing Fan, a pre-doctoral fellow at the Energy Policy Institute, University of Chicago, (EPIC) released the findings of an innovative piece of research that converted particulate air pollution concentrations into their impact on life expectancy,[1] thus quantifying how many years of your life you lose, depending on the extent of pollution you've been exposed to by living in different parts of the world.

For Delhi, it is 10 years, their website calculated through its Air Quality Life Index (AQLI) tool.[2]

EPIC's AQLI tool goes a step beyond the Air Quality Index (AQI) (which measures the extent of pollutants in the ambient air) by communicating the health risk from inhaling the microparticles in that polluted air. This tool thus converts the particulate air pollution contained within the AQI into its impact on life expectancy, perhaps the most important metric we care about.

So, by living here, in Delhi, my mother had essentially shaved 10 years off her life. To know – even in theory, even simplistically – that I would have had 10 more years with my mother had she not breathed in polluted air all her life filled me with rage. It made me furious that every single person in India's capital city was unknowingly dying faster because of its polluted air, full of toxins such as PM (particulate matter) 2.5, ozone, benzene, dioxins, microplastics, chlorides, lead and so many others not even measured by the government's AQI measures. I knew already that the worst culprit was microparticulate PM2.5.

'Particulate air pollution shortens lives globally. There is no greater current risk to human health,' says Dr Greenstone.[3]

Globally, the reduction in life expectancy is two years, making particulate pollution more devastating than communicable diseases like tuberculosis and HIV/AIDS, and behavioural killers like cigarette smoking – and even war. In China and India, where the level of pollution is far greater, just bringing particulate concentrations down to the World Health Organization's (WHO) guidelines would increase average life expectancy by 2.9 and 4.3 years respectively, the UChicago website calculated through its AQLI tool. Thus, AQLI not just quantifies the causal relationship between long-term human exposure to air pollution and life expectancy, but also then combines this research with hyper-localized, global PM measurements, yielding insight into the true cost of air pollution in communities around the world.

But even before there was a numeral attached to the number of extra years of life I could have had with my mother, an inarticulate anger just flowed, like a red river of pain, helplessness and fear, as India's famed medical system fanned around us, its tentacles capturing us in a fierce, ruthless embrace. I want to forget those feelings now. I had seen the face of medical tourism on my way down in the elevator – worried Afghani and African women in their customary clothing, speaking in tongues I didn't understand, but whose expressions I did. Worry, love, concern, suffering, pain – these didn't need a language. And they understood mine as we stood in lines for scans and X-rays, comforting each other through look, gesture or touch, something I won't ever forget.

Meanwhile, doctors prescribed physical therapy for my mother's weakening lungs, and to the plethora of machines in her room was added a colourful respiratory exerciser with red, yellow and green plastic balls that she had to blow at through a plastic tube to help with lung function. Lung function was key. The better the lung function, the better the organs' capacity, rate of air flow and strength. Even yoga, with its emphasis on pranayama, recognizes the benefits of breath and focus on breathing.

'Look!' I remember my father pointing to a squirrel in our garden when I was little, trying to feed fussy, six-year-old me an egg. 'See how rapidly it breathes? And see Bijou?' He pointed to our black Tibetan spaniel, lazing in the sun, one eye on the squirrel. 'And that black bird with the yellow beak up on that tree?' I looked dutifully up at the frangipani tree. I knew that bird. It usually sat with its friends in our custard apple trees in the rambling backyard of our tiny government home.

'See the difference in the rate of their breath? That's how you measure how long a living being remains alive,' he said, coaxing the last bit of loathsome egg into my mouth.

According to my father, animals which had long, slow breaths lived longer than those with shallow, rapid breathing. His theory has always been that all living beings have a finite number of breaths allotted to them when they are sent to this world. If you use up your number of breaths quickly, in rapid breathing, you die earlier. The longer your breath, the longer you remain alive.

'So the squirrel will die before Bijou does,' he told me then, but noticing my childish distress at the mention of death, stopped hurriedly.

Much later in life, I conclude that his theory is two fold. One, that animals who breathe rapidly have lower life expectancy, and those that breathe long and slow have higher life expectancy. And two, at a more philosophical level, that we all come into this world with a finite set of breaths. When that number runs out, we die. This is his belief, and it was his father's belief before him.

I have no way of questioning and validating these theories. All I know is that my father continued his version of the family tradition, especially with the pranayama he performed daily under a neem tree, as his father did before him. My paternal grandfather died at the ripe old age of 90-something, ramrod straight till the end, the pranayama he had done all his life, breathing in the crystal-clear air of the Kumaon hills – where he lived, where my father was born and raised and from where my family originates – keeping his lungs strong till the end. The difference is that I have compelled my father to move his practice indoors, in a room with air filters, because the air under the neem tree is no longer fit to enter human lungs, laden as it is with toxins. And it isn't just one poison. Delhi's air consists of all of the Big Five – SOx, NOx (lethal oxides of sulphur and nitrogen), ozone, PM10 and, the deadliest of all, PM2.5 – which make up India's AQI, a weighted average simplified to one number. The composition may differ from region to region, what scientists and experts call airsheds, and the fraction of PM2.5 to PM10 or even solid to gaseous pollutants may differ in proportion between airsheds, but there is no part of India that has air quality at the levels that the WHO deems 'healthy'.

The discipline of my father's childhood in the crisp, clean air of his Kumaoni village, fringed with deodar and pines, hopping and skipping 6 miles to his hilly, informal *taat patti* municipal school in his early years, a youth spent clambering up and down slopes, may also be what continues to protect him despite years of abuse later as a smoker after he moved to more polluted areas, first to study in the prestigious Allahabad University and then to live in different parts of the Indo-Gangetic plain.

Compared to his childhood, my mother's, in the smoky sugarcane belt in the dusty plains of northern India, probably impacted her lungs from an early age. Meerut, where she grew up, just 64 kilometres from Delhi, was a satellite town to the bustling capital, achieving growth milestones in ungainly leaps and bounds, like an adolescent, eager to grow. Surrounded by sugarcane, paper, cement factories, brick kilns, power plants and other industries that belched out emissions, Meerut's air was further fed with dust from unending construction, rotating cement mixers, endless dug-up foundations and the burning of garbage. Another fact I want to forget but can't.

Her married life began in sooty, sophisticated Kolkata, whose air was probably heavy with the maximum pollution, but still under the radar, because at the time there was no real radar. In fact, Kolkata was the original city defined by black carbon in the air, soot that made its trams – and everyone's clothes – grimy. In the early 1980s, it was the *Telegraph*, then the city's young and feisty paper, that published what were probably the first air pollution stories in India.

Umesh Anand, at the time with the newspaper, who reported the findings of an early researcher in urban air pollution remembers that people in government just wouldn't accept that the air was so polluted. Anand now lives in Delhi and is the founder and publisher of *Civil Society*, a magazine that covers the work of social change agents. 'The stories I wrote in the '80s could have been written today,' he says.

It's not as if rural India is pollution-free. If you travel by road through the countryside you will be accompanied by the pungent odour of burning biomass. It comes from burning cow-dung cakes, which are used as fuel in the village kitchens. This smoke mostly affects women, as they are the ones cooking three times a day over earthen stoves, burning wood or smouldering cow dung. Cow dung causes the maximum smoke as it smoulders without catching fire.

It is during regular monthly breakfast meetings with the late Dr Kirk Smith,[4] Professor of Global Environmental Health at University of California, Berkeley's School of Public Health, who almost single-handedly shone a searchlight on household air pollution, that I will first realize the critical impact of indoor air pollution on ambient air. He is one of three pollution experts who has mentioned how the smell of pollution in India is different from that in China – the latter smells more industrial, whereas India's ambient rural air smells more of biomass.

As many as seven independent published scientific studies[5] have proven household sources to be the largest single source of ambient air pollution in India. The burning of solid fuels like firewood for cooking and heating in millions of households across the country contributes to the PM2.5 load of ambient outdoor air pollution.

As India industrializes and grows without any sustainable planning, our skies get darker and I try to forget many uncomfortable memories, thoughts and facts related to my mother and her struggle to breathe. I am compelled to remind my father to forget the old ways. To forget the clean, crisp air of his mountainous origins, the long inhalations of his meditative *sandhya* outdoors, the fragrance of pine-scented air, swapped now for the sharp fumes of city emissions, of fuel and garbage burning. Forget.

What's the point? the words often slip back in. But in the middle of this Pandora's box of wretched despair, illness and sadness, a tiny green shoot of hope unfurls. Perhaps it is still possible to drive change, I tell myself. Make others aware of how close this killer has reached, so that together we can vanquish it.

2

India's

June 2009

'Are you sure, man? You know you can change your mind any time. You can still stay back.'

It's my husband's 'boss'. He has tried everything to keep my husband in Palo Alto. But a promise is a promise. I strain to overhear my husband's response, while also trying to pour more vodka and schnapps into the paper cup my Polish American neighbour is holding. She and I have been giggling over our weird, common anxieties, suspicious nature and absolute conviction that bad things are poised to happen all the time. Her hazel eyes are sparkling with laughter. We are wondering what in our disparate backgrounds and childhoods could possibly have made us so similar to each other. We are also occasionally teary-eyed, promising each other we will remain in touch. We are all a little drunk.

Our belongings have already been sent to India and our home is mostly empty. Our hearts, though, are full. The evening sunlight enters unfiltered through the bare windows. We have invited all available neighbours and friends to help us finish 47 half-empty bottles of various kinds of alcohol, the ones the moving company can't transport to India. Everyone is sad, but also in high spirits.

'I love it here. We all do,' I hear my husband say and see him gesturing towards us. 'It's been awesome, but the plan was always to go back to India.'

'So what, man? Plans change. Your family is happy here, everyone's happy,' his boss counters. 'You guys are so settled. By this time, next year, you'll get your citizenship. The L-1 converts real quick. Work is good. The new product is going to be a game changer…'

My husband is laughing now. 'This is a farewell party, man,' he says. 'My container has left! It's too late. All our stuff is currently bobbing on the high seas!'

'Stuff! What's stuff? We'll buy you everything. Replace it all. I have the budget. It's not too late. It's never too late. We want you to stay. You're making a mistake.' His voice is suddenly serious, deep, the lightness in it gone. I turn around in surprise and he waves me over urgently, but I smile and ignore his gesture. My husband and I have agonized over this decision. Everything is done now. Signed and sealed. I can't go through one last thought, even in jest, again. As I refill our paper cups, the amber liquid sloshes onto my neighbour's outstretched hand.

Later that night, after we've cleared up and pressed the remaining bottles of alcohol into the unresisting hands of our friends, we finally wriggle into our sleeping bags on the bare floorboards in the echoing house, exhausted. But we can't sleep. It's been a long, eventful day. We talk in low voices about our time in this welcoming suburb of America. How I had resisted the move here for years, almost forcing a split in the family as my husband flew back and forth alone while I stayed back with my toddlers in New Delhi. I hadn't wanted to move away from family and friends, even if it meant moving to the land of milk and honey, and cupcakes and burgers. But my husband's company grew even as my family did, and the board voted to acquire him along with the company, relocating us across the ocean, like any other asset. We had no option.

'Remember all the fights and tears?' I whisper to him now, and I see him nod in the streaming moonlight, mouth turned down. 'Do you feel a sense of déjà vu too?' I ask.

We can hear our kids whispering and talking in the next room, the novelty and excitement of sleeping in sleeping bags in an empty room keeping sleep at bay.

'It's going to be fun. There will be friends, family and Indian food. And you love parathas as much as pizzas. And I can eat as many samosas as I want. And chaat.' I can hear my always-optimistic daughter reassure my always-slightly-anxious son, forgetting to keep her high, piping voice down. My son responds in that fake-nonchalant tone I recognize so well, 'Well, they've promised we'll come back every summer, and summer is the funnest time, and I'll be able to meet Jack and Graham. And Taylor.' His self-soothing words add another spike of doubt to the ones always floating around in my head, and I look at my husband. Moonbeams entering through the windows behind his head make farewell patterns around us, filtered only by the leaves of the trees whispering outside. 'Are you sure you'll be able to swing that? He takes promises very seriously, more than other kids.'

'You know the company doesn't want me to move. They need me here. I'll be flying back and forth more than ever,' he reminds me, unworried. I sigh. Yes. That is one of the reasons why I have just turned down a potential job in New Delhi. My husband's job is high-octane and his firm is generous to us. But his travel and frequent absences are what compelled me to give up a job I loved after I had my second child.

I'd managed to get back to work after birthing one child, but I knew I couldn't do it with two. Without adequate help or good day care options, parenting two infants, born 21 months apart, and reporting internationally for a wire agency felt overwhelming.

I often wondered how single parents coped. I wasn't a young mother to begin with, but I had a supportive, encouraging boss at Dow Jones Newswires in New Delhi. Yet, my head knew, anyone can be replaced at work. At home? That's where I was indispensable, my heart told me.

What finally led me to decide on being a stay-at-home parent was the accident my daughter had 10 days before I was to rejoin work, for which she needed surgery under general anaesthesia. She was two. It may have been at the exact moment when I leant over her as they gave her anaesthesia, my tears falling on her delicate face framed by wild curls, while my three-month-old waited to be nursed downstairs in the hospital lobby in my mother's arms. Or, it may have been when I signed the hospital documents alone, releasing the hospital from all culpability. My husband was travelling.

After I resigned, I had barely learnt the new skill sets needed to be an active parent and full-time house manager while continuing to freelance when his job moved us to California and I slipped into the default role of a trailing spouse. The same challenges remained – except, now I had no family around. The parenting buck stopped with me.

Palo Alto was good to us, the diverse community kind and welcoming. I made many friends, some of them becoming like the family I missed. Very quickly, we began to feel like we belonged.

My learning curve was steep. I grappled with pages of detailed instructions on every sort of domestic machinery in order to escape domestic drudgery. I read reams of paper on every kind of insurance there was, and researched subjects as diverse as children's summer camps, income and property taxes, zoning laws, identity theft and fraud, and window retrofits. There was always something new to learn to survive the entirely new environment. I was always exhausted.

But it was fun. We rediscovered our passion for jazz and Western classical music, attending symphonies, and arias, operas and open-air reggae concerts, until my senses were dazzled, my mind overwhelmed. I took writing classes at Stanford, cycling across El Camino Real to the beautiful palm-fringed campus, sitting in a class along with goth teenagers and 85-year-old Holocaust survivors, listening to Tobias Wolff, George Saunders, Pico Iyer, even the Dalai Lama. My children celebrated Christmas and Hanukkah in addition to Diwali; Easter and Pesach along with Holi; Rosh Hashanah and Yom Kippur with Dussehra. They made close friends, learnt to ice-skate in winter, and skateboard and rollerblade in the summer. They set up lemonade stalls, went camping with friends and learnt to trick or treat for Halloween. We had turkey for Thanksgiving, chocolate eggs for Easter and *thandai* with the local Indian-American community during Holi. We loved it here. It felt like home.

The tone in my voice when I told people that we planned to return to India – return home – in a few years changed from suppressed excitement to gentle regret. Along the way, I started feeling that 'home' itself was a construct.

But I still worried that my children wouldn't be Indian enough.

'Remind me,' my writing group partner asked me during my final class at the Stanford campus, 'why are you moving back to India?'

'My children,' I mumbled. 'They're becoming American.'

'And that's a bad thing?' his nostrils flared. He was a high-school teacher.

'No, no. Just that…they're forgetting who they are. Where they come from. We want them to know their Indian heritage, relate to it. Their terms of reference have changed. There's nothing from India here. They celebrate their own festivals so…self-consciously…' I trailed off.

Even our Indian-American friends didn't understand. Their children were learning Hindi, Bharatanatyam, tabla, mridangam, in structured classes at local community centres, connecting them to their origins. Why couldn't mine?

'It has to be organic. Immersive. Not imposed externally,' I insisted. But in my heart, I trembled. I knew the move back would be difficult, and yet I was hopeful that it would build resilience, grit.

'Doesn't Palo Alto feel like home to you?' another friend burst out, her eyes displaying her hurt.

'It does. It is home. I love it. This has been the best time of my life. We've all thrived. But it's time to head to the homeland,' I replied, squeezing her hand. Gradually, the difference between home and homeland has become clearer to me.

This is home, but we will always be exotic in this setting. We have no history here – our cultural context will always be something we have to fiercely hold on to rather than take for granted. My children won't know what *pithoo*, kabaddi, kho-kho and cricket are. Hindi will be alien to them, despite my attempts to make them watch cartoons dubbed in the vernacular. How will they learn who they are, what their identity is, where they have originated from? It will just not be possible in Palo Alto's colourful, well-equipped public school, with experiential pedagogy taught by gentle teachers with twanging accents similar to theirs.

'You came here on an L-1 visa? And you've all had green cards for, what, two years now, right? So why don't you move back, like, next year?' an Indian-American friend asks, quickly calculating exactly how long it would take for us to convert the permanent residency into citizenship.

'But if we convert the L-1 into citizenship, we'll have to surrender our Indian passport and our Indian citizenship, right?' I ask.

It had been a tough decision. The timing was critical. Soon, my malleable tweens would turn into sullen, suspicious teens. Expecting them to navigate geographies and cultures at a time of natural rebellion when they were already traversing a transition between childhood and adolescence would be unfair. I was also wary of settling into the groove of that permanent limbo, where each year, we plan to move back 'home' the next year, and 'next year' kept getting pushed back, until the concept of home itself transformed. Yet, in many ways it had also been easy. India beckoned. And now, tonight, was our last night in this lovely suburb.

I inhale the crisp, clean Californian air as memories flow in with the silvery moonlight, vivid, sharp in the clear night.

These bittersweet feelings of longing and loss, pollinated with an underlying spike of excitement that I've been feeling all week, are so similar to those I had felt while making the reverse move. The wistful feelings of nostalgia cling to me in a lingering, sepia-tinted dream state long after the memories sink away, like seawater absorbed by the sand.

When I awake, my eyes are wet, my heart heavy with melancholic longing for something for which I have no name.

August 2009

'Mommy, why can't I drink water from the tap? I'm firsty!' asks my eight-year-old son, his American twang cutting through the thick, moist heat of a Delhi August, his missing teeth making him lisp in the way I adore and he hates. His face is red and shining with sweat, his hair stuck to his forehead. His eyes look big in his face, which seems to be losing its healthy fullness in this heat. He has just returned from his new school, where he is having trouble – a lot of trouble – settling in. It hasn't been a fun summer for him. Actually, it has almost been a baptism by fire. I can feel his sadness, and it makes my heart ache.

It has been just two months since our move back, and already my children have had to unlearn many things, like waiting their turn; give up some habits, like cycling and walking alone to the library, crossing roads at zebra crossings; learn to ignore some things, like stray dogs, the beggars at traffic lights. The initial horror and pity both my children expressed on their first encounters turning into a stoic, unemotional empathy. In the first week back, my daughter wept inconsolably for hours after I refused to hand over everything we had, every last thing in the car, to the children clustering at our window at the traffic signal, while my son looked on silently, seriously, processing the huge inequality in which we occupied the advantageous end. Now, we keep biscuits and colouring books and crayons in the car, handing them out at signals. My children are growing, maturing in my India. They will never take their privilege for granted.

'I'm firsty, I'm firsty. I want water! Why can't I drink it?' A petulant note is creeping into my son's voice. It's been hard to explain to his logical mind why he shouldn't drink tap water here. (But why don't they just clean it, Mommy, like in 'Merica?)

'Why can't I drink from the tap?' he persists, and I know he won't stop till he gets a satisfactory answer. 'I always did, back home in Palo Alto, remember?' he says, as if it wasn't mere months ago. His eyes cloud over, wounded, when he says, 'home in Palo Alto', stopping me from correcting him.

He is going through behavioural changes that the school counsellor says are worrying. He wants to belong but is desperately lonely, his twang making him the butt of jokes. I'm consumed with guilt for having lured him here with stories of friends, family and food.

'Mommy?' He tugs at my elbow and I sigh. He will not let go till he critically evaluates my answer to his satisfaction. Just two days earlier, it had taken me half an hour and a scary experiment at a zebra crossing to prove to him that cars do not stop for pedestrians at zebra crossings in India, often even when we raise our hands in the international stop sign.

The heat has been relentless and he's been at school, getting bullied, while I've been out looking for apartments to move into as we wait for our container to show up. I suddenly remember the little shop in the basement of the towering building where our serviced apartment is located and suggest going there for an ice cream. Two little faces brighten, look at each other in surprised delight and within minutes we are there, buying water, buying ice cream and other junk to lift our drooping spirits.

Delhi has grown, transformed in the brief time we have been away. It feels like everything has changed and I have come back to a city on steroids, urgently moving faster and faster. The slow, innocent Delhi of my childhood has all but disappeared, something that had begun even before I'd relocated to Palo Alto. This Noida condominium where we are staying temporarily while we wait for our container to dock is one of those hundreds of gated communities that have sprung up in our short absence from the Delhi we left. It is beautiful, aesthetically landscaped, with well-laid-out tennis courts, a turquoise pool, dancing fountains, a clubhouse, a gym and a play area for children. It even has 24-hour security and power backup. You could be in a tony Californian suburb, except for the way the light is so different, the sky a softer hazier blue, despite the fierce sun. I have passed by many such gated communities, with glamourous, outlandish names newly embedded within the India I used to know well.

But, just outside the gates is another India. It assails your senses, unapologetic, aggressive, reminding you it is there, with its traffic noises, dust, grime, loud horns, two-wheelers of every kind sidling between four-wheelers of all sorts, a grim poverty in the eyes of the vendors and beggars at the traffic lights, hopeful aspiration in the shiny nylon garments of every girl and boy, their mobile phones stuck to their ears as they look ahead at so much more that they want from their lives.

Along the sidelines sit the hutments and slums of the invisible people who built these gleaming new buildings, migrant labour lured from rural areas by the promise of jobs and money, living in tented huts with bright-blue plastic roofs to keep the rain out, the smell telling me that toilets are an unknown luxury. The construction workers include women with newborns suckling at their breasts as they carry bricks on their heads, their older children looking up at a blazing sun. Urbanization and migration, landlessness and construction, homelessness and new homes jostle against each other, the inequalities starker than ever, sharper from just a few years ago and adding to the guilt I carry within my privilege.

I look down at the tired, sweaty faces of my children and feel a sudden rush of love so huge that I can barely contain it. I smile at their obvious delight at the cheap pink (fake strawberry flavour) and orange (fake mango) iced lollies, full of food colouring and chemicals that I know I shouldn't let them have, and my heart melts at the uncomplaining way in which they are beginning to face their little trials and tribulations – a foreshadowing of life's big ones yet to come.

We've all faced them. Lived them. Lived through them. And become the tougher for it, more resilient. Wasn't this one of the reasons we chose to come back home, uprooting our children from an idyllic, fairy-tale-like childhood? So that they learn resilience, become tough, go through experiences similar to those we had? Isn't this why we threw them, head first, into the rigorous curriculum-heavy Indian school instead of the gentler, holistic American Embassy School (AES)?

Well, now it was time to walk our talk.

3

Omnipresent

2010–12

I can see my children in the yellow August afternoon from my kitchen window as I wash the vegetables I have just bought and prepare to clean them with my newly acquired ozonizer. The thick haze of dust suspended in the air makes the sun look like a dim, red fireball, but the trees outside have begun to sway eagerly, and it looks as if it may rain again.

The children are playing with a ragamuffin kitten we have brought home from an animal shelter and which they have named Spirit. I mechanically go over a debate we have been having endlessly – whether or not we should return to the US. It's not a real option – I couldn't bear to move again, so soon – but my husband's job is an always-beckoning beacon. Our neatly stacked green cards call out to be converted to full citizenship. We will need to decide soon; the paperwork of paying taxes in two countries takes up too much time, effort and energy.

It is my son's troubling behavioural changes that are causing me anxiety. He was always an intense, tranquil child, somewhat hyper-sensory, prone to taking life a bit too seriously, overthinking every decision, uncomfortable with spontaneity, but happy in the shadow of his extroverted sister. A quietly content, inventive child. But ever since our move back, I notice, he laughs less, seems more angry. Last week, he deliberately smashed a glass bowl to the ground before bursting into unaccountable tears. I have talked to endless counsellors, educators – even two psychologists – to figure out what is causing these personality alterations. I'm concerned that perhaps the move to India will turn out to be his undoing.

The dull yellow sky is turning grey, darkening ominously. I anticipate a quiet afternoon mulling over our options, as I watch sheets of rain from the window, over a cup of tea and perhaps samosas, the classic fantasy those who grew up in India carry with us wherever we go.

But right now, I have more immediate chores to finish, which include washing off the toxic chemicals and pesticides sticking to the vegetables and fruits I've just bought. California has made me hyper-aware of chemicals and pesticides in my produce, antibiotics and hormones in my dairy and meats, mercury in my fish, and carcinogens in skin and hair products.

I've figured out the difference between conventional and organic produce, obsessed about wild-caught versus farm-raised, cage-free, grass-fed and kosher until I've finally understood the meaning of 'ignorance is bliss'. But the thing is, once you know something is bad for your children's health, it's difficult to un-know it.

So I triple-wash my fruits and vegetables in water and potassium permanganate before ozonizing them, will always choose glass and steel containers over plastic to avoid toxic BPA and am constantly looking for better ways to filter my drinking water, balance its pH and minerals. To assuage my guilt, I try to save the gallons of water that my reverse-osmosis water filter throws out by attaching its long, thin pipe to a 50-litre tank that captures the waste water and reuse it to clean the house and water the plants.

I've developed a reputation as the crazy lady who stops the drivers in my neighbourhood from hosing down their cars, requesting them to use a bucket and cloth instead. My next-door neighbour dislikes me for insisting on using *kaccha paani*, the unfiltered water that smells of sewage, in my garden. 'It stinks, you know? Can't you smell it?' she wrinkles her nose. And when she realizes I won't listen, she tells me that the bacteria in it will make my children sick. 'It's good for the soil,' I insist stoutly, but her words hit home.

I know that microbiological pollution is good for you, that it builds immunity. I learnt this lesson early, when my now-husband returned from the US after completing his engineering degree at Stanford nearly 20 years ago. Unable to figure out why he kept falling sick in his first year back, he went to a top medical research institute to understand the issue. There, the head of gastroenterology explained to him that the human body takes roughly a year to get used to local bacteria and develop immunity to native microbes, and it takes just as long for gut flora to readjust and familiarize itself to the new assault. This knowledge has helped to keep me from becoming a paranoid parent. When I restart my writing, mining my own life for 'Chai Latte', one of the columns I write, I talk about organic versus conventionally grown produce. The concept of 'organic' is still very new, and the Indian courts have recently taken note of excessive pesticides found in vegetables at the *mandis*. I'm relieved and hopeful that the court's attention will bring the change we need, as I note in my column.[1]

I had promised myself I wouldn't turn into the sort of returning Indian that everyone loves to hate. And I have embraced Delhi, warts and all – easy, because I was born and mostly raised in this city. But poor health is something else, and I've been traumatized from miscarriages and premature birth already. My daughter has undergone surgery before she was two, been in a burns ward before she was three and been on an intravenous drip at a military hospital before she was five. I have sat at enough hospitals to loathe the smell of antiseptic and the white lights that accompany the pain of seeing a loved one suffer.

'Mommy! Come quickly,' I hear the panic in my daughter's voice. I run out and find my two tweens huddled around their kitten, who is not moving at all.

'What happened?' I ask, drying my hands, my heart full of dread.

'Spirit shuddered just now. Very hard. Now she's not moving,' says my son. 'Is she dead?

'Mommy, she can't die!' My daughter's voice is firm, but my ears catch in it a note of hysteria.

'Don't let her die. I'm not going to let her die. Can we take her to the vet?'

While I drive to our new vet, I note that Spirit is breathing, but only just. I wonder what awaits us as I remember the vet shaking his head over the kitten just a couple of days ago, asking me sotto voce if I knew what I was doing adopting such a sick kitty.

The muggy, yellow afternoon has turned dark as heavy grey clouds follow our car out of our verdant neighbourhood. I narrowly miss a peacock that is shaking its brilliant turquoise tail at us, but both children have no eyes for anything but the raggedy kitten in their arms.

I don't see much hope, but we wait at the community centre where the vet is located. Outside, it starts to rain; the smell of wet earth is balm to my senses. But I'm also dreading what I know will be a tiresome drive back home; because Delhi can't handle any rain, the roads will quickly get waterlogged, traffic lights will go on the blink, and honking and stalling cars will pile up quickly. For now, I sit there and inhale the smell of the Indian monsoon, among the sick animals and their hopeful humans and I feel content.

But Spirit survives and we drive back home.

'Leave Spirit in her basket and have a bath, you two. I don't want any bacteria from the sick animals on us. Plus, we're all a little wet from the rain. I don't want anyone getting sick here,' I'm already instructing the kids as I park.

'Some bacteria are good for us,' remarks my son. 'I learnt that on the internet.'

'You're only saying that because you don't want to have a bath, stinky,' says my daughter, who is slightly OCD about cleanliness and baths, and hates sharing her organized room with her messy brother.

'Not true! Did you know that to keep your immune system active, alert and fit, you've got to give it some bacteria to fight against, otherwise it gets lazy?' he challenges her with his new-found knowledge. They are both in high spirits, their kitty is alive, but I can see they are tired, hear it in the higher-than-normal pitch of their voices. I'm dreading a meltdown.

'Of course, I know that! And if you live in too sterile an environment, your immune system can turn against you, because it has no bacteria to fight, and that's how you get allergies. That's why so many of my friends at Ohlone had so many allergies. Palo Alto was too clean,' retorts my daughter, cuddling Spirit and kissing her forehead, to my chagrin. My son is silent. I wish she hadn't brought up the old school, the old neighbourhood. I ruffle his damp hair, sticky with sweat.

He doesn't look at me. He is standing on the driveway, washed clean by the rain, looking down. Then he shoots an angry look at his sister. His mouth is turned down.

'You're both correct,' I say hurriedly. 'Without some bacteria to fight, your immune system can get lazy – or crazy and begin attacking itself. But, right now, you probably have a lot, which is much, much more than some. Your immune system is your private army...'

'Consisting of white blood cells and good gut bacteria, which fight the enemy, the bad bacteria. By washing hands, keeping warm, eating well and sleeping long, we help the good guys fight the bad guys,' the children chorus, and I see some serious eye-rolling as they look at each other. But at least they are united again, no longer spoiling for a fight to release their emotional stress. A bath will ease their tiredness – and wash off all the bacteria, I decide, as I take Spirit gently from them and herd them quickly towards the washroom.

That night, despite our best efforts, Spirit dies. Surprisingly, it is my son who is inconsolable, my daughter stoic as we prepare to bury her. A picture of Spirit's furry orange face is added to our shiny chrome refrigerator door, right next to the re-pasted list of the Environmental Working Group's 'Skin-Deep' database that tells me which personal products from soaps and shampoos to sunscreens have the maximum toxins and the 'Dirty Dozen' and 'Clean Thirteen' that has survived from my refrigerator in Palo Alto – produce that absorbs the maximum and minimum pesticides and chemicals.

It is Dussehra, 2010. We have been back just over a year. We are standing, along with hundreds, or maybe thousands, of others around the giant effigies of Meghnada, Kumbhakarana and Ravana that rise imposingly from what is normally a parking lot in Khan Market. The scene is surreal, set as it is amongst the chrome-and-glass frontage of designer stores. We are waiting for a local politician to shoot the fateful arrow that will explode Meghnada's effigy into a shower of fireworks and flames. Meanwhile, the sounds of the dholak and other folk instruments beat on our eardrums. I draw the children closer to me. I've never liked crowds, and now that I have young children crowds feel more menacing than before. My mother's anxieties have slowly become mine. But 'Ravana-burning' has been an exciting part of my husband's childhood, and something he had missed the most while we were away.

At this point, our children are looking wide-eyed at the imposing structures, the colourful wood-and-paper caricatures from the Ramayana. They already know the story of good and evil, Ram and Ravana, and now they are getting infected with the palpable excitement of the milling crowd around us.

'The whole of Ravana will burn?' asks my son.

'Meghnada and Kumbhakarana also, silly! Everything will burn, go up in smoke,' says my daughter. She is excited, almost as much as her father, her eyes shining. I ask her to remain close. My son looks around. He is thinking.

'Mommy?' He tugs at my hand insistently. There are balloon sellers, and today they are also carrying bamboo and cardboard bow and arrow sets, swords and *damrus*, bringing back memories from my own childhood. It feels like home; these sights, smells and sounds have taken me back to another era. It feels so familiar, but also so different. I realize with a sudden shock that like my city, I too, have changed.

'Mommy? Where are the fire engines?'

'What fire engines, baba? Are you afraid of a fire?' I ask.

'The fire engines,' he insists. 'There will be so much burning and so many people, so much smoke, shouldn't there be a fire engine, you know, in case?'

It's a valid question. I remember the earthquake drills their school had in California and how I couldn't relate to them. When the inevitable earthquake did happen, the children were under the dining table in a trice, holding tightly onto the sturdy table legs. Meanwhile, I stood petrified, dinner dishes in hand, wondering whether to run outside with the children or stand under the doorframe, as I'd once read I should. They called out to me in one voice, 'Mommy, come, duck, cover and hold,' as they dived under, within 20 seconds of the first rumble. Their disaster preparedness had impressed me, but also made me realize how the unique cultural context of fatalism can inform action – and I wrote about this as well.[2]

Now the drumbeats are rising to a crescendo, the politicians have come, the speeches have begun. Before we know it, the theatrical Rama, Lakshmana and Sita, in their saffron robes, are standing before us, ready to unleash the fiery arrows at the effigies. The first to light up is Meghnada, Ravana's thunderous brother, followed by Kumbhakarana, the other brother, who sleeps for six months of the year. Then, it is Ravana's turn, the learned Brahmin whose one mistake doomed him to being a villain in Indian mythology. Flames burst into the sky, fireworks go off, and the effigies burn in thick ropes of smoke that rise into the air. The smell of explosives enters our nostrils. We look up admiringly at the sky that is now lit up, and the children squeal with joy, all their fears forgotten.

Afterwards, as we walk home, I pick up the fire engine conversation and try to explain how cultures differ in their disaster preparedness, and how the Indian concept of fate and destiny sometimes limits our ability to plan for and react to natural disasters. I can't recall a single fire or earthquake drill during my own childhood, yet the drills in the schools back in California had been wonderfully reassuring to me as a parent.

We walk along, crossing the streets carefully, my son leading the way, looking in both directions. He has finally learnt not to trust Indian zebra crossings and traffic lights, and has become a cautious road-crosser. The children chatter on about the fireworks and the mythology of the Ramayana, all of us occasionally correcting each other. The smoke and smell of explosives is still in the air.

'Winter is coming,' says my daughter blithely. She clears her throat. 'I can smell it in the air. Winter in Delhi smells just like this. Mommy, when will the melas start?' My son walks along silently, occasionally rubbing his eyes, which I notice are turning red. The October evening air has turned cool, but it also smells acrid, sharp, the fumes of the explosives that have gone up in smoke still hanging low. My eyes are stinging too, and I blink hard but remain distracted by thoughts of my childhood triggered by a particular smell, the fragrance of seasonal autumn trees intermingling with the smell of expended Dussehra fireworks. It is good to be home, I think, even as, unknown to us, we continue to breathe in particulate matter many times over WHO-prescribed limits.

Exactly 19 days later, it is Diwali. This is our second Diwali back home, and my house is lit up with tiny oil-filled terracotta lamps.

Last year, this evening was a blur of friends, family, too much food and too much expectation to live up to. We had marvelled at how different it was from Diwali in Palo Alto. There, when I tried to light diyas and place them outdoors, I was warned that the fire department may knock on my door, and so I ended up standing a tense guard and finally bringing the lamps in. We were the only Indian family on the block. Later, we had found others, who met at each other's homes, played cards and ate spicy Indian food. Once, we even burst some firecrackers in their backyard, right by a creek that flowed through it, although none of us was sure if that was even allowed.

But here, diyas and *patakhas* are everywhere. Except, this year, my children have taken a pledge in school against burning crackers. They are being taught about the ill effects of crackers, about child labour and how tiny hands are used by Sivaskasi factories to fill finely ground explosives into delicate paper, while young lungs inhale the toxic, metal-and-chemical-laden particles. But they had looked so longingly at the rockets and Catherine wheels at some of the melas we had gone to, that I had quietly bought a few. When I bring out the handful of crackers at night, the children's faces light up in excitement, but then cloud over when they realize they'd be breaking their pledge. Despite my urging them, they refuse to light the crackers. But for all the fireworks we don't light, our next-door neighbour more than compensates.

A single wall separates Pavan and Neera Varma's home from ours. The middle-aged couple have the advantage of a little over a decade on us and live on the first floor of their family home with Pavan's feisty 80-year-old mother who still looks like a yesteryears Hollywood film star. Her elder son and wife live on the second floor in the sweetest joint family set-up I have ever known. To me, in a certain way, they epitomize Delhi.

Pavan and Neera were among the first to welcome us into the neighbourhood, showing up at the door when our container arrived, asking if they could be of any help. Pavan is an electronics engineer and runs authorized service centres for over a dozen electronic companies. He is that combination of dynamic, masterful and genial that has created the foundation of services in Delhi as we know it today. Neera is his soft power, his inner strength. They know everyone in our neighbourhood, troves of backstories included. We've loved everything about them so far – except the long *ladi*s Pavan insists on lighting Diwali after Diwali. It's his thing – his pride, his machismo, his tradition, his baggage, and he won't let go, however much anyone asks.

'That's Dad,' says his son with a shrug. He is a budding engineer and entrepreneur, who literally built a car that runs on water in their garage in 2005. On water! What could be cleaner than that! Unfortunately, apart from some newspaper articles, he hasn't got any traction, no encouragement from the government or investors mainly because there are no certification companies in India that will proactively offer him validation. 'I've given up,' he tells me.

Still, we raise our voice in complaint, politely, firmly. But being relative newcomers to this friendly neighbourhood we are jovially ignored, when we aren't repeatedly being asked to join in. So we stand back disapprovingly and watch in silent dismay as sackfuls of fireworks go up in smoke. The odour of that cocktail of chemicals, metals, explosives and paper burning hangs low in the air, without dispersing in the stillness of the night. The next morning, the smoky air still looks ghostly. The street sweepers are out there with their long bamboo brooms, throwing up more dust as they collect the burnt embers of last night's celebrations into little mounds. Then they light these, to leave smouldering embers of blackened ash nestled between more plumes of smoke. Pavan smiles genially at me from across the wall that separates our homes, the smoke distorting his features. I don't smile back.

The following year, on Diwali, we have the same conversation. Pavan is still smiling as he continues to light many firecrackers; specially his famous *ladi*, which stretches from one end of our lane to the other, around 500 metres, singeing the air with its light, bursting with its sound and fury for a full five minutes. It is always his grand finale.

My smile is strained by now, though my children seem more pragmatic. They no longer look wistfully at others lighting crackers, they still enjoy watching the sky light up. They've stopped saying, 'Isn't this like the 4th of July?' and no longer refer to their festive traditional wear as 'costumes': my son in his kurta pyjama and my daughter in all varieties of ghagra choli and salwar kameez. I notice lazily that their references have become more Indian, their Hindi near-perfect. Sometimes when I hear my son speaking to my mother in Hindi, a language she has a master's in, I feel that the angst and experience of moving back is validated. Although my son still hasn't settled in fully, his behaviour is no longer as worrying as before. My husband and I discuss the logistics and decide we are ready to take the plunge to give up our green card.

In December 2011, we park our car a little distance from the US embassy and walk in to give up our green cards. An incredulous young man, blonde and clean-shaven, repeatedly asks if we're 'absolutely certain' of our decision as he checks our application to voluntarily surrender our lawful permanent resident status in the United States.

We nod in unison. We're sure.

The room is empty. We are the only people who want to give up this document. We're making a mistake. At least, that's what my son is saying to me. He has been quiet, thoughtful the whole morning.

'I don't want to give up my green card, Mom. Why do I have to?' I hear him say abruptly.

'You don't *have* to. None of us *have* to. We're *choosing* to give it back.' I sit on my haunches until I'm at eye level. His long-lashed, brown eyes look steadily back into mine.

'I'm not choosing. I don't want to give it up,' he says. His words bring back all my doubts.

'Why? Aren't you happy to be back in India?' I ask.

'But why do we have to give up the green card? Doesn't this card ensure that one day I can live in Palo Alto forever?' His eyes are pleading now, and I'm at a loss for words.

'You can give up yours if you want. I'm not giving up mine,' he says, suddenly stubborn. 'I'm telling that man at the window. I'm telling him I'm sad. I want to go back home.'

Home! He still considers Palo Alto home. A thousand thoughts go through my mind before I hug him close and tell him how we can't live without him. Luckily that hug is all he needs to nestle obediently back into the family fold. By the time the clean-shaven man has read through our three-page Form I-407, abandonment of lawful permanent resident status applications, asking us again if we're certain, if we're aware that we will be giving up all our rights, if we're aware we will become non-resident aliens, my family is one again. We tell him we understand our rights and won't be changing our minds. He stamps 10-year visas on our Indian passports, and we leave American soil, stepping outside, into the wide Delhi roads and a weak December sun.

But my son's pleading eyes stay with me and I redouble my efforts to help him settle down. My mother is my strongest ally and has already presented him with a large Casio piano. He takes to it like a duck takes to water; his behavioural tics improve. He becomes calmer, happier, more settled. Serendipitously, I find a piano teacher right across the park, a Korean woman who loves music and children. With the switch from the tabla to the piano, his musical journey takes on a new life.

By Diwali 2012, I have not only stopped insisting stonily that Pavan desist from lighting his Diwali crackers, but we've also stopped joining our otherwise near-perfect neighbours during this part of the festival evening, no longer standing outside with them and their friends while they light their heavy cache of fireworks, along with the *ladi*. He pretends not to notice, and I pretend not to care. I try to not let it bother me.

This year has been fulfilling in so many ways. My children seem to have finally settled in. They have started teaching the children of all drivers and cooks in the neighbourhood how to use computers and, in the process, made many friends. This had never been a problem for my extroverted daughter, but what delights me is my son's soccer-crazy 'gang' – the same children whom he teaches digital literacy. A few months later, Joao, a Portuguese boy exactly his age moves in next door. He is equally sporty and joins the gang. My son seems much happier. His piano teacher has left, but we've bought a real piano, a well-loved upright from a departing expat, and he is now immersed in music. It has transformed him.

There is only one problem. Recently, I've started feeling something is very wrong, started dreading the Delhi winters, something I used to enjoy so much. I've begun noticing that the number of people who sniff, cough or get sick in the winter seems disproportionately higher than when I was here as a child. In the last two winters, someone or the other in my house has been sick, each time with respiratory issues that have lingered on. I myself have had a bad bout of asthma, something I'd suffered from briefly as a child but haven't had for years. My walking partner, a young

American mother whose children keep getting ear infections, has now got pneumonia Her children are not the only ones. All my children's friends seem to suffer from some respiratory disease or the other right through the winters. Many carry inhalers in their school bags. If my elderly parents have caught colds or developed a cough after November, it has invariably ended up stretching through the entire winter.

I can't resist keeping a count of the instances I encounter. I decide I've become the paranoid NRI I'd promised myself I would never be. This is normal, this is India, I tell myself; I must accept, surrender, go with the flow, do whatever people do to adjust. I take a deep breath. Then another. And another. I feel slightly calmer.

That's when I meet Gen.

4

Invisible

Winter 2012–13

Genevieve and Robert Chase arrive in India in September 2012 from their posting in Addis Ababa. Rob's job with the World Bank had seen them live in different parts of the world, and they're excited about being in India.

When I meet Gen for the first time on a cool October evening in 2012, we connect instantly. She is originally a California girl, and we talk excitedly about Palo Alto and Delhi, how rich both places are in such different ways – the similarities and dissimilarities. We promise to stay in touch; then, like it always is, we lose contact.

It will be another year before she and I actually begin to talk about our experiences with pollution and what it is doing to our families. It will be later, after I've joined her cohort of pollution warriors, after she has returned to the US and joined the Environmental Protection Agency (EPA) in Washington, after my mother has succumbed to lung cancer, that we will piece together the story of the invisible killer, phone call by weekly phone call.

'I fell in love with Delhi almost as soon as we arrived. It was magical, beautiful. There was this mystical sort of haze surrounding everything,' Gen says over one of these calls, her voice sounding wistful. 'The school was great, we were happy, everything seemed wonderful… Until the headaches started. My daughter was a track-and-field athlete but running seemed to give her headaches and made her feel sick. She was otherwise a healthy tween and had never had asthma or any respiratory problem in the past. But now she just always seemed to be sick.' Gen's background, including her master's degree in public health, made her more sensitive, telling her something was very wrong. 'First, it was just headaches. Then, one or other of us always seemed to be sick.'

'In our first winter in Delhi, we were all sick at different points in time,' she reminisces. 'Naturally, as a mother, I was very concerned. I kept thinking there was some weird virus that was around.' By the end of that year, Gen had dived deeper into the research.

I ask her if she had read Heather Timmons's news reports on Delhi's air pollution being worse than Beijing's, the most recent of which appeared in the India Ink blog of the *New York Times* in January 2013, just months after her arrival.[1] Gen can't remember reading that article but what she does remember about that January is a meeting in the headmaster's office at her children's American Embassy School, in which the usually receptive headmaster brusquely dismissed her fears. 'It left me feeling very uncomfortable,' she says.

It is only later that Gen will find out that fellow Americans who were diplomats had access to pollution statistics that she didn't, and surmises that the embassy school most likely already had access to those numbers as well, given that many of those diplomats were school parents. 'They probably already knew. They certainly had more information than I did,' she says. But back in January 2013, she didn't connect the dots. 'No one used to wear masks then, so I didn't think about air pollution to begin with.'

The irony was that before taking up the Delhi posting, Gen and Rob had actively considered another position that was available in China but had passed on it due to the high pollution levels there. 'No one talked of air pollution in Delhi back then, so we chose to come to Delhi over Beijing,' Gen tells me. Having worked as a public health consultant in two countries before moving to India, Gen knew that dirty air harmed health. But since the secret of Delhi's air remained hidden in plain sight, it took some time for her to make the connection.

New Delhi's American Embassy School didn't encourage her fears and didn't engage with her, she says. 'Very early on, the school [AES] didn't want to talk to me about this. I was new to India, to the system. I was shy. I didn't want to be thought alarmist or unreasonable. I didn't want to be seen as that crazy, obstreperous mother. But more and more, I could see, something was wrong.' So Gen persisted steadfastly.

'Then, when I found the numbers, I was appalled.' The numbers she is referring to were of PM2.5, and, at first, Gen couldn't believe how high the levels were.

'I couldn't understand why no one was talking about that level of pollution,' she wonders. 'But I was still too new. And I was bashful... And no one mentioned PM2.5.' In fact, people in the international community only talked about PM10 – fine dust.

Heat and dust are what define India to foreigners; everyone talks about the dust in India. But PM2.5 isn't dust. It's much smaller, the finest microparticles that bypass all the natural barriers the human body has, including nose hairs that trap dust. Once inhaled, these particles go deep into the lungs and are absorbed into the bloodstream, thus travelling to all organs of the body. These particles are toxic for our body, which tries to fight them with the only defences it has, creating in the process mild to severe inflammatory responses and oxidative stress. The damage PM2.5 causes the human body goes beyond the respiratory system, lungs or heart. This harm is irreversible.

Since the bulk of the initial research conducted on air pollution's health effects had been done on respiratory and cardiovascular health, less is known about other health harms caused by air pollution. Doctors in Bengaluru say that around 20 per cent of the severe cases of heart attacks admitted in ICUs are due to air pollution.[2] But apart from hypertension and heart arrhythmia, which lead to heart attacks and strokes in Indians as young as 16 years old,[3] polluted air triggers many other lifestyle and non-communicable diseases. It can lead to diabetes, cancer, obesity, kidney and liver disease. It affects neurological pathways, thus causing cognitive and psychiatric impact, and triggering autism, dementia, Alzheimer's, depression, bipolar disorder. It also results in infertility, prenatal, neonatal and postnatal health harm and childhood leukaemia.[4] Air pollution affects every human organ, writes Damian Carrington, the *Guardian*'s environment editor, quoting scientists from the Forum of International Respiratory Societies who state that air pollution may be damaging 'acutely as well as chronically' every organ and virtually every cell in the human body.[5]

It would be at least two more years before we slowly found out how ubiquitously, holistically these particles affect the human body, our knowledge deepening like a horror story in slow motion. It was like unpeeling layers of an imperceptibly decomposing onion to get to the dark, rotten core, invisible from the outside. Over time, I would find out through the tweets of Dr Maria Neira, the director of public and environmental health at WHO, that there were more than 70,000 scientific papers linking air pollution to health harm.[6] But in 2013, we were still fumbling for information, some of us, still in denial.

Meanwhile, Gen ploughed ahead. 'I turned to the internet. I went to the EPA [Environmental Protection Agency] site, the WHO site, the NIH sites, the Johns Hopkins site. And the more I studied this problem, the more I panicked. And the more I panicked, the more I started talking about it to everyone who was willing to lend me an ear,' says Gen.

Healthwise, things seemed to improve briefly for her family later in 2013, but that was probably just the pollution season easing as the approaching summer burnt off the smog. It happens every year when the season changes after it rains in February or March and, with wind velocity increasing, Delhi's air improves to its best levels by April.

Another clue for Gen was that whenever they left Delhi – in their initial excitement to explore this vast, new country, they took several short holidays over long weekends outside the capital – her family's health seemed to improve miraculously. Yet, when they returned to Delhi, a strange miasma seemed to get hold of them, and they were down again.

'Sick. Down. Low on energy. Just not feeling good. Something, we didn't know what, was getting hold of us,' she says. What was this mysterious vapour, she kept thinking. An unknown virus? By the end of that year, with her observations, research and the data she found, Gen had come to the realization that this wasn't a virus that was affecting her family.

It was air pollution.

'But the worst part was knowing that we were only suffering the short-term effects of air pollution. There were other, longer-term, irreversible effects that I would be carrying back with me when I left the country,' Gen says, her voice heavy with regret.

At that point Gen went on a mission to educate others. She pushed friends to talk and write about this issue. Among these friends was Gardiner Harris, the *New York Times* correspondent, who had just arrived in India.

'I encouraged, actually, nagged him to look at the numbers being published by the Central Pollution Control Board. We moved in the same social circles. I urged him to look at the numbers being published on government websites, hidden in technical and bureaucratic jargon,' Gen tells me. It wasn't just Harris Gen would talk to about this, but whoever came in her radar. 'I wasn't strategic about it – I just wanted all this information on air pollution out there in the public domain,' she says. As far as Gardiner was concerned, Gen says, 'I just wanted to leverage the incredible reach of his voice.'

Gardiner had been the public health correspondent for the *New York Times* in Washington DC, a sharp, if eccentric, journalist, with searchlight-blue eyes and the typical curiosity of an experienced newshound. Delhi was his first international posting, which probably explains why he didn't fit the role of the lethargic purveyor of second-hand stories, something I'd seen many foreign correspondents who arrived here end up falling back on.

I knew Gardiner too, though in a different context. He and my husband were tennis partners, his wiry, 6-foot frame and athletic body giving my husband more than his match. His wife, Elizabeth, was one of the early members of my serious-readers-only book group and had become a friend. They lived a two-minute walk away in a charming white bungalow with a palm-fringed garden that faced Delhi's zoo, with just an old stone wall separating it from the zoo's green acreage.

Within months of moving to Delhi, their young son Bram suffered from the effects of the city's air, developing asthma and being put on inhalers, nebulizers and steroids. I still recall in vivid detail how Elizabeth once phoned me in utter distress during a scary episode of breathlessness her son experienced that left us both shaken. In some ways, it is the epiphany I had after that April evening's events that made me realize the dangerous levels of air pollution we were all breathing.

It is in April 2013, and I am at another journalist friend's birthday celebration. We are laughing so loudly on her terrace I almost miss hearing Elizabeth's phone call. She sounds panicked.

'It's my son,' she says without preamble. 'He can't breathe! What do I do?'

At first, I'm confused.

'Is it an allergy? Did he get stung? Do you have an EpiPen at home?' I ask, painfully aware that she is alone at home, with her two children. I know Gardiner is travelling because no tennis has been scheduled. I can feel her panic. I've been that mother, alone with two young children in a foreign country where I had no family while my husband travelled on work, so I hear her, hear her loud and clear. And unlike in the US, where at least I had the advantage of a 911-type emergency rescue, a huge comfort and one of the only things I miss even now, in my own country with its erratic healthcare system, there is no emergency rescue I can recommend to her. I want to help. But how?

'Who do you call here when there's a medical emergency?' she asks. I hear the suppressed tension in her voice.

'Er...family, mostly. But mostly, I pray I never have an emergency.'

'What should I do? Bram can't breathe. He seems to be having a sort of an asthma attack,' her voice rising in fear. She says she thinks it's the air. The air? Oh gosh.

Without a 911-type emergency rescue that most Americans depend upon, Elizabeth has found it hard to cope with these sudden attacks. This is her first call to me, though later, there will be others.

'Do you have a nebulizer at home?' I can feel panic rising in me along with sympathy. We've spoken about the bad air in Delhi and how it affects children in a desultory sort of way often enough, but suddenly I feel perhaps I've been in denial. This is so real, so scary. So immediate.

'What should I do?' She is sounding breathless herself. What should I say?

I move away from the laughing, chattering group of people to a quieter side of the terrace so that I can hear her better. If I were home, I could have run over to her house, even just for moral support. Because, the truth is, I don't really know how I can help.

Once Elizabeth realizes I'm not in the neighbourhood but at a party some distance away, she thanks me distractedly, innately polite, and hangs up. I can't stop thinking about what she and her son must be going through and call her back after a while, but her phone is busy. When I call back later, it keeps ringing.

I'm unable to enjoy myself the rest of the evening, much as I try, and on my return, I ensure we drive by her house. Everything looks peaceful. I wonder what I was expecting. My husband is flying to New York later that night and is in a hurry to get home, but I double back after dropping him at home.

'I'll just check from outside. I just want to reassure myself that everything is okay,' I promise him, before driving away quickly. He has warned me not to barge in, not to do things Indian-style, not to bother her; he is very politically correct and often embarrassed by his more spontaneous wife.

I park outside, then realize I don't actually know what to do. My husband's warnings ring loud in my ears. Elegant palm fronds framing Gardiner and Elizabeth's garden sway gently in the night breeze, waving to me to leave. Almost immediately, I get a whiff of smoke – perhaps someone burning leaves inside the zoo or within the neighbourhood. With so many trees and greenery, there are bound to be leaves aplenty – and many will take the quick-fix route of burning them instead of composting. It is late, so I don't want to ring the bell and disturb her. I convince myself that everything is fine and leave.

Elizabeth tells me the next day how awful it was. She is sure it is the polluted air. Bram has been sensitive to the air, but he has never gasped for breath in that exact way before. The hospital says he's lost lung function, and she is considering flying back to the US. I'm speechless.

A week later, I get a late-night email.

Jyoti, are you awake? The air is just horrible again. G says he will start prowling around at night to figure out where it's coming from, but really, will that make any difference? Even if we do find the source (what if it is in the zoo, for example? That's my guess), is anyone really going to do anything about it? I think it's more realistic for me to find us an apartment across town. Now is the time when so many expats are leaving, and so the time to look at flats. It's heartbreaking, but I think the more practical thing to do. YUCK.

By September 2013 she's hired a realtor, and by October, barely a year after, they move into a house right across town, a modern, cookie-cutter home of chrome and glass in Vasant Vihar. There, they can seal all the windows and doors tightly, and with the air filters running all the time, they will be able to sanitize that bubble, keeping their children safe, protecting themselves as best they can. Their school, AES, has already begun planning indoor air purification. This is how they manage for the next couple of years.

I remember thinking that this is not how it should be. This is just not how it should be.

That Diwali, we stay away from fireworks, which has become usual, but celebrate by getting ourselves a dog. My children are over the moon. We decided to name her Lila.

Between experiencing first-hand his son's reaction to Delhi's toxic air and the constant stream of data he received from Gen, Gardiner began writing for his newspaper what is now an entire body of stories linking poor air quality to poor health outcomes.

As Gen became more deeply entrenched in the local expat community and made more friends in her AES school circles, her increasing conviction that US embassy and state government employees seemed to have access to better information on air pollution than she did was validated by a new friendship when she met Beth Kotis, a fellow school parent.

Beth Silverman Kotis and Samuel D. Kotis had arrived in India a year after Gen, in August 2013. Sam was a diplomat at the US embassy. Thanks to Gen and others talking so openly about air pollution, their family was quicker to reach similar conclusions.

'One winter is all it took,' Beth tells me.

The Kotises weren't new to poor air quality. They had moved to Delhi from London, a city whose air holds high levels of nitrous oxides, NOx, from its vehicular diesel fumes. Since 1991, they had also lived in Jakarta, Tunis, Baghdad, Amman, Singapore and Budapest – and knew what poor air quality looked, felt and smelt like.

'Our first interaction with bad air had been in Jakarta during our posting there from 1992 to 1994,' Sam tells me. 'When I arrived in New Delhi to begin my assignment, the bad air here was already an increasingly distressing issue for many, especially in the embassy community,' says Sam, in his measured baritone. Not only did these people have the option of choosing not to live in India, but they were also much more aware than most local Indians. Ironically, those most affected by pollution are least aware of its harms. It is an inversely correlated curve.

Sam agrees to be interviewed only after he retires from his job with the US Department of State. I speak to the Kotises in a joint interview when I'm trying to work out the timeline of how pollution research became more mainstream in the country.

Were they taken aback by the extent and levels of pollution when they arrived, I ask, especially considering it wasn't as widely written about as the pollution in China?

'We were taken completely unaware,' says Beth. It was a shock, something they were unprepared for.

'There was lots of paperwork, of course, but air pollution didn't show up as a factor anywhere,' says Beth. 'If I recall correctly, there was some mention of air pollution being an issue in the country report for India, but nothing that struck us as alarming at the time.'

'At first, we had no data to attach to why we were feeling so crappy. People [who were posted here] weren't aware until they got here,' he says.

'In any case,' breaks in Beth, 'we certainly weren't focused on air pollution. We just arrived excited, to go experience a new country. We'd been warned about the chaotic traffic, some health issues, crime, safety and other big red flags, but air pollution certainly never showed up prominently in those conversations.'

However, Sam's job at the embassy gave him first-hand access to all environment data, data that Gen had to struggle to find.

But he also had to face the classic problem that all expats have – especially those on a diplomatic passport. He couldn't openly criticize his host country and had to remain under the radar. How do you tell your host country, for instance, that their air is so dirty that you can barely breathe? It's a bit like being a guest in someone's home and telling them their home is filthy. It's just not kosher – and definitely not diplomatic.

'We were part of the same social community,' says Gen, 'but very soon I realized that Beth and Sam, by virtue of being American diplomats, had better access to air pollution data.'

This was because the US embassy had already installed five expensive EPA-standard air quality monitors (AQM) in New Delhi and its consulates in Mumbai, Kolkata, Chennai and Hyderabad. Updated hourly, the readings were available to all mission personnel through the embassy's intranet system and to family members through a password-protected weblink. What's more, the data was available in an easy-to-understand format keyed to the EPA's AQI and accompanied by EPA-approved health guidance for various levels of pollution.

'We could only see this information on our work computers,'

says Sam. Which meant that American diplomats living in India were sole beneficiaries of this information, while others living in India could not access it, including other American citizens, like Gen. Gen was outraged at what she perceived as double standards. It was this knowledge that made her decide to set up her own website that would disseminate information on pollution freely to everyone. Technically, this information was freely available – displayed in plain sight on the CPCB website, but not easily understood by a layperson.

'The data was there,' admits Gen, 'but not easy to find. And often,' Gen says, 'the system went offline for extended periods of time, without explanation. Especially when the pollution seemed to be at its worst,' she adds significantly. 'The embassy air quality data seemed much more reliable and unbiased.'

She wanted to unpack the complexity and mystery around pollution statistics and spread awareness. The internet seemed the easiest way for that, because, while at one level air pollution is just dirty air, at another it is a complex science, involving meteorology, atmospheric science, data, monitors, methodologies, protocols and climatology. And, if you're interested in its impact on human health, epidemiology.

Beth and Sam were also taken unawares by the informational asymmetry.

'I was dismayed to learn that no one else had access to this pollution data generated by our AQMs,' says Sam. 'It just didn't make sense that a US mission would not share helpful health information with other US nationals living here and with India's citizens. I began asking why.' He was told that senior leadership was opposed to publicizing the embassy's air quality data, and that that position was very unlikely to change. The opposition was based on two assumptions. 'One, that official Indian government air pollution data was already available for anyone who was interested, and thus there was no need to publicize ours,' says Sam, 'and, two, it was best not to do anything to call attention to India's air pollution as that might generate a negative backlash.'

'So what did you do?' I prompt him.

'Well, I discussed this with colleagues in any number of spontaneous "bad air" conversations that would come up,' he says, unhurriedly. Most colleagues were equally concerned but shrugged their shoulders and accepted the status quo.

By December that year, the middle of what is now recognized as high pollution season, relations between India and the United States came to an all-time low after a senior Indian foreign service officer was arrested very publicly in New York for visa fraud and strip-searched, leading to public outrage and retaliatory actions by the Indian government. This was the winter of what is now popularly referred to as the 'Khobragade incident'.[7]

'After the Khobragade incident in December [2013] relations went off a cliff. [The embassy's] decision makers were rightly cautious... The political decision was already made complicated by the prickly relationship. We didn't need to add air pollution to the mix,' says Beth.

From a diplomatic standpoint, this was the worst time to focus any attention on India's poor air quality. But Beth's almost daily interaction with Gen, the knowledge that Sam now carried with him and the fact that not only were American lives being compromised by the high degree of air pollution, but that that information was being, in a sense, withheld from the public, compelled Sam to focus on what was right even if it meant sacrificing diplomacy.

Meanwhile, Gen renewed her efforts to get her children's school to recognize and acknowledge the poor air quality. 'The least they could do was link outdoor aerobic activity to air pollution and ensure that our kids weren't running around exerting themselves in the terrible winter air,' she says. The school didn't have any specific protocols for outdoor play during the high pollution peaks, and Gen worked tirelessly to get something started. But for every policy or change, the first step is awareness and acknowledgement, and that was difficult to come by. By this time, more and more people, mostly diplomats still, were beginning to question the smog that settled on Delhi and most of north India in the cooler months, and a small cohort of American diplomats who had access to the embassy's air pollution data were sharing it, unofficially, with their friends. A hushed panic seemed to be taking hold of the expat community, and drawing-room conversations on winter evenings rarely ended without consternation around Delhi's polluted air. And now there was embassy data leaking through the social fabric to validate these fears.

Ironically, many of these heated discussions about Delhi's poor winter air were taking place in coruscating evenings by these newly aware people standing around coal-burning sigris in the lush gardens of embassies and high commissions, or even private farmhouses, sometimes lit up by hundreds of candles. As my social circles grew and intersected, I felt pulled in two different directions.

When I was with friends from my school and college days, those of us who had been born and raised in India, I felt as if polluted air was a figment of my overactive imagination. But when I met my growing cohort of expatriate friends, families who had lived under bluer skies and cleaner air and could more easily differentiate between degrees of pollution, I would hear worrying statistics and arguments that would confuse me again. Was I overreacting or under-reacting? I wasn't sure.

With Gen's nagging paying off, Gardiner's first story in the *New York Times* appeared in January 2014. Its headline, 'Beijing's bad air would be a step up for smoggy Delhi' catches everyone's attention. It is a well-researched story, quoting WHO statistics, public health experts and studies showing that Indians have the world's weakest lungs, with far less capacity than Chinese lungs.[8] The article cites a study by Pune's Chest Research Foundation that says that half of all visits to doctors in India are for respiratory problems.

'Fine particle pollution has been strongly linked with premature death, heart attacks, strokes and heart failure. In October, the World Health Organization declared that it caused lung cancer,' the article says, citing multiple reports and research. It also quoted the chief executive officer (CEO) of a Swiss-based manufacturer of air purifiers saying sales were hundreds of times higher in China than in India. 'In China, people are extremely concerned about the air, especially around small children... Why there's not the same concern in India is puzzling,' Gardiner quotes the CEO as saying.

He also quotes Dr Angel Hsu from the Yale Centre for Environment Law and Policy as saying, 'It's always puzzled me that the focus is always on China and not India. China has realized that it can't hide behind its usual opacity, whereas India gets no pressure to release better data. So there simply isn't good public data on India like there is for China.'

Meanwhile, Sam kept trying to do what he could do about the situation.[9]

'First, a conference was convened in New Delhi, of officials and academics from India and California involved with the India–California air pollution mitigation programme,' says Sam. 'California's experience offered a compelling, positive story of how an American state had overcome significant environmental challenges and had simultaneously grown its economy substantially. It was a story I felt would resonate in India, and it was something I began to stress in discussions on the issue. These took place between February and April 2014, as an initiative that offered practical, actionable recommendations on ways to improve air quality in India in an affordable and technically feasible manner.'

'In April, a few of us at the embassy met with the Lawrence Berkeley National Labs scientist Dr Josh Apte, who had been doing research on New Delhi's air pollution for several years,' continues Sam. 'Apte's slide presentation[10] was a concise, powerful, easily digestible summation of the factors contributing to Delhi's bad air, the health impact it was having on the population, the importance of raising public awareness of the problem and the steps that could be implemented to begin making a difference. Those of us in that first meeting were so impressed that we proposed that he give his presentation to the ambassador.'

A few weeks later, Dr Apte did just that, and its impact was critical. 'In a short span of time, [then] Ambassador Nancy Powell became a supporter of publishing our data,' says Sam. 'She often cited Apte's briefing as a turning point in her own understanding of the importance of acting on air pollution and how it could fit into our diplomatic engagement with India,' says Sam.

The result was that all restrictions to publicly sharing air quality information were lifted.

'After that, it became just a matter of getting different people to see the value of it,' concludes Sam. 'We weren't trying to make a splash, just put it out there.' And put it out there they did.

The stage was now set for India's invisible killer to be exposed.

5

Toxic

January 2014

I'm late to pick up the children from the bus stop and I still haven't finished writing my 'Startup Gigs' column that is due later today. I also have to send out emails inviting every one of my girlfriends in Delhi – from the newly acquired to the ones I've almost lost touch with – to help me celebrate my birthday this year. I've decided to host a lunch at the Ethiopian Cultural Centre. They're going to be shocked. They know me, and know I dislike acknowledging my birthday, let alone celebrating it. But it's time to celebrate. I finally feel like everyone in my family has settled in, and I'm relieved that both the children are finally in the same school. As I wait by the side of the road for their school bus, I begin to feel sleepy in the warmth of the car. The hazy mid-January sunshine is comforting, the weak sun half hidden behind a thin blanket of winter fog.

Across the road, the graceful Gol Gumbad sits alongside a red-brick church, both blurred by mist and the ubiquitous haze. Less than 100 metres away, I can barely see the arc of a flyover. I smell vehicle exhaust and wonder idly whether Delhi's air is really as polluted as some of my expat friends say it is. I wonder why the city smells so different – not just from other cities I've lived in, or from Palo Alto's magnolia-scented suburban air, but also from my childhood memories – and why the sunshine here seems to be so muted and grey. In this too, compared to my childhood memories of golden sunshine, winter picnics under clear blue skies and shelled peanuts, today the city's landscape seems muted, hazy, almost dystopian, with misty, grey mornings and dull clay-coloured afternoon.

The school bus still hasn't arrived. So I start composing my message to my friends on my phone – a long, persuasive email, as it's going to be a challenge pulling them away for a Monday lunch – and send it. Then I sit back and let a feeling of smug anticipation wash over me.

That afternoon is the happiest, most content I have felt since my return. In retrospect, I should have known that feeling for what it was – hubris. Because in just a matter of time nothing would ever be the same again. Outside, everything looked perfect. Beautiful, beckoning with possibilities, mysterious, all outlines and edges blurred by the smokiness of the afternoon. Inside, I basked in self-congratulatory complacency while killer air swirled and eddied around me, unrecognized, undetected.

A week later, following up on the birthday invite, I have to relay painful news to my friends – that our darling new puppy, Lila, whom we brought home barely three months ago on Diwali, has been run over by a car right outside our gate. We are going ahead with the lunch, but I don't want to talk about her, and don't want them to mention her to the children, who will be joining the group straight from school. When I trace it back now, it is after Lila's death that my well-settled life begins to unravel, unpicked layer by layer by the dawning – and draining – knowledge of the contents of the very air I'm breathing.

I've just pressed 'send' on the email and am trying to overcome my sadness, when a news notification about Delhi's terrible air catches my attention. It's Gardiner's story in the *New York Times.* He is saying Delhi's air is worse than Beijing's![1] This is the first time I'm seeing in black and white the essence of the conversations I've been having with so many of my friends. As I read, I recall how embarrassed China was during the 2008 Olympics when the country's air became a burning issue, focusing the world's attention on it, and how it scrambled to get back its blue skies – going to lengths like engineering rain clouds to cleanse it. Now it's official that Delhi's air is worse. I also clearly remember the time, in 1992, when the United Nations declared Mexico City the most polluted place in the world. At the time, I was a cub reporter in my first job. Travelling by public transport – the Delhi metro had not yet appeared on the scene – passing the congested ITO crossing every day where information on the city's sooty air quality was displayed on digital boards, and noticing how my face, hands and white clothes became grey and dust-ridden by the end of the day, I was constantly reminded that Delhi was not far behind.

A Supreme Court order mandating all public transport to switch to the less polluting compressed natural gas (CNG) as fuel, diligently executed by the government of the time, had saved the city from certain disaster. There had been protests, but the government had stayed firm. The black-and-yellow three-wheelers became green and yellow, and Delhi's air improved quickly. But I feel now that that success lulled us into a sense of complacency.

Subsequently, the number of vehicles on the roads grew at a faster rate, and with frenzied construction activities, burning and combustion following, here we were, 20 years later, back to square one, breathing in worse carcinogenic toxins – now invisible – microparticles, aerosols and gases every day, with every breath. Mexico City had cleaned up its air, leaving Delhi behind. Maybe it was good that Lila had died, I tell myself. Dogs breathe the same air as we do, and we're all going to die, choking and gasping on this toxic air, I think morbidly as I slump over my desk, obsessively rereading Gardiner's news report.

—

I wake up on the morning of my birthday wondering why I'm feeling so low and then I remember Lila. I sigh, but quickly arrange my face into a smile as my children burst in, singing happy birthday to 'mommeeee'. Packing them off to school feels like a chore, and the only thing I'm looking forward to is meeting my mother.

Since moving back to India, I have kicked off every birthday with a visit to my parents' home, to touch their feet, get their blessings. I felt no such urge as a rebellious teen, and remained unconventional and argumentative until I moved to California, but after living away from them, in another country with absolutely no close family around, I've discovered afresh the value of rituals as well as relatives. On my way back from their home, I'm disturbed that my mother still hasn't shaken off her winter cough and that both my parents seem older, weaker, smaller somehow. But I shake off the beginnings of anxiety with the thought of meeting my friends at lunch, certain that they will cheer me up.

This is the first time I've called all my girlfriends without curating the list of invitees. In a wild burst of enthusiasm, I've really mixed it up – Indian, foreign, in between, extrovert, introvert, old, young. I wonder who will get along with whom.

Over the past year, I've begun to notice that there is only one area where my friends from India and those from other countries differ – and that the difference is starker during the winter. Come the end of October, my expat friends check among themselves about air quality before deciding to send their children to school, while my Indian friends laugh at me when I talk about air pollution and its terrible impact on our health. As for myself, I've been unsure whether I'm overreacting (Yes! say my Indian friends) or underreacting (Yes! say my expat friends). Just this morning, the *New York Times* has published another of Gardiner's stories, this time on its blog.[2] My first instinct is to avoid reading it, but as the day progresses I cannot get it off my mind. I recognize now that the entirely human response of denial hasn't allowed me to accept how badly air pollution was affecting my own family's health. Feeling fidgety and scattered, en route to the venue, I look up 'denial' on my new phone – a birthday gift that allows me to access the internet. There are many variations of the same definition.

> *Denial: n. In the psychological sense, denial is a defence mechanism in which a person, faced with a painful fact, rejects the reality of that fact. They will insist*

> *that the fact is not true despite what may be overwhelming and irrefutable evidence. Either they will deny the fact altogether, or minimize it, downplaying its seriousness. Another form is transference denial, when the painful fact is admitted, its seriousness is also admitted, but one's moral responsibility in the situation involving the fact is downplayed. Any of these forms of denial lead to distractive or escapist strategies to reduce stress and help cope.*

So, one thing is confirmed, I tell myself – that it is denial that is keeping me going, as it is several of my friends.

I'm still thinking about this when I reach the Ethiopian Cultural Centre and enter its white-pebbled courtyard. Soon, my friends begin to arrive, and we stand in the open courtyard of the cultural centre in the dappled, weak sunlight, chatting. Perhaps because of the thoughts plaguing my mind since the morning, or because all my friends, Indian, foreign, expat, are together at the same place at the same time, the difference that had earlier occurred to me in their attitudes to the quality of air they breathe appears starker today. It is probably also because so many of my expat friends are directly or indirectly involved with public health, at the WHO or the World Bank, that they are more aware about the issue.

Many of them are talking about Gardiner's story, which has stated that Indians have the weakest lungs in the world – a 38 per cent lower lung capacity than North Americans and lower also than Chinese.[3] Meanwhile, my Indian friends mutter darkly about how the report is typical of Western journalists – filtering India through the lens of disease and poverty – because the report has also mentioned dengue, open defecation and bacterial infections as contributing to the poor health of Indians. It has additionally quoted a medical doctor from Pune's Chest Research Foundation saying that the nightly burning of mosquito coils is equivalent to smoking 100 cigarettes. But everyone burns these, I think to myself, so we're all smoking 100 cigarettes each?

Gardiner's story is clearly divisive. As I flit from group to group, introducing those who are meeting for the first time, and catching up in two-minute conversations, I overhear ongoing exchanges.

'...worse than Beijing. The story backs it with data...very high PM levels.'

'Which? PM10 or 2.5?'

'How does it matter? And how are they different?'

'It does, actually. PM2.5 is worse – it goes into your bloodstream. The particles are tinier, totally poisonous...'

'Is it really worse for children?'

'That's what public health experts are saying. AQI levels just keep rising, but schools remain open here. It wasn't like this in our last posting – and the air there was slightly cleaner.'

'Are you planning to keep your kids home this week?'

'I'm working, actually. It will be so inconvenient. But I think I will. It sounds terrible.'

'Did you read the story in the *New York Times*? Two days ago? I think it was front page.'

'No, I saw the one on the NYT blog, though. Is that different?'

'Yes, different, but similar... Do you think this is hyped? Why doesn't anyone here seem to care?'

'Hi! Happy birthday.'

'Thanks. What's this you guys are talking about?'

'Gardiner's story. Did you see it this morning?'

'Yes. It was scary. Is it all a little OTT? I really don't know what to think...'

'Over the top? No way! I've heard some of the foreign missions have sent an internal circular making India a non-family station. Home rents are coming down!'

As I move along, diverting, delightful accents assail my ears. Spanish, French, German. The Australian drawl, so different from the American. Thanks to a game my children play in which they mimic accents, beginning with their version of the Indian accent, I'm even able to discern the Scottish one from the Irish.

My voluble Italian friend, gesticulating with intensity, is complaining about her children's preschool in Lajpat Nagar, which hasn't installed air filters. She beckons me over.

'What about you? Will you send your kids to school?'

'Yes,' I say unhesitatingly. I'm thinking of them moping and brooding at home, thinking of Lila.

Disbelief.

'Are you serious? You're usually so particular.'

'...really? But the air is really *filthy*! I can hardly breathe myself. Actually, I still can't believe you chose to come back here – and I heard you've given up your green card. Is that true? Now you can never go back!' More exclamations.

'Weren't you in California? Cleanest air to dirtiest! Why would you do that?'

'Hey, do you know Gen Chase?' someone asks. 'Cali girl. She's been tracking this whole air quality thing. She posted Gardiner's story on Facebook – she's obsessive about air quality.'

'She was the one who nagged him to write – he's even said so on FB!'

'Really? I'm not really active on FB,' I say apologetically. But I remember a laughing face and excited chatter under an October sky from more than a year ago, as well as a couple of chance meetings with Gen. Each time we've promised to meet for coffee, but it has never happened. I really should make the effort, I think. Maybe she can shed light on exactly how serious this matter is.

'Isn't she in public health? Or was?'

'Well, she's big on citizen science. Wants to do something about Delhi's toxic air.'

Toxic? The word stays with me.

I move to the next group, friends from my schooldays, a different cacophony of excited high-pitched voices, different accents.

'...you mean the *New York Times* story, or today's piece in the blog?'

'Both, *yaar*! It's the same hyperventilation – dirty, polluted, diseased, that's what India is to Western eyes...'

'India-bashing comes easy. If everything is so filthy, why come here?'

'Oho. Because it's exciting, exotic, ancient. And so many affordable servants!'

'...oh, and don't forget the emerging market, so much growth, so many people. There's bound to be pollution, no?'

'Anyway, it's not just air pollution. Apparently over 50 per cent of the population defecates in the open, and that also causes pollution.'

'Wow. Did the story really say that? I must have missed it. You mean air pollution is because of faecal matter in the air? Ugh!'

'Nope. Bacterial toxins, cooking with cow dung... That's what he says. I read it twice.'

'...but aren't *uplas* supposed to purify the air? My *daadi* used to tell me...'

'I've started lighting *guggulu* and camphor. It's supposed to remove negative energy. Definitely removes mosquitoes...'

'Anyway, Indian immunity is legendary. Even our lungs are *fouladi*! We don't need masks!'

'*Fouladi*, but with stunted growth! Hey, don't look at me! The story said that...'

'If Indian lungs are so strong, then why are they smaller, *haan*?'

'...did you read the stuff about mosquito coils? Do you want to die of dengue or pollution? I'll choose pollution.'

Flippant words, I think to myself.

'Anyway, who uses coils any more? There are alternatives we all use.'

'Well, if those alternatives can kill mosquitoes, what do you think those chemicals are doing to your body?'

'...Hey, how was your vacation?'

'Oh, we almost couldn't go. The fog, you know. Two nights in a row, our flights got cancelled. So we missed our connection. Can you believe, we were on a flight on New Year's Eve?'

'It's not fog, *yaar*. It's actually smog. Caused by the pollution. Like the one in London?'

'Hi, have you met each other?' ...

In the days following my birthday, at every dinner, lunch or social gathering I go to, the subject of air pollution seems to pop up from the most unexpected sources. I have animated arguments – ironically across smoking sigris in the gardens of homes that have air purifiers running in every room – over whether it is fog or its evil twin, smog, that delays flights in the winter months, how much we are endangering our children's lungs by sending them for sports practice on smoggy mornings and the benefits of exercise over the cost of exercising in polluted air. These conversations only convince me further that awareness about air pollution among my Indian friends is low, and that I myself have limited information. I feel a greater urge to delve deeper into it.

I've already read two reports I wish I'd never laid eyes on. India's air pollution monitor and controller, the CPCB, has commissioned Kolkata's Chittaranjan National Cancer Institute to carry out two studies – and the conclusions are frightening. The first is an epidemiological study with the clear objective of assessing air-pollution-related respiratory symptoms and pulmonary dysfunction at the cellular and subcellular level among the residents of Delhi.[4] The second assesses the respiratory health of school-children chronically exposed to ambient air pollution in Delhi and notes the degree of lung function impairment among them.[5]

The former study was done between November 2002 and August 2005 in various parts of Delhi, during different seasons. It surveyed, through questionnaires and clinical examinations, 6,005 healthy people between the ages of 21 and 66, who had been residents of Delhi for ten years or longer. The results from these people were compared to those of a control group of the same age bracket from rural areas. The findings of the 339-page detailed report, peer-reviewed by the Indian Council of Medical Research, revealed, among a host of other data, that 40 per cent of healthy adults living in Delhi had reduced lung function (and more women were affected than men), 16 per cent suffered from depression linked to pollution, 33 per cent from advanced respiratory diseases and 36 per cent from hypertension (four times more than those not living in Delhi).

Halfway through the second study – a 229-page report of a survey and tests similar to the first conducted the following year, this time on children – I can't fathom why there hasn't been more public outrage about these reports. A year later, an Indian newspaper will highlight the quiet burial of this report,[6] but such thoughts do not cross my mind as I comb through it. The study covers 11,628 schoolchildren from 36 schools in different parts of Delhi and was conducted in different seasons. It offers evidence that every third child growing up in the city has reduced lung function. There is a marked increase in a number of biomarkers, like alveolar macrophages (the first line of cellular defence against inhaled pollutants) in the sputum of children that shows greater exposure to particulate pollution. The sputum of Delhi's children is recorded as containing four times more iron-laden macrophages, indicating pulmonary haemorrhage (internal bleeding in the lungs that is invisible and largely without overt symptoms), than that of children from cleaner environs. The level of these toxic biomarkers is found to be higher in children living in areas with high PM10 levels.

Toxic. That word again.

> Toxic (adj;) *poisonous, venomous, virulent, noxious, dangerous, destructive, harmful, unsafe, malignant, injurious, pestilential, pernicious, environmentally unfriendly; fatal, deadly, lethal, mortal, death-dealing.*

During our interviews much later, Gen tells me that she posted Gardiner's piece on her Facebook timeline on India's Republic Day, 26 January, in 2014, with the message, 'This won't be a huge surprise for anyone living in Delhi – but it's important to share. The mystery for many of us is why Beijing's air quality gets so much attention and India's gets none. Awareness can lead to change. Thanks, Gardiner Harris, for the great article.' She also remembers writing back to a friend who seemed surprised by these developments and commented on the fact that the air seemed worse than when she visited India six years ago. The post said, '@Cheryl, yes, it has gotten a lot worse. Word is that last year was the worst in 30 years, and this year is already worse than the last... You can absolutely feel it. It's scary.'

Gardiner replied to her post, appreciating her for egging him on,

'I did this story because I knew Gen wouldn't stop hassling me until I did. Shows the power of persistent and steady advocacy. Thanks, Gen Chase!', to which she replied, '@Gardiner, it totally pays to be a pain in the @#*$. I think you know this better than most!'

I love Delhi in March. It has the fragrance of hope and new beginnings. Every roundabout in central Delhi starts bursting with flowers. But this year is different. With the winter smog lifting, burnt away by the swiftly rising temperature, I've semi-abandoned the research I had begun on the health harm caused by breathing dirty air. It has been more disturbing than I expected, and I'm really not sure I want to know more than I've already learnt. I feel low and disheartened – though I can't tell whether this is the direct effect of the polluted air I've been inhaling or brought on by the reports that say that Delhi residents have a greater tendency to get depressed from air pollution, a point that is going to be highlighted by national and international media in later years.[7, 8] Also, with the winter haze gone and the smell of spring in the air, it is easier to shrug off the gloom. But, subconsciously, I'm beginning to feel I can't afford to be in denial any longer. If there are so many invisible toxins in the air, isn't there some way to measure them, a part of me wonders – a machine or monitor that can 'see' or 'feel' these micro-particulates/aerosols or gases?

On 21 March, I spot a post on the Delhibabies online community, a resource for parents living in Delhi. Someone named Gen Connors is recommending a consultant who can measure the air in your house for pollutants. I write to the air quality consultant immediately. He replies within hours and offers to come by to test the quality of air in my house. He can do it tomorrow, his email says. This is how I meet Barun Aggarwal. He has recently relocated from Atlanta in the United States and is the son-in-law of Kamal Meattle of the Paharpur Business Centre, who led the fight against benzene levels in India's air several years ago.

He walks in the next day – tall, pleasant-faced, with smiling eyes and a receding hairline. I am utterly charmed by his polite manner and permanent smile, and his portable DustTrak. This, it seems, is that magic machine that can 'see' the invisible toxins and measure their concentration.

The DustTrak, Barun explains, is a multichannel laser photometer that can measure real-time aerosol readings, and it is immediately clear that he is inordinately proud of it. I notice that he carries it like a flag, a venerable object of pride, holding it out in front of him. 'It can measure both mass and size fraction of dust, fumes, mists and smoke and is suitable for engineering control evaluations,' he tells me as he prowls around my house, measuring the contents of the air my family breathes.

'It'll probably be quite low here compared to other neighbourhoods,' I tell him lightly, following him around. 'This is one of the greenest neighbourhoods in Delhi.'

Barun smiles at that – though I don't instantly understand why. 'A hundred and eighty-seven,' he announces in the bedroom.

'*What?* Isn't that high? I thought it would be lower. Didn't you just say the safe limit is supposed to be...'

'Fifteen,' he nods. 'But sixty for India.'

We move on to other parts of the house.

'Two hundred and three,' he says in the children's room.

'A hundred and sixty-five,' he pronounces in the guest room, which has the least furniture.

'Two hundred and fifteen,' he says in the drawing room. And 219 in the hall.

I'm beginning to feel slightly sick. I almost wish I hadn't called him and allowed this awful machine into my house. We step out the glass doors into a sunny March morning. My garden is full of flowers. I inhale deeply. The air smells fresh.

'Two hundred and sixty-six,' says Barun. I stop in mid-exhale. He is amused at my reaction to the numbers. My suspicion that there is something toxic in the air around us led me to invite this smiling stranger with the illusion-destroying machine into my home, but to see these numbers first-hand, to get confirmation that toxic particles are secretly swirling in the air around us, is terribly disorienting.

I begin to ask him question after question, probing, poking, provoking. He neither loses his smile nor his patience, answering each question thoughtfully, thoroughly.

We move to the little room at the back of the house, where I meditate and pray. Its soothing fragrance of sandalwood and jasmine calms me a little. Barun holds out the DustTrak. The particle counter reading shoots up.

'Three hundred and fifty-nine,' he says, matter-of-fact.

Wait, what?

'Do you light incense here?' he asks, sniffing.

'Yes,' I say, confused. What has that got to do with anything?

Turns out it does. Anything we burn – including candles, incense, coal sigris, barbecues, cremation pyres – creates smoke and the tiny, noxious particles that are deadly for human health. I'm feeling nauseated now, and ready to buy anything he will sell me to save us from this slow poisoning by breathing. I ask him more questions, something I'm good at. I feel like I'm grilling him, but the look on his face tells me he's heard this before. All of it. An hour later, he is still smiling, and I'm still asking questions. At some point during this exchange it occurs to me that Barun still has the option of moving back to the US – unlike us, he has not given up his permanent residency card and has converted it into citizenship – but he shows no signs of wanting to. How does he protect his family, his children, I ask him.

He tells me that there is a machine that filters the air and cleans it of these malignant particles. It's a simple technology and there are many companies who manufacture such machines. He has tested 28 brands and his company sells the ones they trust. Yes, they provide a full solution from monitoring to cleaning. Yes, it's expensive, but not more valuable than my family's lungs. His parting shot fells me.

'These numbers, what you see today, they're actually relatively low,' he says gravely. 'Pollution peaks in the winter, when there is temperature inversion and heavier, colder air gets trapped under warmer air that rises to the top. All the particulate matter that colder, heavier air contains sits there at ambient, breathable levels, ready to be inhaled by all of us.' His smile has finally faded. His voice is grim.

'So, you mean our lungs absorb all these microparticles? Our lungs *become* the filters, and these…these…toxic particles get absorbed by our bodies?' When I say the word 'toxic' now, it doesn't feel over the top at all. Barun is quiet. He is letting the information sink in.

'And what do mean by "relatively *low*"? That the numbers are higher in the winter?'

He nods silently, face unsmiling, eyes bleak.

'How much worse is it?'

'Much, much worse. The PM level can be three times, four times these levels.'

'No way! Then why aren't people talking about it?' My voice comes out louder than I intend it to. I clear my throat, embarrassed. He looks at me, his face troubled. He is weighing something in his head, clearly some information he isn't sure he wants to share.

'Actually…' he hesitates. 'I recorded a PM2.5 reading of 3,200. On Diwali night, last year,' he shrugs. 'That is literally…I mean literally, off the charts.' Government monitors don't go beyond 999, he tells me.

That's over 300 times the WHO's annual 'safe' limit (I will discover later that there are actually no safe levels of air pollution exposure.[9]) I look at him in stupefied silence. I clear my throat again and find a chair, feeling a sudden urge to sit down.

'I'm going to check all this on the internet,' I continue weakly. 'It all sounds quite…quite…' *Unbelievable? Frightening? Sinister? Ridiculous?* '…er…alarming. I'm quite, er, alarmed. I really need to look into this a bit more.'

I'm not *just* alarmed, actually. I'm wounded. I've always prided myself in being a very aware person, especially in matters of health and parenting, and this has been quite a blow. How could this killer have been stalking my children and family so stealthily while I have remained completely clueless? Now I want Barun to leave so I can quickly get to my computer and revive my research. My mind is racing. My training of so many years as a journalist is kicking in, and I'm making mental notes about where and whom to get the best, most credible information from.

I notice Barun is looking at me quizzically.

'Actually, I did read some reports…' I admit, in response to his unspoken question. 'But I wasn't sure… I guess I didn't…' *believe them*, but I leave that unsaid, '… pay attention.' Is this what denial is?

'I'll send you some links,' he says quietly, unsurprised, and gets up to leave.

I have one last question, though I think I know the answer.

What about immunity, I ask him. I know that some amount of microbiological pollution exposure is good for us – it builds our immunity against bacteria and viruses. Will I get used to the purified air his machine will dispense? Will it lower my immunity? His response confirms what I had suspected – that, unlike microbiological pollutants, exposure to even tiny amounts of particulate matter is bad for us. It doesn't build immunity. Getting eight hours of PM-free sleep gives our bodies some respite. It is like smoking cigarettes. Smoking none is best, but if you're going to smoke anyway, then smoking five is better than smoking fifty.

By the time Barun finishes, I'm sold on his motto, 'Davos air in Delhi,' and have bought two air purifiers from him. I am also making a mental list of family and friends whom I need to educate. After he leaves, I rush to my laptop and read up furiously on everything we spoke about, fact-checking and validating his information. Sadly, it all checks out. There is nowhere to run from these immutable facts. In the process, however, I stumble upon the work of Indian and international pollution analysts, atmospheric and environmental engineers, meteorologists, climatologists, public health researchers and scientists – encoded masses of information hidden in silos, waiting to be excavated and shared.

In fact, on the immunity question I'd posed to Barun, I learn further that unlike minimal exposure to germs and viruses, inhaling even small amounts of microparticles *reduces* immunity rather than building it. Simply put, inhaled microparticles cause inflammation and oxidative stress on every organ they touch, beginning with the lining of the nose all the way to the lining of the lungs and beyond, releasing free radicals and reducing overall immunity. Unlike immunity to bacteria and viruses, the build-up of particulate matter over the years probably explains reduced immunity, greater sickening, faster ageing and many other symptoms. People confuse immunity with endurance. It crosses my mind that it probably also explains why my parents seem to get sicker faster each winter.

I use my research to familiarize myself with how to measure and monitor air pollution. It is complex, an entire science that I was unaware of, involving physics (air flow), chemistry (composition of air) and math (the measurement of that composition). To measure a dynamic situation where the air, a complex mixture of chemical compounds constantly forming and transforming into other compounds, is moving at various speeds with no boundaries is challenging, but I recognize its importance. We can't fight an enemy that is invisible. It is important to understand and wield tools that shine a light to expose them. To take it one step further, like Michael Bloomberg said, if you can't measure it, you can't manage it.

I focus on AQI, trying to understand what exactly it means[10] and where I can easily access its daily levels. The AQI, I learn, indexes the value of the current pollution status in the city in terms of how polluted the air presently is.[11] The EPA in the US calculates daily air quality as an index for five major air pollutants – ground-level ozone, particulate matter, carbon monoxide, sulphur dioxide and nitrogen dioxide. I discover that different countries have different indexes for pollution, depending on what their local pollutants are, that countries like Mexico, China, France, Hong Kong and the US have implemented smog alert systems. I cannot find anything similar for India, not even an Indian AQI. It is as if the government believes that by ignoring pollution and not acknowledging its existence, it will go away.

Six weeks after Barun's visit to my home, on 8 May, when the WHO declares Delhi the most polluted city in the world, I'm no longer shocked, just bemused that it hasn't made more headlines in Indian newspapers. Again, it is an article by Gardiner in the *New York Times* that seems to be attracting maximum attention. This dubious distinction attracts reactions ranging from outright denial to evasive downplaying. Some Indian newspapers carry the explosive information but bury it in the inside pages. Then, in a controversial decision that risks diplomatic ramifications, the US embassy quietly goes public with its own pollution measurements – thus bringing the issue of India's poor air quality front and centre, and making it undeniable, for the very first time.

This sequence of events aligns perfectly with Sam's recollection when I interview him later, in 2019. Sam recalls how the WHO announcement helped the US embassy to go public with its own pollution numbers, measured by the EPA-standard monitors installed on the compound of the US embassy in Delhi. 'After the WHO released its list of cities suffering [from] high air pollution levels and New Delhi was identified as the worst in the 1,600-city worldwide database in May 2014, it became easier to talk about air pollution publicly. In June 2014, with the Indian elections behind us, all of our senior leadership agreed to make our AQM data available on our public website,' Sam tells me from Washington, sounding satisfied despite the passage of time. It is in recognition of his contribution in naming the elephant in the room publicly, for bringing the issue of airborne pollution in India to the forefront of not only US policy but also global engagement in general, despite his bosses initially advising him to keep the information under wraps – a tricky diplomatic manoeuvre – that Sam is honoured with the William R. Rivkin Award for Constructive Dissent by the American Foreign Service Association on 9 June 2015.[12, 13]

While the initial reaction to the embassy going public with their data was subdued, mainly because June is a 'low pollution' month in New Delhi, the Indian media later began to report the embassy's public numbers with regularity. That set of data quickly came to be considered a reliable source of trusted information, especially as a few national news channels and newspapers, taking courage from the WHO's damning statistics, began to give more comprehensive coverage of India's bad air. One of the major dailies started to print an air pollution box that included the embassy AQM data every day. This helped bring pollution into mainstream conversation among expats and Indians alike, says Sam.

It wasn't that the Indian government did not release its air pollution data. It did. But, unlike the US embassy's data which was linked to the EPA's Air Quality Index and accompanied by EPA-approved health guidance for various levels of pollution, the government data was practically inaccessible, hidden in plain sight, released as it was in hard-to-understand formats that only experts could make sense of.

Data empowers and easily accessible information democratizes issues. One has to know what one is fighting. This was the first time ordinary people were able to make sense of pollution data in India. It is the same in other countries. Sam tells me that it was easier for the US embassy to publicly release air pollution data in China – which had led to greater international attention and pressure to clean up – because they could justify on the basis of language that it was ostensibly meant for American citizens living there. This was not possible in India, where pollution data was freely available in English, even though few could make sense of it, even among the educated and aware. With the embassy relaying this data publicly in India, more people began to understand the problem.

Meanwhile, I continue to dig deeper, into basic questions and more advanced ones. What causes pollution in India, I wonder, and find that the answer is not as straightforward as I would have thought. The major sources of air pollution include inefficient modes of transport, household fuel and waste burning, fossil fuels, coal-fired power plants and industrial activities – undeniably, it is a 'burning' issue. However, not all air pollution originates from human activity. For example, air quality can also be influenced by dust storms, particularly in regions close to deserts.

The more I read, the more I worry about my loved ones. In August, I call Barun and order another air purifier. This one is for my parents.

They live near Anand Vihar, not far from the inter-state bus terminus which I later find out has the highest PM2.5 levels in Delhi and the National Capital Region (NCR). I know it's going to be a long battle to get them to start using this device. However, I'm determined that they must adopt the practice.

'If I'm not going to fight to protect my family, then who will?' I reason aloud when I'm ordering their machine from Barun. I can almost hear his smile on the phone.

'Good luck with convincing them!' he says, and we both know he is referring to the generational resistance. If this pollution had been visible, like the sooty particles in the air in the early 1990s, perhaps it would have been easier to persuade my parents. But the PM2.5 particles of today are less visible than the black carbon of 20 years ago. For the longest time, smog has deceitfully hidden in the garb of fog and been reported as such, with misleading headlines each winter saying 'fog delays flights', making the nasty cocktail of toxic air sound like mere weather change. Perhaps if I had his DustTrak to expose the hidden microparticles in the air by measuring them, like a microscope reveals viruses by magnifying them, it would be easier to convince them, I tell Barun. My father is a student of chemistry, a 'first class first' graduate in the subject from the renowned Allahabad University, as he often reminds me, and can ask more questions per minute than anyone else I know. If I can convince him, my mother will be an easy target. In the end, I decide I will just have to improvise. Maybe show them pictures of their visit to California and point to the dazzling periwinkle sky to remind them what clean skies look like.

'What's this? What have you got?' my mother asks. I dread telling her that the package I'm unloading isn't something artsy or a carton of her favourite Oil of Olay. Yet, I'm convinced this will bring her more long-term joy, improve her immunity, allow her to sing for longer periods without getting those nasty winter colds and coughs.

'It's an air purifier,' I tell her.

'Oho. That thing you keep talking about these days, pollution? *Beta*, everything dirty isn't terrible. Krishna used to eat dirt, and when his mother peered into his mouth, she saw the whole *brahmand*,' she responds, immediately losing interest in the carton.

'You know, if you live in too much cleanliness, your immune system has nothing to fight, and becomes lazy?' My father has joined in the conversation. 'This is not America. We are not Americans. When in Rome...'

'We also grew up breathing the same air. We are all okay. Stronger than your generation, in many ways. Why do you think you won't be?' asks my mother.

'It isn't the same, Ma,' I counter. 'You yourself keep saying how the food my children eat today is so adulterated that you're shocked they're even growing. In your time, the grain was nutritious, the fruits tastier. There was none of this genetically modified nonsense.'

I see my mother exchange a look with my father. I know that look. *You've become too Westernized,* it says. I see my dad shoot a warning look back. *Don't say it. Don't say anything. She will get annoyed. She means well.* But my mother can't stop and I get the whole nine yards from her: from how tasteless the perfect-looking giant red-and-yellow tomatoes in Palo Alto were when they visited despite being grown in clean air and water to how the food used to taste in her father's house, and ending with how, ultimately, everything is fated and no one can control what is meant to be, so what's the point of my constant worry about the air – it's going to get me nowhere.

I've heard these words so many times that I zone out and get busy setting up the purifier. It doesn't take much; these simple devices are plug and play. This one has a brand-new HEPA filter – a filter that will trap the tiniest of microparticles, allowing only pure, clean air to blow out. Barun had shown me how the readings of his DustTrak had fallen when he placed it near the outlet, and again I wish I had his measuring device, or at least that I had remembered to bring my own purifier's filters. It is only September, and already the filters in the air purifiers at home are filthy, the pre-filters clogged, the HEPA filters already greying.

I manage to get my parents to consider using the new machine by telling them it will help with the snoring and my father's lungs – his COPD worries her. They look delighted at that. Cunningly, I also tell my mother it will increase her breath for her *alaap* and *taans*, make her a better vocalist. By the time I leave, she is at least a little more willing to try the device.

The very next month, I find news reports of a National AQI (NAQI) being planned for India,[14] something that Prime Minister Modi will launch the following year.[15] The NAQI takes eight pollutants into account – PM2.5, PM10, nitrogen oxides, sulphur dioxide, ozone, carbon monoxide, ammonia and lead – and will initially be available in 10 cities. 'It will help people in these cities take precautions on days when the air quality is particularly poor,' the report states. Particularly poor, I think. I still can't get Barun's number of 3,200 out of my mind. I note that the NAQI has no actionable plans on how to reduce pollution associated with it, nor a health advisory attached to different levels, but it's a beginning. Transparency precedes accountability and change, I comfort myself.

The festive season is approaching. This year, as the air cools, my concern about air quality grows. I briefly run into Gen at another social evening and she mentions she is working on some sort of a repository of air pollution stories – a sort of informational site. Once again, we make plans to meet and once again they fall through the cracks. Years later, after she has moved to Washington and I'm interviewing her, phone call by painstaking phone call, I discover how my lived experience of that time overlaps with hers. As we piece together the past and match timelines, we find we were leading parallel lives as far as tracking pollution was concerned, although she was ahead of me on the journey. Because right around this time, when I'm still floundering in the newness of all this knowledge, she has already launched delhiair.org.

October–December 2014

'I launched delhiair.org in October 2014, just before the winter pollution season,' Gen tells me in a phone interview in April 2019. 'A soft launch – one of my friends threw a party, and suddenly there it was. All my friends said this was citizen journalism at its best,' reminisces Gen. 'I monitored it in the early days, and found almost 10,000 people visiting the site, around 300 people a day.'

One of the reasons Gen had launched the Delhiair website was that she wanted credible data to be accessible to others like her who were struggling to understand what was making them sick. Her site hosted air quality data from multiple sources, including the five US embassy monitors in India.

This was also around the time, in October 2014, that she began increasing the pressure on her children's school to come up with protocols for outdoor sports to protect the children, especially with winter approaching. 'I was the squeaky wheel that was making the school nervous,' she admits, self-consciously. She had three meetings with the school's directors, and even provided AES with a file full of protocols other schools around the world had put into place. Schools in places like Mexico City and Thailand. But when that had no effect, she pulled her children off the field.

'Oh, they were all very respectful when I insisted that the school had a role to play in protecting our children. But no one *did* anything. It was very frustrating,' she says.

'By now, I was emboldened by the science behind me. I was 'that crazy air pollution lady' and people were palpably nervous at parties and gatherings that I would only talk about air. And they were right to be. I'd heard that a scientist called Josh Apte had made a presentation at the embassy earlier that year. I heard he had a lot of data and evidence to prove how toxic Delhi's air was, so I tracked him down and got him to come and make a presentation to the school. He presented to the faculty and parents in November 2014. His clarity and conclusions made a huge difference,' says Gen. Delhiair.org was gaining recognition. 'It was honoured at an Earth Day event in April 2015. It's funny, but I recall Indian government officials mostly wanted to know if I could tell through the site analytics if Americans or Indians were the ones looking at the site!' Gen reminisces. Worried parents wanted to know what they could do. 'We had a couple of meetings, trying to figure out what we could do, if we could even *do* anything. Then one day, soon after, you joined... Remember the day you walked into the meeting room?' Gen comments with a laugh.

I remember that day. It was almost six months after I'd bought the air purifier for my parents, when the seasonal high pollution seemed to be receding. A story in the *Guardian*[16] which cast doubt on the Indian government's air quality figures, implying things were actually worse had rattled me further.

In those six months, during the time Gen was launching delhiair.org, I found myself nudged into becoming the president of my children's school's parent-teacher association (PTA). Although I didn't know it yet, this reluctantly held position would hugely influence my journey in the field of air pollution in more ways than I could imagine.

PTAs across the world can be divisive, agenda-ridden and deeply politicized, with strongly held views on the part of all the stakeholders: parents, teachers and staff. But across the six schools in three cities that my children have been to, nowhere has this been more apparent than at their present school. The earlier PTA body at the school had the same handful of people running the show for eight years, and seemed to have multiple agendas, none of which were visibly benefiting the children. I really don't want to put my hand inside this snake pit, but a few dynamic and charismatic young mothers entice me, infect me with their optimism, and together we are excited to steer things in a new direction.

One of these parents is Haripriya, an energetic, quixotic lawyer with sparkling eyes and an infectious laugh. I instantly like her and instinctively trust her, so I go against my better judgement and allow her to pull me in. Also, I feel I must rescue her from her own idealism. She is the only person I know whose caller tune plays *Vande Mataram*.

'Seriously?' I ask her the first few times I call her.

She laughs her belly laugh. 'Can't give up on my country, can I?' she asks.

The other is the soft-spoken, spiritually inclined Gayatri whose gentle diplomacy hides a steely determination to do the right thing. Quietly. The three of us begin scouring the school for parents who will replace the current PTA, individuals who will complement our skills and offset our faults. We scan through class lists, make hundreds of phone calls, spread the word through a new feature of an easy technology called WhatsApp which allows us to create parent groups and, very soon, between our hard-nosed plans and soft skills, we have a fully – and fairly – elected Executive Council in place. We form committees for security, uniforms, canteen, sports and transport. At first, we aren't popular with the teachers and school staff, but over the first six months, they begin to grudgingly recognize our work and slowly, very slowly, warm to us. 'Fix the problem, not the blame, and do it respectfully,' becomes our quiet mantra, winning us reluctant friends within the teaching community.

Slowly, the PTA swallows any free time I have. My family is dead against my PTA activities, with my children now old enough to be embarrassed at seeing their mother anywhere near their school.

'Don't you have better things to do with your time?' sniffs my husband.

'You have no idea how horrible the sports teacher has become to me since you joined the PTA!' whines my son.

'All the teachers *officially* hate me now,' announces my daughter cheerfully. 'And they make no secret of it.'

By March 2015, she is fed up and wants to leave her present school, and eventually persuades us to allow her to switch to an International Baccalaureate (IB) school-leaving board. It will teach her critical thinking, analytical skills, we reason, though privately we wonder if she realizes exactly how challenging the move will be. Through it all, lurking somewhere in the back of my mind is the thought that perhaps an IB degree will also allow her to escape India's pollution after she graduates from school. As someone who's always wanted her children to get at least their undergraduate degree in India – it will strengthen their umbilical cord to their motherland – I push that thought out of my mind and try to stop worrying about pollution, bad air, toxicity, poor health, disease, lung cancer. All the scary stuff. Over time, the uneasy relationship of the PTA with the faculty dissolves into mutual respect, and although I don't know this now, some of the teachers will end up becoming closet pollution warriors. At any rate, the school becomes a fertile ground for me not just to push my pollution awareness agenda – in the time I am the president of the PTA, we conduct eight presentations for teachers, two for parents and three for children – but also to execute pilot projects experimenting with a few solutions to the problem.

6

Air Pollution

2015

I love this city. I also hate it. Both are strong emotions and the conflict between them tends to be intense.

What I love about the city are the broad, leafy avenues of central Delhi – punctuated by confusing identical-looking roundabouts – and how each neighbourhood has its own character. The dignified, old trees in north Delhi's stately avenues are a study in contrast to the chaotic frenzy of the western and eastern parts of the city with their energetic markets and Lego-like homes stacked one beside the other. Old Delhi's Chandni Chowk, Kinari Bazaar, Paranthe Wali Gali – their evocative names more romantic than the actual places – where narrow lanes criss-cross before doubling back in a confusing labyrinth, the sky obscured by a maze of wires so thick that minimum sunlight passes through, is a marvel of old-world charm. Every neighbourhood boasts of the ruins of a centuries-old mosque, minar or tomb, the red sandstone usually hidden behind overgrown creepers. What I hate about Delhi is its grimy, dusty and polluted underside, its unacknowledged, illegal split personality, hidden from the privileged, but providing for them – us – in so many ways, swollen with the throb of unauthorized activities, undisposed garbage.

I was born here, yet often feel foreign to it. On the day of my birth, at the grand Willingdon Hospital, the entire city was aglow because it was

Republic Day, as my father never tires of telling me. 'The night I drove your mother to the hospital, India Gate, Rashtrapati Bhavan, North and South Block, all glittered with lights. That's why we named you Jyoti...' Yet, if I attempt to replicate that journey in January now, all I will see are the dim outlines of these grand buildings, Bikaner House, Baroda House, Hyderabad House, Jamnagar House, and the National Stadium standing in hazy sibling salute to the elegant silhouette of India Gate. They are barely standing up to pollution and are in danger, I imagine, of vanishing into the smoky toxicity of Delhi's winter smog. Rising whispers of a plan to change the entire layout of this central vista add another layer of doom to the stately buildings.

Delhi is a city rich with the legacies of many pasts. There is the pure, geometric, faded beauty of Jantar Mantar, the landscaped serenity of the Lodhi Gardens, the symmetric beauty of Safdarjung's Tomb, the imposing Qutub Minar surrounded by hundreds of monuments scattered around Jamali Kamali, the charming Jama Masjid, Purana Qila and Red Fort. Occasionally, melodious notes of Hindustani classical music spill out of the undulating landscape of Nehru Park, and Sufi music, qawwalis or dissonant jazz are heard from the premises of Humayun's Tomb. You can hear the bells on the feet of a Kuchipudi danseuse performing against the majestic, glittering Purana Qila, the flames of thousands of little lamps flickering around the stage, and watch live performances at the sprawling Indira Gandhi National Centre for the Arts. Delhi is a grand city, rich with culture, music, dance, food, but the scourge of its air poisons everything. To imagine this strumming, thrumming metropolis without the shroud of pollution is a dream that feels ephemeral.

One of my earliest childhood memories is of the Republic Day parade. Every year, on 26 January, my father would faithfully switch on the television in the morning and I would watch the parade, entranced by the pageantry, my internal bubble of excitement growing till the grand finale when the jets roared into the air, painting the sky with the colours of India's national flag. For all the years that my family lived in Delhi, that was the signal for me to run out into the garden to look up at the blue sky stained with saffron, white and green, feeling my heart swell with pride.

In 2015, though, Republic Day is different. It is the first one since I have become hyper-aware of the polluted air around me, and I am anxious about stepping outdoors without a mask. The gradual awareness that the shadowy haze I see during my early-morning or evening walks is poisonous is an uncomfortable fact that I have taken time to get used to. This year, Barack Obama, the President of the United States, is to be the chief guest at the parade.

In keeping with family tradition, I switch on the television at 8.30 a.m. and tune in to the familiar sounds and scripts of compères, practically unchanged from 45 years ago. This Republic Day is a turning point in my own awareness as I see the US President and my countrymen, including Prime Minister Narendra Modi, peer through the haze obscuring their visibility at the parade followed by the ceremonial centrepiece of the jets streaking across the sky. As the bands march past followed by the *jhaankis* and then the dancing schoolchildren, all I can think of is those tiny toxic particles settling deep into their lungs, as well as those of the people standing innocently along Rajpath, cheering.

I've grown up hearing the boom-boom of drums and early-morning practice marches for Republic Day, but now, all that sound does for me is remind me that out there, in the menacing smog, innocent countrymen are inhaling poison voluntarily, unaware of what they are doing to their bodies.

As the jets roar above our heads, I neither step out nor ask my children to. It's the first time this has happened.

Among the treaties signed on defence, business, trade, investment and commerce, clean energy and climate change during the visit, President Obama and Prime Minister Modi include 'cooperation on air pollution' in their joint statement.[1] That night, after everyone is in bed, a notification pops up on my computer. It is an article in *Bloomberg* titled 'Mr President, world's worst air is taking six hours off your life'.[2] David Spiegelhalter, a statistician at the University of Cambridge who specializes in quantifying risk in a way that is understandable to the public, has calculated how many hours President Obama has shaved off his expected lifespan since Air Force One descended into New Delhi's acrid smog on a January night. In the article, Spiegelhalter states that breathing that air is like smoking 'roughly eight cigarettes a day.' He goes on to elaborate: 'Those levels translate roughly into an estimated loss of two hours a day in life expectancy. I think Delhi is a wonderful city, but this pollution is harming its residents.'

'Inhaling the world's most toxic air...'The words stay with me. Later, when I search for how researchers estimate the mortality rate from air pollution, I find the same scientist explaining a 'hazard ratio' – the average risk of dying for every extra unit of particulate matter that people inhale.[3] In the United Kingdom, a committee on the medical effects of air pollution uses a 6 per cent figure.[4] This implies that the risk of dying increases by 6 per cent for every 10 micrograms of PM2.5 one inhales.

A little bit of rain has helped, but despite that the American embassy's monitoring station has recorded an AQI reading of 222 that week, a level the US EPA classifies as 'very unhealthy'. There is nothing anyone can do to treat the air outdoors, but the embassy tries hard to protect its President, as diplomatically as possible. I find a report[5] that says the American embassy in Delhi has bought 1,850 high-performance portable indoor air purifiers from a Swedish company for President Obama's visit. A temporary fix, like applying a Band-Aid to a gaping wound. The only person who seems overjoyed with the embassy's purchase is Bengt Rittri, the founder and CEO of the company that makes the devices – BlueAir. The company issues a press release[6] making the most of this public relations opportunity.

In 2019, when we're piecing together the full story, Josh Apte remembers those machines and how effective – and expensive – they were. 'The consular staff began to be issued air purification units. It was a great expense, because each one of those systems was just shy of a thousand dollars, and many of the larger official residences were given as many of the systems as was required. And if you think of the number of diplomatic staff there are, I'd speculate the cost was millions of dollars a year,' Josh says. Millions of dollars. Just to try to combat Delhi's air pollution.

By May 2015, BlueAir, with manufacturing plants in Sweden, the US and China, is on an expansion drive and has increased the number of its stores in India to 24. In July 2015, Unilever buys BlueAir, giving Hindustan Unilever an immediate foothold into the air purifier market.

Air purifiers have been available in India for over 20 years, but it is only in recent years that they have become popular. The market for them is expected to grow to ₹1,400 crore by 2021, according to a report by TechSci Research.[7] There are over two dozen companies in India selling air purifiers. Ever since the WHO declared India to be home to 11 of the 20 cities with the worst air quality in the world, companies that manufacture air purifiers seem to have set their sights on getting rich by offering personal solutions.

Again, I wonder why Indian newspapers don't carry more stories on air pollution, considering all the pollution statistics available in the public domain. Why does all the excellent peer-reviewed research and evidence, available for the asking, remain buried in scientific silos? Why did it need expats and foreign journalists to point out our truth to us? I gather that one reason is that, until now, the connection between air pollution and its negative health impact hasn't been revealed emphatically enough in India. Also, until India's economic reforms opened up the country, fewer Indians were travelling abroad and experiencing clean air – and the reverse. Added to that are the vast resources of the internet, aiding transparency.

Josh and I try to analyse why the years between 2012 and 2015 seem to be the tipping point for improved awareness. 'There were already good Indian journalists reporting on air pollution before,' says Josh. 'What really changed things is that those reports were not getting much traction. Once the *New York Times* started putting it on the front page, I think it gave greater legitimacy to the Indian journalists.' He recalls the *Indian Express* and the *Times of India* as those being at the forefront of the reporting. 'Gardiner's writings basically gave courage and a platform to Indian journalists, made it easier for them to highlight their stories and make it the big deal that it was,' he says. It amplified the existing truth.

On 31 March 2014, the *Indian Express* launched an investigative series ominously called 'Death by Breath'[8] on Delhi's air quality, which began with a disturbing story[9] that pointed to governmental apathy in the face of sharply rising pollution from 2008, a year before I moved back. Over the next few years, this series would cover – and uncover – many missed opportunities to act, at least 15 important research studies that went unheeded,[10] and one in which the then Delhi chief minister herself talked of lobbies that blocked attempts to improve air quality.[11] But something it missed was a law Punjab passed in 2009, meant to preserve groundwater levels there but inadvertently intensified pollution levels as well.

By April 2015, India finally has its own NAQI, launched by Prime Minister Modi.[12] By the end of 2015, however, I will find out that in addition to the eight toxins that comprise India's NAQI – that is, solid particulate matter PM10 and its more lethal cousin PM2.5, heavy metals like lead, gases such as sulphur dioxide and its associated compounds (commonly called SOx), nitrous oxides and their associated compounds (NOx), ozone (proliferated more in the summer months), carbon monoxide and ammonia – Delhi's air also contains several pollutants that the government's NAQI *doesn't* measure. These include mercury and other heavy metal residues, several volatile organic compounds and persistent organic pollutants (POPs) such as dioxins and DDT in the air. Then there are benzene, microplastics and other polycyclic aromatic hydrocarbons, all of which are known carcinogens that mainly come from diesel and other dirty fuels as well as burning of plastic and rubber (often from Delhi's notorious 'waste-to-energy' plants).[13]

While gaseous pollutants mainly affect the respiratory system and are potentially carcinogenic, air toxins like heavy metals and POPs can cause acute organ damage and cancer. These air toxins are particularly harmful because they are long-lasting compounds that bioaccumulate in the human body; that is, their chemical concentration increases over time. PM is one of the most complicated pollutants because particulates can consist of hundreds of chemicals and toxins that can be absorbed through the lungs into the circulatory system. When PM is inhaled, it can cause severe damage to the lungs and other organs, triggering life-threatening conditions including cardiovascular disease, respiratory infections, chronic respiratory disease (like asthma and COPD) and cancer. Reducing air pollution can significantly decrease the burden of disease from stroke, heart disease, lung cancer and both chronic and acute respiratory diseases.

The more I read and research, the more alarmed I get, and more helpless in the face of the sheer enormity of the problem and the lack of mass awareness and, thus, action being taken. Now that I've stopped avoiding the issue, overcome my denial, there is no going back. One cannot un-know facts.

'Do you know Gen?' Barun asks me at a friend's party on Holi that year. I've just rubbed pink powder on his face and he on mine, and we have both commented on the sun splashing down on us, after months of grey skies. 'She's set up an informational website on Delhi's air. That's how I got to know her. She's here too today,' he says.

Everyone seems to ask me if I know Gen,' I tell him waspishly as I look around doubtfully at unrecognizable faces stained with pink, yellow, purple, green.

But it isn't until May 2015 that we pick up this conversation again and the three of us are finally able to meet, when I run into Barun at another friend's dinner outdoors and comment on how clear the sky is.

'You know now that it's not just the winter pollution that's bad,' he says. 'It's bad all year through, but in different ways. We keep complaining about it in the winter and forget about it in the summer.' Disturbingly, he tells me that although I feel the air is cleaner in the summer, actually, ground-level ozone is the worst at this time of the year, so I'm still breathing poor-quality air, and my family's lungs are still being negatively affected.

'Now some of us are planning to create an organization. We need solutions.' His usually smiling eyes look serious. 'We have a meeting next week. Join us.' It is neither a question nor a request. I like the idea of converting the negative energy of complaining to each other into something more constructive. But my work with the PTA at my son's school has been more time-consuming and tiresome than I'd first thought. In his inimitable style, Barun persists, gently, insistently, asking me to at least join one meeting of a core group of individuals who want to do something to spread awareness. I ask him to send me an email, hoping he'll forget. He doesn't. The email promptly arrives, and I reluctantly wake up early on the morning of the meeting and head over to AES. The first person I see when I walk in is Gen, who welcomes me with a broad smile.

'Jyoti! This has taken so long to come together!'

I also meet Tina Haskins Chaddha, Aurelia Driver, Manjali Khosla and Jai Dhar Gupta. We all have children, and each of us has independently arrived at the conclusion that Delhi's air is a cause for serious concern and is probably making us all sick. Our paths to this realization may be unique to each of us, but it is a relief to find others who feel the same way.

Tina Chaddha is a typical straight-talking, no-nonsense yoga-loving New Yorker married to an Indian and has three young children. She is blonde, blue-eyed and self-consciously aware of what she calls the 'optics'. 'This problem needs to be solved – and be seen to be solved – by local Indians. Clean air must be accessible to all,' she says. Sitting next to her is Aurelia, who is from South Africa and a mother of two. Across the table is Manjali, who has a PhD in analytical chemistry and has researched asthma and migraine in relation to North America's pharmaceutical industry. She's had pneumonia twice in her first winter since she moved to New Delhi from Canada with her three children in August 2012. Both times, her left lung was affected, and she was put on three weeks of strong antibiotics. She knows the ill effects of Delhi's air up close, she tells me with a friendly smile. Jai has also suffered from Delhi's insidiously venomous air. He is sporty and fit, a runner who has never smoked, yet suddenly, in October 2013, he was diagnosed with having a patch in his lungs. He is a huge believer in masks. Masks are how he managed to get off all his medicines, nebulizers, antihistamines and antibiotics when doctors weren't able to figure out what was causing the constant discharge of phlegm in his lungs. 'A sort of bronchial asthma,' he says.

From our very first conversations, I begin to feel these people are knowledgeable and ethical, and all of them strongly believe that clean air must be accessible to all. *This is my tribe*, I think suddenly as I look around the room at their serious faces. They are throwing out numbers, facts and data, talking about the science, reinforcing the facts I have discovered in my own research. I learn more about air pollution in those two hours than I have in the past two years. They validate my doubts and fears, solidify my knowledge and show me a way ahead. The feeling of isolation and helplessness that had overwhelmed me just weeks ago begins to subside.

Currently, the group wants to focus on awareness; it's the only way to begin, they say. We brainstorm ideas and decide to begin with schools. Children are more open-minded than adults, who hold strong views. We will begin with the schools of our own children – low-hanging fruit. I offer to begin with my children's school – we will present to children, teachers and parents. After all, if the president of the PTA can't educate parents and teachers, then what's the point of that thankless job? Plus, the school is full of the children of bureaucrats, politicians, judges – people who legislate and execute policy, make laws. When they realize how bad the situation is, they will effect changes in policies, we think naively, optimistically. Everyone agrees enthusiastically. Gen is looking thrilled, beaming at me from across the oval table. I turn to look at Barun. He can't stop smiling. There is a knowing look in his eyes. I smile back. These people, I feel, will help me bring about change. The meeting marks the beginning of something that grows to be much bigger. Later, Gopal Sankarnarayanan, Bhargav Krishna, Abhishek Bhartia and Anita Bhargav join what becomes the founding team of CFA, our non-profit organization seeking to develop public awareness about air pollution.

Before I leave the embassy school, Barun walks me through its premises, pointing out classrooms where he says the AQI is usually under 10. I can't believe it, but he should know. It is his company that has provided the school with its entire indoor air pollution protection, bringing its AQI down to WHO standards. Children and adults working in these buildings are breathing cleaner air than the rest of the city, than the children in other schools. The kind of clean air that should be everyone's right to breathe. The American embassy is paying a steep sum for the clean air – it can afford it. Those of us who can't must continue to breathe the dirty air outside.

'But what happens when they step outside this bubble you've created?' I ask. Barun shrugs.

'The same thing that happens when you step outside your air-purified bedroom.'

'Air is the ultimate democratizer,' Tina had announced earlier, during our meeting. I understand this experientially now.

I understand also that environmental justice is being flouted yet again – that like tap water made potable using machines at home, we now have to make our own clean air. Air pollution is a social iniquity.[14] Even though my children aren't getting clean air in their classrooms, their canteens, cafes, libraries, auditoriums and indoor public spaces, at least they are getting clean air at night in their air-purified rooms, reducing some of the harm done to their bodies. But what about those who can't afford purifiers for their indoor spaces? And, worse, those who have no indoor spaces to call their own, the homeless who sleep on Delhi's pavements or in the night shelters? Those whose jobs keep them outdoors, the daily wagers, construction workers, traffic policemen, autorickshaw drivers, couriers and delivery staff? They are facing the maximum brunt, taking on the heaviest load of pollutants in their lungs. I understand that we're looking at profits in the pockets of the polluters, and ill health and organ damage for the poorest of the poor.

Profits are accrued privately, but the costs and penalties are paid for with our lungs. I understood that we had to do something. And quickly. But where were we to begin?

I notice a trend. The usual trickle of expats choosing to leave Delhi citing pollution as the reason has gathered momentum turning into a deluge this year. With farewell messages every few weeks and offloading of used purifiers on Delhibabies and other sites at a peak, the summer of 2015 is the peak of what I privately call the Pollution Exodus of Expats from India.

This accelerating exodus of expats, especially those with young children, catches media attention with Gardiner and Elizabeth's very public decision to leave India, fed up with the polluted air and constant worry about the health of their children. Gardiner's parting shot, a dispatch he writes in the *New York Times* in May 2015, creates a ripple of unease among the English-speaking community, diplomats, expats, Indians and especially the journalists based out of New Delhi. This is also when Gen and Beth leave the country, a bittersweet time when they choose their families' health over the beguiling charms of a city that has fascinated and dazzled them.

Headlined 'Holding your breath in India'[15] and highlighting the tragedy of a city that is quietly suffering from a dire paediatric respiratory crisis, Gardiner's report is damning. It quotes a study[16] that reveals that nearly half of the city's 4.4 million schoolchildren have irreversible lung damage from the city's poisonous air. He writes, 'We gradually learned that Delhi's true menace came from its air, water, food and flies. These perils sicken, disable and kill millions in India annually, making for one of the worst public health disasters in the world… For most Indians, these are inescapable horrors. But there are thousands of others who have chosen to live here, including some trying to save the world, others hoping to describe it and still others intent on getting their own small piece of it.' Are expats in India pursuing their careers at the cost of their children's health, he wonders.

In his article, he is able to put into words what many foreigners living in India, and in Delhi in particular, are grappling with – their conscience, and guilt if they have young ones. It is enough to nudge fence sitters to hasten their departure. By talking about his son's struggle and trauma, Gardiner humanizes an environmental problem that has hitherto been discussed in facts and figures, bringing it uncomfortably close to home. And by calling out the unacceptably high personal cost of living with pollution while exposing the lack of public outrage on the part of a resigned or unaware citizenry in the capital of a major developing nation, he shames Indians.

Gardiner's natural irreverence for most things – hierarchies, institutions, guidelines, diplomacy, attributes that go towards making a good journalist – also ruffles many feathers. His expat-centric piece stirs much controversy and receives predominantly negative reactions in India.

'His article didn't surprise anyone who was following the issue. But his account of his son's struggles got under the skin of Indians who may never have thought of pollution before, or not realized how bad it was, or even argued that it was necessary if India had to catch up with the developed world. And that hurt,' writes the *Guardian* in a follow-up article.[17] Columnist Salil Tripathi hits the nail on the head when he tweets, 'Seems many are more upset with @GardinerHarris than with urban pollution in India! Is it that they resent that he can leave, but they can't?'[18] In the face of clear and present danger, the primitive instinct is flight. Or fight. For those with little option of moving out, Gardiner's words act like a red rag; some become hyper-critical, others vow to fight the scourge.

In that first wave of an exodus many expats leave India; Gen, Beth and Gardiner among them – Gen for Washington DC's blue skies; the Kotises for Montreal, where the AQI on an average is one-twentieth of what they have become used to breathing in New Delhi. They leave regretfully, for they have made many friends and still have so much to learn, experience and enjoy, they tell me. They say they have been 'driven away' by the air. 'I loved Delhi. But in retrospect, I wouldn't do it again,' Beth says matter-of-factly.

In their wake they leave behind a cohort of aware professionals. We have the haziest of plans of effecting a transformation. All we know is that first we need to grow our tribe.

'Ready?'

'Yes, ready... Good morning! There is an invisible killer in the city, and we're here to tell you about it. It's lethal, and it's around you, everywhere. It's called air –'

'Stop kidding around! We don't want to scare the kids!'

Some things are so big, so serious, that the only way we can make sense of them and make them seem manageable is through humour.

'Okay, okay! Ready? Good morning. We'd like to introduce ourselves, and then explain why we're here. Delhi has an invisible problem. It affects all of us. Does anyone know how much air you breathe in in a day?'

It has been a very rough summer for my family, between a reluctant house move, fire falling from the May sky and my daughter's appendix bursting before the first moving truck is loaded. Our new landlady is an ex-royal, and her eccentricities are reflected in an enchanting garden, wild with flora from the mountains and plains alike. It is what has attracted my family to this creaking, whitewashed house with green shutters and purple creepers.

This is where we now sit, amidst captivating greenery, pine, palm and bougainvillea intermingling incongruously with rib-high basil plants and a baby weeping willow. Empty cups of coffee and brownie crumbs indicate how long we've been working here, drawing up and practising an air pollution presentation that will become the base of CFA's awareness and outreach programme.

Awareness is the first step. Until people know, they won't care. We have decided to begin with students, and their parents and teachers. Then we plan to talk to neighbourhood resident housing societies, hospitals, doctors and corporations. We hope our awareness drive will lead to 'clean air ambassadors' and will seed change. The government will then be forced to listen to us, and new clean air policies will be made, we think in naive excitement. We are full of enthusiasm and passion.

We begin with my children's school, as planned, and announce it as a 'parent-ed' programme, spreading the word on WhatsApp. Barun and Jai will present to the parents. On the day of our first official presentation, several PTA volunteers stand ready with flyers, quivering with information. We've even managed to procure a Dylos air quality monitor in an attempt to make the invisible visible to parents. However, from a cohort of parents of 2,800 children, only 70 show up. The PTA workshops committee and the volunteers are crestfallen, disappointed by the turnout.

Once we are a few presentations old, I decide to ask Haripriya to join CFA, impressed with her acumen, optimism and idealism. She has just had her third child, whom they've named Arjun Gopal, has an open mind and is an engaged, active parent. I corral her one morning after a noisy PTA meeting and tell her how I've gradually realized how terrible Delhi's air is and how the pollution affects young children the most. I explain that because the lungs of young children are still growing and their respiration rate is faster compared to their body mass, they absorb more toxins than adults, and also, because they are smaller, their noses and mouths closer to the ground, they tend to inhale the worst of it.

By now I have a lot of the science, data and information at my fingertips. I tell her how children under five are 60 times more likely to die from dirty air in poor countries than in rich ones, how the lung function of Delhi's children is lower than that of other children,[19] how air pollution retards lung growth, and thus children from Delhi have smaller lungs compared to American children.[20] She listens to me attentively, her eyes widening in shock, then narrowing as she absorbs the facts.

She admits to not knowing any of these details, and surprises me with the information that her husband, a lawyer at the Supreme Court, has also been worrying about the terrible quality of air in north India. He wants to move the entire family away from Delhi, perhaps back to the south, where they are both from, especially now that they have a newborn to care for.

'Why don't you ask my husband instead?' Haripriya says. 'He's been wanting to do something. A petition in court, use the judiciary to help – I don't know. Something concrete.' Their older children, both under six, suffer from repeated respiratory troubles, ear infections and adenoids that are aggravated every winter to the extent that the children are put on steroidal medication. Their paediatrician has warned them to brace themselves because October to March is the season of allergens and pollutants. The doctor also indicates that she is treating many children with similar symptoms.

Steroids. For children under six. I am shocked into silence.

'But why are you still here, then? You have a newborn!' I finally exclaim.

'We're lawyers,' she replies enunciating clearly, as if talking to a child. 'Lawyers. The Supreme Court is in Delhi. Our careers are entirely based here. It takes a long time for lawyers to create a niche for themselves. I've spent seventeen years here. I'm not ready to give it all up,' she continues, her voice implacable.

Later, when we're piecing together the timeline of the petition in 2019, it becomes clear that at that time, in July 2015, Haripriya didn't know the extent of damage the pollution was causing to her children. She is sitting cross-legged in a black-and-mustard sari on my sofa when I interview her. I've caught her en route to the high court, which is close to my home. She tells me that her two girls coughed incessantly 'to the extent that we used to keep mugs by our bedside at night because they would throw up because they coughed so much'. But she thought it was caused by seasonal allergens and irritants, because that is what their paediatrician had said. 'Initially we were not aware enough to restrict their outdoor activities. It was only gradually, when we started investigating, that I began to realize that it was caused by PM2.5. That it is retained inside, forever. These tiny particles were affecting their lungs. Irreversibly.'

'By the time Arjun was born,' she continued, 'we began suspecting there may be some long-lasting effects, but we were still not aware how extremely dangerous this particulate matter was. There just wasn't adequate info...' Their gradual, though rude, awakening as knowledge set in, layer by layer, bringing with it awareness and alarm, spurred the lawyer couple into action.

When I meet Gopal at Haripriya's insistence, I'm struck by his firm determination. He is wearing a 1960s-style Homburg on his head, which immediately endears him to me. My father used to wear these as a young man.

'I've been thinking of a petition,' he says, his keen eyes assessing me from behind his old-style, black-rimmed spectacles. I tell him about CFA and our focus on awareness. Will he join us?

'I'm not sure awareness is the way forward,' he says before he clamps his mouth shut. I also get the impression that he isn't in favour of working with foreign nationals, and he's clearly not going to take a decision without weighing and assessing everything. I begin to wonder if he will fit in with our awareness-driven, expat-heavy group.

I try Barun's strategy. 'Just come for one meeting. With an open mind,' I tell him.

He is circumspect, non-committal, but agrees. Just one meeting.

My initial reservations about Gopal's fit with the group turn out to be unfounded. The others love him and hang onto his every word. He even manages to convince Tina, who is the most vociferous about awareness trumping advocacy, that the courts in India are the only way things get done. I listen to their heated but civil discourse and applaud silently when he manages to convince the group about the necessity of advocacy. And just like that, he is in!

Over the summer of 2015, while on the one hand the flight of expats intensifies, so on the other does the fight of those left behind. Gen and Beth remain committed to CFA. Gen has joined the EPA in Washington DC, which adds a synergistic value to our mission, and Beth and she keep delhiair.org updated – it is still the only website in India that is focused solely on air pollution – encouraging the rest of us from afar. We continue to meet monthly at the AES library, continue to build awareness, school by school, improving and updating our presentation based on questions that we encounter from schoolchildren.

Meanwhile, Gopal, along with two of his friends who are also lawyers – Saurabh Bhasin and Amit Bhandari – prepares to file a writ petition in the name of their three toddlers, asking to exercise their fundamental right to breathe clean air under Article 21 of the Indian Constitution. In September 2015, Arjun, Arav and Zoya petition the highest court of the land via their 'next friends', their fathers. Led by little Arjun, not yet six months old, the petition is formally named 'Arjun Gopal (and Others) vs Union of India (and Others)' – although it soon comes to be known as the 'firecracker petition'. I feel sure that if there is any saviour for all of Delhi's children, it will be Arjun Gopal.

As Saurabh, who later joins CFA, tells *Mint*,[21] 'The interim aspect of our petition was dealing with fireworks, but the petition itself is much broader in nature, dealing with everything from crop burning, dust from reckless construction, vehicular pollution, etc.'

Why a writ and not a public interest litigation (PIL), I ask Gopal, who drafted the petition.

'Filing it as a writ made it easier to make it admissible in court because a writ is a guaranteed right. In a PIL you are advocating for other people's rights,' says Gopal, explaining his drafting process in a separate interview on another afternoon. He is impeccably dressed in the penguin colours of lawyers and has grown a thin moustache. 'Whereas a writ may also advocate other's rights, a PIL can't advocate private rights,' he adds. So, in effect, this did both. Plus, filing a petition in the name of children was 'unprecedented', he says.

'The petition did target the many causes of pollution – dirty fuel, road dust, construction dust,' continues Gopal. 'But we had to be practical. Fireworks was where the court could actually do something immediately. Besides, it was the only cause which had no positive value. Fireworks are just used for entertainment. Their production and manufacture involves child labour, and their use creates endless amounts of garbage. And air pollution.'

Meanwhile, CFA continues to make presentations, notching up several schools. But before we can seriously scale up to the next level, another issue comes up. Both Barun and Jai are in the business of air-purifying systems, air-filter machines and masks. Both come from business families and have spotted the commercial opportunity for personal and indoor air filtering solutions and are looking to grow their businesses. There is that little matter of a conflict of interest that is rearing its head. It is making the rest of us uncomfortable.

'When we make a presentation like this, the idea is to make people aware of the pollution and how it affects their health. Once they are aware, they also become anxious about how to protect themselves. It seems a little pat that we then also say – here, we're also peddling solutions. Buy this expensive purifier, that mask,' says Tina, putting her finger on the crux of the problem.

'Well, these aren't really solutions, are they? Clean air is the real solution,' says Aurelia, her lilting South African accent cutting through our confusion.

'So, what shall we do?' Manjali is looking around at us, her large eyes questioning. She has tried every mask available, every purifier.

'Well, we ourselves do use masks for protection. And they help make this invisible problem visible. But maybe we should not call them solutions – let's call them...palliative measures? Protective measures?' we ask each other. We settle on calling these 'mitigating measures' and decide to create a code of conduct that we will all sign so that we are better able to separate commerce from education, awareness and advocacy. We could perhaps explain away one co-founder commercially selling indoor air purification solutions, but two would be difficult. So, regretfully, we part with Jai, whose business is more focused on masks. We reason that since Barun is in the business of cleaning indoor air and we are working to clean *outdoor* air, perhaps we can sidestep the conflict more easily. Besides, some industry participation is important and we want to be inclusive.

'Actually, our job is to drive you out of business,' I tell Barun. This is true. I'm only half joking. The group laughs nervously. Conflicts make us uneasy. Also, we all like Barun. He has taught us much. Barun laughs with us, an awkward sound. This must be as uncomfortable for him, I think suddenly. I feel bad, but we need to call out the elephant in the room. Better now than later.

When the laughter dies down, Barun turns and looks me in the eye. 'I will be the happiest if you can drive me out of this business. If I had to choose between clean air and my business, I would choose clean air. I want to run outdoors again,' he says. As a runner and golfer, he's often told me how he misses the outdoors since moving from the cleaner air of North Carolina and Atlanta, where his children could play outside without compromising their lungs.

'I started testing air quality after my children became asthmatic in Delhi. Tested 28 different air purifiers before choosing the optimal one. It's only after that, that I made this my business. At first, it was personal. Very personal,' he says, telling me about the time he went for a long run late one November night and couldn't stop coughing up black sputum for almost an hour after he returned. 'It was frightening,' he says.

But he was lucky. Jai's case was worse. He was training for a marathon in October 2013, when his doctor discovered a patch in his lungs. 'I'd never smoked, I was at the peak of my fitness – and then this.' For Jai, it was more than his own health. His son, who had never had any respiratory issues, had an intense asthma attack, so severe that the school had to rush him directly into intensive care. 'He had gone blue in the face. It took injecting an EpiPen directly into his heart to revive him,' says Jai. Actually, I tell myself, like Gen, Heather, Gardiner and many other expats, Barun and Jai are the Paul Reveres of our times, warning us of dangers to come and enabling us to be prepared to fight them off.

But these concerns and conflicts slow us down only temporarily. Tina takes the lead on how we should separate the commercial aspect from our collective dream of clean outdoor air. Under Gopal's guidance, we collectively draw up a code of ethics, which everyone signs.

As CFA continues to thrash out the process, presentation, plans, mission and goals, the group grows. Abhishek Bhartia from the Sitaram Bhartia group of hospitals joins us, bringing with him Anita Bhargav, an ex-PayPal entrepreneur who has already tried to clean Delhi of its garbage with her 'Let's Do It Delhi' campaign. Garbage is a very important component of air pollution. Anything that our landfills don't absorb is burnt – and municipal solid waste burning makes a large contribution to Delhi's air pollution.[22] Different research papers attribute a different load to garbage burning, but the fact remains that it is a significant contributor.

Delhi produces almost 10,000 metric tonnes of garbage every day, and its four landfills can together only absorb 7,000 or 8,000 metric tonnes, although exact estimates vary. This would imply that 2,000 to 3,000 metric tonnes of garbage is being burnt *every day* – the smoke from our own garbage going back into our lungs. When I first hear these numbers, I can hardly believe it. But some years later, when I read news reports about Delhi's garbage mountains becoming taller than the Qutub Minar[23] and the Taj Mahal,[24] my disbelief is replaced with outrage. This is especially because compared to other sources of pollution, where one can debate a potential clash between development and environment, no one can argue that improving waste management reduces growth and development. If at all, it only improves productivity, and thus growth. Yet, what we see on the ground is baffling. Part of the problem – one of the simplest issues not being resolved – is due to the multiplicity of authorities meant to be responsible for it and a lack of clear accountability.

Anita is initially focused only on cleaning dirty surroundings;

dirty air is invisible to her. A video she saw in 2010[25] inspired her to start a campaign to clean her city of garbage, beginning with her own neighbourhood. Within months, she had conducted 125 clean-ups across Delhi and devised a plan for a mammoth one-day clean-up at Bhikaji Cama Place. Her method was to set up systems in one area as a perfectly working pilot and then make them scalable and replicable across the city. She threw herself into waste removal, using self-reporting, data, scorecards, accountability and the existing civic system and bureaucracy. Soon, she had extended her work across 18 wards around Delhi. By 2011, she had become a pro bono consultant to the commissioner of the Municipal Corporation of Delhi (MCD).

'The idea was to fix the problem, not the blame,' she says, echoing a familiar mantra of mine, as she tucks her thick, white mane behind her ears. By 2012, she had become chief of staff to a municipal councillor and hoped to use the ward as a lab to transform it. But the bureaucratic hurdles she faced disillusioned her, even though she had citizen and political support. 'It failed,' she admits. 'I couldn't scale it up to the rest of Delhi – 18 wards were getting better service at the expense of other wards.' This meant that municipal workers, their contractors and subcontractors were throwing the garbage of one area that was getting public attention into another area that wasn't. 'I realize now that I should have involved the judiciary too. It is only with a pincer-like movement of all arms of democracy – the legislators, the executives and the judiciary – could I have hoped to make a lasting difference,' she says, sounding regretful.

With CFA, the plan is to have Anita work on the garbage disposal factor in air pollution. Open trash burning is one of the single biggest sources of air pollution in Delhi. 'No wonder Delhi is a gas chamber,' she says. She wants to find innovative ways to handle the city's garbage. Segregating and composting are only the basic steps, she tells us, pointing out the uselessness of household segregation when all the segregated bundles are tossed together at the landfills.

The next to join is air pollution scientist Dr Sarath Guttikinda, who becomes our scientific adviser. He has recently set up Urban Emissions.info and wants to democratize air pollution research. An early pollution migrant, he has escaped Delhi's filthy air and relocated his family to Goa.

Dr Joshua Apte, who has been measuring air pollution in Delhi since 2007 as a doctoral student, also becomes our adviser. And when Bhargav Krishna – a young research fellow at the Public Health Foundation – joins, the group's health data and research focus get a boost. These three are among early data scientists who understand that air pollution science needs to become accessible to more non-specialists to create impact.

Bhargav is part of the technical team of the Government of India-constituted Steering Committee on Air Pollution and Health Related Issues that is helping write a report for the central government. This committee's report[26] is ready by August 2015 and released in the public domain in January 2016, but like most government documents that highlight uncomfortable issues, it sinks without a trace. The report conclusively and clearly states, 'We believe that reduction of both emissions and exposures are important to protecting public health but a health policy driven prioritization of options has to be principally driven by exposure, since that ultimately determines health outcomes. Therefore, while we very much recommend reduction of emissions as much as possible to reduce overall population levels of exposure, the highest immediate priority has to be accorded to sources that lead to the greatest levels of exposure and adverse health impacts.'

Despite being the first Indian government report on the health impact of air pollution, the excellent report doesn't get the attention it deserves, even from the media.

Over the next year, we plan to extend and expand our reach to more schools in Delhi. We realize what is missing is mass mobilization and want to develop a Hindi version of our presentation and reach government schools, to make this more of a mass movement. We want children in all north Indian schools to become aware. Actually, what we want is for air pollution to become a conversation in every tea stall, every pharmacy, every adda. But we have limited human and financial resources – we are funding everything ourselves – and are unsure of how to navigate government corridors.

'If we can't do it directly,' I tell the group excitedly during one meeting, 'let's embed our curriculum obliquely.' A few years ago, I had met and written about Teach for India, a start-up modelled on Wendy Kopp's Teach for America that tries to improve outcomes in the field of education by embedding its fellows in the poorest municipal schools. Now I think perhaps we can speak to some of those bright minds and big hearts, or even the founder of the movement. There may be other avenues too – Khan Academy, some of the more effective extracurricular edu-tech start-ups. I feel confident that many people can be convinced through data and science to do their bit. After all, science is on our side. It will be a full year and many hours of my time later that I will realize how naive I have been about the politics of clean air.

Arjun Gopal's writ petition is a strategy to bring the central government to the table – because air pollution has been a long-standing problem and the government has done very little over the years. Earlier rulings by the Supreme Court to limit the duration of lighting crackers and noise pollution are hardly followed. After the petition is filed in the Supreme Court, even though the government requests deferral in hearings, newspapers and broadcast media pick up the 'firecracker petition'. Three toddlers pleading with the mighty Supreme Court captures public imagination. Between the systemic and strategic delays, deferrals and procrastinations of hearings, the case will take about a year to fully gain traction. But by Diwali 2016, there is a national furore.

Gopal, Saurabh and Amit are seasoned enough to play the waiting game and know that nothing moves fast in the courts. Their aim is to create awareness about air pollution, make it a political issue that people vote on and get the government to act. 'We want the government to put a stringent pollution control mechanism in place. Advocacy is our larger aim,' Gopal tells *Mint* in November 2015.

We discuss the case during our CFA meetings. 'Episodic spikes in air pollution lead to many more deaths, disease and disability. There is a direct correlation to heart attacks, strokes and health issues,' Bhargav tells us sombrely.

'So, every Diwali, when there is a spike, more people end up in hospitals? Isn't there a way to correlate them? Is there any research on this?' I ask.

'I've been trying to get data from hospitals in India,' he says drily. 'No one wants to share this information.'

I recall the director of the All India Institute of Medical Sciences (AIIMS), Dr Randeep Guleria, telling me of a study they were conducting in 2017, linking emergency admissions immediately after Diwali and other celebratory occasions, from weddings and cricket match wins to New Year's Day and Guru Purab.

It is now perfectly clear to me that the real effects of air pollution aren't felt in our environment. They are felt in our hospitals, and inside our bodies, beginning with our lungs. I resolve to ask other doctors I know for such data.

In November, I reel in a feisty friend, Dilshad Master, the proverbial 'crazy Parsi', to help me set up a website for CFA.

Dilshad is like an indestructible India rubber. She has had 13 surgeries in her life, her first when she was in college. Her face has been mauled by her brother's dog, she has been in a car accident and, most recently, has survived cancer. I have only seen her cry once in the 25 years I have known her, and that wasn't over physical pain.

'Okay, tell me. What kind of website do you guys want?' Dilshad asks in her quintessential style, cutting directly to the chase as she walks in with her laptop and plonks herself down at my dining table on a grey November morning.

At first, Tina and Aurelia are startled at her no-nonsense style, but soon we are sitting companionably together, trying to figure out how to set up a website.

'It should be simple, easy to understand, but completely science and evidence-backed,' Tina and I decide. 'We should have our existing programmes up there – maybe an email address?' we say tentatively.

'How good are you guys on social media? Are you on Twitter? Snapchat? Insta? YouTube?' asks Dilshad briskly, tapping away on her laptop. Its fuchsia neon silicon cover hurts my eyes, but I've known her long enough to know that like her ever-changing hairstyles, this is her signature statement.

Our combined social media retardation keeps us silent. Dilshad's sharp eyes take in our dejected body language.

'Well. Okay. Then I'll just begin with a simple Weebly page. Do you have a domain name? A GoDaddy account? Do you want YouTube? I'm assuming you already have an email address? Shall I create a tab for response? You want new volunteers, right? Sub-tabs? Pull-down menu?' Dilshad barks out questions at her usual breakneck speed.

We nod, shake, nod our heads mutely.

She types and clicks, muttering to herself, clicks some more. Then she swivels around saying, 'Okay, here,' and shows us a page with snow-blue-tipped mountains, blue skies and a clear lake reflecting the orange glow of the sun – and our logo! It's beautiful. It's real. *We're* real! But there's no time to admire it. Dilshad is barrelling ahead.

'Now, the content. Who has that? We can do it right away. C'mon, come *on*!'

Thankfully, we have lots of *that* at hand. Now, suddenly she's the one learning. She listens attentively as we give her facts, numbers, data, evidence, research. So much content. How will it fit in? Should we have a section on air pollution myths? Her eyes widen as we get to all the health harm PM2.5 causes. She has a little girl of her own.

'What's this particulate matter? Smaller than dust? Like smoking cigarettes? My kid is smoking cigarettes?' Dilshad's slightly hooked nose is quivering in alarm as she clicks and saves. I quickly explain to her how it is the health impact of smoking cigarettes that researchers measure, but she has caught on to the scarier fact.

'Are you serious!' She turns around. 'It doesn't just harm our respiratory system? Wait, what else did you say is affected? Cognitive skills?[27] And it's irreversible? Childhood cancers?[28] Oh, don't say childhood cancers!'

Now she is holding her head, mussing up her chicly styled salt-and-pepper hair. It stands up incongruously, framing her sharp, attractive features. Her shoulders sag in the now-familiar gesture of someone who is getting overwhelmed by facts on air pollution and how it affects every human organ. We look at her sympathetically, wait while she absorbs the deluge of information, then gesture her back to her neon laptop. Her usually animated face begins to look troubled; her questions don't stop. Our data doesn't stop pouring out.

'You mean, my kid is breathing toxins daily and they're never going to come out of her system in her whole life? Pollution is stunting her growth?' She's looking at me now, her voice turning nasal, high-pitched, her eyes shocked at what we're telling her. I nod. She falls silent, her lips turned down. Then she takes a deep breath, throws her head back in a typical gallant gesture and resumes clicking away, her forehead wrinkled in thought.

'Come on, guys. We have work to do. The website. Do you want to make it informational or interactive? What's your goal?'

'Awareness,' says Tina, steadfastly. Aurelia nods. 'That's the first step to driving any change.'

'Can we add our motto?' I say. I've suddenly thought of something. Three enquiring faces turn towards me. 'Awareness. Advocacy. Change: Clean Air for All.' There is silence. There! In seven words, we've captured the essence of the movement.

'Brilliant!' Everyone agrees, and it's done.

When the rest of the crew see the new website up and running, they love it. In particular, Barun loves the tag line the most. I often catch him muttering to himself 'Awareness-Advocacy-Change' like it's some sort of mantra.

In early December, there is a completely unforeseen announcement by the newly formed Aam Aadmi Party (AAP), which was sworn in in February 2015 to govern Delhi-NCR. AAP leader and Delhi's new chief minister Arvind Kejriwal says Delhi will experiment with a road-rationing scheme to reduce pollution from its skyrocketing levels. Kejriwal, who has had to leave the city in order to cure himself of a chronic bronchial cough and has labelled Delhi a 'gas chamber', says the 'odd-even' road rationing will begin in January 2016, before schools reopen from winter break.

This is the first time a government – even though it is a state and not the central government – publicly acknowledges air pollution. With this announcement, air pollution finally stops being seen only as a problem of the rich. It may have taken a long time to turn air pollution from an elite to an *aam aadmi* narrative, as Josh puts it, but the AAP must be congratulated for the part it ultimately played in converting pollution into *'pradooshan'*, a middle-class narrative.

Vehicles will be allowed on the road on the basis of their licence plates – dividing them into those ending in odd numbers and those in even numbers. This should get more people to use public transport – and it is strategic to do this while schools are closed, so that the existing public bus fleet is fully available. Because this is not just a policy announcement but an action that directly disrupts the lives of the residents of Delhi-NCR, the gravity of the situation percolates to the common man, making it an absolute game changer for awareness and bringing it into the radar of those affected most by the dirty air.

What this means for CFA is that suddenly we get no pushback from schools and hospitals. In fact, we are getting sought out.

Gopal is doggedly pursuing the toddlers' petition. The next hearing is in December. He has managed to get the venerable senior lawyer Mr K.K. Venugopal to mention the matter for him in court in order to give it more weight. The night before the matter is to come up in court, Gopal asks us to help with some facts, data and research. A group of us huddle in Mr Venugopal's chambers with Gopal and his younger colleagues, bouncing ideas off each other, sharing research. We talk about how diesel – a dirty fuel – is subsidized and cheaper, and how the refineries of Reliance and Essar export all the high-quality, clean Euro-6-quality fuel abroad, selling the dirtier BS-4 fuel here. We talk of how the Essential Commodities Act protects Indian interests by controlling the production, supply, distribution, trade and commerce in any commodity that is considered 'essential' and 'in the interest of the general public'. Clean fuel should be an essential commodity made available to Indians first, before allowing exports, we say. The lawyers listen attentively, taking occasional notes.

It's after 9 p.m. when we get up to leave. Gopal casually asks us if we'd like to see the proceedings inside the Supreme Court. Barun, Manjali and I immediately say yes. As a reporter, I have covered Parliament, but this will be my first time at the Supreme Court of India. Gopal asks Barun to bring along his DustTrak, to 'show' the bench the invisible particles in the air.

Thanks to his invitation, the three of us get a chance to view the petition proceedings the next day.

Black-robed, white-shirted lawyers mill around as we enter the majestic high-domed courthouse. By the time the case is called, it is close to 1 p.m. Barun has brought his DustTrak and measures the PM levels as the three-judge bench comprising Justices Madan Lokur, R. Bhanumathi and A.K. Sikri look on. When the lunch recess is called, Manjali has to leave, but Gopal leads us to Mr Venugopal's chambers, where we make some calls to get additional data. Barun and I stand through the post-lunch session, trying to understand what is going on and after a few hours we are ready to leave. Walking through the red sandstone building, past graceful pillars, down the grand stairs, dotted by flowerpots bursting with colour, I feel overawed, an immense sense of pride. I also feel sobered by the thought of the mammoth task that lies ahead of us. Somewhere in my head, I hear the rousing strains of *Vande Mataram*, playing like a ring tone.

'Shall we take a selfie?' asks Barun. His eyes are shining. As a mother of two teens, I've always been conflicted about selfies, looking down on them as an act of narcissism. But this time I can't resist. In the weak sunlight of 15 December 2015, we take a selfie with the grand dome of the Supreme Court of India in the background, the tricolour flying high atop it. Barun promptly posts it on his Facebook timeline.

The odd-even road rationing scheme will begin in January, before schools reopen. For the holidays, I'm trying to get my family out of smoggy Delhi. It has become important to do this, even if it's for a short while, to give our lungs a break. I'm very aware of the irony of flying to our destination, fuelled by polluting jet fuel.

I look out my airplane window at the haze over my beautiful but toxic city. I feel that familiar tug of love, of belonging, something I always feel when I travel. But today, for the first time, as I look down at the city I was born and raised in – and made the active choice to come back to – I feel another, newer feeling. For the first time, I'm considering that perhaps I should encourage my children to leave this place. I had so wanted them to get their undergraduate degree from India. Today is when I decide I will leave that desire behind. Delhi's air is sickening us all. It isn't worth breathing, and it is definitely not worth compromising their health for.

7

Is Sickening

2016

In January, the people of Delhi adopt and actively support the 'odd-even scheme' announced by the Aam Aadmi Party. The scheme dictates which vehicles will be allowed on the road through the week based on their licence plate numbers, and aims to cut down pollution in the city. The ready compliance of the people shows not only that there is some degree of awareness about the ill effects of air pollution, but also, that, when required, Delhi's residents will cooperate.

Sadly, the scheme does absolutely nothing to bring down levels of air pollution, as research confirms later.[1,2,3] Some reports even say that, counter-intuitively, pollution levels likely increased.[4] The reasons for this are many, the two main reasons being the lack of adequate public transport as an alternative to private vehicles and the many exemptions allowed under the scheme.

Since Delhi's public transport system is inadequate for the population to begin with, any extra burden only creates more scarcity and chaos. Around the time that the odd-even scheme is launched, newly launched taxi services like Uber and Ola see a sharp rise in demand. Since public transport is unable to ferry all the commuters, people turn to taxis, and the overall demand for and usage of taxis increases while the scheme is in place. Furthermore, Uber's 'surge' pricing policy attracts many Uber drivers not registered in Delhi to enter the city to meet the sudden demand. Since taxis with an all-India licence don't necessarily have to be CNG-fuelled, as is mandated for all taxis registered in Delhi, there is an increase in diesel fumes being emitted because of the influx of taxis from other states. All of this results in no actual drop in the number of vehicles on the road. Also, the total actual mileage travelled by the vehicles doesn't drop in the same proportion as their presence on the road. Odd-numbered cars do more kilometres on odd days, ditto even cars on even days, keeping the total numbers of kilometres travelled more or less the same.

The second and more important reason is that two-wheelers – with their two-stroke engines that use a mixture of gasoline and oil as fuel which cause more pollution – are exempted from the scheme and remain on the road. There is thus little real effect in the efforts to clean the air.[5] The oil-gas fuel of older models emits more smoke, carbon monoxide, hydrocarbons and particulate matter than the gas-only four-stroke engines found in newer motorcycles. Making matters worse, many two-wheelers carry extra passengers during this time, making the engines work harder and burn dirtier.

Since inexpensive two-wheelers form a staggering 75 to 80 per cent of traffic in most Asian cities, reducing pollution depends on stringent emissions standards for them. India is no different. Two-wheelers (75 per cent) and three-wheelers (4 per cent) constituted about 80 per cent of the total number of vehicles in 2008.[6] In addition to strict emission standards India needs an effective vehicle-inspection programme, fiscal incentive programmes to replace existing two-stroke engines with four-stroke ones, and the development of efficient public transportation systems, none of which are addressed by the odd-even scheme. In India, government data[7] shows that two-wheelers consume 62 per cent of petrol. Cars consume less than half of that – only 27 per cent. This skew is not unique to India. Measurements of how much pollution two-wheelers emit are rare, but one study of traffic intersections in Bangkok found that two-wheelers contributed to up to 47 per cent of particulate matter in the air. Similarly, when two-stroke scooter taxis were phased out in Dhaka in 2002, particulate concentrations dropped by up to 40 per cent and the levels of carbon monoxide and hydrocarbons fell significantly. Dr Mukesh Sharma estimates that in India between 25 and 40 per cent of total vehicular pollution is caused by two-wheelers. 'Two-wheelers in India travel 1 trillion kilometres each year,' he will tell me some years later, and that number is so staggering that I have to ask him to repeat himself.

Lastly, diesel vehicles and large trucks are still at large – so the biggest contributors to pollution aren't controlled. Another survey, done by Nielsen, shows that 19 per cent of diesel vehicles are used for agriculture and 66 per cent for transport.[8]

National news channels ask for CFA's views on the odd-even scheme. 'Target the dirty fuel, the polluting engine, not the licence plate,' I say multiple times on different national television shows. But no one seems to be listening.

As a group, we support any measure taken by the government to address the problem of air pollution, however small, ad hoc or reactive – it's better than nothing being done. But, instead of targeting number plates, the Delhi government needs to tackle real issues, beginning with the still-subsidized dirty diesel fuel, then figuring out how to retain the better, cleaner, BS-6 fuel within the country instead of it being exported, and looking into effective engine models. It is, after all, a fact that – India exports 'cleaner' cars to Mexico than it sells to its own people. What is not as well known is that Indian refineries export cleaner fuel to other countries, while selling cheaper, dirtier fuel produced domestically. There is talk of moving to BS-6 fuel by 2020, but now that I know how harmful polluted air is, I don't understand why it should take so long to switch. Years later, even by 2019, the government will be subsidizing fossil fuels over nine times more than its subsidy to renewable energy, a fact that will continue to bother me.

Despite its flaws, CFA decides to support the scheme whole-heartedly because it has raised awareness like nothing else has. It has helped do in one stroke what CFA and other organizations like ours couldn't have done in years. Overnight, awareness about pollution has become more mainstream, a fact I ascertain by the sudden surge in the mention of the word – '*pradooshan*', the Hindi for pollution, on television programmes, news channels, in the regional media, advertisements and conversations among people alike. When people sitting at tea shops, vegetable vendors and autorickshaw drivers start talking about pollution, that is when I will say awareness has reached a critical mass.

'In many ways, the Aam Aadmi Party was the first political party to champion available water or breathable air... I don't recall the Congress or the BJP leadership in Delhi doing this the same way as the AAP – presenting these as clear and present dangers with an existential thread,' says Josh.

Josh is in the habit of speaking to taxi and autorickshaw drivers whenever he visits India, and it's not just to practise the smattering of Hindi he knows. He always talks to them about pollution. Taxi drivers across the world are the best informed and know the pulse on the ground, as most journalists know. Before WhatsApp and social media, they were literally the veined network that information informally passed through. Josh casually brings up pollution as a topic of conversation during his commutes, like most people would ask about the weather.

'What's interesting is that till then [the odd-even scheme came into effect], whenever I'd ask the cab drivers what they thought about air pollution, they would say, "Oh, this is just fog." It just didn't really register.'

Yet, this was the time when, he says, you couldn't go to any gathering of 'expats or very well-connected people in the upper echelon of Indian society' and *not* talk about air pollution, 'because pollution was so front and centre of what was in their minds'.

However, by 2016, overnight, auto and taxi drivers seemed to catch up. They had become aware of *pradooshan*. 'One of the challenges was that the narrative took a really long time to become a middle-class, sort of "*aam aadmi*", if you will, topic. I think it was seen as a very elitist concern, something that only the rich contribute to and worry about,' Josh says. This was probably because emissions from cars were perceived to be the primary contributors to pollution, when in reality, it was also the more middle-class two-wheelers as well as burning of trash, cow dung and biomass that contributed equally to the pollution.

One of Josh's studies was done from the back of an autorickshaw in 2010, when he was a doctoral student, which he recorded in a YouTube clip.[9] The four-month study showed clearly the spikes and high levels of toxic air Delhi commuters were exposed to on a daily basis. He found that levels of pollution in traffic are 1.5 to 8 times higher than urban background readings measured by official monitors.[10] 'Our on-road pollution measurements in Delhi rank among the highest...anywhere in the world,' he says. It is shocking to know that in traffic we could be breathing up to eight times the amount of pollutants being recorded by official monitors. Katy Daigle, an Associated Press journalist, came across this paper in 2014, and we met in Delhi to talk about it. She then decided that we would re-enact the study to take photos and do some data journalism,' says Josh.

While the odd-even scheme is going on, someone adds me to a WhatsApp group called 'Help Delhi Breathe.' Reecha Upadhyay, the lead campaigner for the Purpose Climate Lab, is a part of this group. Tina, Aurelia and I have earlier had a couple of intense meetings with her international team and her to look for synergies, and now I keep bumping into her at pollution-centric meets. The group discusses organizing public events to bring attention to the declining, lethal air quality, and decides to start a campaign with the same name. The plans include a rally, petitions, videos and a clean-air fair. For the rally, they want to invite scientific experts, doctors, air pollution researchers and activists. People such as Anumita Roychowdhury from Centre for Science and Environment (CSE), Vikrant Tongad from Social Action for Forests and Environment, Parthaa Bosu from Clean Air Asia, Sunil Dahiya from Greenpeace India and Dr Randeep Guleria from AIIMS are considered. There is also talk of getting artistes and troupes such as Shilpa Rao, the Delhi Drum Circle and Astitva to perform at the venue to help raise awareness.

The group's 'charter of demands' includes, among others, a better public transportation system, smog-alert systems and strictly enforced measures for heavily polluted days, phasing out all diesel-operated vehicles and machinery, and the continuation of the odd-even car-rationing system. They use social media to leverage publicity – the event is publicized via Facebook and by mid-January it has 1,700 'interested'. Reecha and her collaborators manage to reach the middle and upper class among Delhi's population by some intelligent power-mapping and savvy leveraging of social media and technology. 'We brought the event together with lots of help from civil society. We used the networks of some of the more woke and influential members of society to help us get this going,' Reecha told MobLab, a Greenpeace offshoot, in a detailed article[11] partly funded by Purpose Labs. It is Purpose that funds the event – with help and favours from collaborators.

Take a deep breath.
Can you smell it? It's the scent of death.
Until a few months ago
Even I didn't know
That the sky was so grey,
That the 13,000 litres of air I was breathing every day
Was so poisonous, so polluted
And that this particulate matter was rooted
In my lungs, seeping into my blood-stream.
When I found out, I wanted to scream.
Because all those frequent headaches I got
Were because of the air which left me so distraught.
Lung cancer, stunted organ development, respiratory diseases
All because we drive our Mercedes?

Yes, you heard that right.
Cars cause 60 per cent of the pollution – just because our sight
Is not designed to see these invisible particles
Doesn't mean we should ignore those articles
In the newspapers, which talk about how
Every day in the city that seems so pretty is somehow
Bringing us closer to bad days.
But this is OUR city. We're not going to run.
Instead of feeling sorry and scared for our sons
and daughters and mother and fathers,
We can find a solution
For this terrible, terrible air pollution.
Trust me it's possible – but only if we work together.
Seeing everyone gathered here, despite the cold weather
Is a step itself, to make a change.
It gives me hope, that someone, somewhere wanted to arrange
An event like this.

On 17 January 2016, my family participates in the Help Delhi Breathe event at Jantar Mantar. My daughter, a newly minted slam poet, writes these lines and performs to the crowd, intersecting her desire for environmental justice with youthful creativity. Young people in the crowd cheer her on before the music begins, and I feel a sudden sense of shame that my generation will leave a much dirtier world for our children.

Jantar Mantar is a UNESCO world heritage site, and the street next to it has become the seat of all protests. It is an appropriate place to voice our demand that the government give us back our right to breathe clean air.

I've done my bit to spread the word through CFA, making a few calls and putting up posters at schools. Most protesters are wearing masks. We are hoping this event will raise awareness about Delhi's pollution and help us push for measures to mitigate it. Give us back our public spaces. Because breathing outdoors has become injurious to our health.

It is Sunday, just a couple of days since the odd-even trial ended.

Already, news reports are saying that though the 15-day pollution-control experiment did little to improve Delhi's air quality, it has raised awareness and is being 'widely acknowledged to be a valiant effort to find a solution to the horrendous problem'.

The media is present, which makes this gathering appear like a protest, though no one wants to actually call this a protest – the organizers emphasize that this is 'not a protest but a plea to the government to continue the good work by implementing policies to lower air pollution'.

'This event is a very good articulation of public concern,' *Scroll* reports Anumita Roychowdhury as saying. CSE has an excellent body of work in air pollution and has been at the forefront of trying to highlight this environmental hazard for years, but like The Energy and Resources Institute (TERI) and other established organizations, it hasn't successfully managed to bring conversations on dirty air into the public domain or channel existing outrage into action or policy change. It is this work that we want to bring out into the public domain. Amplify that research, convert it into public outrage and channel it into better enforcement and stronger clean air policies. Despite the masks, I recognize several long-time pollution activists in the gathering, which makes me realize that we are still preaching to the choir. Instead, we need to step out of our echo chambers, and reach the masses.

The loudest message that emerges from this public movement – the first time citizens have come together and demanded clean air – is that 'more steps need to be taken to clean Delhi's air'.

It is around this time that I begin to realize that pollution isn't just a Delhi-centred problem. I've attended enough seminars and read enough research by now to know that airsheds over the entire northern part of India show high AQIs. NASA photographs are beginning to show the entire Indo-Gangetic plain as being covered by terrible air.[12] The next round of WHO data shows that almost 92 per cent of India is breathing polluted air in differing degrees. Of the 20 top polluted cities in the world, 14 are in India, and all in the north.[13] Part of the reason why more cities are being added to the list is not because they were clean earlier and have recently become polluted, but because the pollution levels in these cities were never being measured. India needs almost 3,500 monitors. At present, it barely has less than 10 per cent of this number. While numbers are increasing every day, the rise is not happening at the rate required.

'One mistake we made was that in our initial petition for clean air, we should have asked to include these 14 cities. It could have had an all-India impact,' Gopal tells me during our interview. But perfect vision always comes post-event.

The government is considering moving to cleaner BS-6 fuel from April 2020, but now we want to exert some pressure to ensure that it happens earlier. Gopal has been wondering how to use the might of the court to move faster towards cleaner fuel among other measures to lower emissions. Two days after the Help Delhi Breathe event, on 19 January, he files an interim application seeking urgent orders from the court to selectively ban diesel, documenting that it is carcinogenic, ban the registration of new diesel vehicles in 13 polluted Indian cities, remove import duties and incentivize cleaner CNG fuel and hybrid vehicles, as well as push for filters at polluting thermal power plants. It is a detailed application and the hearing is set for 21 January. At the hearing, Gopal specifically names the Reliance and Essar refineries which have been quietly exporting all their clean BS-6 fuel to the USA and Europe, and asks to divert the clean fuel for domestic sale and consumption. 'We did not need to wait four years for clean fuel in our country,' he tells me. A national daily carries news of his plea on its front page[14] but his application is kept pending as the judges assigned to the plea change.

'We kept putting pressure until the Petroleum Ministry decided in November 2017 that they will advance the date to roll out BS-6 to April 2018 in Delhi and subsequently to the rest of the country,' he says.

That year, I start hearing about more protests, though most are still in Delhi. I sense the momentum building and decide to devote my time entirely to writing about air pollution. I stop my start-up column. This is the best way I know to contribute to something more meaningful. I will focus on writing about pollution research in simple terms in order to make the messages more accessible and amplify them. Simplify and magnify, I pledge to myself. But I forget about the resistance newspapers have to what I call broccoli journalism – writing about things that are actually good for you – over the instant gratification junk that is becoming more and more common, the sort that thrives on television rating points (TRPs) and loud debates. Alas, in March the air quality is improving and no one wants to talk or read about air pollution any more. It is the same story every year.

When the 'Global Burden of Disease' report – the most comprehensive worldwide observational epidemiological study that describes mortality and morbidity from major diseases, injuries and risk factors to health at global, national and regional levels – is released, it declares air pollution as the second-largest killer in the world.[16] I use that as an opportunity to write an opinion piece[15] about the topic. I want to highlight that air pollution is not just a Delhi problem but a pan-Indian one that may eventually create pollution refugees. In the piece, I also highlight the sort of environmental migration it can lead to. I point out that the 'Make in India' policy being pushed by the Narendra Modi government won't be possible without cleaning the air, as rising pollution is in the process of creating a cohort of environmental refugees.

I send it to the op-ed page editors of three of the widest-read newspapers. They all push back – air pollution has never been an exciting topic – but I eventually manage to get it published. Over time, I find other articles and writers using terms like 'pollution migrants' and 'environmental refugees' in the context of air pollution and related health harm and feel relief. If journalists can continue convincing the media to cover this topic, perhaps we can drum up some interest and support and embed these conversations into public memory.

There are also several more ideas that I want to roll out. I plan to take all new air pollution research that links it to health harm and create simple, accessible one-pager flyers in different languages and distribute them widely. I also want to write a series of myth busters – for example, how pranayama under a neem tree at peak winter pollution levels does not strengthen or protect our lungs. On the contrary, doing so causes more PM to collect in our lungs. This comes from seeing a hospital flyer asking people to do pranayama outdoors to strengthen their lungs in winter that we at CFA have exclaimed over. People need to know that unlike microbiological pollutants, humans never build immunity to particulate matter – in fact, their immune system weakens – and that intense aerobic activities like running marathons in high pollution can worsen matters.[17] We plan to get people affected by pollution to write first-hand accounts on the CFA blog, 'Care to Share'.

CFA is still managing to present to two schools each month. We have spoken at schools such as Sardar Patel, Modern School, Vasant Vihar and Delhi Public School, and have gone beyond schools to present at Vedika, a unique management school that caters to women. Meanwhile, Abhishek Bhartia asks us to start hospital presentations, with the first one scheduled to be at the Sitaram Bhartia Hospital.

'Let's talk to some pregnant women. I will also get as many of our doctors to attend as possible,' Abhishek tells us. This will be our first presentation to doctors and expectant parents. We are a little nervous, especially about answering questions posed by experienced specialists. We've decided that having a public health researcher present and tweaking the presentation to make it more technical is a good idea, and Bhargav's strong scientific background and tall, stolid presence is reassuring.

Abhishek, slim and dapper, is standing at the steps of the graceful, old-worldly Sitaram Bhartia Hospital to welcome us when we arrive, another reassuring sight. The conference room is full of expectant parents. We tell them how the air they are breathing is going to affect their unborn children and how microparticles cross over from the placenta before birth, setting up their babies for a lifetime of ill health. We are harbingers of bad news. We don't want to scare them – at least not too much – but we also want to make sure those newborn lungs are protected. Many of these babies will be born in the winter – which, in my head, has been firmly designated the 'pollution season'.

'Black carbon particles have been found in the foetal side of placentas, greatly increasing the risk of diseases at birth,' Tina tells the audience, as I take notes of reactions and prepare to answer questions.

The presentation goes well. At the end, there is the usual stunned silence, followed by an outburst of questions as faces turn tight with anxiety and concern. We take the questions and answer them to the best of our ability. For us, it is mildly shocking to hear that doctors have such little awareness about the ill effects of air pollution on the human body.

After the presentation, I find myself wishing we could cover every hospital. Once all our doctors are aware, this awareness will pass more easily on to the masses. People listen to their doctors. Unfortunately, as Dr Kumar says, the healthcare sector has failed to disseminate information on air pollution – even in the capital city, 92 per cent of residents don't know the difference between PM10 and PM2.5 – or, as he calls it, *dhool* and *dhuan*.

Abhishek thanks us profusely as he drops us at the gate of the leafy lane that houses the hospital. We thank him back. This has given us confidence.

'We should do more of these,' says Bhargav, echoing my thoughts. Everyone else agrees. Unfortunately, Abhishek himself has recently moved out of India, driven out by its foul air, to Toronto, and spends his time juggling between the two countries, trying to minimize his children's time in Delhi during the high pollution season. He is among the early pollution refugees, a number that will swell as more Indians become aware of the risks of air pollution and migrate to cleaner cities because of dirty air. The Pollution Exodus of Expats is spreading to local Indians. I see this as a second wave, an exodus more poignant, because, unlike expats leaving India, here no one is returning – they are leaving home.

These moves aren't easy. People who never wanted to move are uprooting themselves, moving away from their homes and families. Apart from Abhishek, who moved countries mainly because of the pollution, leaving behind his family-owned hospital, his ageing parents, I start to hear of several Indians who have taken a similar drastic step, despite being as culturally strongly rooted in traditional Indian values as Abhishek. He admits that his being a pollution refugee is a nuanced reason, and is especially challenging to understand for those who have never lived elsewhere.

So Abhishek and his wife, Saru, try to stay and leave at once – be present for their family in their homeland and absent from its pollution. It's something they both feel sorry about every day, but they won't compromise their children's health.

They have the luxury of doing this, and life is good. But they have traded off, for now, a certain groundedness that comes from residing in one country with the restlessness of belonging to two. They have traded their children's identity, culture and heritage for better facilities, clean air and nature.

And what about his parents? What did it feel like to leave them behind?

'It was hard for them to understand my decision,' admits Abhishek. 'They thought I was being too extreme. They weren't happy.'

But that was then. After two more polluted winters, his parents started saying that his decision to leave was a wise one. And now, in his third year of juggling life in two countries, 'they say, *bahut theek kiya,*' he says. But they won't join him.

'For people of that generation, this isn't even a conversation.' It's not that Abhishek hasn't tried his utmost. 'They can't even imagine relocating. Their sense of identity is too deeply tied to their country, their city and their community,' he says. 'The elderly don't have a choice. At least the young are mobile.'

Kalyani and Akshaya Gulhati's story reflects this mobility. They are a young, professional couple – she is a computer scientist, he a management consultant. After living in London, Chicago, Washington DC, Poughkeepsie and New York, they moved back to New Delhi in 2010 with their two children to live in the family home with Akshaya's parents. 'The idea was to raise our children in our home country,' says Kalyani. Akshaya's father, Dr Shashi Gulhati, is a retired IIT professor who coincidentally taught my husband a civil engineering class in the

1980s, and Rashmi, his wife, coincidentally ran the preschool my children went to years ago. Kalyani and Akshaya's move to Delhi was meant to be a permanent move. They had their third child right here in 2011, before they realized how toxic the air was and how sick it was making their children.

'Our son would get sick every winter, wheezing often, and with an almost non-stop cough throughout the season,' says Kalyani.

It was heart-breaking to see the children sick so often. Her in-laws couldn't understand it. 'I don't think they thought the pollution was contributing. In fact, I remember my mother-in-law explaining to me that kids "build up immunity" and "everyone living here is doing fine."'

But Kalyani was part of a community of young parents who were very aware about how the air was affecting everyone's health, several of them expats. Not wanting to move anywhere, now that they had finally reached 'home', the young couple persevered. 'My husband and I had been so determined to move back to Delhi. We had spent 10 years planning our move back home. This was meant to be our final destination. We wanted our kids to go to college here,' she says.

'Once we realized how toxic the air was, we tried to have the kids wear masks, but weren't very successful. I think they were too young and playful. The novelty wore off after about a week. We had air purifiers in almost every room. We made sure we didn't open the windows for too long in the morning; had the kids play indoors a lot. I know this sounds crazy but some days I would even have them take an extra shower to get their nasal passages cleaned a bit more with the steam. It would also help with the coughing.' They even tried to get away from Delhi in the worst time.

'We'd go and stay with my parents in Himachal [Pradesh] for a good part of the winter, as well. We knew the air was cleaner there, even though the temperatures were much lower.'

But instead of getting better, things got worse.

'The last winter that we were in Delhi, even our youngest daughter started to cough incessantly,' Kalyani says.

To get out of Delhi's air, without moving out of the country, they briefly and desperately thought of relocating to Palampur in Himachal, but a lack of good schools and job opportunities restrained them. This is the problem faced by many young professionals who don't want their children to suffer, but find their own jobs tying them to cities with toxic air. Finally, reluctantly, the young family decided to give up their dream of 'home' and moved back to the West. After 10 years of planning their move back home, relocating, trying everything they could to stay back, suddenly, the dream was over.

It wasn't an easy move back either, since Akshaya had to wait to get a job to his liking, which didn't happen until two years after Kalyani and the children moved to Seattle in 2016. 'But ultimately, I remember my husband and me thinking – what are we doing here if our kids can't even breathe? And I think once that thought took over, it became pretty easy [to move],' says Kalyani.

'Pollution was absolutely the only reason we moved out. We are in cleaner air, but I miss being a one-hour flight away from my parents and extended family,' she says ruefully. It's always tough to go back on what you thought was a permanent decision.

In fact, now, in a reverse move, Akshaya has managed to persuade his ageing parents to relocate. Rashmi and Shashi have sold their charming old family bungalow at a time of falling prices, almost a distress sale, packed up and left to join their children. And this is how India loses highly educated professionals from its workforce.

A couple of years later, I run into Rashmi, Kalyani's mother-in-law, close to where they used to live. She has settled into her new life in Seattle and no longer believes that inhaling Delhi's toxic air builds immunity, a common myth among many older Indians. She has figured out the difference between microbiological immunity, where the human body learns to adapt to and resist viruses and bacteria and develop immunity to them – and endurance. 'You should leave too,' she tells me, looking at my son.

There are several young couples like Kalyani and Akshaya who have moved to Goa, others abroad, only because of pollution: MapMyIndia CEO, Rohan Varma, and Namrata and their two young boys. *Highway on My Plate* anchor Mayur Sharma and Michelle and their two young children – and many others. Their stories are resoundingly similar. This second wave of this exodus has many more young, aware, Indian families.

Whereas Gardiner, Gen, Beth, Marina, Aurelia, Tina, Claire, Sue, and many other expats left India in the first wave, before the local exodus, this second wave was also triggered by Delhi's dirty air. As Gardiner noted in one of his reports, his church pastor lost an entire congregation, a fact independently and anecdotally corroborated by my children's orthodontist. But there were many more, as expats continued to come to India, lured by its exotic attractions, its growing economy, its large markets and its accessibility via the English language. Most who arrived here initially didn't know how polluted India's air was – remember, it was China's air that always got the bad rap – but within one winter season, got to know Delhi's best-kept open secret: Its foul air. Once they realized this, they would move out, especially if they had children.

'I don't think it's possible [for anyone] to understand how air pollution will feel until you've felt it,' says Nicole Baute, a writer and teacher, from Canada. She grew up on a farm in south-western Ontario and has lived in several Canadian cities including Toronto and Vancouver – which have some of the cleanest urban air in the world, before coming to India with her partner.

I immediately understand what she's saying. Foreigners coming from environments with cleaner air don't understand pollution because they've never lived with it. They don't know what dirty air looks or smells like, aren't aware of its health harms, haven't experienced the dull headaches, smarting, watering eyes and daily respiratory distress that accompanies any outdoor mobility. Indians who have been born and raised in pollution don't understand it either, because they don't know what clean air looks and smells like.

'Many people back home still think China is the big air pollution story,' Nicole says.

That belief has finally changed, not just among foreigners who are posted to India, but also Indians who live here.

'There's definitely been a spike in local awareness over the past three years,' says Nicole. She adds, 'At first people spoke of getting used to the air, as if it was something I didn't have a tolerance to as an outsider. But now I think people have a better understanding of what's going on. My closest Indian friend keeps an air purifier in her bedroom now. I think that awareness will continue to increase as more and more stories and statistics emerge.'

This second wave of exodus quickly spreads to aware Indians, and those who have the option to leave, do so. Others keep trying.

I know this because I talked to many of them. True, this is anecdotal and not based on scientific data, but if there had been an exit interview that recorded the reason for educated professionals emigrating from India between 2015 and 2017, air pollution would have been right there on top, especially for those who had young children.

In fact, I get unexpected corroboration of my premise from one of Delhi's top orthodontists when he shares his anecdotal experience with me one afternoon while he is doing dental work on my teenage son. Since this is someone who works with adolescents, hundreds of children go through his hands, literally, every year. If I have to trust anecdotal evidence, this is a better source than any. He is reluctant to share his name but is absolutely sure of his numbers.

'I know almost 100 to 150 Indian families that moved out of Delhi between 2015 and early 2018 due to air pollution,' he tells me, scrolling through his computer.

'Are you sure?' I ask. In all the years I've known him, this is the first time we are talking about air pollution.

'Of course.' His eyes from behind his square-framed spectacles look directly back at me.

'How do you know?' I persist.

He takes off his surgical mask. I can see his face now. He isn't smiling.

'I know because they were all my clients. Their children were my patients,' he says.

His next statement shocks me further. 'I don't see myself living in Delhi,' he says. But he has no idea where he will go. His son goes to a well-known school close by and his practice is well-established, a family practice with his father and wife. Despite such strong roots, familial as well as business-related, he says he is waiting for his son to finish school.

I feel sad when I hear his words. I've known him for five years. He is well regarded, with a thriving practice. I look around his modern, airy office, and recall the pains he took over remodelling. It looks aesthetic, at par with other international dental offices I've seen. His practice is flourishing, he is well-settled – and I wonder how many others who have worked so hard to establish thriving practices will be forced to leave a city that can't clean its air.

By 2018, corporate human resource heads tell me that they are seeing executives *asking* to be transferred out of Delhi-NCR, and in fact many were even willing to take a cut in their salary if only they can leave the city. A senior Cushman & Wakefield official corroborates this exodus from Delhi – home prices and rentals are falling as more people want to move out. In 2019 the online travel agency MakeMyTrip (MMT) conducts an in-house pollution survey among its 1,039 employees to find that almost 70 per cent of its employees have considered moving out of Delhi due to its winter smog.

This pollution survey, shared with me by MMT's CEO Deep Kalra via email, is amongst the most fascinating surveys I've come across in this field. Nearly 45 per cent of MMT's employees report that someone in their family has 'air-related allergies and breathing issues', and an astonishingly high 65 per cent of employees say they'd be willing to trade in their increments for better air. It is also sobering to note that the families of MMT's employees are spending an average of ₹14,905 each year on fighting air pollution, which goes up to ₹17,807 if there are children or seniors in the home and a whopping ₹22,888 per year in households where someone in the family has breathing issues (45 per cent of the total, as stated earlier). I wish every company based in polluted locations would carry out such surveys.

Quality of living surveys by companies like Mercer include AQI. The latest survey in 2019 shows Hyderabad topping the list of Indian cities for living standards.[18] The AQI there is at the 'moderate level', according to CPCB data.[19]

It almost seems to me that the more we teach people about air pollution and its impact on their health, the faster it catalyses their exodus. At Care For Air, we were running out of volunteers. We were also getting tired of running hard to stay in the same place.

A new tribe of immigrants – variously being called environmental migrants, pollution immigrants or environmental refugees – were now emerging. Indian youth primarily left the country for greener pastures, lured by better facilities, more money, a better quality of life, which were all 'pull' factors. Push factors[20] like poor air quality, were practically unheard of. But the current rising trend of pollution and the accompanying awareness around it is leading to a very different type of migration.

In February 2016, my children's school principal asks me to get the PTA to intervene on a transportation issue with parents.

'Please arrange a meeting at the earliest,' she said in her politely imperious style. 'We need the PTA's help. I'll explain.' When the PTA committee troops in to the principal's large, open office overlooking the school's red-brick facade and landscaped foliage, we realize this is an ongoing issue that the school had tried to resolve earlier as well.

For several years, the Bangladesh High Commission across the road from the school has been complaining about the twice-daily traffic jams that occur when parents drop off and pick up their children from the school. Other embassies on the road have also been complaining, as diplomatically as possible.

'This has been going on too long. We need a solution,' says the principal, looking directly at me. One of her ideas is to get more children to use the school bus, thus reducing the number of cars. 'We need the PTA to encourage parents to sign up for the school buses.'

I learn that of the 2,800 children enrolled in the school, only 650 take the school bus. It is a shockingly small proportion. This is one of the simplest and easiest ways for the school to reduce its air pollution footprint. Why can't school buses be mandatory and not optional, I ask, but the principal dismisses that, citing the various pro-choice concerns that parents have. Later, I find out that that idea had never got any traction.

The principal looks around the room, her burgundy hair glinting in the sunlight that is coming in from the large window. 'Well?' she asks.

By increasing the buses and reducing the cars, we will be able to contribute a little to lowering the air pollution. I really want this to happen, but I also know that the school needs to own this idea and take the lead.

Through personal experience, I know how forbidding the school's transport incharge is. At the same time, many parents, concerned about the safety of their young children, are reluctant to send them in buses unsupervised by teachers. I myself have been through one awful, harried afternoon when I was waiting at the bus stop to pick up my daughter, then a new student in seventh grade, and she didn't get off the school bus. No one, including the teacher on the bus, seemed to know where she was. Thankfully, that afternoon hadn't ended in a tragedy, even though the drama was something I could have happily done without.

I tell her about that incident and other parents share their own experiences as we brainstorm ideas to make this transformation from private vehicles to buses work. However, for school buses to be pushed as a desirable option for the children to travel, it is the principal who needs to make a push for it. The PTA should only be seen to be playing a supporting role.

'For more parents to sign up, we first need to address their concerns around safety,' says Haripriya. She heads the PTA's transport committee and is on multiple WhatsApp groups, connected to hundreds of parents.

We discuss this and try to find out what other schools do. Some, like the Noida school my children had first attended when we moved back to India, had two teachers, a conductor and guard in each bus. But my son's school, with the lower fee it charges, will not be able to afford that.

'How about bus mothers or bus didis?' someone asks.

'That's a good idea,' says the principal. 'But who will pay for it?'

After we thrash that out, another parent suggests 'bus buddies', older kids who will look out for the younger ones and help the bus didis. Someone else suggests house points for kids who take buses, so that kids are incentivized, perhaps cool wristbands for those who take the bus. Ideas have begun to flow.

'Next, we need routes to be rationalized, so that the buses can serve as many locations and children as possible without making the journey very long. Buses compete with car pickups, which get kids home much faster,' Haripriya says. It is at this point that the principal comes up with a trump card: making the road outside the school a pedestrian-only area, with only buses allowed during the pickup and drop-off hours. That means, cars can come in earlier than buses in the morning and leave after buses have left in the afternoon.

This is brilliant. It cuts right to the root of the problem. By switching timings – only allowing cars into the road *before* buses in the morning and *after* buses leave in the afternoon – the incentive to use individual cars for an incremental time advantage will be equalized.

A babel of voices break out as we speak excitedly among ourselves.

'Also, the air quality will improve,' I add. No one pays any attention.

'The air quality,' I say, louder now. 'More children on public transport will mean less cars, less idling emissions. And less cars will mean less vehicular pollution and less traffic jams right outside our school where children are breathing tailpipe emissions from those huge SUVs. Especially the little ones – it's almost at their nose level.' Now I have their attention. 'There's actual research to show that poorer schools have better air quality around them than richer schools, where hundreds of parents drop their children off individually in cars running on petrol and diesel,' I say. Suddenly, everyone is listening closely.

I'm not joking. I remember a seminar I have recently attended at the American Centre, where I've heard the director of the multilateral organization Clean Air Asia's India talk of ambient air around schools.

A strategic plan begins to form. 'I can get someone to measure how air quality is affected if that helps convince parents to make the switch,' I add. I'm thinking of Barun's trusty DusTrak. He is a school parent and will be heavily invested in clean air outside his children's school.

I want this push towards school buses to succeed. Some parents are still looking uncertain. I talk hurriedly of my children's remembered bus experience, which has been great. 'When children travel in school buses, they learn to make more friends across different classes and they become more social. It allows them to integrate better than when each child is commuting in his or her own car, alone. Also, by having children take the bus to school, we will create a cohort of people comfortable with taking public transport,' I slip in.

It is March by the time I'm able to find and reach out to Parthaa Bosu, the India director of Clean Air Asia (CAA). I've liked that his presentation at the seminar suggested solutions, something I felt we desperately needed to begin focusing on. I wanted to find out more. CAA is internationally funded and works in the area of clean air in a low-key sort of way.

My meeting with the bearded, bespectacled Bosu is a few days before Holi, and as I follow him up the narrow staircase of the CAA office, I feel certain he will be able to help me with the information I need. The friendly and knowledgeable Bosu mentions a 5-school study CAA had just conducted along with IIT Delhi in 2015 that shows that air pollution outside schools tends to increase during drop-off and pickup times. It's a straightforward explanation. 'Many more parents drop their children by cycle and on foot in lower-income schools,' he says simply. Later, he sends me a more formal note.

'During a study conducted along with IIT Delhi, we observed that schools tend to have higher air pollution during the start and end of the school day when parents were coming to pick up and drop children apart from the existing school transport. The air quality during these hours deteriorated by nearly 8–15 per cent.'

That's how Barun's team from Breathe Easy Labs end up outside the school on several morning in April to measure air quality in 'before and after' test that checks to see if reducing the number of vehicles outside the school helps improve air quality.

'The improvement was approximately 30 per cent on PM2.5 almost immediately,' says Barun. 'Before we actually ran the tests, we were a little sceptical. But the results confirmed our hypothesis that using the school bus and carpooling can help reduce tailpipe exposure for hundreds of children.'

This pilot makes me think – if only the government could make school buses mandatory – or at least an 'opt-out' rather than 'opt-in' system, then cars and private vehicles outside schools would reduce sharply, leading to improved air quality. We could replicate the success of our single-school experiment across the city.

But implementing this is impossible. We need more volunteers, people who could follow this up.

Haripriya swings into action pulling in her supportive husband as well. The committee shortlists bus mothers that the school can hire, brings in mapping company MapMyIndia to help us rationalize routes, meets the Delhi Transport Corporation chairman to negotiate for more buses, navigates between the taxi and minicab lobbies that have quietly been mushrooming, obstructing instead of encouraging parents to switch to buses. We devise ways to make taking the school bus the 'cool' thing for children to do, lobby with teachers to support this initiative and, most importantly, lobby with parents to make the swap.

The school's transport administrators don't like this degree of parental interference. There are confrontations, some polite, some not, fiery emails are exchanged, threats to resign are made.

But in the end, we manage to double the number of children taking school buses. The number of buses goes up from 17 to 34. We also get parents and older children to volunteer to walk younger kids through the car-free zone. The principal seems happy and is often seen enthusiastically helping the teachers as they walk the youngest children to the school gate along the car-free pedestrian-only zone.

I try and share this experience with other schools to encourage them to replicate this model and increase bus transport, but don't get much traction. I give up my attempts to scale fairly quickly – all the drama has left me exhausted.

The success of the move towards increased bus usage leads to more conversations around air pollution and spurs on more members of the PTA to bring up their concerns around air pollution. They bring up the health harm to our children from outdoor aerobic activity during high pollution days but are met with passive hostility.

We'll look into it, we're told, in a polite, deadpan manner.

At a couple of meetings of the school management committee, which is supposed to include six representatives from the PTA, we propose that school timings be pushed back to later in the day during the severely polluted winter months. We also tentatively explore whether the school would be open to parents getting air purifiers installed in classrooms – or at least common areas like gymnasiums, the auditorium, libraries.

'We will look into it,' echo the principal and the elegant chairperson of the committee who is the ex officio spouse of the top serving bureaucrat. We know what that means.

But at least we manage to get one small win – the school's sports days for junior, middle and senior students, scheduled in the winter, when the air is at its worst, are moved to cleaner months.

At first, the school's resistance to anything to do with alleviating air pollution make some of us who are now aware of the lethal effects of PM2.5 very angry. How can they take a risk with the lives of our children, we discuss. It's only later that I realize that parents themselves are divided. There are enough disbelievers. A few are confused enough to choose outdoor play – thinking it is great for children – even if the air is polluted. Then there are those still unaware, who prefer to let their children play outside in hazardous air because they just don't know about the terrible damage that the air is doing to their children. There are also those who fall for the myths – that like microbiological pollution, microparticulate pollution will ultimately build resistance and immunity, and that Indian lungs are used to the air and are the stronger for it. In reality, we know they're smaller, weaker and more irreversibly damaged as compared to lungs from other countries

But even if every parent in the school had been convinced that their children should be kept indoors in classrooms with clean filtered air during high pollution days, it wasn't really a solution and is logistically impossible. As the principal points out to me during one impassioned discussion, what about inter-school sports competitions? Should our schoolchildren stop competing at inter-school level and excuse themselves when most sporting events took place in the winter months? Her well-modulated voice sounds reasonable. I'm the one who ends up sounding extreme.

Frustrated and angry, I write to the directorate of education of the Delhi government from the CFA email address asking, pleading, actually, that they direct all schools to link outdoor aerobic activity – all sports, matches and competitions – to prevailing AQI levels. This is the only way to protect children from pollution-triggered health harm – especially since they have no agency and must follow instruction. There is no reply, not even an acknowledgement.

This problem of linking outdoor air pollution to air quality will be an abiding conflict I will face in my own sporting family as well, especially with my sports-crazy son. I will face it when I oppose public marathons and inter-school football and cricket tournaments. Even until 2019, I find myself filled with frustration when the newest CFA governing board member Chetan Bhattacharji, the managing director of NDTV and one of the most air-aware parents I know, is compelled to sit outdoors in AQI over 300 at his child's inter-school football match in November 2019 at a school in Noida.

Noida, if it's possible to imagine, is even more polluted than Delhi. Parents who have to sit and watch as their children run outdoors in polluted air don't have a real choice. This is a CBSE inter-school tournament, part of their children's curriculum, mandated by the central government-run board.

'Ironically, the only person wearing a mask is the medico on the tournament. And my daughter – briefly – on the field, and me,' he will text me from Noida.

It infuriates me that after years of fighting this, there are still Indian children playing matches that have been scheduled by the government's education department – an education department that should be teaching them how harmful it is for the children to indulge in any outdoor aerobic activity. We are setting up our youth for poor health, handicapping them from a young age. But no one seems to be seeing this.

But in 2016, when I realize the division among parents, the question CFA grapples with is – how are we to build greater awareness, quickly? One of the ideas we have is to make an informative and accessible video on air pollution to help spread awareness, especially among the young. I've also started thinking of podcasts – my experience in national radio has taught me about the reach of the spoken word early in life. The group agrees these would be great ways to spread awareness. We are confident of the content curation for this – but where do we get funding for the project?

Over the next couple of months, CFA suffers a body blow in the form of Aurelia and Tina's exit from India. Both of them have been a part of CFA's journey from the very beginning. I always knew Aurelia's stay was going to be transient – her husband was on short contract with the

Hindustan Times – but since Tina's husband was of Indian origin with a family business and they lived in his family home in Delhi, I had rather hoped for her continued presence. But the air has driven out her young family – she has three children under 10 – and after tentatively exploring some cleaner air countries not too far away, they decide to move to Bangkok. Team CFA is devastated, and I know I'm going to miss her the most. Her communication skills have been excellent for us and we make a good team. She promises to continue working remotely. When we bid the two oldest CFA members goodbye, we adopt the Eagles' 'Hotel California' as our theme. You can check out from CFA, but you can never ever leave, we tell them unhappily. Around this time, Gen connects us to Christa Hasenkopf who founded OpenAQ. The core of OpenAQ's work is an air quality platform (openaq.org) that aggregates, formats and makes real-time and historical air quality data available from public sources. This is an open source platform on GitHub.

The true impact of their work is the community they're building. Christa firmly believes that openly available data organized in an easy-to-access fashion truly enables and empowers the public around air quality issues. OpenAQ conducts workshops in places facing air inequality and connects air quality scientists, software developers, journalists and others passionate about open air quality data. After conducting a session in Ulaanbaatar, Mongolia she wants to do one in New Delhi. Barun, Sarath and I decide to attend this workshop.

This workshop will be one of the events that also makes me realize anew something that grassroots campaigners often say: 'We can't manage what we can't measure'. Even in 2019, when the number of Continuous Air Quality Monitoring Stations (CAMS) goes up to 232, Ekta Shekhar, lead campaigner for The Climate Agenda will lament, quite rightly, that 87 of them, (38 per cent) are located in Delhi, Bengaluru and Hyderabad, with the remaining 145 distributed over the rest of the country. Later, urban scientists like Ronak Sutaria of Respirer Living Sciences and Namita Gupta of AirVeda, build a network of low-cost sensors that allow one to 'see' these microparticulates, in their attempt to democratize awareness.

My daughter – who has taken up environmental sciences as one of her subjects at her new school – is running some tests on air quality at home for a class project. Others in her project team are also asking very pertinent questions. I request Barun to help by showing them his lab. 'Actually, another young girl is coming to my lab to learn about air pollution,' he says. 'Why don't you send the girls at the same time?'

That's when I get the idea to run a programme for high-school children to teach them more about air pollution – not in the way the CFA presentation does (that's more of an overview and quick primer), but in a more in-depth way. The Pollution 201 to our existing Pollution 101. I ask Barun, Gen and Beth for their thoughts and they are all excited and enthusiastic. In fact, Gen and Beth respond almost immediately with a first draft of what this curriculum should look like. Gen's job with the EPA turns out to be very useful in helping with content and resources.

We have many experts collaborating with us and need to sort out the logistics. Once we have the basic framework in place, finding a space is easy – both the British School and the AES in Delhi happily agree to host us. We recruit some excellent, enthusiastic new volunteers from both schools to help spread the word. Student applicants are asked to either write a 500-word essay or make a two-minute video on why they care for the air and send it to us before 31 August.

Here is one of the emails we use to reach out to schools and invite their students to apply.

> *Care For Air (www.careforair.org) is an awareness and advocacy platform formed in Delhi more than two years ago. Our mission has been to educate, dispel myths, spread awareness and inspire action around the issue of air pollution among the influencers of tomorrow.*
>
> *In Fall 2016, we are launching an intensive, first-of-its-kind programme: the Care For Air Student Ambassador Programme. This unique, customized programme will be offered to secondary school students as a twelve-hour module over four weekend days from late September to November 2016 in New Delhi. Credible and highly respected air pollution scientists and air pollution analysts will be part of the teaching panel.*

Our organization is supported by experts in this field such as TED Fellow Dr Sarath Guttikunda and Dr Joshua Apte from the department of civil, architectural and environmental engineering at the University of Texas. Bhargav Krishna from the Public Health Foundation of India will be overseeing all technical content of our programme. We are in the process of finalizing our teaching faculty for the first module. At least three of the four teaching sessions will be held on campus at the British School and the American Embassy School.

High-school students applying for this unique, highly specialized programme will learn about the causes of air pollution, how pollution travels, the impact of weather and other factors, its impact on human health, the current state of pollution in Delhi and the policy and regulations around it, among other things. Students will also get laboratory time to learn the science of air pollution measurement (and perhaps even learn to make their own sensors!) from among the best in this field through a series of interactive and practical in-lab sessions led by experts especially chosen by us.

Two students from each school will be chosen based on their essay submission on 'Why I care about the air, how air pollution impacts life and what I'd like to learn about the air we breathe'. Upon completion of the course, they will be certified as Care For Air student ambassadors. They will have the opportunity to share their learnings and personal insights on the official Care For Air website and blog, as well.

Through this programme, we hope to trigger greater passion for our environment among our youth and create a cohort of more aware and environmentally conscious young people, in whatever professions they go on to choose.

The entire CFA team reaches out to schools, trying to explain why we are doing this. 'With knowledge comes empowerment and greater social responsibility towards our air,' we tell principal after principal. It doesn't take long for schools to warm up to this ready-made programme – at no additional cost to either the schools or their students.

'We will select two students per school, preferably one male and one female. We are looking for students with knowledge, passion, commitment and leadership potential,' we tell schools in our emails. Within days we have 150 applications for the 25 available spots.

'The quality of most of these is excellent!' I tell Tina excitedly over a call. 'I wish we could take all these kids. I wish we could teach this course multiple times a year!' Despite having moved out to Bangkok to get away from Delhi air, Tina is still actively involved with CFA and has volunteered to help with shortlisting the students.

But we have to do it well the first time – and we are still few in number. We divide up the applications and, with the help of some numerical parameters, judge which ones will make the cut. By September, our Student Ambassador Programme (SAP) is ready to be launched.

We get a boost when a non-profit research institute called RTI International offers to loan us its MicroPEMs (Personal Emission Monitors) and send them over from the US for free. These are monitors that individuals can wear around their necks which measure PM2.5 wherever the person travels, thus being able to calculate the daily personal exposure to air pollution, and we receive these well in time for the SAP.

Gopal sponsors professional equipment to record the entire workshop on video, and other volunteers take care of getting brochures, bags and files made. New volunteers include Mayur Sharma, co-anchor of a popular food show *Highway on My Plate* and his wife Michelle, who pitch in enthusiastically. Mayur entices a professional communication company to help with recordings, and we plan to use this material to make educational and promotional videos to build awareness. The communication company offers to make publicity material from the documented video, and we decide the in-house expertise of Sarath, Bhargav, Barun and Gopal will be enough to create a high-quality, world-class programme. I also invite a close friend who is a Johns Hopkins and Stanford-trained medical doctor and increasingly aware of pollution to speak on the health harm associated with dirty air at this training session. Like many pollution emigrees, Dr Gita Sinha, a public health consultant, relocated from Gurugram to Toronto the previous year. It is important to have medical doctors speak out, I argue at a CFA meeting, where I realize for the first time that turf wars between public health and clinical medicine can be a very real challenge. Fortunately, she is visiting Delhi over that period and agrees to share the opening session with Bhargav.

Broadly, the Student Ambassador Programme will cover these issues over four sessions: 1) What exactly is pollution (composition) and how does it affect human health – Bhargav and Gita will explain this, with Mayur kicking off the session with an icebreaker; 2) Where does it come from/who causes it (source apportionment) – Sarath will fly in from Goa to dive deep into this with students; 3) How do we measure it and how accurate is that measurement (monitoring) – Barun will take the high schoolers to his laboratory and they will learn to make their own monitors; and 4) What are the regulations around it and what can we do to reduce it (policy advocacy) – Gopal will speak on laws and regulations including how to use the judiciary to advocate for clean air.

At Barun's invitation, Mr George Sibley, the American embassy's minister counsellor for economic affairs and environment, science and technology, who Sam Kotis used to report to, also speaks to the student ambassadors at the final session in early November.

'Let's do this three times a year!' Barun says enthusiastically as we hand out the certificates on the final day. The students have loved the programme and their feedback is enthusiastic. Even though it has expanded to 16 hours of training, they have been fully engaged, with not a single absentee.

We are exhausted, but happy. The pilot has succeeded. After the newly minted student ambassadors leave the AES campus, Sue, a recent CFA volunteer invites us home, which is on campus since her husband teaches there, to celebrate with wine and lasagne. She is leaving Delhi soon, but by now we are used to the transience of our volunteers. But we still don't know what next. We still need a way forward...

Just around when our Student Ambassador Programme finishes, I see news reports of some mothers and schoolchildren protesting at Jantar Mantar wearing masks.[21] I've also been hearing of people protesting via masked picnics at Lodhi Gardens. These events are very interesting and get me very excited. Awareness – at least among some – is growing, I think to myself. I make a mental note to bring this up at the next CFA meeting. Maybe we can reach out to these aware parents and their children – perhaps they can be the legs we have been looking for, the vehicles for all the big ideas we have.

In November, Delhi begins gearing up for the Airtel Delhi half marathon. It is scheduled to be held on 19 November, during the period when the pollution is at its worst. Already Delhi feels like the gas chamber its chief minister has been calling it. To encourage people to run outdoors in this air feels almost criminal in its negligence. I wonder where corporate responsibility is. Then I wonder why permissions to conduct this murderous marathon are being given at all. That should be treated in the same way as deliberately causing harm – as a criminal offence.

But none of us at CFA are activists – we don't know how to fight giant corporations to get them to stop something that is clearly bringing them great publicity. 'No one will listen to you,' my husband tells me. He too has signed up to participate and has begun training for it. He participated back in 2014 too, but I wasn't as aware about the ill effects of PM2.5 then. Now that I am, I try to convince him not to put his lungs at risk. But we end up getting into a debate about the positive impact of outdoor exercise over the negative impact of PM deposits in lungs. I write a letter to the company and send it to an email address I find online. It is a half-hearted attempt and I'm not surprised when I don't get an acknowledgement.

As it is, I have already begun butting heads with my soccer-playing, tennis-crazy son. My daughter, also an athletic youngster, is less of a worry as she has been off strenuous exercise since her appendectomy. It helps that her school is more aware and that she has set up a Clean Air

Club and is updated with all the latest research. This year, ahead of their sports day, her school had sent a circular to all parents saying that the decision to go ahead with the sports day would rest with the pollution gods. The British School is very proactive and checks air quality before outdoor aerobic activity for children is permitted, unlike my son's school. He and I have our battle lines clearly drawn.

Still elated with our successful SAP, we are thinking of what to do next. Gopal suggests organizing an event with an electric bus. He has a client in South India who is ready to loan an actual electric bus. How about we offer free rides to people along a crowded Delhi route while telling them about air pollution? Delhi needs to convert all buses to electric. Sarath's calculations tell us we need from 13,000–15,000 electric buses to meet the demands of Delhi's population. Delhi barely has 3,000 – and they aren't electric. This is a great idea. The media is sure to pick it up and we can build awareness quickly. But again, we are hamstrung by a shrinking cohort of volunteers. Also, this will be a brand-new experiment, like the SAP pilot. Would it be better, instead, to build on top of what has already worked? We need to decide if we can go ahead in this manner, picking up projects in an ad hoc way and trying them out.

We wonder if we can replicate, scale, codify and make this a people's movement, in different languages, and continue to focus on building awareness or whether we should focus more on trying to influence policy at a government level. Shall we file a PIL and use the judiciary as the route to advocate for clean air? We don't have answers to these questions and no time during our monthly meetings to dive deeper into what we should do next, the road ahead, the vision, mission and goals of our group.

What are the institutions we can use as ordinary citizens to drive change? In a democracy, the main institutions are the legislature, the executive and the judiciary, with the fourth pillar being the media.

Anita is interested in using the executive. 'The trick is to find a good bureaucrat who understands the importance of a problem and then works through the system to achieve the goal, using measurable outcomes,' she says. Gopal, of course, believes in the power of the judiciary. I feel communication is key and media is critical for awareness. Only the most idealistic among us feel the legislature will help drive change.

Some of us have been talking about converting CFA into a non-profit, so that we can get funding to hire full-time employees and guide them to implement some of the ideas we have. Our learnings have been derivative and experiential, but we have a lot of knowledge by now, knowledge that is as broad-based as it is deep. Though we aren't researchers or scientists ourselves, we have learnt to parse the science.

It's time for a huddle, a focused retreat that will help us decide the way ahead.

We meet at Anita's house one evening to thrash out these issues, and vote on whether we should make this a people's movement – something like the 'Occupy WallStreet' phenomenon of a few years ago, or an 'Arab Spring' for clean air – or go down the route of becoming a non-profit. As a non-profit, we can apply for the Section 80G tax exemption status, get funding and replicate some of the initiatives that we have already begun on a larger scale.

Anita always brings up *The Starfish and the Spider* by Ori Brafman and Rod Beckstrom as a Bible of what can happen in leaderless organizations, like an Alcoholics Anonymous group. 'Look, you have to see what happens when there's no one in charge. It's about what happens when there's no hierarchy. You'd think there would be disorder, even chaos. But in many arenas, a lack of traditional leadership is giving rise to powerful groups that are turning industry and society upside down,' she tells us again and again. I think of Tahrir Square and the Arab Spring – but for air pollution? We're not there, at least not yet.

After a marathon six-hour session that Gita joins from Toronto, we discuss all our options and finally decide to go ahead and apply for non-profit status. It is the beginning of a new chapter for us.

In December, I get an email from the British School, and it is interesting to see how it is focusing on pollution – even going to the extent of implementing changes in its school calendar.

> *12 December 2016*
>
> *Dear parents and colleagues,*
>
> *I am pleased to share the summary calendar for the academic year 2017–18. This calendar has been reviewed and altered primarily to build in a cushion to safeguard children against the predictably poor air quality days during the post-Diwali and early January periods. We have ensured that there is no loss of teaching time and that students taking external examinations in May 2018 are not disadvantaged.*

So this *can* be done. I wonder why some children's lungs and health seem to be valued more than others. I show this circular to some parents in my son's school, which is showing no signs of accepting air pollution as a menace. They're probably waiting for a government notification to tell them so, a parent notes, wryly. The principal herself has air purifiers at home. The junior school headmistress was among the first buyers of air purifiers for her own home. She bought them from Barun, which is how I know. When I tell the other parents, there is a collective sigh of surprise at these double standards.

'Don't be so shocked,' I say, and show them a photo someone has forwarded to me of Arun Jaitley, India's current finance minister, in his office. He is getting ready to present the country's budget, carrying that famous bag with the budget documents and striding out of his office. Behind him sits an air purifier. 'Probably bought from taxpayer funds. The babus and the politicians make their own air clean but don't lift a finger to clean our outdoor air,' I say bitterly. Information has been trickling in via the media about the government's increasing spending on air filters for the bureaucrats and the politicians.[22] Another CFA volunteer has been working with his lawyer colleagues to file an RTI petition to get more details but information has been hard to come by.

We all sit in silence, the negative energy swirling around us like the thick, menacing air outside. 'Let's try and get purifiers at least for our junior classes,' chirps Haripriya's optimistic voice suddenly. We shake ourselves out of our despondent reverie and resolve to have another go at the school management.

Now that school is breaking up, everyone is trying to escape from Delhi. My once-lovely Delhi with its bright winter days and long holiday picnics no longer exists. But we vow to come back in the new year to resurrect our demands for air filters in classrooms.

8

Our Children

January 2017

By now it is clear that we're headed straight into the vortex of a national public health emergency and that our children are the most deeply affected.

Every day, I find new studies that validate this fact, such as the one in the *Yale Global Health Review* which says that Delhi's children are the most vulnerable to the toxic effects of polluted air, resulting in decreased quality of life and increased mortality rates.[1]

Another study, led by pulmonologist Prof. S.K. Chhabra, former Director-Professor, Department of Pulmonary Medicine at Vallabhbhai Patel Chest Institute and current Head of Department, Pulmonary Sleep and Critical Care Medicine, Primus Super Speciality Hospital, provides powerful evidence that children growing up in the polluted environs of Delhi suffer from reduced lung growth, as compared to children growing up in developed countries.[2] Accepted in the journal *Indian Paediatrics* in July 2016 and published in its September issue,[3] the ICMR-funded study[4] finds that while both Indian and US children have nearly the same lung size till the age of eight, when the lungs complete their normal physical growth, subsequent growth is different between the two countries: both boys and girls in India have lungs that are about 10 per cent smaller by the time they become adults.

Dr Chhabra tells me he wasn't surprised by these findings when he conducted this study. 'Air pollution retards lung growth in Delhi's children. Even Indian adults have smaller lungs than their US counterparts. Smaller lungs mean poorer exercise capacity and greater vulnerability to respiratory symptoms and diseases. In fact, air pollution retards the overall growth of children,' he says.

The scariest report is a news story I read[5] that correlates air quality to patient admissions and quotes pulmonologists and paediatric chest specialists recommending that people leave Delhi. Data from the Vallabhbhai Patel Chest Institute shows that the number of patients admitted in its respiratory wards increased by almost 80 per cent in the 10 years between 2003–04 and 2013–14.

'What is most worrying is that 10 to 15 years ago, when air pollution levels had come down, our average OPD attendance and admissions in respiratory medicine at AIIMS saw about a 20 per cent decline. We seem to have lost out on our own achievements. As pollution levels have gone up, our public health success has been reversed,' the report quotes Dr Randeep Guleria, the then head of respiratory medicine at AIIMS, as saying.

Later, when I interview Dr Guleria, he will also tell me that children are more vulnerable not just because they respire at a faster rate but also because they play outdoors much more and thus their overall exposure to pollutants is higher. 'Additionally, in children you have a lung that is still growing, evolving...so exposure [to polluted air] hampers the growth of lungs,' he says, referring to Indian and global studies that show that children growing up in areas where pollution levels are high have stunted growth and lower lung capacity. He also suggests that air pollution may be playing a role in 'recurrent chest infections in children, predisposing them to weaker lungs and higher chances of chronic bronchitis and respiratory problems later in life'.

In June 2017, AIIMS will begin an ICMR-funded study that will go on to show that there is a high onset of respiratory symptoms leading to increased morbidity and mortality even with short-term exposure to air pollution.

Practically every day I find myself spotting new research linking air pollution to health harm. Studies link air pollution to Alzheimer's,[6] dementia,[7] depression,[8] obesity,[9] arthritis,[10] breast cancer[11] – the list is endless. I wonder why others can't see this menace, and then remember that I too was blind to it until three years ago.

At CFA, the path before us was clear. It all boiled down to the question of how we could better link air pollution to disease, disability and death in order to appeal to the larger public consciousness. As a group, it occurred to us that if CFA couldn't do more, perhaps the best way forward was to document what we had accomplished so far so that others could build on our work. At our next meeting, one of us suggests that we archive our work in an easy-to-understand video, as spreading our knowledge base visually would make it more accessible.

It is January and team CFA is sitting in the garden of yet another, smaller rental that my family has recently had to move into, discussing how we can push ahead on awareness and advocacy. This house has lots of glass and light, and though the move here hasn't been as traumatic as the last, it has had its share of tribulations. Owing to a bit of bad luck, I slipped and hurt my foot a couple of days before the packers arrived and had to hobble in a cast through the move. But in a bigger scare, an entire glass door in the new house disintegrated on my daughter in a freak accident, cutting her chest and wrist, scarily close to her ulnar vein, requiring several stitches in the middle of the night.

Everything else remains the same around me, despite the new environment; our awareness about air pollution grows and deepens, even as frustration with the lack of resources builds up. While discussing our plans to archive CFA's work, Holly, one of our newest volunteers who is a young Fulbright scholar, offers to help sift through the excellent, but not easy to understand, air pollution research that we have come across, unpack, simplify and condense it into one-page summaries. After all, what is the point of all this in-depth research, if it's not able to drive change? And, for that to happen, research and evidence need to translate into actionable policy.

Other ideas begin to flow on how to bring the conversation on pollution and its prevention into the mainstream. Manjali has been trying to collaborate with a friend to stage plays so that information is relayed in varied formats. Gopal brings up his suggested event with an electric bus. He is firmly of the view that Delhi needs to convert all its buses to run on electricity. We also decide to integrate delhiair.org with careforair.org, and Holly volunteers for this project as well. The idea is to keep the identities of the two websites distinct since they approach the problem in different ways – one focusing on information, the other on action. What we need urgently, we realize, is a community manager to grow the tribe. Other ideas we have revolve around making community-specific short videos that we could circulate on WhatsApp; educating potters and brickmakers to opt for cleaner firing technologies such as zigzag draught, vertical shaft or other cleaner kiln technologies;[12] researching innovative solutions so that farmers don't burn crop stubble; and translating all our presentations into Hindi and other regional languages, embedding an air pollution curriculum into academia from elementary school. With so many great ideas, I am reminded again that CFA is full of thinking power, but it's the implementation that needs more work. It all comes back to the fact that we are a self-funded volunteer-run organization, with a dwindling number of volunteers.

At our next meeting, Bhargav informs us he is temporarily moving to Boston to pursue a PhD. He will be a doctoral candidate at the Harvard T.H. Chan School of Public Health. As a visiting scientist with the exposure, epidemiology and risk group at the department of environmental health, he will have more access to top research in the field, and this will be beneficial for CFA. Holly will also leave soon when her Fulbright programme ends. I email the Fulbright director to see if we can get other volunteers like her and also invite Dr Pawan Gupta of NASA, to become a scientific adviser.

This is also around the time our group begins talking about the need for a centralized, accountable authority that can focus on measurable outcomes at the government level. We decide to call out air pollution as a national health emergency and try to get more doctors on board.

'People, especially Indians, will believe anything medical doctors say,' says another one of our newer volunteers drily. She is a public health researcher who validates my observation that while public health workers have been trying to highlight the health impact of pollution for years, medical doctors and clinicians are yet to treat the problem with the same gravity. Perhaps if doctors made a bigger deal about it, the public would finally realize how we are all hurtling towards disease and death, we tell each other, and try to come up with ways to involve doctors. Thus far, we haven't actually tried to use our personal networks or the power of social media. Maybe it's time we did.

When I call around and talk to friends who are pulmonologists and ENT specialists, they complain about the challenges they face in trying to build greater awareness while also diagnosing and treating, in the tiny fragments of time they get with each patient.

I don't know this yet, but the following month is when I will meet Dr Arvind Kumar, who despite being a busy lung surgeon of repute, has made it his mission to spread awareness about air pollution. From within the medical community, he will be the one to call out doctors in failing to preventively communicate the health harm caused by dirty air, and subsequently, to rally the medical community behind him. But, in 2017, doctors, nurses and the allied medical community, the critical piece in this puzzle, are still missing in action.

That night, with a greater social media push in mind, I log on to CFA's Facebook page and appoint more page managers in the hope that with more people, we will be able to amplify the pollution stories. In the following days, very reluctantly, I also learn to use Twitter, and relaunch the CFA account, set up in October 2015 and previously managed by Tina, Gita, Sue and other volunteers. We decide to create an Instagram handle. For our storyboard, we consider launching a global campaign called 'Humans of Air Pollution', along the lines of the 'Humans of New York' handle, with stories of real people grappling with air pollution – people such as waste segregators, landfill workers, children who work in the firecracker industry, coal miners, traffic policemen, autorickshaw drivers, marathon runners, among others. I set up a YouTube channel and reach out to a Finnish mojo – a mobile journalist – who lives next door and makes all her shows on her smartphone for a Nordic channel and even take a short training course in social media. I try and learn about Pinterest, Snapchat, TikTok, before I begin to feel overwhelmed and decide to look for young interns who will be digital natives, unlike me. We need stories around air pollution. We need to humanize it.

Pollution is our grim reality, and it needs to enter our art, literature and consciousness in every way. I want to embed conversations surrounding pollution into Delhi's art and popular culture, and leverage the outrage generated into action for policy change. Over time, I've seen some hard-hitting art that effectively manages to bring to light the hidden danger of pollution to the public. One such project, a series of photographs by a Frenchwoman living in Gurgaon, consists of Delhiites posing with masks and holding an X-ray film of their lungs against their chests.[13] She has created over 50 such portraits: bicycle-mounted milkmen, domestic maids, schoolboys, pregnant women and elderly people standing against varied backgrounds such as highway traffic, construction sites and trash dumps. I decide to reach out to her for a collaboration.

Just the previous year, in January 2016, the India Art Fair had an installation by artist Shahid Parvez – a 6-foot bust in the style of Ravinder Reddy's *Heads*, but wearing a heavy-duty pollution mask. Its torso and hair were made up entirely of tiny, colourful cars. Also in 2016, a Spanish artist called Lucas Munoz created a public installation called *Delhi Lung*[14] – 36 metres of thin muslin cloth with 21 fans inside a round bamboo structure, meant to reflect what Delhi's air does to human lungs. The mobile installation was first displayed on 30 January 2016 at Bikaner House before moving to perform at diverse spots in Delhi including the

Instituto Cervantes. I interviewed Lucas, and he permitted me to upload photos of his installation on our website. After 30 days in Delhi's air, the muslin cloth was meant to pattern what lungs of Delhi residents look like. 'It will be like an imprint,' the artist had said. And it had – much faster than he expected.

Seven million people die prematurely every year because of air pollution. This issue needs to be more deeply embedded in our collective consciousness, in our art, our music, our corporations, our literature, our films – in fact, in all popular culture. We especially need our youth to become more aware so that their generation can fix what previous generations have broken. I want CFA to do its bit to insert air pollution in every area of mass culture.

On a pleasant March morning, my father, mother, brother-in-law, husband and I visit the Garden of Five Senses in South Delhi. The bright sunshine washes over us, and I can actually smell flowers – the air doesn't have its usual smoky smell. For once, my eyes are watering due to the bright sunlight and not the pollution. Both my parents have been sick simultaneously, and my brother-in-law has swooped in and transferred them to Saket, where he and my sister live. This is the first day they've been allowed to leave home. It's no fun getting old, I can see that. Both of them look weak and pale. They've been under 'house arrest' due to poor outdoor air, trapped in their air-purified rooms. The PM2.5 level is at 'just' 145 today – a relatively clean day. The good news is that they've had no respiratory troubles this past winter.

'Finally, the AQI is improving,' I tell my mother as we walk. 'Now, you should start walking outdoors, get some exercise. Get your appetite back.' She finally vaguely understands AQI. Like most air pollution facts and figures, AQI too doesn't lend itself to easy understanding.

She is unusually quiet, her cane tap-tapping along. I look at her face. In the bright sunshine, I can see every wrinkle. My father walks ahead with a full head of brilliant white hair. He can still walk without a cane. They are both past the age of 80, but neither looks it.

'*Beta, ab akele rehna mushkil lag raha hai*. We will have to move closer to one of you,' she says, so softly that I have to stoop to catch her words. The sentence pierces my heart. I know how independent they are and have always been. They've never wanted to depend on their children, trouble their sons-in-law, or live with their daughters. Now, it seems all this is going to change.

'Let's think about this when you're feeling stronger, Ma,' I tell her bracingly and take her hand. She lets it sit in mine for a bit, then wriggles it away.

'No, *beta*,' her voice is stronger now. 'It is time.'

I broach the subject with my brother-in-law when we return and are sitting on his sunny balcony. My sister is not home. She and her husband live in a builder's flat that belongs to their son, my nephew, an investment banker who lives abroad. It's a good arrangement. At least they don't keep getting tossed out by landlords like we do, I think wryly.

I look out of their balcony appreciatively. It is a narrow, relatively quiet street in Saket, thick with parked cars, flanked by two large yellow-and-green iron gates to filter traffic.

'Aren't there other flats like these available close by?' I ask tentatively. I've been thinking of what my mother just said. 'Well, right now, the ground floor and second floor are both empty,' says my brother-in-law. 'The ground floor owner is an elderly non-resident. He visits occasionally. I think he's getting too old for the back-and-forth travel travel. Why?'

The idea is overwhelming in its simplicity. We are fortunate that at this point three of the four siblings live in Delhi. What if my parents downsized, sold their beautiful, park-facing bungalow in the government cooperative in which they lived, close to the most polluted part of Delhi, and with that money bought a smaller, more compact flat closer to all of us? This way, they would never need to feel dependent on any *one* of us, and we could support each other in the final leg of their journey.

'Can you ask him if he will sell?' I ask, turning to my brother-in-law.

And now it is September and so much has changed. The past months have been eventful. My father has managed to sell the bungalow he built after retirement, to buy the ground-floor apartment in the building where my sister and brother-in-law live. Given that I've moved house three times in three years, I've been put in charge of packing and moving all of my parents' things across town. The move has been fraught, because it has been hard to get my mother, the ultimate hoarder, to throw away *anything*.

Meanwhile, there is another packing and moving I'm helping with. My daughter, my nestling will be flying off to college overseas – to cleaner air, I keep reminding myself. I've been preparing myself emotionally to let go of my firstborn. Sometimes I still feel a flare of anger. If India's air hadn't been so polluted, she would have remained here, like we'd always planned.

Somewhere in the middle of all this, I discover that in July, an organization called Asar has launched a Clean Air Collective to pilot what it calls a 'strategic framework for coordinated action', a 'collective impact'[15] model introduced by the Stanford Social Innovation Review[16] to address the 'wicked' problem of air pollution. Led by Brikesh Singh, an environmentalist and avid bicyclist, Asar aims to create an unbranded network of organizations, individuals and groups working on air pollution and help them to collaborate, complement each other's work and align on strategy.

I learn about the collective later, in September, by which time both mother and daughter are almost settled into their new homes. I decide to reach out to Brikesh to see how we can work together. There are around 15 organizations which have banded together collectively under this umbrella.

It's end-September, still summer-warm, when everything is finally done in my parents' new home. The flat is compact, they have much less space, but they seem to be settling in well. My father looks happier, though my mother is missing her old life, her weekly music group and local friends. She is also complaining of feeling a little breathless, which surprises me, since this is a time when Delhi's air is relatively clean. I get their air filters checked and cleaned for the coming winter. I decide to help my mother settle into the new place by creating a new music group around her. Fortunately, I know a couple of her friends who live close by. All I need to do is ring them, arrange that first session and schedule it as a regular meeting. But my mother seems resistant to the idea. I'm taken aback.

'Why?' I ask.

'I'll do it next week. I feel a bit tired right now,' she says. There is a certain weariness about her that I've never seen before. I put it down to the house move. It has probably taken a bigger toll on her than I imagined. I hadn't considered it possible, for this was the woman who had moved house effortlessly from her parental home in Meerut to Calcutta in 1955, then Bareilly, Sitapur, and many other small north Indian towns, including Kanpur in 1969, before moving to Delhi in 1983 for the final stint.

We siblings decide we must throw a house-warming party for my parents, but even to this, my feisty, uber-social mother demurs, surprising us all. It is unlike her to want to be alone.

'How will all your friends know where your new home is?' coaxes my older sister, who lives one flight of stairs above them. She is the extrovert among us.

But my mother shakes her head.

'I'll get you a new sari to wear,' my eldest sister declares. This is her way of cajoling, a secret language that only she and my mother share. As her firstborn, she knows my mother best and is able to persuade her to do virtually anything.

'Oh, let her be,' says my father. 'You know she's not been feeling that well.' But he looks thoughtful.

Delivering the ninth P.N. Srivastava Endowment Lecture on 'Air Pollution and Health' in October 2018, almost a year later, Dr

Randeep Guleria would say that human health was affected by 'genetic predisposition and the environment'. 'Genetics loads the gun, but environment pulls the trigger,' he said. 'I see a lot of individuals who come to Delhi to study or work. These are the people who have never had any respiratory problems until their move to the city, but they start complaining of cough or chest congestion after they start living in the capital.'

My mother had lived in this sort of polluted environment all her life, and the pollution load of years of inhaling PM2.5 had pulled the trigger on the loaded gun. Air pollution had been stalking her for years and had finally found her. We just didn't know it yet.

9

Killing Us All

October 2017

We have overruled my dad and gone ahead and invited all my parents' relatives and some of their friends to their house-warming party. In fact, we've decided that the occasion can double up as my mother's birthday celebration. She loves celebrations. We schedule the party for 29 October, two days before her birthday. Email invitations are sent, phone calls are made, preparations begin.

In early October, the air quality in Delhi starts to worsen. It isn't Diwali yet, but with the temperature falling I begin to taste and smell the acrid air. Soon, crop stubble will be burnt in the states neighbouring Delhi and heavy smoke from the farm fires – so large that they can now be seen by satellites – will shroud the city in killer microparticles. I'm concerned about my family. My father has been diagnosed with COPD – likely a throwback from his years as a smoker – and in hopes of alleviating the problem somewhat, I have placed 12 NASA-recommended snake plants (sansevieria) that produce oxygen at night in their bedroom and replaced all the clogged filters in their air-purifying machines, following Barun's advice of six plants per person.

However, my father still refuses to wear a mask when he steps out, complaining that it is too restrictive. He is excited to find a park close to their new apartment and insists on walking there every morning. My mother had begun accompanying him, but lately she has been too tired to join him. 'At least her lungs aren't getting fresh deposits of toxic ash,' I say to myself, and plead with my father to go outside only after the sun has burnt off the worst of the PM. Surprisingly, he agrees and changes the timing of his walks to around noon.

We have been fortunate with wind speeds this year. The already heavy load of particulate matter is being blown away, and concentrations aren't yet at suffocating levels. But Diwali is early this year, and soon there will be smoke from firecrackers. I worry about strange things now. Wind speed and direction. Falling temperatures. Rains. Harvesting in neighbouring states. Festivals – Diwali, Lohri, Holi – all of which have a component of open burning.

Northern India's geography ensures that pollution generated locally doesn't easily disperse. The Himalayas form a barrier in the north, preventing dirty air from dissipating. The wind dies in the winter, turning the Indo-Gangetic plain into a giant bowl. A bowl of filthy air for residents to inhale.

Around me, I notice, awareness has grown and, more importantly, people now seem to want to *do* something to fight pollution. I see different approaches by citizens to counter the killer air. A group of Delhiites who call themselves Vasant Vihar Divas are active on a WhatsApp group and are pushing to get doctors to validate the ill effects of pollution for this. I recognize in the group, names from the protest on 6 November last year. They have since delivered a petition to bring down pollution levels to anyone they thought could help, from the chief minister to the chief justice and even the President of India. But nothing has been done in terms of any real action. As has happened earlier, once the season changes and nature does its annual clean-up act, things fall silent.

This is the real challenge with activism in air pollution. Even those who genuinely want to make a difference get intimidated by the science and the gigantic, seemingly unsolvable problem. And once the elements blow and burn and wash away the smog, people forget, their efforts wither. The protest group which has been silent for almost a year since the protests, reawakens now, in early October 2017, right around the time the farm fires start belching out their smoke. As Delhi's AQI levels start soaring, the group mobilizes organically, self-catalysing, its chatter becoming more pollution focused. Meanwhile, the PTA's request for air purifiers to be installed in classrooms and common areas of the school has been met with resistance from the school's management. The unofficial reason being offered to us is that the school – predominantly consisting of children of senior government officials – doesn't want to appear to be elitist. We are appalled. Clean air is being perceived as a luxury that only rich schools can or should provide their students. It is being likened to air conditioning.

I've tried to explain the difference at more than one management committee meeting. I'm all for toughening up our children, and have resisted air-conditioned buses and classrooms. But air purifiers aren't for physical comfort. They prevent further health harm by filtering out toxic particles before they enter our children's lungs. Our children, who are involuntary smokers just because they live in Delhi, in India.

A new principal has taken charge in the new academic term earlier this year, which energizes the PTA to retry arguing our case for installing air purifiers. The open plan of the school means that centralized air purification systems can't be installed. We could at best install space air purifiers in each of the 50 classrooms – but that would lead to the carbon dioxide paradox. To explain this paradox simply: with roughly 35 children in each classroom, if we seal the space for an air filter to work most efficiently inside a room, we can get the PM2.5 down within minutes; however, the exhaled air from those 35 children will quickly build high levels of carbon dioxide in the room. Carbon dioxide is also a pollutant – one that causes cognitive harm. It is the lack of oxygen and the excess carbon dioxide that causes that drowsy feeling of tiredness that the human body often fixes by yawning. So, for any system that is installed, we will have to find some way of circulating the air as well as cleaning it. Additionally, unlike the night-oxygen-producing plants I place in our bedrooms, placing day-oxygen-producing plants for 35 children would mean classrooms will need a mini-forest, it seems, because, according to Barun, four shoulder-high areca palms or bamboo plants are needed per person.

But, despite the new principal acknowledging the seriousness of air pollution, the school doesn't approve even our basic action plan. This includes delaying school timings to escape the worst air quality on cold mornings, when pollutants stay trapped close to the ground at inhalation levels; linking all outdoor aerobic activity to current levels of PM2.5, flagging high pollution, as 'bad air' days and, on such days, moving physical and sporting activity to the indoor gymnasium or other spaces such as the dance and yoga rooms; and covering all dusty, untarred areas with grass or concrete to minimize dust. I feel defeated and write an apology to all parent representatives, telling them that we haven't been able to convince the school management to install air filters even though several parents willingly volunteered to pay for air purifiers themselves.

It is clear that the only thing we have managed to achieve is that there are now many more 'pollution-aware' moms and some parental bonding over pollution.

On 9 October 2017, Gopal finally wins a favourable order on his petition on behalf of the three toddlers.[1] After two years, several hearings and much back and forth,[2] the Supreme Court finally bans the sale and distribution of firecrackers though it allows manufacturing to continue. The firecracker industry is up in arms because of the judgement and joining the cacophony are religious groups who claim that firecrackers are a Diwali tradition. Television channels suddenly begin sprouting panels filled with political and religious leaders at increasing decibel levels.

'Why are they making this about religion and politics? It's about our health!' we ask each other, confused. We try to figure out what our public engagement and narrative should be. A quick internet search confirms that historically firecrackers were a Chinese import first used in India by the Mughals. Diwali traditionally only involved the lighting of oil lamps. So, in reality, this is about commerce, not customs, culture or even religion, we realize.

Then, the firecracker industry makes a tactical error in getting involved.

'The order had only banned sales and distribution. But then industry got involved and in the process, ended up scoring an own goal,' Gopal parses the order for me while also giving me the inside story of how it all unfolded in court.

'When the [firecracker] industry opposed our petition in court, one of the arguments its representatives made was that firecrackers burst during Diwali are responsible for "just" 2 per cent of the total pollution in Delhi. Now, causing 2 per cent of the annual figure in just two nights…you can do the math,' says Gopal, sounding triumphant.

We turn to our experts – back-of-the envelope calculations tell us this number is correct. The numbers are huge. The high load of smoke and emissions from firecrackers, calculated on an annual basis, comes from the sharp episodic spikes in PM2.5 in the two nights around Diwali. 'The firecracker industry itself provided this information based on a source apportionment study carried out by an Austrian group,' says Gopal.

We quickly realize another thing. Firecrackers not only add to the PM2.5 – just one of those tiny hissing 'snake' tablets emits 64,500 PM2.5[3] – but also to heavy metals in the air. The colours in the fireworks[4] come from strontium, barium, copper and aluminium sulphates, nitrates and chlorides that add to the strong sulphurous fumes that cause the unique smell of explosives that pervades Delhi's air on Diwali evening and in the days following. This is how pollution due to crackers probably contributes 2 per cent of the annual load of pollution. From just the two to three days of bursting highly polluting, high-emission crackers, I think to myself. I've never thought of Diwali in these terms before.

Later, Dr Guleria will tell me about a multi-centre study funded by ICMR that he led from AIIMS which tracked emergency patient admissions between June 2017 and February 2019 and found that in the two to four days after higher episodic levels of air pollution, such as Diwali, not only did the number of emergency admissions increase, but higher respiratory symptoms led to increased morbidity and almost doubled mortality rates. Data also shows that more patients visit the hospital even six days after pollution levels have subsided. Dr Guleria says[5] that there was a rise of 20 to 40 per cent in patients visiting the emergency ward as air quality worsened. 'The concern we have is that many of these patients become sick and require ICU care. Indirectly, it also leads to higher morbidity and mortality.' He also tells me how PM2.5 is the most lethal of all pollutants that can go deep into the lungs. 'Toxic particles also get attached to these,' he says – which is why the post-Diwali smoke is probably the worst cocktail of air to inhale.

Gopal's writ petition includes nine different factors that cause pollution. It has also pleaded to stop crop residue burning, curb the export of all of India's cleanest BS-6 fuel by India's top refineries, including privately owned Essar and Reliance, and remove import duties on electric cars.

Based on this new order, NDTV's Sonia Singh anchors a panel discussion with eight well-known medical doctors – radiologists, pathologists, cardiologists and pulmonologists, both from the private and the public sector, where, for the first time, it seems to me, the entire panel is in complete agreement with each other. The panel emphasizes that pollution isn't just a Delhi problem, that it affects all socio-economic classes and that it doesn't just harm our lungs but all our organs. The doctors also unanimously say that children are the most vulnerable and that the country is facing a public health emergency. Anyone watching this show would be convinced about the health harm pollution causes. Unfortunately, NDTV addresses a limited, mostly English-speaking audience and faces the same challenge that CFA does. What we need is mass awareness, because it is only when the voting masses start understanding how the dirty air they breathe is pulling them back into poverty and killing them, that they will begin to demand clean air from their representatives and political parties. This is the only way any real and serious change will come about.

Later, I find out this panel discussion is Shibani Thukral's brainchild. Shibani, is one of the mothers who was at the November 2016 protest, and the force behind the social media hashtag #MyRightToBreathe (MRTB), which I notice gains in popularity following the panel discussion. The hashtag was an attempt to make this a citizen's movement for clean air.

When I reach out to Shibani, she walks me through the timeline of the movement.

'We started with peaceful protests at Jantar Mantar in November 2016. It got good media coverage for a day but was overtaken the next day by the news of demonetization in India and the US elections,' Shibani says, tucking her long, black hair behind her ears. 'So, in October 2017, we launched a campaign with NDTV, spearheading it with doctors,' she says.

The NDTV show on pollution creates a big buzz on several of the WhatsApp groups I'm on. There is a lot of networking, reaching out, connecting and collaborations via social media to bring air pollution centre stage. One of the results is a press conference that is arranged at Le Meridien with doctors, cricketers and other celebrities. The MRTB mothers and citizen activists want to use the Supreme Court order to build momentum against pollution. Someone invites me as one of the speakers, but I am hesitant. My main reservation is that I don't want air pollution activism to become – or be seen as – another fleeting, elitist fashion statement, a social 'flavour of the month' among Delhi's party circuit. The presence of so many celebrities congregating in a five-star hotel makes me uncomfortable. But celebrities do have powerful networks. Maybe they could be used to make a difference and take pollution mainstream, a friend points out to me. She's right. I've been frustrated with our slow progress in bringing pollution research and evidence out of silos, and to the masses – perhaps celebrity endorsement will help make it more mainstream.

In the end, I don't go. Had I gone, I would have met Ravina Raj Kohli, another pollution warrior and founding member of My Right To Breathe who will later become its face and de facto leader.

The press conference takes place at Le Meridien's 'Desire' on 11 October. Gopal is on the panel, along with doctors such as Dr Anupam Sibal, a senior paediatrician, and Dr Sidharth Sahni, a breast surgeon, both from Apollo Hospital; Dr Arvind Kumar, chief thoracic surgeon, and Dr Neeraj Jain, a senior pulmonologist, both from Sir Ganga Ram Hospital; Dr Randeep Guleria, director of pulmonology at AIIMS; Dr Nitin Verma, senior paediatrician, Max Hospital, and Dr Harsh Mahajan, a radiologist. Also on the panel are Shamsher K. Sheriff, secretary general of the Rajya Sabha, and cricketer Kapil Dev. Ravina is the moderator. Arjun Sharma, who is chairman of the Select group, which includes a posh South Delhi mall by the same name, brings in the Avian Media Co. to handle publicity. A total of 42 media houses across electronic, wires and print media attend the event. The press release is titled 'Prominent citizens and social influencers call for celebrating a smoke-free, green Diwali.' The organizers manage to get popular public figures such as Virat Kohli, Kapil Dev, Rohit Sharma, Ashish Nehra, Virender Sehwag, Rannvijay Singh, Nina Gupta and Arjun Nagpal to voice their support for a cracker-free Diwali and share video pledges on their social media accounts to spread awareness about air pollution.

By all accounts, the event is a success; the collective effort of some of Delhi's best-connected influencers who pull in some of the best-known doctors from the medical community creates a media splash and highlights the health harm caused by pollution.

Until this involvement, the medical community has made no concerted effort to communicate the seriousness of the health harm triggered by air pollution, a grave omission. Few doctors have used their positions to build awareness for preventive healthcare or advocate for clean air. Even now, it isn't doctors or the medical community initiating this, but the pent-up anger and fear of several of the city's residents who have begun to realize that air pollution is causing serious health harm that propels the clean-air movement forward. It is after 2017 that doctors will get more openly involved, led most prominently by a handful of pulmonologists, such as Dr Kumar, Dr Trehan, Dr Guleria and Dr Vivek Nangia.

When I finally meet up with Ravina a month after the press conference, I excitedly ask for details about the 2016 'black-and-white' protest, remembering how inspired I had been to see others from civil society protest against pollution.

'Oh, that? That was something we managed literally overnight,' says Ravina breezily. 'It was basically a group of mothers who collectively managed to pull in their networks to highlight air pollution... We asked Thud to get us police permission on Friday and on Sunday, 6 November 2016, we were out there, protesting,' she says. How many people attended it, I ask.

'Oh, there must have been at least a couple of hundred...' For an overnight protest, that's pretty good. Who is Thud, I ask.

'You don't know Thud? Rajiv Luthra,' she says with a laugh.

I should have guessed. He is my soft-spoken Sanskriti treasurer Gayatri's lawyer husband and her complete antithesis. I've met him a few times and quickly understood that not only does he literally know anyone of any importance, but that he is a mini force of nature. If you need anything done, he is your go-to guy.

When I'm piecing these events together, I discover another component of the jigsaw in my own backyard – a young mother, Ayesha Chenoy who runs a digital media and advertising company. She's the one who created My Right To Breathe's original name, logo, Facebook presence, 'somewhere around October 2016', as she tells me. 'Arjun [Sharma] is a friend, neighbour and mentor,' she adds.

Ayesha sends me the link of the original Facebook page. It was created on 2 November 2016, before the current new page and logo came up on 2 December 2017.

'I left it to the others to take the movement forward,' Ayesha tells me. 'It was becoming too exclusive for my liking. I wanted it to be more inclusive.' Ayesha's mother is a professor at JNU and there was talk of involving students. 'But some of the members started saying that will make it too political,' Ayesha says wryly.

Socialites versus the socialists? Listening to Ravina and Ayesha, that is what it feels like.

Ravina takes up the story from here.

'We got many public personalities and opinion leaders involved,' she says, naming Bollywood celebrities and politicians.

What did you do at the protest? And what did you do after that, I persist.

'Ummm. I was there in the morning, up on stage, and spoke non-stop for almost three hours to keep the crowd engaged. Then we got those people to sign a petition to the chief justice, the President of India, to everyone who mattered,' she says, going through her phone. I ask to see the petition, and she sends me a copy. I am impressed to find its demands are fairly comprehensive. It asks for the following:

- Develop a better environment-friendly public transport system
- Strict ban on firecrackers and air pollutants throughout the year
- Stop burning crops (sic) in and around Delhi at all times
- Create proper waste-management systems
- Restrict construction pollution
- Restrict entry of trucks in the city by creating bypasses
- Shut down thermal power plants

It is after I meet Shibani and another MRTB founder Radhika Kapoor that I realize what Ravina meant by 'glamorous moms and their networks' and how they pulled this off. Radhika is the one who arranges the 2016 meeting with the then President of India, the late Pranab Mukherjee, as well as a meeting with Chief Justice T.S. Thakur. To both, she and her daughter, Nyrah, submit the petition signed by Delhi's children and adult citizens in the name of #My Right To Breathe.

'I went representing the moms who organized the Jantar Mantar protest. Nyrah represented the children who had signed petitions,' Radhika texts me when I ask her to recall those days.

'We also met Kejriwal. Made him sing that song he sang at his oath-taking,' reminisces Ravina. This is a meeting her friend Parul Sharma Jesudasan, then the corporate and marketing communications head, Star India, arranged at the residence of Arvind Kejriwal on Children's Day. 'The children gave him red roses, and he promised them a mask-free Children's Day in 2017.[6] Of course, that never happened.'

In the first instance, the focus is on Delhi. The idea to convert these protests and events to highlight overall pollution emerges later.

'That's not all we did,' Ravina tells me. 'We also tried to stop the Airtel half marathon. We – Jaidhar [Gupta] and I – filed an instant petition challenging the holding of Airtel Delhi half marathon,' she says and forwards me the petition. The instant petition notes the reason as 'the present air quality in the city of Delhi which has, in fact, reached toxic levels. On account of the severity of the air pollution in the city of Delhi, holding of the said half marathon would cause serious health hazards for the participants therein, specially the children and senior citizens.' It goes on to say that the 'very high level of air pollution in the city of Delhi makes it wholly unfit to hold the marathon… The prolonged exposure, during the course of strenuous exercise while running the marathon has the potential of causing serious damages to the life and health of the participants.'

'Two Ranji trophy matches which were to take place in Delhi have been cancelled recently,' the petition pleads, adding that 'the deteriorating air quality in the city of Delhi has endangered the health and life of the participants, thereby violating their Right to Life under Article 21 of the Constitution of India'.

Ravina and Jaidhar petition the court to cancel the 9th Airtel Delhi half marathon.

When I hear this, I understand that she is serious about the issue. This group isn't a flighty looking-for-a-cause-to-espouse bunch of glamourous women after all.

'Of course, I didn't file this case to win it – we knew we wouldn't win. There was no way Airtel was going to move the half marathon out of Delhi or even postpone it. This was mainly to highlight the problem,' she adds.

When I had written to Airtel in 2016 about their half marathon, it hadn't even yielded an acknowledgement. But now I'm wondering if, with the weight and heft of so many more, a jointly written petition to the company asking to move the half marathon to a less polluted time may help exert more pressure. When some on the group start questioning the wisdom of running a marathon in so much pollution, I tell them of my failed attempt from the previous year and we decide to draft a joint plea. CFA will be MRTB's knowledge partner and back the plea with scientific evidence on the perils of outdoor aerobic activity during high pollution. I start drafting a letter that will be sent jointly from us. One day, in one of the conversations around how we should send the letter, I recognize one of the names added to a WhatsApp group I'm part of. Bharati Chaturvedi was someone I knew in school 30 years ago, some years my junior. Since then, I learn, she has earned a master's in history, got married to an Indian diplomat and founded Chintan, an environmental non-profit that works in waste management while also attempting to uplift recyclers, *kabari* wallahs and waste pickers in India. She is also on a Delhi Pollution Control Committee (DPCC)[7] and writes for *Down to Earth*, the magazine of the environmental think tank, CSE. She and I reconnect eagerly. At first, we get caught up with a controversial issue – the exact role and effectiveness of the controversial Supreme Court-appointed Environment Pollution (Prevention and Control) Authority (EPCA) – and we end up having an exhaustive – and exhausting – conversation on air pollution, arguing with the support of facts and figures. Although Bharati has worked in the environment and waste-management space for years, she has only recently connected the dots to air pollution and is getting increasingly active in the area. I share what some of CFA's members have pointed out to me – that EPCA is riddled with conflicts of interest and is a drain on public funds. My biggest grouse with the Supreme Court-mandated authority has been that it had a very real, strong chance to clean Delhi's air, and yet it failed. It is important to note that EPCA isn't an agency, but an actual authority – which means its diktats must be followed by law. Despite being vested with enormous powers since its inception 20 years ago, it hasn't ordered a single penalty for polluters, functioning instead as a defensive entity, giving 'suggestions' and 'recommendations' to polluters and governments. Till date, knowing how terrible the air gets every winter, with the turn of the season, it only reactively 'advises' the government to close schools when pollution shoots up, rather than ordering closure and ensuring compliance. I am also of the opinion that it has weakened its own power by kowtowing to the interests of lobbies – some of which have infiltrated the organization itself.

I'm telling Bharati all this when she mentions that she knows an environmental lawyer whose work I admire – Ritwick Dutta, who founded the Legal Initiative for Forest and Environment. Exactly one year later, Ritwick will write a short report as well as a two-part story[8] that encapsulates every argument[9] I make to Bharati that day – and more. 'While we didn't entirely agree about EPCA ours was one of those rare chats that has been deep, long term and often,' says Bharati. Years later, I will discover that she serves on the board of CSE.

'The reason why EPCA is an authority, and not just an advisory committee, is because it has powers similar to those enjoyed by the Centre. Specifically, it can issue directions in writing to any person, officer or authority, including for – but not limited to – stoppage of electricity, water and other services. If its directions are not followed, it has powers to file criminal complaints [under Section 19 of the Act] before courts,' Ritwick says in 2018.[10] He points out 'serious issues with respect to the EPCA's independence and objectivity' because of the conflict of including not just the automobile manufacturers, whose 'main role is to promote the growth of the automobile industry [its members have stated[11] in public that they are opposed to any restriction on the use of diesel cars],' but also Sunita Narain, the Director General of CSE. In fact, he debunks her justification that the EPCA 'prepare reports and monitor the implementation of court orders', stating firmly that an authority's principal charge is to serve as an effective grievance redressal forum.

Additionally, he questions EPCA being headed by retired bureaucrat Bhure Lal, saying, 'His is perhaps the longest ever appointment in any statutory committee and/or authority in the Government of India.'

The following year, in November 2019, he will write an equally damning follow-up[12] on EPCA, ripping apart a report it submits,[13] which he calls 'a testimony to helplessness and passing the buck'. Bharati and I don't know this then, but one of the repercussions of this report by the EPCA will lead to another bogey, a red herring that the Supreme Court will unwittingly swallow as bait when it directs the central and Delhi state governments to install two smog towers in the capital city at a cost of roughly ₹18 crore each – public money wasted in an inefficient non-solution.

Tellingly, Dutta concludes his 2019 piece with 'we must recognize that the biggest crisis facing the capital city and its neighbouring areas is not air pollution; it's the collective ignorance, institutional failure, a culture of denial, inaction and a bloated confidence in technology'.

After our conversation, I look Bharati up on LinkedIn. Her profile says she 'offers action and leadership for sustainable consumption, resource efficiency and waste management for a *swachh* Bharat'. I discover that in the intervening years that we've lost touch, Bharati has become passionate about trying to save India from the ugly fate of drowning under its own trash. 'The pollution in rivers and in drinking water from landfills means we are literally drinking our trash. Burning it means we breathe trash. But what is even worse is that we have failed to acknowledge and improve the lives of the 20 lakh Indians who recycle over 20 per cent of our trash – the waste pickers, *kabaris* and sorters. They are called the informal recycling sector,' she writes on LinkedIn.

In Bharati, I immediately recognize the missing link. Since she works directly with the exact class that is most affected and least aware – the poorest and most underprivileged – our scavengers, landfill and waste workers, she is the best vehicle to spread awareness about air pollution among them. She is the equivalent of CFA's Anita Bhargav, just at a more long-term grassroots level.

It will be another year before I understand that in reality, waste pickers are among the most aware – and most disdainful of the rich who don't bother to segregate their trash. Their knowledge and awareness doesn't come from books and research but through their everyday lived experience.

Bharati suffers from asthma and feels just as strongly about advocating the perils of outdoor exercise in Delhi's filthy air as I do. When we draft the letter to Airtel, she is among the first to join the discussion. But, in the larger group, I notice something strange unfolding. When I share a draft of the letter to Airtel asking the company to reconsider holding the half marathon under such poor health conditions on the different WhatsApp groups for inputs and feedback, it goes through many changes. In each iteration, I find it watered down. Members of the groups whom I don't know personally start ringing me, asking me to either hold off or suggesting several changes. One day, a very vocal member of the MRTB group calls to tell me to leave the letter to him. He will not just write it, but he will also ensure it gets delivered 'to the right people, at the top', he says authoritatively. Fed up with the constant pestering, I am ready to agree to his request, when Ravina informs me that this man is somehow connected to Procam, who, I discover, is one of the organizers of the event.

I'm shaken by my gullibility. The reach of corporations is very long, I've come to find.

Ravina, on the other hand, has already understood this. I much prefer to leave the letter to Bharati. We decide to meet in person but will let Diwali pass.

My suspicions are further aroused when I notice that I'm getting pushback on an opinion piece I have submitted for publication in a national newspaper – just because the article involves Airtel. I receive an email from the op-ed page editor that is overly polite, with too much explanation being offered for the response to sound entirely natural. It reads:

Hi Jyoti,

I think I will have to pass on this. My colleague who writes on this issue feels that it is not the job of corporates to be responsible, but that people should be responsible for their own health and decide whether to run in marathons or not. Apparently, many marathoners steer clear of Delhi. Maybe you could look at another issue for me.

I receive this email on 27 October, the same day that I meet Ravina for the first time in person. It has been eight days since the Diwali phone call informing me of my mother's lung cancer. These eight days have been full of tests, the family's hopes rising and falling in line with the reports and second opinions as we huddle together, recalibrating our new feelings and altered lives, despair and hope jostling one another. We have also begun the search for a competent and trustworthy oncologist as we begin to navigate the Indian healthcare system. It is all a bit surreal, because our mother seems so normal, so not terminally ill, that we're still in a state of disbelief. We still haven't told her the full extent of what the tests are revealing, though it's getting harder to sidestep her questions. Our hopes now hang on a remaining retest that a promising potential oncologist has prescribed for her. The result will be out later today.

I meet Ravina at the library lounge of the India Habitat Centre. Although the usual post-Diwali pollution hasn't yet gripped the city, the evening is grey and gloomy, a light haze beginning to settle into the horizon. Accompanying Ravina is a younger woman who looks like she is in her forties. She is wearing jeans, a black top and impossibly high heels. Later, I will know that that is Parul Sharma Jesudasan's standard dress code. Parul, says Ravina, has just left her job at Star TV and is helping with the communications and publicity for the campaign. They seem uncertain about exactly what they are going to do next. They are considering registering this undefined movement or hashtag, whatever this is – as a non-profit.

'Some of us want to register this as a non-profit,' Ravina says, sounding uncertain.

'Don't do that,' I blurt out.

'Why?'

'The protests and all that you have done until now have been so organic, so pure,' I say. 'Keep this as a movement. Call it whatever you want but keep it a movement. It should be free, organic and belong to everyone.' They are listening attentively, nodding in instant agreement.

I tell them about our movement to spread awareness and share our learnings, the pros and cons of volunteer-led movements, our missteps and failures. Registering CFA as a non-profit has taken us a long time and has diverted our energies. We now have to worry about compliances and all sorts of paperwork even though we are only continuing to do what we've been doing so far. 'So, unless you plan to raise money, don't go down that path,' I advise Ravina. I really want this new group to succeed. We need many more groups like this – groups that understand the science and realize how serious the problem is.

'I agree,' Ravina says at last. 'This must remain a movement.' Her voice is firm. Parul nods, looking thoughtful.

'We're happy to share our learnings, be your knowledge partner,' I tell her. Anita joins us at this point – I've invited her to tell them more about her waste-management campaign and to share our conclusions that what we need is an independent, empowered, centralized and accountable authority with a time-bound goal to reduce air pollution by specific amounts each year.

Anita is giving them a detailed download when my phone rings. The screen flashes the name of Dr Navin Dang in whose laboratory we've given in my mother's cell block samples for a retest. The dread in my heart grows. I excuse myself and step outside in the thickening haze of the early evening air to take the call.

We've double- and triple-checked, hoping against hope that my mother's diagnosis is somehow a big, giant mistake. Navin's warm voice gives me the bad news gently. There is no mistake with the diagnosis. After the call, I try to recompose myself before going back inside. I look out at the grey miasma that is shrouding my dying city and wonder how many more people are afflicted by deadly diseases triggered by breathing this malignant air. I rejoin the others, but the rest of the discussion is a blur to me. I don't remember what else is said, or even how I reach home. But that meeting with Ravina and Parul is a turning point in my fight against pollution, because I am finally able to overcome my scepticism about this group of citizen activists and join in their conversations with wholehearted enthusiasm. As I get back into the groove of things, I reply three days later to the editor of the newspaper daily.

Hi [redacted]

I strongly disagree with your colleague. I would have agreed with him if it was full disclosure and people were well aware of the severely harmful impact of running in this toxic weather and still chose to run. That isn't the case. Given that almost 95 per cent of those participating will be completely unaware of the ill effects of running in this air, it is unfair and irresponsible for corporates to exhort people to come out in large numbers.

Actually, your colleague's arguments are exactly the same ones that the tobacco industry used to oppose spreading information on the ill effects of smoking. It took 75 years to enforce having the warnings that are now added to cigarette packaging statutorily. I don't know if these marathon sponsors are unaware themselves, or just don't care about anything apart from their brand building and profits. Airtel and others should use their brand-building exercise to make others more aware, not put them at greater risk via marathons.

I'm old enough to remember how the tobacco industry had fought tooth and nail till the end, even negotiating to get the simple message that 'Smoking kills' diluted to 'Smoking is injurious to your health' on cigarette packs. I realize that this is going to be a long battle. I resign myself to the fact that the newspaper is unlikely to carry my op-ed piece. But as a last resort, I turn to Aparna Gupta – whose son used to be on the same school football team as mine. She works on persuading the Indian Medical Association (IMA) to declare air pollution a national medical health emergency. The IMA comes out with a formal statement.[14] This leads to wide media coverage and reports like the following:

> *In view of the deteriorating air quality of the capital, the Indian Medical Association on Tuesday declared a state of 'public health emergency' in Delhi. IMA president Dr K.K. Aggarwal requested people to avoid stepping out and asked schools to remain closed.*
>
> *The medical body also requested Delhi Chief Minister Arvind Kejriwal to cancel the Delhi half marathon scheduled for 19 November. The city saw a sharp fall in air quality today with various places, including India Gate and Rajpath, enveloped in thick smog. The city's air saw a huge rise in air pollutants – PM2.5, PM10 – which was counted at 452 and 336, respectively. As per international standards, the permissible range for PM2.5 is 25.*
>
> *Earlier, on Monday, Bharti Airtel, the sponsor of Delhi half marathon, said it would stop its association with the event if the authorities refused to address the issue of air pollution in the capital. 'Air pollution poses serious health risks and it is important that these concerns are addressed urgently and appropriately by the authorities for Airtel to continue associating with the event next year and beyond,' the telecom major said in a statement.*[15,16]

In fact, the organizers, Procam International, call the IMA's call for cancellation of the marathon 'shortsighted and misplaced.' When I read these reports, my anger grows. Bharti Airtel has cleverly and conveniently thrown the onus of responsibility into the court of the 'authorities'. Nowhere does the company acknowledge or take responsibility for exacerbating these health harms by encouraging people to run in such high levels of pollution. It isn't the only corporations holding marathons, of course, as I have seen 'fun runs' being advertised for schoolchildren by other companies. State-owned banks and companies aren't far behind. In fact, the authorities themselves are holding marathons – I see the Border Security Force and the Central Reserve Police Force marathons advertised in the most polluted of times. The Indian prime minister himself asks the people to 'Run for Unity' on 31 October 2017[17] and flags off the run from the national stadium.[18] The PM2.5 is several times over WHO-prescribed limits that morning. In retrospect, I realize that we – and the IMA – should have made our demand more generic, without singling out any one corporation.

I read all this while I'm sitting with my mother in her new apartment. It is her birthday, she has just blown the candles on a tiny cake I brought her and we've sung to her. I can see she is short of breath. My older siblings mill around as she begins packing for hospital. Tomorrow, we will admit her so that the fluid from her lungs can be drained out to give her some relief. We are still hopeful that the first line of treatment will help her.

While she packs her personal items, I open up my laptop and carefully study event charts of marathons listed and realize that there are runs organized every week. It is almost as if there's a collective death wish – and all this despite doctors making public statements on how any exercise in Delhi's air is harmful. In fact, Dr Arvind Kumar has publicly said[19] that 'running marathons in these air conditions can deposit approximately two tablespoons of toxic ash in your lungs'. Two tablespoons for every run. 'A normal adult breathes approximately 6 litres of air per minute at rest, but while exercising, they may inhale up to 20 litres, thus causing more toxicity,'[20] he says.

The controversy around the Airtel half marathon makes me understand the contradictory nature of the MRTB group. As long as the focus is on fireworks, everyone is united. But the minute it hits closer home, affecting industries with a large air pollution footprint, such as construction, power, steel and cement that many in the group were involved with, or the high-consumption lifestyles of some of the members, the motley collective starts to crumble. Instead of using their valuable social capital to teach the masses about the need to reduce air pollution, their main focus reverts to protecting their own profits and interests.

I recall Ravina warning me not to wait for a consensus on the group, and her words, 'MRTB is just a hashtag under which all types of people try to coexist. We can never have total consensus' now hits home.

Now, in November, her messages become even more direct. 'The group has become very politicized,' says one message. 'Sorry, I need fearless people, not people who are afraid to lose business or a party invite,' reads another such text. But, creditably, she manages to keep My Right To Breathe apolitical, non-commercial and detached from lobbies. '#MRTB must belong to everyone,' she repeats ad nauseum.

In the end, that year too, our efforts come to nought, and the Airtel half marathon goes ahead as scheduled on 19 November 2017. But we don't give up and try again the following year. By then, Ravina has fully established her credentials as a pollution warrior – and so has Dr Kumar. In fact, on 30 October 2018, when the WHO holds its first-ever Global Conference on Air Pollution and Health in Geneva, it is Dr Kumar and Ravina who are present. India doesn't send a single senior government official or minister to represent the country with the most polluted cities in the world. The only other Indian representative is a Member of Parliament from Amritsar.[21] Dr Kumar[22] is sponsored by the WHO, but Ravina goes on her own steam. Viewing their WHO-endorsed presentations,[23] I find they have become firm air pollution warriors. The satisfaction I feel at seeing their continued commitment is deep and fulfilling.

While the three are representing a billion people in Geneva, the Indian prime minister back home is once again asking people to 'Run for Unity'[24] on 31 October 2018. 'Despite a thick blanket of haze that engulfed Delhi, nearly 12,000 people took part in the marathon. This included 3,000 school children, 300 ex-servicemen and a number of senior citizens,' according to media reports.[25] India's home minister flags off the run from Delhi's national stadium on a day when the PM2.5 level is over 15 times the WHO-prescribed limit.

In Gujarat, the prime minister inaugurates the world's tallest 'statue of unity'. 'Air pollution is the new tobacco,' says WHO's director general in Geneva, while Indians smoke by just drawing breath.

By November 2017, I'm becoming busier with my mother's illness, talking to oncologists, pulmonologists, lab diagnosticians, even epidemiologists and friends who are cancer researchers, double-checking everything told to us at the shiny hospital. I also ensure I validate suggested tests with my cousin who is himself a chest specialist at a government hospital.

At home, my war against pollution begins to sow discord in my family, increasing confrontations with my sports-crazy son. I've always admonished him for playing outdoors without checking air quality, but after the shock of my mother's diagnosis, I find I've become more fanatical and less conciliatory with his very natural desire to play. There have been so many arguments, always beginning with a laconic request and ending in a stand-off and sulking teenage anger.

A typical argument begins with him casually informing me of soccer or tennis practice and ends with his storming off rudely after I point out yet again that the air is polluted and playing outdoors bad for his health, and he should excuse himself:

'I have soccer practice tomorrow, early morning. Just letting you know,' he will begin.

'I'm sorry, the AQI is 379, I really can't let you play outside.'

'This is not just play, Mom. And you yourself have taught me that sports and exercise is good for health.'

'I know. And it is. But not in this disgusting air. It's like smoking 30 cigarettes.'

'Last time you said 20.'

'Maybe I did. Maybe the AQI was lower. But the bottom line is that it is injurious to your health. I can't allow you to compromise your lungs. You're not going.'

'But I feel fine. So do my friends...'

'Why are you arguing? I've explained to you that feeling fine doesn't mean the pollution isn't harming your body. Those lethal microparticles are just collecting inside your lungs. And I've told you a hundred times it doesn't just affect your lungs but every organ of your body. With irreversible impact. Isn't your health more important than play?'

Familiar panic and anger build up inside me. My son is looking at me mutinously, anger blazing in his eyes.

'It's NOT just play. This is *soccer*, Mom. It's the *school team*. I'm in the team, remember?' tinged with the typical sarcasm of a teen.

'Yes, I remember. From yesterday. And the day before. And last year. But I'm sorry, the air is still bad, you know very well what it does to you. I can't allow you to run around outdoors. Why can't you just wait till the air is better?'

'But it's never better. When has AQI ever been at WHO levels?' says my 11th-grader reasonably. 'You said the same thing yesterday and I had to skip practice. The rest of the team went. I'm defence. I have to go.' By now, he is gritting his teeth, trying to control himself.

He's right. There are hardly any good air days. This will finally get documented in 2018, when there isn't even one day of good air quality. A fact that is never talked about by the government, though vigilant Greenpeace activist Sunil Dahiya will tweet it[26] and *Al Jazeera* will write about it,[27] adding that there are zero people being held accountable for the state of affairs, despite myriad laws to that effect. Later, a Parliament question on air quality will deftly change the focus to talking about satisfactory AQI levels but conveniently omit to mention that the entire year didn't have a single day when AQI was at levels acceptable to the WHO.

'No. Please stop arguing. This is non-negotiable. You can play when it isn't so polluted,' I say harshly, unrelenting.

Then softening, 'I'm doing this because I love you, and it's my job to protect you. You'll thank me for this later.'

It will only be after a global pandemic grips the world, adding a lockdown to an economic slowdown in India that AQI will fall to unbelievably low levels in March–April 2020, already low pollution season. Later, in the usually lowest pollution monsoon months when the rain washes remaining pollution away, Delhi will see a level of 41 on 1 September 2020, the lowest since records have been maintained – and it will make headlines.[28]

'How come my friends are all allowed? You think their mothers don't love them? Everyone else plays, except me. And what do I say? "My mommy doesn't want me to breathe the bad air?"' I can see his anger and frustration growing.

'I can't comment on other mothers, maybe they're not aware of exactly how terrible the air quality is, but this mother won't let you go.'

Silence.

'What if I wear a mask?' he says suddenly.

'But you hate it! You say you can't run well and that your skin breaks out.'

'I just don't want to let my team down. Plus, now another kid on the team also wears a mask, so I won't be the only one.'

'Will you promise me you won't take it off? It has to fit tightly.'

To be honest, this isn't the best solution. Even to be effective, they have to be fitted just right, made of HEPA filters of the finest mesh and even then, there can be uncomfortable carbon dioxide build-up, despite a valve. Running with a mask isn't advisable either, what with the build-up of carbon dioxide and the extra effort the heart and lungs have to make. Dr Guleria will reiterate this expressively when he tells me 'masks give us a false sense of security'. But in the same interview, he has emphasized that 'we often underplay the long-term effects of continuous exposure to high levels of air pollution on children. As they get older, they will have to pay a price.'

'I hate that mask. It makes me feel dizzy. I sweat inside it while running.'

'Well, that's better than getting all sorts of diseases and lung cancer.' (How lightly I used to say this before!)

'And my team can't hear what I'm saying across the field.'

I hate wearing masks myself and have recently discovered nasal filters that are much less uncomfortable. But the real solution is clean air.

'Do you want to try the nasal filters again?'

'They fall off with all the running and sweating. No point.'

'Then you're not going.'

I'm tired. We've had this argument about a hundred times.

'Okay, fine! I won't go. You just don't want me to play soccer. You just don't want me to be on the school team. Anyway, you hate sports!' he shouts and a door bangs.

The next day, without any warning, he drops out of his school team. He had worked hard to be selected for the team and now he's out.

'There was no point. I was letting my team down by not showing up for practice,' he tells me, resigned. 'I hate this pollution. I hate Delhi. Why do we live in a city where I can't play soccer?' he says, sounding dejected.

I ask myself this question every winter. I know some of the other mothers do too. One of them, Aparna Gupta, also has a soccer-crazy child. Fed up of constantly worrying about his health as he went for practice morning after polluted morning, Aparna took the difficult decision to send him away at the tender age of 14 to a country with cleaner air so that he could follow his passion.

'I had to send him away. There wasn't a single day when I could let him play without worrying about the terrible air, I got tired of the daily fights,' says Aparna, who took this call in 2015, before many parents had even realised what pollution was doing to their children.

She ended up choosing a tiny boarding school, known for its excellent football academy deep in rural England. So off went Daksh uprooted from his home, school and country due to pollution, just because he loved football and wanted to play it professionally.

Aparna is sensible and straight-talking – and very aware of the privilege of having the resources to move her son to England. 'It was so disruptive for him and us. His dream was to play for India. He wanted to be here. But it wasn't worth his lungs and life. Between the politics at all the leagues and the toxic air, it was best to send him away,' she says. Once there, Daksh thrived. 'His energy levels were much better, so was his lung power and stamina,' says Aparna.

Daksh Gupta has recently been chosen by Crawley Town FC, a professional association football club based in West Sussex. 'But his dream? I don't know if that will ever happen. Clean healthy air is a basic and rightful need for any human being, leave alone a sportsman!' says Aparna, her voice filled with regret and anger.

Her personal experience with pollution has made her a clean air activist.

November is also when I notice that a terrible, leaden ache has settled on my chest. I feel it when I wake up from an exhausted sleep every morning, as I remember what is happening to us, to my mother, how this feisty woman is fading right before our eyes. I carry this ache with me as I make my daily way to the hospital for my shift from the flexible roster that my siblings and I follow to ensure my mother is never without someone from the family.

Through this journey with my mother, I learn which signs of distress to look out for where her breathing is concerned, and other details about her ailment. In all of us, the pleural cavity aids optimal functioning of the lungs while breathing. The fluid in it acts as a lubricant for the pleurae to slide effortlessly against each other with each breath. When cancer grows and there is effusion – a build-up of extra fluid – it is an almost sure sign that the disease has metastasized and spread to other parts of the body. I measure the fluid's constant build-up in my mother's lungs, noting down its colour and amount as part of a personal protocol my nephew and I devise for the family to keep ourselves abreast of the treatment. We know well that often, between a doctor's hurried directions and the nurses' blind execution, there is an abyss of oversight a patient could easily fall into. Language barriers, human error, sheer exhaustion, or just a gap in hospital protocols and processes – anything can cause this. So we try to bridge that potential breach, checking and rechecking instructions, medication, augmenting communications during shift changes at the hospital, trying to anticipate and integrate what the oncologist, pulmonologist and executing doctors say. We are on high alert.

But the malignant liquid continues to form endlessly, not responding to any medication, draining out into a plastic pouch through the thin needle attached to her left lung. When I help my mother to the toilet in those early days when she can still walk, we carry the bag of fluid between us like an illegitimate child, not mentioning it, but hyper-aware and careful not to drop it. I often wonder what they do with it afterwards.

What happens when the hospital staff throws away this pouch, and the hundreds of other pouches collected in this hospital and other hospitals throughout the city and country, I wonder. Do they all burn along with other medical waste in some landfill or unregulated incinerators? If so, those fumes will rise into the air and go into other bodies, bodies of my loved ones, entering through their lungs, coursing through their bloodstreams, to collect and mutate or trigger new cancer cells, triggering other diseases. This process will continue until we are all dead.

Breathing is what lies between being born and dying. Standing in hospital queues, waiting for elevators, doctors and more tests, I find myself hemmed in by morbid thoughts. I realize it isn't so much the dying I mind. It is the suffering before the actual death, the struggle to breathe and the pain – not just of the patients, but of their families, their mothers and fathers and sons and daughters. My pain was linked to my mother's pain, the number of years of life lost, its quality degraded. I minded that. I minded that a lot. An inarticulate anger just flowed, like a red river of pain, helplessness and fear, as India's famed medical system fanned around us, its tentacles capturing us in a fierce, ruthless embrace.

Even later, when we brought her home, when November turned to December, and my daughter, my mother's granddaughter, came back from her first semester away at college and was shocked to see how frail her naani had become, it was the suffering that we all minded. The suffering and the daily humiliations.

Dying of cancer was one thing, but the smaller humiliations and inconveniences, like bowel movements in bed and the indignities of being dependent on another to even brush your teeth were what chipped away her spirit and ours.

Even the sunshine and characteristic youthful optimism of my daughter, unrealistically buoyant as a rule, withered away against the visible decay she could see from visit to visit in the body of her beloved naani. The naani she is afraid she may never see again once she returns to college for her spring term, in January.

'A hospital,' she announces from the folds of my lap, her voice muffled and nasal with spent tears, 'is where pain and its suffering are imprisoned inside a building.' I'm struck by the poetry of her words.

'So, by bringing Naani home, we've tried to release some of that pain, isn't it?' I say, tucking her wayward hair behind her ears. I'm trying to make her feel better, but the truth is that the suffering that rose like a miasma in the hospital has followed us home, and I know without being told that the way the home nurse is treating her naani as a body, just a body, brushing its teeth, applying Hexigel, replacing the BiPAP mask, laying it back on the angled hospital bed, is difficult for my poet child to stomach.

'This side, Auntyji,' Manju, the sweet-natured day attendant will say, deftly flipping my mother to one side, her hands gentle, her round face shining with sweat, as she sponges her with long, practised strokes as I stand by, ready to help.

'She is remarkably well preserved for her age,' I remembered the words of one of her doctors. Remarkably well preserved. But that didn't save her. In the end, the very air she inhaled, consumed her.

'Open your mouth, *aaaaah*,' Nilu, the night attendant will say, archly, in a high falsetto, her hands rough and quick, as she swipes a dollop of Hexigel with an efficient, indifferent forefinger inside my mother's mouth after hurriedly brushing her teeth. I often want to smack Nilu, for her detachment, the shortcuts she takes, for her very presence, her emotional absence, for the times she looks out of the window, bored, or WhatsApps away furiously as my mother struggles to breathe or call her name. For the bedsore that she doesn't point out in time, for the ungentle way she sometimes angles the bed, the sharp voice she sometimes uses when she thinks no one is listening. But when my own daughter points out the same things to me, I console her, defending Nilu.

'She's helping us. We are all emotionally exhausted. At least she is saving us physical exhaustion,' I tell my daughter, who is unhappy with the situation, with the disorienting knowledge that such a terminal illness lives inside the very first person who held her at birth, the one who later delighted her by telling her secrets and stories of her mother's childhood. Most recently they have bonded over laughter – at my daughter's mother and my mother's daughter – together.

I stroke her curls gently, waiting for her to process what I'm saying as I point to the nurse. 'See how young she is? It's not a fun job, being a hospice nurse, being placed from one dying patient to another. I bet she didn't choose it. It must be emotionally exhausting. She is emotionally exhausted.' She is emotionally dead, I think but don't say.

My anger wasn't directed at Nilu, personally. It was equally directed at the world outside my mother's window, a world that continued, oblivious to the laboured breathing and suffocating misery inside. The vegetable seller who called out his wares, the people who bought from him, the Uber driver who stopped outside, the man who got in to go – to work? The airport? It was directed at the pharmacist who ran out of adult diapers, at the phlebotomist who arrived late to take her blood sample, at the physiotherapist who looked sadly at the spirometer as her lung function declined, at the lab which informed us that the EGFR tests were negative, so the first line of treatment, our best chance, would likely fail.

I can't remember the exact moment my anger coalesces into a smouldering, simmering rage, rumbling subliminally like a storm about to burst. Anger at the suddenness of my mother's diagnosis, anger at the way I find out, on a glittering Diwali night when I am already fuming at the firecrackers polluting Delhi's sulphurous sky. Irrational anger at the unequal power dynamic of the doctor–patient relationship; anger at the manner in which my mother is sometimes treated like a billable client rather than a patient, anger at nurses, doctors, attendants and cleaners, and other people in uniform, who keep coming in and waking her up, just as she has dozed off; anger at the look of hope on my mother's face, every time someone in a white coat comes towards her, at her plaintive sentence series repeated every day at first, then less often. 'I only feel a little breathless, a little tired. Are you sure the test is correct?'

And now? I hadn't heard it for days, now. Not since we brought her back in the ambulance through the narrow streets of Saket, up the black granite stairs into her new room, the one with the blue accented wall to match her elegant 'arty' quilted bedspread. Words so full of hope, so soaked in denial.

Afterwards, when a cough develops, when the breathlessness keeps her up and I order an inclined backrest to ease her nights, and later, when her angled hospice bed takes over the job, and she stops asking the question, my unreasonable, inarticulate anger bursts and drains away like a pus-filled sore, leaving in its place a resigned sorrow.

At first, my mother had the will, but the demands were so exhausting. We had so much to learn, but no idea how much. Between breathing tubes and machine screens blinking and beeping, talking to us in a tinny vocabulary we didn't understand, between spirometers to measure and improve lung function and learning that respiratory physiotherapy was actually a profession, learning to read oxygen saturation levels and take blood pressure with an analogue machine, between all of this, somewhere along the way, I stopped being just a daughter and became more of a caregiver.

It isn't as if I wanted that role. But day after endless day of watching her suffocate and feeling helpless to ease her suffering, I just forgot how to be a daughter. To just sit with her, talk to her, share her fears, help her articulate them. She – we – were unprepared to engage in any end-of-life talk. Always somewhat secretive, she didn't end up sharing her innermost thoughts. Meanwhile, we were all so busy trying to ease her physical discomfort, that none of us thought to empathetically engage her in comforting conversations that would disclose her inner thoughts, her private wishes.

Over time, she spoke as little as she could get away with, sometimes sulking silently, at other times muttering angrily as her electrolyte levels fluctuated and low-sodium-inspired fits of depression or alternately aggression fuelled her days.

In the middle of those dark days, I recall one vivid afternoon that stands out as an island of incandescent happiness in a roiling sea of grief. That day, my mother tried to sing, gesturing to me to join her. Her voice was a bare croak as we sang together. She switched seamlessly from song to song, melodies I remembered from my childhood.

Her day attendant, nurse and I had moved her from her bed and out of the blue-walled room into the yellow-walled living room, so that she could recline on a chair. The weak December sunlight streamed in to create a halo around her as the round-faced Manju tenderly massaged her swollen feet. The image of my mother that luminous afternoon, whisper-singing, without her mask, lives inside me, flickering like a shiny, jagged piece of glass at the bottom of a muddy stream.

The optimistic, buoyant mantras that doctors told us to chant to her 'you'll get better, soon, very soon', were false, yet, we had no other. I truly wish we had understood the emotional trauma she was undergoing even as she continued living in deliberate denial of her inevitable acceleration towards oblivion. Understood it so that we could hold her hand through it. But we were all so busy processing our own feelings of sadness, anger, loss and emptiness that we defaulted into the common script prescribed by others.

The last time I had a semi-lucid conversation with her, I observed a new look descend on her face; the grim look of someone who has come to terms with a private compromise and a fiercely private grief.

Sometimes we sisters cried, huddled together. At other times we fought until the walls vibrated with our rage. Emotions raged, anger swelled, quick, extraordinary, almost disconnected from the cause, which could be anything. Who was supposed to order the adult diapers, whose turn was it to monitor her medical chart, had someone fed her tender coconut water already? Once, an angry showdown was even planned in advance, enraged WhatsApp messages from my eldest sister warning us all what to expect. It was New Year's Eve. The last night of

2017. That night, my mother had her first serious bradycardia episode. An overseas house guest, an in-law of my sister jump-started her heart with the epinephrine she was carrying in her doctor's bag.

Once, my mother was a young girl, with hopes and dreams and ambitions. Now I watch her sit, consumed and spent, an old woman in an angled bed, her life punctuated by fits of coughing and low-sodium-induced rage. We are watching her dying and she is watching us watch her, helplessly.

Some memories never leave our bones; they sink into our very marrow, like oxygen in the air we breathe, giving us life. And soon, like salt in the sea, they become an elemental part of us. The memories of our mothers and our fathers, our first and forever friends, whom we love in the most primal way. And when they are gone, their absence becomes their presence.

10

My Mother, Your Mother

January 2018

'Didi, *paani*?'

I shake my head: No. Her eyes are red. She's known my mother for almost nine years, from the time she first came to work in the house soon after I moved back from California. She had wanted to attend the cremation, but her husband didn't allow her. Women aren't supposed to go to cremation grounds. She waits, then leaves the glass of water on the dining table, where I'm sitting, and returns to the kitchen. I drink it absent-mindedly.

I've just returned from the crematorium, a short ride completed in silence, and don't know what to do with myself now. There is no script with directions on how to react to big, momentous occasions in your life that you experience for the first time, even if they were expected.

The house is completely silent. Everyone is somewhere else. There is still an hour to go for lunch. I decide to go for a walk. Maybe I will feel better. Maybe I will feel. I have learnt to get my cardio exercise at the optimum time of the afternoon during Delhi's polluted winters so that I'm not imprisoned indoors for the duration of the season. I step out into the dappled sunshine, weak for mid-January. My neighbour accosts me almost instantly, even before I've strapped on my pollution mask.

'Hi! How are you?' I debate this question silently. How am I?

'I haven't seen you around recently. All well?' she continues breezily. She doesn't know.

Do I want to tell her? If I don't, and just stand around and chat for a few minutes, perhaps I can pretend that nothing has changed. It may help me to feel that my mother is still alive. Or I can tell her the truth. 'I'm fine. My mother just died. I'm back from electrocuting her body in a dark, metal cavern. Everything feels raw. My life is now forever divided into "before Mom" and "after Mom". I don't know what to do next.' But the words stick in my throat, their newness scratching like a first-time contact lens in the eye. All I know is that I don't want to make eye contact with anyone, I want to avoid finding pity in their eyes. I hurry past her, with a brief nod and a gesture, not caring if it looks rude. I resolve firmly not to think about this morning, or about the last three months. I want to feel peace.

At the corner of my street – there are 148 homes in my neighbourhood, neatly laid out around small parks – I walk past a white-haired security guard, the one with the crooked smile whom I always see drinking tea, and he raises his hand in a half salute, chai in his other hand. I raise my hand back. I know him because he is one of the guards I have bought thermals, a blanket and a set of pollution masks for last winter. He and some of his friends used to burn leaves, twigs, trash to keep themselves warm and spend their hours on duty coughing into the smoke. I've had many conversations with him, the last one just before Diwali a few months ago.

'Do you know this smoke will get into your lungs and gradually kill you?' I asked.

'Yes. It's not so bad when I burn wood, but when I burn plastic or rubber, I feel short of breath.'

Oh god. He burns plastic, I thought. *Other watchmen and security guards must be doing the same, all across the city, across the country.* No wonder we have microplastics in our air!

Two years later, when I interview Dr Jamie Schauer, the scientific adviser to the US embassy, and he tells me that they have found dioxins and microplastics in Delhi's air, I'm no longer surprised. Dioxins are endocrine disruptors and lead to birth defects, decreased fertility, immunity suppression and reproductive disorders. Unfortunately, instead of curtailing plastics, the Delhi government in 2015 has inaugurated a new market, a 'toxic mall' in Tikri Kalan village,[1] which the EPCA will later identify as a hotspot for the presence of lethal pollutants due to the open burning of waste that can't be recycled.[2] 'If you feel short of breath, why do you burn them?' I'd persisted.

'*Kya karein, memsaab. Thand mein thithurtein hain.* What to do, madam? We shiver in the cold otherwise.'

'Why don't you dress more warmly, add another layer?'

'More warmly than this?' He had gestured towards his uniform, a knitted sweater, its synthetic newness unable to hide its thinness. I felt the guilt of privilege pinch me and had maintained a guilty silence. 'I wear my warmest clothes... This is new, see? But the cold is chilling.' I remember smelling the tobacco *khaini* he was chewing, even though I stood at least 3 feet away.

'What if I gave you some warm blankets?' I asked, struck by an idea. His heavy-lidded eyes, tranquilized by the tobacco and chuna, limestone, suddenly opened wide.

I thought about asking the Residents' Welfare Association (RWA) to give blankets to all the neighbourhood guards for Diwali, and getting the residents to fit their guard shacks with inexpensive electric heaters, like they did coolers during the summer.

We all see how people who are exposed to the elements because of their work or their living conditions burn anything they can lay their hands on – trash, leaves biomass, plastic, rubber tyres – for warmth in the winter, which adds to the pollution. It's unfair to ask them to stop burning trash for warmth without providing them with an alternative – but imagine the cleaner air everyone would breathe with this one, small change? The non-profit organization Chintan had estimated in February 2015 that at least 30,000 small fires are burnt every night from November to February in Delhi, usually by security guards trying to stay warm in chilly weather.

'Burning fires, locally and across the city, pumps poison into us all. Most of all, it pumps poison into those who seek warmth from it,' according to Chintan founder and director Bharati.[3] Burning rubber is even worse. Western countries impose fines on burning rubber tyres.[4] In India, the open burning of rubber tyres has been banned by the National Green Tribunal (NGT) since 2014,[5] but I'm not sure anyone follows it. Certainly, it is not enforced.

However, RWAs are notoriously political and I didn't succeed with my request. Instead, I distributed limited numbers of blankets, masks and warm clothes among the guards.

Today, again, I point to my own mask. *Where's yours*, I gesture as I pass by him and he points to his chai, indicating that if he wore one he'd be going without his tea. I smile, but he can't see that, so I wave again. This is our routine, and it feels strangely comforting. Sometimes, the comfort of strangers can be immensely consoling.

I see Shanti with her large broom. The municipal sweeper waits courteously for me to pass. Dust motes surround her – she has been sweeping the road, an activity that is as energetic as it is useless. I've told her hundreds of times that sweeping up dust is bad for health – and of no use as a solution for pollution, unless those little mounds she creates are compacted into bricks or somehow 'fixed' into the ground. She understands this when I explain, but has to do her job, she has told me. She isn't wearing the mask I have given her, but has her sari pallu wrapped around her face so I can only see her eyes. They crinkle at me, and she points to her sari. I wonder dully what she is indicating, then suddenly recognize it as my mother's. I remember now that she had given some of her cotton saris to Shanti when my father and she had come to spend a day with me, something they would try and do a few times a month. It hurts to think I will never make that uniquely weak, milky tea that she loves, ever again. I try to blank out my thoughts. I don't want to think about my mother.

I walk past her, past the pista-green tiled, three-walled concrete garbage *dhalao* just before the turn into my lane. I notice three large metal barrows perched next to each other, labelled clearly as '*jaivik*' (organic), '*geela*' (wet) and '*sookha*' (dry). I'm surprised to see this, because one of the things I've been trying to work on through CFA has been garbage segregation. I've never seen these barrows before – but then, the last few months have passed by in a blur of soul-crushing grief and burning anger. Perhaps these barrows sneaked past my inert eyes.

Delhi is among the greenest cities I've seen in India – but with the canopy of trees come leaves. Huge quantities of them. Until 2016, burning leaves wasn't even illegal. I feel certain that Bram, Gardiner's son's, breathing troubles were exacerbated by their proximity to the zoo, where leaves were openly burnt. Since 2016, burning of leaves has been made illegal.[6] As I continue to walk, I also notice that some local parks have large wire baskets installed to collect leaves to be composted. I recall meeting some RWA members in 2016 and asking them to implement garbage segregation as well as leaf composting, something I had recently begun experimenting with in my own home. I had enthusiastically shared my resources – I had just started using the Daily Dump's terracotta *khamba* – and a quirkily named recycling company called PomPom,[7] which aimed to convert your 'trash to cash'. Unfortunately, PomPom folded; my home composting flourished, however. My household waste dropped by almost 80 per cent – and I never had to buy organic compost again. I had wanted to scale this to every house in the neighbourhood, but I hadn't bargained for internal RWA politics. Deciding this was a snake pit I was not going to put my hand in, I had withdrawn swiftly. I'm glad to see that the changed law has forced my RWA to install the leaf composter.

Delhi generates anywhere between 9,500–10,000 metric tonnes of garbage every day, of which its four landfills have the capacity to absorb 7,000–8,000 tonnes. Where does the rest of it go? It is mostly burnt – illegally, because garbage burning is outlawed – its smoke adding to the already heavy pollution load Delhi's air carries. Research shows open burning of 2 to 3 per cent of Delhi's municipal solid waste occurs each day. Municipal solid waste burning contributes nearly 10 per cent of PM10 and PM2.5 to ambient air in winters, says Bharati, and adds to the implosions of methane and fires at the landfills. As anyone who drives by can clearly see, the Ghazipur and Bhalswa landfills have been burning silently for years. Still under the radar are the waste-to-energy (WtE, or, as I like to refer to them, waste-to-pollution) incinerators.

There are currently eight WtE in India, including three in Delhi – in Ghazipur, Bawana and Sukhdev Vihar-Okhla. The one in Okhla is located just 35 metres from residential areas in upscale South Delhi, putting the health and lives of more than half a million residents in danger. This is despite the government's Municipal Solid Waste Management guidelines,[8] which state that a WtE plant of this capacity needs to have a buffer zone of 500 metres around the zone. For some homes in this residential area though, the plant is literally a stone's throw away.

Local residents have been fighting against this for almost 10 years, refusing to bear the risks of dioxins and saying they don't want electricity at the cost of their lungs.[9] In 2009, they filed a case in Delhi High Court, which was transferred to the NGT in January 2013 after 28 futile hearings. Representatives from Delhi government failed to appear before the tribunal to defend permissions given, but despite that and despite escalating protests, including those by waste pickers who said such plants are a blow to their livelihood, the NGT in 2017 decided in favour of incineration[10] and allowed them to continue. The CPCB told the NGT in 2017 that it doesn't have in-house mechanisms in its laboratories to analyse dioxins and furans,[11] but I recall reading a detailed report in the *Wire* that said paradoxically that two CPCB investigation reports in April and September 2013 showed high levels of dioxins and furans as well as particulate matter. The emissions of these two carcinogens was one of the primary contentions of the petitioners – they were found to be in excess of the standards on several occasions. Inspections carried out on 28 to 31 March 2013 had found them to be present in amounts 120 times above levels considered safe.[12]

'In one of the protests against the plant recently, we had many doctors join us,' says Huma Hashim, president of the NGO Centre for Changing

Societies and a resident of Sukhdev Vihar. 'They joined specifically because they observed an increase in the past few years in the number of patients suffering from cancer, asthma and tuberculosis from nearby areas.' Knowing all this now makes me wonder what else we're breathing.

I ask Karthik Ganesan, an engineer who works in energy and air pollution and lives quite close to the Okhla plant what he thinks. 'Living within a couple of kilometres of the Okhla WtE plant, there are many days when the air is putrid with the smell of "burning" waste. It is invariably during the nights. Is it poisonous? I don't know but it certainly prevents me from stepping out or having my windows open. It can be quite suffocating,' he says.

Burning garbage is neither clean nor renewable.[13] Whether open trash burning or municipal solid waste incineration, it has a negative impact on health[14] though the jury is still out on the formation of dioxins and furans.[15] The science may say it is okay – and Singapore is a shining example of how to use WtE well – but it really depends on the technology used, its efficiency as well as how well WtE plants follow regulations. The Okhla plant doesn't seem to be doing either; the plant has been incinerating 1,500 tonnes per day against the approved 750 tonnes.[16]

The International Solid Waste Association, a global association of waste management companies, is clear in its evaluation: 'Municipal solid waste incineration is only considered suitable in "mature" waste management systems, where the waste collection is working properly, where the calorific value has a certain minimum level and where the required tipping fees are affordable. India fails on all counts,' *Wire* concludes.

Even the globally respected Environmental Justice Atlas,[17] a teaching, networking and advocacy resource that crowdsources and interactively maps ecological conflict, lists the Okhla WtE as environmentally unjust, calling out the Timarpur-Okhla Waste Management Co. Pvt. Ltd and the Jindal Urban Infrastructure Limited. It cites health impacts from air pollution as well as dioxins among impacts which include socio-economic injustice, biodiversity loss, soil contamination and global warming.

Like most environmental battles in India, there is no sign of resolution. This battle will continue until 2019, when the Environment Ministry will tell the CPCB to carry out an 'ecological damage assessment' and formulate a remediation plan for the plant.

Despite the controversy and the CSE's *Down to Earth* magazine's indictment of WtE plants in January 2019,[18] the court-mandated government-constituted EPCA, which includes the CSE director general, in its special report on air pollution hotspots in the NCR will recommend WtE plants for Hapur and Meerut Nagar Nigam. The report states that 'the proposal…must be explore[d] on top priority.[19] There are plans to set up 56 of these across the country.

But even if we ignore the WtE plants and focus on garbage segregation at source – which doesn't exist – Indian landfills are imploding.

The University of Virginia's Yamuna River Project[20] is an interdisciplinary research programme with the objective of revitalizing the ecology of the Yamuna river in New Delhi. The website dedicated to the project has a section on landfills that seems to have the most accurate information on Delhi's landfills.[21] When the landfills first started to grow, they were not supposed to exceed a height of 15 metres. Now, the tallest one in Okhla stands at 48.5 metres over 40 acres but serves only 18 per cent of Delhi's population. The landfill at Ghazipur, at 45 metres over 71 acres, serves 30 per cent, and the one at Bhalswa, at 40 metres over 71 acres, serves over 50 per cent of Delhi's population. A fourth landfill at Narela serves the remaining 2 per cent. These landfills are hazardous – especially to residents who live nearby[22] who suffer not just from odour, but also health harm from the pollution.

On an average day, 1,000 tonnes of waste is dumped at and distributed among each of these landfills. According to the website, 10,000 tonnes of waste is collected daily and transported up these landfill mountains by trucks 600 to 650 times a day. Between 190 and 246 tonnes of waste is burnt daily contributing to between 7 and 9 per cent of air pollution. By around 8 p.m., fuelled by heat and decomposition, many sections of the landfills begin to burn, sending toxic pollutants into the atmosphere and the city. In addition, 1.4 million tonnes of toxic leachate flows into the Yamuna river, contaminating the city's groundwater.

The startling fact is that the estimate of Delhi's daily solid waste being 10,000 metric tonnes – roughly the weight of the Eiffel Tower – is from four years ago. Official figures predict that by 2021, the waste produced by the city will almost double to 18,000 tonnes a day.

With these thoughts running through my head, I adjust my mask to fit tightly around my mouth and nose. Masks are ineffective if they don't fit exactly, but the backflow from the exhaled carbon dioxide is so uncomfortable that I often switch to less effective nasal filters. I have an array of masks now, with single valves, double valves. Exactly two years later, when a respiratory pandemic caused by a novel coronavirus called Covid-19 sweeps the world and there is a shortage of masks in the initial days, I will have more than enough variety for my family, including unused ones that my mother never eventually wore.

Perhaps I should have insisted more with my mother, forced her to at least wear nose filters, even though I'm painfully aware that masks or filters aren't even close to a solution for air pollution, nor even a preferred or efficient mitigant. These are just survival tactics – and one way to make an invisible problem visible. I try not to think if masks would have protected my mother from getting cancer. I try to block all thoughts from my mind, especially of her. My mother, your mother, all our mothers dying in this city, which is itself dying, from its polluted air.

I see Dular, our local picker-upper of all things that residents want to dispose of and are unsure how to. He is walking away from the *dhalao* and I increase my speed to catch up with him. A migrant from Bangladesh who looks older than his age, with blunt features and a pleasant smile, he lives in the slum behind the neighbourhood.

I met Dular for the first time when we pruned the overgrown bamboo that was sheltering rats in our backyard. I had tried to find out from the RWA office where exactly I should responsibly dispose of garden trimmings and was asked to contact the municipal office, which asked me to call the horticulture department, which asked me to check with my RWA. My gardener, taking pity on me, had introduced me to Dular.

'He takes care of everything,' the gardener had said, indicating that I should stop finding out about the 'right' thing to do and just do what everyone else does.

From a brief conversation, I found out that Dular had been unofficially servicing this neighbourhood since 1977. He still had no identity card, even though he was subcontracted by the Dakshin Dilli Swachh Initiatives Limited (DDSIL) – created specially to serve as a concessionaire of the South Delhi Municipal Corporation which undertakes collection and transportation of municipal solid waste – to sweep the streets and clean the drains.

Now, I approach Dular breathlessly and ask him about the three barrows. He confirms they are recent but has no idea which one is for what. He smiles apologetically, his weather-beaten face crinkling into furrows. It is as I thought. The on-ground training, the grassroots awareness is still missing. Even those households segregating their garbage are doing so uselessly – it is all getting mixed up at the community garbage level. I try to explain the difference between the three barrows to Dular before walking away.

It is Makar Sankranti, when, as my father explained to me, the shadow of the sun is neither long nor short. I have walked around for an hour after cremating the one who gave birth to me, trying not to think of her. But ultimately, I have to return home to face the rest of my life without my mother. Everything reminds me of her. The exuberant pink flowers on the bougainvillea bush cascading down the front gate remind me of the exact shade of her favourite sari; the unique fragrance of the tiny, star-shaped orange-and-white flowers clustered unseasonably on the harsringar tree in the driveway smells like her favourite perfume. I feel a sudden surge of loneliness, a sense of loss and grief so sharp that I need to sit down and take a breath. But at least I'm *feeling* again.

Then, unexpectedly, I am swamped by guilt. I remember the day my mother's cancer diagnosis was finally, irrevocably confirmed. That day, when all of us were unhappily leaving her house to return to our families, our worst fears confirmed, it was me she had asked to stay back. 'Jyoti, you will know what is really happening,' she had said. 'You know all these medical things very well. You will tell it to me straight, as it is. As it really is. Come, sit with me.' And I hadn't.

I had made up some excuse and left. Left her alone with her thoughts, her concerns, her worries, her fears, instead of walking her through them. Why did I do that, I agonize now. I know it was partly because I didn't have the vocabulary to talk to a mother dying so actively. But I was also confused, and my confusion was confounded by the fact that we sisters were bitterly divided about whether to tell her or not. On the one hand, our mother had the right to know. On the other, there was no point. Her illness was terminal – why tell her that and take away her hope? Today, the guilt swoops back to haunt me. That afternoon was the last chance I'd had to be alone with her, just the two of us, before she became the main actor in an absurdly tragic play, permanently surrounded by hovering attendants, nurses and doctors. And I'd let it pass. My last words to my first love had been false. I had failed her. Another thing I know now, with cruel hindsight, adding to the heaviness of guilt and regret, is that I should never, *never* have encouraged her to try chemotherapy. It only increased her suffering exponentially and destroyed her quality of life.

In India, these are the questions that trouble us when a terminal illness sentences our loved ones to death. When my friend Anita Nayar's father got unexpectedly diagnosed with terminal liver cancer – it is always unexpected – the biggest question troubling the three siblings, after the initial shock wore off, was whether they should tell him, or even tell their mother. It was harder for Anita, since she was a doctor and knew more clearly what lay ahead. Today, if I had known how little time my mother had left, that *we* had left together, I would have made sure I found the right, true words to reassure her.

I know them now. A bald, overweight end-of-life doctor, a part of our home hospice package taught me the basics of the vocabulary I needed to approach the finality of death, but by then, it was too late.

It wasn't just these things – the lack of courage and words to reassure her, the bad medical decisions. Later, when her dependence on the BiPAP machine increased, when I saw the muscle and fat falling off her body, leaving skin and bone, her restlessness, anger and depression growing, the increasing weariness in her eyes, when I watched her being stripped of her dignity, a little bit every day, I had prayed for her to be released from the suffering. I had prayed for my mother to die.

That was better, I felt, than to become less and less every day, die in small parts, in full public view, with no privacy, as people cleaned her, fed and medicated her and talked about her in the third person in her presence.

This is how it happened. One afternoon, a few days before she died, just after I had seen the doctor out after his regular bi-weekly visit, I went to my father's room to tell him I was leaving.

I found my father sitting still on his bed, eyes closed, his mouth moving in silent prayer. Hearing me, he opened cloudy eyes.

'What did the doctor say?' he asked.

'The antibiotics have kicked in,' I said. 'Her chest is clear. She's better.'

But she's not going to recover, I didn't say.

'But she's not going to recover,' he said. We looked at each other. There were no words. His eyes were filled with a pain that I could only vaguely fathom. He looked away. When, after 63 years together, a part of you disappears, that is also a sort of death, I thought. Although he and I were joined in our grief, I knew my pain was different from his. We are all outsiders to each other's pain.

'What are you praying for? What should we be praying for?' I asked. I heard the tremor in my voice, and cleared my throat, embarrassed. My father turned to look back at me, the weak sun from the window directly behind him, turning his shock of cotton-ball hair into a halo of brilliant white. He hadn't combed it, I noted. His chin looked unshaven too.

'Jaana toh hai hi. Sabko jaana hai,' he said quietly. 'We all have to go. Myself included. Pray for her release. Help her leave.'

What was he saying? That I should pray for my mother's death? Or did he mean that we should engineer it, find a way to let her go? We'd heard so many stories from people in recent days, including well-meaning cancer relief organizations, about palliative and end-of-life care. I felt confused, but remained silent.

His words hung in the air between us. We both knew she wasn't going to recover, and we didn't want a death for her that wouldn't finish, a death that keeps dying every day, in an endless loop, extending suffering.

And yet.

Yet, this period of bardo-like limbo was giving us time to prepare for her departure. It was for us, not for her.

The next day, I went to the temple, but when the priest asked me how my mother was, I shook my head, unable to speak.

'*Woh paar lagaayega,*' he said, without my uttering a single word. I took it as a benediction.

I'm thinking of all this as I wash my hands, surprised to find that I'm hungry. Guilt and regret are emotions I can still deal with; it is the relief I am unable to understand. The pernicious combination of relief and guilt has never felt as painful as now, when we are sitting at the dining table for lunch once I get home.

'Am I a bad daughter?' I ask my husband and son baldly, without preamble.

Both look surprised.

'No, you're not. Why do you say that?' My son sounds genuinely confused.

'First, I couldn't feel anything,' I say aloud. 'Then I felt regret and guilt. Now I feel relief. What's wrong with me? Why can't I feel pain? Grief?'

'Mom, you've been in pain for so long, I think you'd already let Naani go,' says my son.

'You had been grieving for her even when she was alive. I don't think you even realized it,' says my husband quietly, his brown eyes watchful. This seems to have become his normal expression.

'I have?'

Yes, nods my 16-year-old. I look at him. He has grown up so quickly in these last couple of months. 'You're not a bad daughter, Mom. You're not. You had already let her go,' he says.

'When? When did I let her go? Did I give up on her? Did I let her go when I gave up on her?'

He's thinking now.

'After those tests, remember? The EGFR tests?' he says. 'At least,' he amends, 'you went into a shell.'

A shell. A small, dark place. That is where I wanted to be right now. My son persists, quietly, forcefully. 'You've been in emotional pain, Mom. For so long. You've been suffering with her. Maybe that's why you're feeling relief? She's not suffering any more,' he says.

Between the lightness of relief and the weight of guilt, I swing like a pendulum, a Trishanku in my own private hell. I wished now that I hadn't wasted my time in the medical caring, the double-checking and second-guessing of doctors and a broken healthcare system. If I hadn't spent all that time on the phone and the internet and in serpentine lines to receive reports and get approvals and signatures, maybe I could have just sat and talked to her more, acknowledging her wishes, her dreams and her regrets, singing with her, to her. Somewhere along the way, I had turned from a daughter to a caregiver, and today I was back to being a daughter. It was the caregiver who was feeling relief. Relief from the responsibility. It was the daughter feeling the guilt.

Later that afternoon, when I go back to the crematorium to collect my mother's ashes, her *asthis*, bones, more memories come rushing at me. I walk in to see several wood pyres still burning. So much smoke, so much pollution, my brain observes subconsciously, but for once, I don't care. The electric-fired crematorium is towards the back. I wonder whether more people would choose this option if they made it more aesthetic, less horrific.

I see others who have suffered loss, wandering around like me, cocooned in our individual sorrows, and I recognize the empty look in their eyes. We are each looking for things that are no longer there; we are each looking for direction.

The men who sift through the bones of the dead are toward, the back, closer to the metal cavern where I don't want to go. They are wearing clothes of no colour, wearing them like shrouds, stoic men with dead eyes. One of them sees me and comes up to me. I hand over the small, pink slip that has my mother's name on it. He gestures to me to follow him. I have to buy a *ghada,* an urn, he says. They have some in a little shop up front. I choose a warm terracotta one over the lurid green and blue plastic ones. I buy a red cloth, a *mouli*. The man takes me back towards the metal cavern. The rays of the afternoon sun touch me warmly through the smoke of the burning pyres as I wait, my eyes stinging, my chest tight. I'm unprepared for the unsettled feeling that clings to me like a lingering dream state. He brings some ashes to me, and along with them, a sieve. This is all that is left of my mother. My sister's suspicious words – how will you know which ashes are our mother's – resound in my own doubtful, sceptical mind. How do I know there is no mistake?

I can't know. I have to accept. I have to surrender. I surrender.

When he sifts and pours the ashes into the urn, the fine, dry powder rises up in the air around me and I inhale deeply. I want to keep her with me, within me. Everything I've learnt about inhaling ash and particulate matter seems unimportant at that moment.

11

Every Day, Everywhere

January 2018

I cross the road from the crematorium, holding the terracotta urn with my mother's ashes, its mouth tied with a thin, red cloth. Smoke from the always-smouldering pyres rises behind me and blends silently into the Delhi air, already heavy with particulate matter, construction dust, road dust and vehicular exhaust.

'Got your mask?' asks my husband, and the sudden, painful image of a silicon BiPAP mask attached to the delicate nose and generous mouth of the woman who gave birth to me and whose ashes I'm now holding flashes before my eyes.

'Your pollution mask. You'll need it,' he clarifies soberly as I stare at him, dazed.

I've forgotten to bring my pollution mask. We are going to Haridwar to immerse my mother's ashes in the Ganga and I'm waiting for the hired Tempo Traveller van to pick me up along with the rest of the immediate family. It will be just us, her four daughters, my father and my cousin – my father's late brother's son, who has been designated to perform the last rituals , usually carried out by the eldest son according to Hindu dharma. My father shares a close bond with him.

'Shall we wait in the car?' asks my husband. I debate between sitting inside the mini gas chamber of a car idling in traffic and standing on the main road, breathing in Delhi's air, before consciously choosing the latter. It will be marginally less toxic.

It has been a week since my mother's body disappeared into that dark space inside this crematorium, a week since I last heard her voice, touched her hands, stroked her hair, saw her disappear behind her mask. Loneliness has lived inside me like a persistent virus, and, yet, I have felt like I'm waiting for something momentous to happen. But what can be more momentous than this loss?

I climb into the Traveller when it arrives, and my husband hands me the urn. He and my son have excused themselves from the ritual. They don't believe in religious ceremonies and I don't believe in insisting on their presence if they don't want to come. One brother-in-law – the one who was closest to my mother – has decided to travel with us. He likes to call himself our fifth sister and is more seasoned than us in navigating the end of a life and loss, having lost his mother to cancer some years ago. I now wish that I had heeded his words when he advocated spending time just chatting with her in my mother's last days. Only, I hadn't known they would so quickly become her last days. I don't want to look back now, but I'm also not looking forward to the next two days. They are going to be filled with solemn funerary ceremonies meant to release my mother's soul, make her passing smoother; serious, formal, rigid rituals that I don't understand and I'm not sure I believe in. All I know is that first we will immerse her ashes – do the *asthi visarjan* – and then there will be the *pind daan*, performed to allow the soul to transcend into the afterlife.

I don't know what my mother would have wanted – she was an iconoclast, and we never talked about her passing; she was so vivaciously alive. But I'm not taking any chances that her soul won't be at peace.

'*Mukti dham*,' declares the arch above the entrance to the crematorium. Mukti. Release, salvation. I watch those words recede as the Traveller begins moving with a little lurch.

I sit in the seat across from my youngest sister, trying to overcome this surreal feeling of the whole family being together in a van heading out of town, almost like a holiday, but without the person whose uncontainable vitality and large presence made our family whole. I look over at my father, sitting a couple of seats behind me, and find myself looking into old eyes, grey with cataract and sorrow, his untrimmed bushy white brows falling over them, screening his inner pain.

'Okay?' I mouth across the seats.

Okay, he nods back.

I slump back in my seat. It will take us four hours to reach Haridwar. I've never enjoyed road travel through northern India. Dusty, potholed roads, plastic scattered everywhere and slow navigation through congested 'toilet towns' has taken away the fun I used to have when travelling through these areas as a child. We will pass through Meerut, my mother's birthplace, past sugarcane and paddy fields, on roads that will throw up more dust than dust storms, softening all focus and dimming all light. Five years ago, I would have thought of this as a romantic, nostalgia-tinted image of rural India. Today, I know this haze is silently and unobtrusively sickening and killing the village folk.

Then there will be the long wait at train crossings and perhaps a couple of breaks for tea. I settle down and start singing softly to myself through the lump blocking my throat, trying to remember my mother's favourite bhajans, devotional songs set to classical ragas. I wish I had thought to record her singing them in her unique style. I try to remember the words and tunes but when I notice my soft singing is making my sister cry, I fall silent and turn my gaze to the window.

And there it is. Rural India, just as I remember it from childhood trips with my parents. Not much has changed outwardly in 25 years, except that there is more plastic. Women now carry water in garish plastic receptacles instead of the terracotta of the past. More plastic litter – the wrappers of bhujia, chips and noodle packets are strewn everywhere. I wish we could make the companies selling these items in plastic pouches responsible for their disposal. We pass by fields, huts and luridly painted brick homes, sugarcane fields alternating with wheat fields.

I know that burning of biomass for domestic use is a large contributor to the haze outside. Most Indian villages cook with biomass – cow dung cakes, wood, twigs, coal. They use kerosene for lighting. As many as seven independent studies have proven household sources to be the single largest source of ambient air pollution in the country.

The Collaborative Clean Air Policy Centre – a brainchild of Dr Kirk Smith, professor of global environmental health at the University of Berkeley – specifically states that burning of solid fuels like firewood for cooking and heating, in millions of households across the country, contributes anywhere between 22 and 52 per cent to the PM2.5 load of ambient outdoor air pollution.[1] Even a median value of 30 per cent is much higher than any of the other sources contributing to particulate air pollution, including vehicular pollution from transportation and microparticulates from power plants or factories.

Globally, around 2.8 billion people continue to rely on solid fuels such as wood, dung, crop residues and coal for cooking. 780 million of them live in India, as per a 2015 report by India's Health and Family Welfare Ministry on air pollution and health-related issues[2] partly authored by Dr Smith and Bhargav.

In simple, traditional stoves, biomass combustion produces a range of toxic products resulting from incomplete combustion during cooking, including PM2.5 that is roughly equal to burning about 400 cigarettes an hour. Given that this occurs in places where people are present, a large percentage of the population (particularly women and children who tend to be in the kitchen the most) is exposed to this source of pollution, the report says.

In fact, eliminating *only* household (indoor) sources of air pollution in India would be enough to bring national outdoor air pollution exposure below the Indian national ambient air pollution standards, Dr Smith has told me more than once. 'It may be counter-intuitive, but it's true,' he says, smiling at my surprise. 'Actually, just clean cooking stoves would allow India to meet its emissions standards.' Today, I can see for myself how this strangely beautiful misty miasma that shrouds the northern plains arises from the wood and cow dung cakes burnt three times a day for family meals.

Learning about air pollution from the most erudite and experienced researchers is markedly different from living and breathing it. When I first started learning about air pollution in 2014, I thought it was an urban problem – even specifically a Delhi problem, formed by the perfect storm of its geographical and urban misfortunes. But I have come to understand that pollution isn't just rampant in the Indo-Gangetic plain. It is all-pervasive.

Even in coastal metros like Mumbai, Kolkata and Chennai, is the pollution load is so heavy that even the sea breeze can't blow it away, nor can Bengaluru's frequent rain wash it away. I now see how the countryside fares no better. It is as much a rural problem as an urban one – only the source differs.

I finally understand what happens when you layer theoretical knowledge with actual experience. Looking outside, through the diaphanous beauty of the horizon, I recognize the malignant miasma hidden in the golden dust and the gossamer purple haze and I wonder what it smells like. I part the van's shiny brown synthetic curtains to try and open the window but it is stuck.

I remember Josh telling me how he can guess which country he has landed in by the smell of its air. Each country's air has its own specific smell. 'China is more industrial. Delhi is still more organic, earthy-smelling,' he had said. Dr Smith had agreed. They should know, given that their work always takes them to ground zero of the most polluted places in the world. Josh has worked in Brazil, Mexico and China. 'Pollution smells different in different countries,' he said, explaining how it was a function of the components that made up the air of that region. This is what source-apportionment studies tell us – what factors and how much pollution each emission source contributes to the overall air quality.[3]

By the time I get the window open, a familiar smell of burning molasses has seeped into the van. I recognize this smell from my childhood. It is the smell of the dried sugarcane residue that small local factories burn to make sugar and jaggery from sugarcane juice. *Khoi*! Dim memories of a school field trip to a sugar mill float in my head, triggered by the sickly-sweet smell of what I remember had been called *kolhu,* the thick, sweet sugarcane juice simmering in the industrial-size vessels over open flames fuelled by the *khoi.* We are in the sugarcane belt and have passed Mawana, Khatauli, Daurala and other sugar-mill towns where sugarcane is harvested and processed into sugar, jaggery and white cane sugar from November to March every year. In the distance, I can see spires of smoke rising from sugar mills. This activity adds to the smoke from the solid fuels that rural households burn. I wonder when awareness about pollution and burning will reach these villages. Prime Minister Narendra Modi has made Swachh Bharat (Clean India) his new slogan. But how can there be a clean India without clean air? The dynamic, exciting new campaigns, mottos and catchphrases are all very good, but I often wonder how one can 'Make in India' and 'StartUp India' when one can't even breathe in India.

A 2018 *Lancet* study says that India's dirty air killed an astonishing 1.24 million people in 2017.[4] That is, one in eight people died[5] just because of the air they breathed. Of these, nearly 12,322 fatalities were in Delhi. Shockingly, the study found that 77 per cent of the country's population is exposed to levels of harmful particulate matter that exceed the standard set by the Indian government. That threshold is *already* four times the limit recommended[6] by the WHO. Lalit Dandona, director of the India State-Level Disease Burden Initiative, who conducted the study, said, 'Now, a much larger proportion of the public and policymakers are convinced that something should be done.' However, even before this report, the home-grown 2015 Indian Health Ministry steering committee report[7] referred to the Global Burden of Disease's comparative risk assessment exercise, which showed that exposure to PM2.5 in households from both indoor and outdoor air together was responsible for an even higher number of premature deaths – 1.6 million, to be precise – and 49 million Disability-Adjusted Life Years (DALYs) in India.

Air pollution is now a greater risk factor than even tobacco for a range of diseases. Heart disease and diabetes alone make up a staggering 38 per cent of India's disease burden due to air pollution. But just air pollution – indoor and outdoor (or as the experts say, household and ambient) added together – accounts for 9 per cent of the national disease burden, and comprises the single-largest risk factor among those over 60 a study conducted by India's Ministry of Health and Family Welfare says.[8]

Inadvertently, one of the key initiatives taken by the Narendra Modi government ends up addressing this core issue. The Prime Minister Ujjwala Yojana scheme, launched in 2016, has brought LPG, a clean cooking fuel, to 5 crore homes by 2018. Their target is 3 crore more homes in the next phase of the scheme. By providing LPG, a clean fuel, to first-time users – specifically women below the poverty line – this scheme attempts to replace their clay ovens, or *chullahs*, which use traditional fuels and biomass for cooking. Eight crore new connections will cover almost 95 per cent of India across 715 districts and significantly reduce indoor and outdoor pollution. This is an outstanding achievement. Yet, by choosing to focus the programme on providing cooking gas to the have-nots rather than on raising awareness of the health benefits of cooking with clean fuel, the government has lost two big opportunities. One, any possibility of long-term gains in increasing LPG use through refill cylinders, and two, building awareness about this important issue as well as capitalizing on the political advantage of having its efforts in tackling air pollution at a national level known to the voters.[9]

If the Oil Ministry – which administers this scheme – had collaborated with the Health Ministry through its rural accredited social health activist (ASHA) community health workers, the government could have increased rural awareness of how insidiously air pollution is affecting their bodies as well as demonstrated its good work at one go. Current data shows that new connections are rising at a faster rate than actual use. This means that people are accepting new LPG connections but are either not using them or not refilling them. Without a continued incentive – either monetary or through awareness of improved health – beneficiaries are reverting to old practices of burning biomass. By not continuing to incentivize consistent LPG use and focusing only on increasing access, the government has lost a chance to highlight a key pollution benefit of this excellent programme – which is reducing emissions.

'The government should persuade the middle class more actively to give up its subsidy,' Dr Smith has told me, pointing out that only 20 million have given it up and at least 60 million more need to 'give it up', as it says in the catchy government campaign.

'Perhaps they should make it an opt-in versus an opt-out subsidy,' I suggest at one of our regular breakfast meetings, recalling economist Richard Thaler's book *Nudge*, and his face lights up with enthusiasm.

'Yes, then LPG to all poor households can be offered free.'

Dr Smith says there are three barriers to continued uptake by beneficiary families. 'Informational, reliability and cost,' he says, explaining how a below-poverty-line family will quickly slip back into using free firewood if they aren't aware of the health benefits of LPG, if delivery of LPG cylinders isn't prompt, and if the cost is high.

I can see mounds of cow dung cakes drying in the weak winter sun. More piles are stacked against walls of homes. Burning them beats the subsidized cost of clean cooking gas hands down, because this source of fuel is free and accessible. What if all cooking, heating, lighting in our villages was done *only* by clean cooking gas, I wonder. I imagine the smoky haze shrouding the entire northern plain lifting, disappearing, as village homes become smoke-free. I imagine children across Indian villages growing up healthier and stronger, their overall medical misfortunes (and related costs) lowered, their increased productivity adding to the country's GDP in ways both tangible and intangible and, more than anything else, their suffering lessened and their quality of life much improved.

We have passed my mother's home town, which is also surrounded by sugar mills. This is the smoky air she grew up breathing. It makes me sad to think about it; but now it also makes me anxious. We're breathing the same air she did – worse, actually. With increased industrial activity and more chemical processes added over the years, the air is worse now. There are more carcinogenic dioxins and microplastics in the air. In fact, to test this, back in 2014, Delhi residents had petitioned the NGT, which directed an independent lab to test the air for dioxins after the CPCB and the DPCC found levels that exceeded limits.[10] Air quality in this airshed will only get more toxic once plants similar to the Okhla WtE plant that caused those dioxins come up. Almost two years from now, despite continuing controversy over the Okhla WtE plant, the EPCA in its wisdom will recommend yet another WtE plant in the area we've just passed. Later, when I read that nausea-inducing report,[11] it will remind me of this journey and once again, reflect the enormity of the air pollution problem.

I lean back on the van's Rexine seats and close my eyes. Sudden memories of the clear, iridescent sunshine and bright-blue skies of Palo Alto, its clear, clean air flash through my mind and I take a deep breath. It calms me, and I realize I've unconsciously begun to breathe more shallowly. I'm afraid to breathe deeply. I have never regretted returning to my home country, but I wonder now – would I have come back had I known how filthy the air was? I don't know the answer to that. I just know that the more I learn about the pollution, the more guilty I feel for putting my children at risk.

As if on cue, my phone rings. It's my son.

'Mom? Where have you reached?'

'We've passed Muzaffarnagar,' I tell him.

'How are you feeling?'

How am I feeling? There is no calculus of grief, I'm beginning to realize. This is an emotional landscape which I will have to navigate without a map.

'I'm...okay. I guess.'

'And Nana?'

I look back. My father is talking to my cousin. They look animated. He is okay, for now.

'Nana is very brave. He's doing...okay, I think,' I say.

'Great,' he says, a bit impatient now, 'I also called to ask if I can go for soccer practice tomorrow morning. I checked the AQI today and it was under 200. And the forecast says it may rain. So it will clear it up further. You said I could play outdoors if it was below 150. Anyway, it's just a friendly match, so if you say no, I won't go. But I really want to. All my mates will be there.'

I'm too emotionally fragile at this point to argue with my son. But I can't let him suffer the ill health the lethal January air is definitely going to cause him. Even an AQI of 150 isn't really acceptable – we've normalized bad air.

'Please, Mom! I'll feel less sad,' his voice cracks. I want to say yes. He needs those exercise endorphins, his mates.

But Dr Guleria's words resonate in my ears. 'Exposure to air pollution is bad enough. But for young, growing lungs, it is worse – lung growth is affected, they are weaker, smaller, there are more lung infections, which means there are higher chances of respiratory problems and bronchitis as an adult.'

'No,' I say. My voice is quiet, implacable.

He hangs up.

I didn't think I could feel worse. Now I know there is no bottom to this.

I'm curious about the unfamiliar rituals and ceremonies coming up, conducted mainly by strangers, priests we will never see again. I'm still conflicted about the immersion of the ashes, the last vestiges of her physical body slipping away from us. How much of those we love and lose should we keep alive in our minds and how much should we let go? I wonder when I will start forgetting the intimate lilt of her voice, the familiar musk of her body, the tilt of her smile.

I don't know how to make the time pass faster. Outside, I see every kind of wheeled vehicle – farm tractors chugging along ferrying giggling, goggling women in bright saris; dusty, UP Roadways buses, spilling over with people and luggage, their horns shrieking like piercing elegies. Overloaded Tempos stuffed with cages of live chickens, giant cement mixers lumbering like buffaloes, leaking water tankers, trucks carrying cargo from logs of wood to petroleum products. Another overloaded truck narrowly overtakes us, proclaiming *Jai Jawan, Jai Kisaan,* a thin rod sticking out from the back with the ubiquitous red rag at the end of it fluttering in the wind. This one has cement blocks loaded on it. Like most other vehicles on the road, it is spewing thick, black smoke. The emission standards met by most of these vehicles are probably BS-4 (Euro 4) or even BS-3 (Euro 3).

Taking into account the serious pollution levels in Delhi and its adjoining areas, the Petroleum Ministry decided that Delhi will have Euro 6 fuel available at all its petrol pumps from April 2018 – two years ahead of schedule.[12] But real change will only start when the law demands that all vehicles sold in Delhi have to be BS-6 compliant to be eligible for registration. Until then, this would be a statement of intent with practically no actual impact. Dirty, older engines running on clean fuel or clean BS-6 engines using dirty fuel are both suboptimal. It is only clean, BS-6 engines running on BS-6 fuel that will make any real difference to pollution, something I explain in a newspaper article.[13]

We also urgently need a vehicle scrappage policy, something the ministry of road transport has been promising,[14] to revive growth in the automotive sector. The ministry expects this move will bring down prices by 20–30 per cent. Scrapping old, polluting vehicles will help reduce pollution, but not without other supportive measures. To the credit of the government, in April 2020, India moves to BS6 fuel across the country[15] despite an ongoing pandemic.

Our van slows down again, almost coming to a stop. I sigh. No amount of excellent-quality fuel or improved engines will ever reach the efficiency they are supposed to in the start-stop driving conditions of Indian roads. Research has shown that slow traffic that is not flowing smoothly is much more polluting.[16] This is another reason why we need to improve our roads. But here is where another paradox kicks in. Asphalt in extremely hot weather can generate almost as much PM2.5 as cars, Yale researchers have found.[17]

I look out to see why we are slowing. '*Dharam Kaanta*' proclaims a sign ahead, with a line of idling trucks like colourful, overgrown dinosaurs piling up behind. It's a weighbridge (the *dharam* to prevent cheating, I find out later). These machines are specially designed to weigh the vehicles loaded with goods and cargo. It reminds me of what Barun had told me: 'Every time a truck is overloaded by 20 per cent, its emissions go up 500 per cent.' We need strict penalties on overloading and need to impose fines based on the vehicle's pollution levels – and this should not just be applicable to those vehicles entering Delhi, as has been directed by the courts.

I wonder if all the people out to make a quick buck by overloading their trucks or plying obsolete, polluting vehicles, because they're cheaper, would continue to do so if they knew that these actions were killing their mothers or setting up their sons for an unhealthier life. Often, those who generate pollution and profit from it are not the ones who suffer the most from its ill effects. Industrial emissions caused by using cheaper, dirtier fuel or avoiding the installation of chimney filters may increase profits for the industrialist owners but the pollution caused by the increased emissions affects everyone around those polluting plants. In fact, chances are that the owners don't even live close to the plants. This makes pollution even more iniquitous and difficult to control.

Air pollution is a social iniquity – and independent research proves that.[18] In a further twist to environmental injustice, PM2.5 exposure is disproportionately caused by consumption of goods and services for the rich, but disproportionately inhaled by the poor. On average, the rich have a 'pollution advantage' whereas the poor bear a 'pollution burden' of excess exposure, relative to the exposure caused by their consumption. The total disparity is caused both by how much people consume and by how much polluted air they breathe in. Worsening the inequity is the fact that access to preventive, protective gear, masks and purifiers is confined mostly to the rich. Pollution had become yet another problem, the brunt of which is borne disproportionately by the poor in the country. Later that year, on Constitution Day in November, President Ram Nath Kovind will, for the first time, express exactly this concern, highlighting air pollution as a social iniquity and I will write about it.[19]

Dr Kumar and I have often wondered how to convert action on pollution from a 'class' to 'mass' issue, but it will be another two and a half years before I will hear any political figure say this publicly. Fittingly, it will be Shashi Tharoor saying, 'Air quality is not a class issue but a mass issue and politicians should not ignore it as the poor are the biggest victims of smog and air pollution,' in September 2020.[20] The best part is that he will be speaking to Chhattisgarh's health minister, T.S. Singh Deo, Chhattisgarh's environment minister, Mohammed Akbar, and other senior MLAs from the state on piloting state-level committees to address the issue of bad air quality. Pollution will finally be discussed by states in active terms and no longer only in Delhi.

This journey across Uttar Pradesh has made me realize anew that air pollution is present everywhere, every day.

By the time we reach Haridwar, we are exhausted. A couple of rickshaws take us through the town's narrow lanes, studded with glittering shops selling kitsch and kachoris, to a meticulously restored haveli in the old part of town. The last time we were all at Haveli Hari Ganga together was in 2005 to celebrate my parents' fiftieth anniversary, an event both joyous and reassuring, all of us feeling close to one another. However, the intervening years haven't been kind and the events of the last few months have revealed our ugliest as well as our best sides, drawing us together but also pulling us apart. We have got to know each other in ways we never thought we would and wish we never had.

We enter the haveli's intricate filigreed perfection and see its polished mustard-and-beige stone floors, its old-fashioned, double-sided mirrored doors exactly as I remember them. Unbidden memories of my mother catch me unawares. That memorable anniversary, the music in the evenings, the laughter, the friendly bickering among the sisters and our children, reigned over by my mother. I look for my father. He is standing a little apart, probably surrounded by his own memories. I find in his eyes an emptiness, a tiredness that hasn't got to do with this journey. I wonder if all this has been too much for him.

My siblings and I are all very concerned that my reticent father, who communicated with us more through our mother, will find it hard with his *jeevan sangini* and confidant gone. We're trying to fill the unfillable void she has left.

That evening, when I sit on the balcony of the haveli, looking over the Ganga, as it flows past, the longing to speak to my mother once more intensifies. In the quiet, purple twilight, I hear a velvet voice singing bhajans accompanied by a harmonium. I follow the music through the old-fashioned double doors that lead into the central courtyard to find a gentle-faced elderly man singing. Other haveli guests are sitting in and listening and I join them, but within minutes, I have to leave, afraid I will burst into tears. Instinctively, I look up on my way out, and see my father leaning against the balustrade on the first floor, in the shadow of a beautifully engraved iron pillar, with tears silently streaming down his face.

Journeying back from Haridwar to Delhi with all the ceremonies done, the mood inside the Tempo Traveller is quieter, more pensive. The van no longer feels large enough to hold all of us. We seem to have grown apart. I know there are no families without problems. But this trip has altered family dynamics in a way I still can't process. With our central force gone, we are deflating in a way that is uncharted and vaguely frightening. The tectonic plates of our affection have shifted, changing us in ways that seem irreversible.

Unexpectedly, I am feeling lighter. I put it down to what happened this morning, just before leaving the haveli. I had slipped away from everyone else, to fill a large container with some water from the river, something I wanted to take back with me as a remembrance of this place, of her. I filled my container with the ice-cold water from the swiftly flowing river that is believed to absorb the filth and sins of an entire people and the cities they build, then sat there silently, just looking out at the glittering water hurrying past. They had come then, unpremeditated, the hot tears, released from deep inside a frozen chest, gushing, heaving, unleashing a deep sadness I hadn't allowed myself to feel before. I don't know how long I cried, but the tears flowed like the river, swift, unending, washing away regrets and sorrows. A light breeze touched my hair, like someone's touch, soothing me gently until I was empty. The moment felt timeless, though it must have been mere minutes, but when I finally went back up to the haveli, dragging the large container with me, I felt spent. Spent and somehow, lighter. Even now, in the Traveller heading back, I carry that feeling of lightness with me

It is twilight now, tranquil, mystical. But when I look outside, the once-bewitching evening haze looks ominous, still. Looking at the swaying crop fields outside, I recall an article on crop stubble burning that my mother's attending pulmonologist had written in Hindi for a digital magazine. He was one of the first to tell me, almost casually, that her lung cancer was most likely caused by the polluted air she had been breathing for so many years. He had forwarded his satirical piece to me, and now, I scroll through old messages on my phone to find it. It is as much a rant against the ban on firecrackers as an enraged diatribe on the crop stubble that farmers were burning, causing hazardously high levels of PM2.5.

But he has missed the point. Crop stubble burning isn't new. It is a recurring source of PM2.5-laden smoke that adds heavily to the existing base levels of pollution that north India already suffers from due to an unfortunate convergence of weather and geography. Low wind speeds, dry weather and falling winter temperatures – and their resulting inversion – combine to keep pollutants trapped close to the surface in and around the metropolis. The Himalayas form an additional barrier to the north and the bowl-like topography of the Indo-Gangetic plain doesn't help, further preventing toxic pollutants from dispersing.

Now add to this geographic misfortune and meteorology, man-made pollution in the form of smoke from farm fires so large that they can be seen from outer space. Past years have seen record air pollution events, with levels reaching a hundred times higher than the WHO's recommended limits. Farm fires usually peak to around 4,000 per day by late October. On 31 October 2019, smoke from these contributed 44 per cent to Delhi's PM2.5 level, CPCB member secretary Prashant Gargava stated.[21] Scientists have calculated that on an annualized basis, crop stubble burning contributes anywhere between 5 per cent and 8 per cent to Delhi's pollution load. Since we can't change geography or meteorology, it becomes even more critical to manage man-made issues like crop stubble burning. That's why it is important to understand this issue.

Farmers burn crop residue in northern India because they believe they don't have an alternative viable, economical option. Burning is the fastest, cheapest and easiest method they know to turn around their capital – which is their acreage. But as the first inhalers of that choking smoke, they're also the first sufferers. So why has the problem worsened?

When I research this issue more extensively, I find that crop stubble burning began to contribute more severely to north India's pollution after a 2009 Punjab government order[22] compelled farmers to sow their rice seeds later than before. Rice is usually harvested after 120 days, and this later sowing – in June, instead of April, ostensibly done to preserve groundwater – delays harvest to October and narrows the window of time between the rice harvest and the planting of wheat that follows. The quickest way for farmers to clear the fields in this short window is by burning off the remaining stubble after harvesting the rice. And because by October, winds change direction, smoke from the north blows towards Delhi and its satellite cities. This ends up choking the 46 million people who reside in the NCR.

I'm not even sure that planting rice later is recharging groundwater – but I'm very sure it is suffocating millions of humans. In the course of my research, I find two interesting stories by Arvind Kumar, a technology and economic issues columnist, that theorize why this law came to pass. Both stories, published in the *Sunday Guardian*, allude to this change in sowing time being influenced by Monsanto, the American agrochemical company. The first story[23] details how Monsanto has been lobbying for switching from rice to its genetically modified maize seeds (which have been rejected by Europe because they are known for killing bees,[24] necessary for pollination). The second story,[25] a follow-up that goes deeper into the issue, quotes Dr Hiren Jethva, a NASA scientist who seems to buy into Kumar's exposé.

But even if we discount this theory, one thing is clear: we are growing the wrong crop at the wrong time in the wrong area – something that can be easily changed by simple policy tweaks.

Rice is a high water-use crop, and Punjab, which traditionally grew more wheat and other nutrient-dense crops, isn't the ideal location to grow rice as it needs standing water in its early stages of growth, and groundwater levels in Punjab are low. A minimum guaranteed price that is offered by the government has encouraged farmers to grow more rice. The amount of straw burnt, following harvest, is enormous. A conservative estimate is 23 million tonnes. To imagine what that looks like, this amount, if packed into 20-kilogram 38-centimetre-high bales and piled on top of each other, would reach a height of over 4,30,000 km – about 1.1 times the distance to the moon, a multilaterally funded agricultural research organization estimated.[26]

If the central and state governments genuinely wanted to fix the problem of pollution from straw burning, they would work together with the Agriculture Ministry and research institutions to create strategic, implementable solutions. Soil researchers can educate farmers on how burning not only damages the soil by burning a lot of valuable nutrients, thus reducing soil nutrition and therefore crop yields, but due to pesticides and chemicals in the soil and crop waste, also releases toxic gases in the air. Soil depleted of nutrients, in turn, requires higher external application of fertilizers. Higher fertilizer use means not just higher subsidy costs to the government but also higher input costs for farmers.

Also, the high silica content in the paddy stalks of the varieties currently grown makes them unusable as animal fodder. Agriculture scientists can identify and encourage the use of seed varieties that produce crops with softer stalks that can be used as fodder.

Some of this research already exists and has been written about since 2016. In fact, an economic study in the journal *Science*,[27] conducted by a global team of agriculture and environmental scientists, shows that thousands of farmers in northern India could increase their profits if they stop burning their rice straw and adopt no-till practices to grow wheat. The study shows that direct seeding of wheat into unploughed soil and shredded rice residues is the best option as it raises farmers' profits through higher yields and savings in labour, fuel and machinery costs. Alternative farming practices like these can cut greenhouse gas emissions from on-farm activities by as much as 78 per cent and help lower air pollution in cities like New Delhi, a CIMMYT article says.[28]

Another important area to look into is the farm equipment being used and subsidized. The Happy Seeder simultaneously performs the dual jobs of cutting crop stubble and sowing seeds. Farmers in Punjab seem to be happy with it. But before subsidizing these diesel-run machines, it is important to check that their use doesn't lead to swapping one source of pollution with another. Farmers in Uttar Pradesh growing similar crops burn much less of their stubble than their counterparts in Punjab. A farmer from Bulandshahr told me that crop stubble from basmati seed varieties 1121 and 1509 that they use in Uttar Pradesh don't have very tough, high-silica stalks, so farmers there can utilize most of the crop waste as fodder, animal bedding and compost. I explain all this in more detail in an op-ed.[29] More fundamentally, the op-ed makes the point that the government can easily get farmers to switch back to low-water-use, nutrition-dense coarse grains such as pearl millet (bajra), finger millet (ragi), sorghum (jowar), barley, rye and maize traditionally grown in this region. The food and agriculture ministry could do this by offering higher subsidies via minimum support prices. These grains have a higher iron content and are perfect for a country where large swathes of the population are anaemic. There is no reason to further deplete north India's water table by growing a high-water-use paddy crop in a water-scarce area when these other nutrient-dense native grains can be planted. Since the harvesting cycle is different, these traditional crops would also allow farmers a longer turnaround time to clear their fields so that they don't have to slash and burn so hurriedly. Furthermore, ethanol produced as a by-product can help farmers augment their income. For the country as a whole, this would also help create new employment opportunities and save on oil imports.

But all this is the job of the government, I think indignantly, and they are failing. As a result, we are dying sooner. In 2020, with links between Covid and air pollution becoming more definitive, I write another, more hopeful piece for an international digital platform for global health policy[30] that highlights the Pusa decomposer – cheap pellets that rapidly dissolve into a compost brew that can be sprayed to catalyse and quicken composting. These cost around the same as a box of matches and will be an alternative to burning.

Another simple idea to stop farmers from burning crop stubble is to make it valuable. Farmers won't burn it if they can sell it. We need solutions that reuse farm waste, and preferably monetize it, so that we can incentivize farmers not to burn it. The government could directly pay farmers to deposit crop waste at collection centres or link it to their support price payments. Simultaneously, the government can offer subsidies to entrepreneurs who create solutions such as green refrigeration systems powered by farm waste or ecological crockery, which also reduces plastic use. It will be November when I will find other campaigners to accompany to Swedish company IKEA's India office to discuss their idea of using rice stubble for some of their products[31] as part of its Better Air Now initiative.[32] But it will be another year before IKEA launches its Forandring collection made of rice stubble.[33]

While I've been thinking about all this, we have crossed Meerut again. I wonder if the others realize we are passing our mother's birthplace.

I hear my eldest sister talking on the phone, instructing someone long-distance. Work is her panacea, placebo and pacifier. She was in Kolkata on work when our mother died, the city where she'd been birthed. Eleven years separate us. Eight years separate me from my elder sister, the middle one, the most socially active among us. She has made her friends her family. They are her succour, her support. I turn back to look at her, and as expected, she is on her phone, her spectacles glinting back the blue light, a private smile tugging at her lips, as she texts her friends on WhatsApp.

Once they were young girls and I was their baby sister. Now we are all mourners. I have seen the pain in their eyes, as I know they have seen in mine. Our paths towards acceptance will be different, unique. I already know my eldest sister will immerse herself in work to cope with her pain, and my middle sister will immerse herself in friends. When we pass Sahibabad, the traffic gets thicker, slower as we reach the outskirts of Delhi. Soon we will be home. I reach out and tap my cousin on his shoulder.

'How many more ceremonies are left now?' I ask.

'The *bahravin*, twelfth day.' That is tomorrow.

'And then?'

'Then? Then nothing,' he says.

Nothing. His mother died 30 years ago. Mine, 11 days ago. And now there is nothing.

12

Every Breath You Take

January 2018

My mind buzzes with memories as my hand sweeps away the remains of the twelfth-day ceremony. The people have all left. Now it is truly over. I had decorated the spot where the priest prayed for the release of my mother's soul with crimson rose petals and pearl-like blossoms of rajanigandha. She would have approved of the flowers, I think. I inhale the fresh fragrance appreciatively as I collect the crushed petals to compost.

Air purifiers are running noisily, filtering the smoke from the incense the priest has insisted on lighting. Outside, the heavy air hangs low. The rituals and Sanskrit chants by bossy priests have been somehow soothing and a preset drill directed by well-meaning relatives, vaguely comforting. There is a certain relief in following a choreographed routine in navigating an unknown journey.

Now, the rest of our lives lie stretched before us, scriptless and confusing.

I wander aimlessly in the space that had been her final resting place, the blue room. The home hospice company has been efficient in taking away the angled hospital bed and all the machines. What is left behind are several unopened packs of adult diapers, surgical masks, unused syringes, antibiotics and supplements, the tin of Ensure she hated and her replacement silicon mask – consumables we can donate. There is so much still left to be done that I feel paralysed, overwhelmed, a little out of breath.

Randomly, I begin to clear the room, putting away things without method or direction; her lipsticks, her Oil of Olay, her hairbrush, still tangled with her hair, her saris. I bury my face in her clothes, inhaling the complex matrix of fragrances that defined her. My sisters walk in and I instantly recognize in their eyes the dazed sadness I feel in my heart. Her memories swirl around us, assail us with their finality. There will be no new memories made with her. We talk of our mother and repeat to each other some jewel-like episodes that semi-known, faded aunts have shared with us, helping us to briefly forget the underlying pull of sadness that is fast becoming a constant, unwanted companion. My mother would have called this pull '*tees*', one of those Hindi words she used that I find untranslatable. Each memory flares and shines briefly before burning out of our conversation, lying spent, scattered around us in the late afternoon sun.

Death has a curious way of bringing people together and it is after my mother's death that I reconnect with an old friend, Radha Rangarajan, a post doctoral fellow from the Harvard School of Public Health who has co-founded a drug discovery and development company involved in identifying and developing next-generation antibiotics to treat multidrug-resistant, hospital-acquired infections. My conversations with her make me realize there are probably many more people like my mother, whose lung cancer was likely triggered by Delhi's polluted air. Radha's mother is likely one of them.

'My mother had been living in Delhi for 10 years when she was diagnosed with non-small-cell carcinoma of the lungs,' Radha tells me. Her mother died of lung cancer in September 2016, after having been diagnosed a few days before her 79th birthday in 2014. 'I've long suspected that her lung cancer was triggered by Delhi's toxic air,' says Radha thoughtfully.

Radha's suspicion was reignited when she was attending a medical conference in Delhi just after Diwali in 2017. 'The air was simply awful,' she recalls. 'That was just days after my mother was diagnosed. I've been thinking about it since then,' she tells me when I meet her in Hyderabad, where she lives now. In her own research circles, Radha tried to find out if there is any surveillance being done on lung cancer cases in the Delhi-NCR region, only to find that lung cancer cases have increased sharply in the area over the 10-year period that her mother lived in Delhi.

If she had asked Dr Arvind Kumar, he would have told her that it was not just alarming that incidences of lung cancer were increasing, but that they were doing so at a faster rate for non-smokers and women. Being a researcher in new drug discovery, Radha is very aware of the epidemiology of disease and understands the difference between correlations and cause. No individual case of lung cancer can definitely be attributed to air pollution, which is why air pollution can't be listed as a reason for death in death certificates. It comes back to what Dr Guleria has said about genetics and lifestyle being the loaded gun but air pollution being the trigger. Some people will get lung cancer while others will get COPD, strokes, heart attacks and the other diseases that air pollution triggers. With 70,000 papers connecting air pollution to diseases worldwide, imagine the extent to which India's disease burden would come down if we were just able to remove pollution from our air.

Like my mother, Radha's mother also had no symptoms that one would associate with stage 4 cancer. It was only when she coughed up blood that Radha's father rushed her for a chest X-ray – mainly to rule out tuberculosis. The physician who saw her X-ray knew immediately.

For almost 11 months, Radha's mother's cancer was contained, before it came roaring back. Radha's mother would undergo four cycles of chemotherapy within six months before finally losing the battle.[1]

With cancer, one never knows when to pull back, many friends who have gone through a loved one's battle with this disease have told me. 'My mother was always a fighter,' says Radha. 'She never gave up on anything. So how could we tell her that there was no more hope? She tried so hard to manage all the awful side effects of the drugs in the hope that they would beat the cancer.' We talk about how there are no tools and support systems for families to understand their options well. 'It is so conflicting'. says Radha. Listening to her, a researcher in the field of new drug discovery herself, I feel a strange sense of relief. She is articulating and validating what I've felt. One of the worst things about this emperor of maladies is trying to navigate choices at various stages of the disease. In Radha's mother's case too, the suffering came mostly from the medication. Unlike palliative care in other cancers where pain can be reduced, you can't do much with lung cancer because the person is basically suffocating. 'There is no palliative care for breathing,' Radha says. I couldn't agree more.

In a big step for me, I attend my first music concert since my mother's death. I haven't been able to listen to music. This concert by Shruti Sadolikar celebrates *basant*, spring. She was among my mother's favourite Indian classical vocalists. I wear my mother's sari to the concert and the softly fragrant air at the India Habitat amphitheatre intermingles with my mother's scent when I wipe surreptitious tears with her pallu. I remember how my mother used to welcome each season, with its unique ragas, how she and I had sat right here exactly a year ago for a concert of morning ragas, as she whispered an explanation of the intricacies of the *bandish*.

In March, I learn that a former Associated Press journalist colleague, Ranjan Roy, who has been fighting lung cancer has lost that battle.[2] In my head, I keep replaying our last meeting two years ago, when I had persuaded him to buy a barely used air purifier for his bedroom from a departing BBC journalist friend we both knew, telling him that the poor air was most likely slowing his recovery. We had made plans to meet for chaat, but life got in the way. Now, death had.

Maybe Dr Kumar isn't overstating it when he talks about a lung cancer epidemic.

In the months that follow, as I struggle to find normality, I obsessively research air pollution and lung cancer. I revisit my ideas of creating online content that is both educational and couched in the vocabulary of today's youth in order to spread awareness among the younger demographic, but I find I'm unable to write.

CFA has also gone silent. I consider a revival strategy, but don't have the energy to recruit new volunteers. Our last volunteer, Sujata Bhaduri, a corporate lawyer turned stay-at-home mother is keen on a more formal structure, now that our registration has come through. I turn to Dr Gita Sinha, an infectious diseases doctor who had helped with the CFA Student Ambassador Programme in 2016.

When Gita comes home to commiserate on my mother's passing, we rail against the toxic air. Pollution is why she has proactively moved her family out of India to Toronto. We joke that with three CFA members having moved from Delhi to Toronto in the last three years, it is time to create a Canadian branch.

The weather is getting warmer, causing the pollution to lift somewhat. Some days, the sky even looks blue. The world seems to go on. Gita, Barun, Sujata and I begin weekly online video conferences to discuss creating a more formal structure for the organization. Despite fine-tuning mission statements and goals, adding more organization and structure, we still don't have volunteers, employees or funds. What we do have in place, thanks to Gita and Sujata, is a very clearly structured organization with SOPs, processes and verticals.

Around that time, I decide to travel to take my mind off things and visit Bengaluru and Mysuru with my son. The change of scene is healing, and colours slowly come back into focus. I can even listen to music without crying. The trip to the south also reaffirms my belief that pollution isn't just a problem in northern India. We had briefly considered moving to Bengaluru, where my husband's parents live. But on my visit I witness first-hand Bengaluru's traffic snarl-ups and poor air quality – only slightly better than Delhi's – and drop the idea of moving there. I also start checking air quality levels in Chennai and Mumbai regularly and am shocked at their levels.

Once I'm back in Delhi, I start wondering – and worrying – about the next pollution season. Because it doesn't look like anything is going to change as far as levels of emissions in Delhi are concerned. But at least we can limit our exposure. There is a difference between reducing emissions (which is ideal) and exposure (less than ideal, but a mitigating measure to reduce health harm).

In April, a journalist, Chetan Bhattacharji, who I've occasionally met at air pollution seminars writes to me suggesting starting a movement that will evoke and harness parents' fierce protectiveness of their children. Something akin to the US-based Moms Clean Air Force (MCAF). Created along the lines of the well-known and highly effective Mothers Against Drunk Driving, the MCAF in the US is a community of over 1 million moms and dads who have united against air pollution and committed to fighting for climate safety to protect their children's health.

'I've bought a domain name, and done some basic research to set up a web page, scalability and so on. And while this may well evolve into a more layered site, for starters it's likely to be driven by editorial and tech people motivated by air quality issues, who would in turn build a network of scientists, data pros, health professionals, legal and policy experts and most importantly mothers, and others. Like yourself,' he says in an email, referring to a MCAF, India. He has a broad plan – a funding strategy and executives he's identified. Although the momentum withers away, two years later. Although this doesn't pick up immediately, two years later, in 2020, smack in the middle of a more egregious pandemic, mothers across India will join hands to launch 'Warrior Moms[3]' to fight pollution on the UN International Day for Clean Air and Blue Skies.[4] This time, the venture is incubated by some organizations within the Clean Air Collective. Media reports say the movement is growing, with mothers from Chennai, Pune, Gurugram, Nagpur, Delhi and Mumbai, and Bhavreen Kandhari, an active clean air and climate campaigner tells me, 'We had to become more aggressive, become warriors, because otherwise, no one was listening to us.'

What we have all realized is that unless a strong and durable demand is created by a vocal group, the polity isn't going to respond.

And ultimately, the demographic we can best depend on are mothers, across all strata, who will care the most about their children and be willing to speak up.

In May, my neighbour Pavan alerts me to trees being cut on the section of Mathura Road, which adjoins our neighbourhood. I can't spot fallen trees, so ask him for photos. He's forgotten to take any, but informs me that workers there have told him they have permissions in place. They are making an underpass from Pragati Maidan to the Oberoi Hotel, he texts me. 'More than 60 per cent have already been cut. They cut all through the night,' his text reads. This is worrying, but I can't find any information about any new underpass project on the internet either. This is one of the biggest problems I have with public works – a lack of basic informational transparency, especially on-site. It isn't enough to insert a tiny notice in the newspapers, as I often see happening.

The following month, some vigilant environmentalists report more trees being cut on one of the pollution groups I'm on. This time, there are photos and details.

I'm travelling, so I immediately alert Gopal. By the time I return a week later, several trees along the main Mathura Road as well as the service lane leading into our green neighbourhood have been butchered. The area suddenly looks denuded, bare. Some digging has also begun, but as usual there are no public notices informing anyone of what is going on. This time, I am more persistent and prowl around taking photos and asking questions. The RWA security guard tells me that contractors with large electric saws snuck in at night to cut the trees. When he tried to raise an alarm, they threatened to kill him. I record his version and report this to Gopal, sending him photos and videos.

Since this is during school summer holidays, many of the CFA members are out of town. Gopal decides that the quickest way to file the petition will be through an environmentalist friend, Dr Kaushal Kant Mishra, a Delhi-based orthopaedic surgeon. The additional advantage of this is that Dr Mishra is very articulate – in both Hindi and English – and media-savvy to boot. He becomes the petitioner in the tree felling case.

Gopal flies in from Bengaluru on 22 June to ensure that the petition is admitted to the high court and a notice issued to the opposing parties, which include the state and central governments, the National Buildings Construction Corporation (NBCC), DPCC, Delhi Development Authority and the Delhi Jal Board.

Meanwhile, I get in touch with friends in the press to help highlight the quiet removal of essential greenery, the chowkidars of our lungs. One broadcaster agrees to send a mobile journalist. The RWA is up in arms at this destruction, especially since this seems to be part of a larger plan to build an underpass. Resident architects and lawyers meet at the RWA office and are joined by a stony-faced official of the Public Works Department (PWD) who has ordered the felling. I try to explain the environmental damage to him but my words fall on deaf ears. I manage to get the journalist into the meeting. Neighbours speak up to the television broadcaster, and another hurried RWA meeting is called.

Around the same time, news of 13,000 trees being cut to redevelop seven colonies and build more government housing across South Delhi explodes in the media.[5] The largest of these is in Kidwai Nagar, a South Delhi neighbourhood across from AIIMS. Government-owned construction company NBCC Ltd defends its decision to chop these trees. It says it will also build more parking. Cutting trees for more cars sounds like a death wish to me. But at least now national media has picked up the story.

On 4 July, Gopal appears before Chief Justice Gita Mittal and Justice C. Hari Shankar and manages to get a blanket ban issued on behalf of Dr Mishra. Other environment non-profits, including Chintan, which had moved the NGT, Swechha as well as some advocates who had challenged the Kidwai Nagar NBCC project are also present. Gopal is happy with the outcome and texts me a few details to share with the RWA. 'The chief justice was very vocal in expressing her dismay at the manner in which the government and the authorities had proceeded without applying their mind to the factors of air pollution, water requirements, traffic burden, sewage courses and solid waste disposal,' he said.

Thankfully, though the Delhi government has shockingly approved the massacre of the guardians of our lungs, the high court stays it.[6] With Delhi's lieutenant governor getting involved, it becomes another political blame game.

However, in my locality, the felling continues, always at night. The contractors browbeat the night watchmen, waving notices and permissions that are now outdated by the court's omnibus ban. We quickly realize that their calculation is that once the trees are cut and they have hauled the truck away, the action is irreversible.

I send Gopal the phone numbers of every official I can find, and he steps up to personally make phone calls to the PWD supervisor and contractor, warning them of contempt of court. He also formally sends them the order. Finally, on 6 July 2018, the felling stops.

Trees and plants not only provide oxygen, but some varieties can also absorb volatile organic compounds and 'clean' the air. While they cannot remove the deadliest microparticulate (PM2.5) from the air, their roots help in controlling dust (PM10). NBCC's claims that they will plant 2,00,000 saplings would have made me laugh if their action wasn't so tragic. I wonder how many years it will take for these saplings to grow to the size of the grand old trees that have been mercilessly chopped. In the aftermath of all this chopping, cutting and digging, Mathura Road, especially between the National Zoo and the Supreme Court looks awful, with debris from digging everywhere. Dust hangs in the air, the busy traffic giving it no time to settle back down.

India generates an estimated 150 million tonnes of construction and demolition (C&D) waste every year. This is just the official number – unofficial estimates of the total waste generated in the country put the figure at three to five times more than this, a CSE report has analysed.[7] The official recycling capacity is a meagre 6,500 tonnes per day – just about 1 per cent of the official estimates, CSE highlights. By 2017, 53 cities were scheduled to set up recycling facilities but until 2020, only 13 will have done it. What is worse, there is still no uniformity in characterizing and segregating C&D waste across the country, and recycling from the government's own infrastructure projects – like the NBCC projects – is a non-starter. With no strictly enforced regulations in place, debris remains strewn across landfills or in plain sight everywhere, leading to air and water pollution and other environmental damages.

'Heaps of concrete, bricks and metal waste from construction are choking waterbodies, green areas and public spaces in our cities. Toxic dust particles from the debris are polluting the air at a time when cities have to reduce their particulate pollution by 20–30 per cent by 2024, under the ongoing National Clean Air Programme (NCAP),' says CSE's Anumita Roychowdhury at a national online round-table meeting in August 2020.

At a time when the building and construction industry faces a materials crunch, recycling C&D waste would be an economically sound decision. But little effort is being made to do this. What we need is a circular economy that can turn C&D waste into a resource. This can help reduce energy intensity and environmental footprints of buildings and infrastructure.

Actually, 33 per cent of the waste generation can be avoided if architects design for waste mitigation during the pre-construction stage, the CSE report says, suggesting strictly enforced rules to reduce, recycle and reuse C&D waste on-site.

A large proportion of Delhi's pollution comes from the city's permanently dug-up C&D waste. Planting new trees can help fix the soil and dust into the ground. But cutting mature trees and replacing them with saplings that will take decades to grow, if they survive at all, is just not right, I think as I look sadly at the dry, empty spaces left by the old green saviours whose shade I've walked under so often.

One day, on one of my pollution groups I find someone with the exact skill sets CFA could use. Amrita Bahl has a doctorate in health education and until recently, has been an aide to Puducherry governor Kiran Bedi.

She is self-motivated and best of all, knows the values of collaboration and cooperation in the development sector. I get the others' permission to invite her to join our governing board. This gets me thinking about other past networks I could leverage.

Amrita is also helping MRTB to execute some of their ideas, and we discuss how CFA as well as MRTB are limited by the fact that we only work in one language – English. This isn't going to help either of us to convert this issue into something that resonates with the grassroots workers – farmers, autorickshaw drivers, construction workers, traffic policemen. The people most affected by air pollution, but who are unaware. But we also realize we have to play to our strengths. Through CFA, we have tried spreading awareness to schools, hospitals, RWAs and private gatherings. Along with MRTB and others from the Clean Air Collective, we've tried to incentivize recycling agricultural waste, even meeting senior IKEA executives to discuss this issue. But the impact of all these efforts has been marginal. We know it is time to take awareness out to the larger world in a bigger way. I wonder if perhaps younger companies and start-ups will be more willing to listen, learn and spread the word.

I go through a mental checklist of all the successful entrepreneurs I know, and from among those, I shortlist the ones who are not just business-savvy and intelligent but who could also bring additional weight to strengthen an authentic and credible cause. After much thought, I pick up the phone and call Deep Kalra, the founder of MMT. He immediately understands the purpose of my call and asks me to follow up by email. I send him a detailed email with CFA's background and mission and also my idea of having a session on air pollution awareness and advocacy – highlighting the role of start-ups and entrepreneurs in driving change towards clean air – embedded in The Indus Entrepreneurs' (TiE's) glittering annual conference, TiEcon. TiE is a Silicon Valley non-profit that supports start-ups through networking and the raising of capital. It was founded in 1992 by a trio of Indian American angel investors. TiEcon is its flagship event and one of the largest conferences for entrepreneurs. The event takes place in New Delhi every November or December.

I propose a pan-India competition to find the most effective solutions to pollution and go so far as to suggest that the theme for the 2018 TiEcon should be air pollution. I know this is a long shot, but I put it down anyway. Simplify and amplify beyond echo chambers is my new mantra, and this is the best place to begin.

Deep replies to my email almost immediately, copying in TiE secretariat's executive director, Geetika Dayal. It helps that I know her, having first met her over 20 years ago in the offices of the *Economic Times* when TiE began. She replies that at last year's conference, air pollution had been a key area that the committee members had been very keen to propagate. They had planned a session called 'Clearing the Air: Making Delhi Cleanest' with speakers that had included senior management and founders of various green technology companies and environment organizations as well as the power secretary of the Delhi government.

Geetika writes, 'To our great surprise, the session did not evoke the kind of interest we had anticipated, considering the importance of the issue. Barely a handful of people were in the room and it became terribly embarrassing.' There was no further interest to do such a session again. 'We still don't want to give up on it as it is critical,' she continues. But she wants a focused group to create a session that comes up with some action points or other tangible output in addition to creating awareness. 'Jyoti, it would be great if you could share some ideas and thoughts of what you think is needed and who you can pull together for this discussion. We can then table it and see how best to address or incorporate it,' she concludes.

Feeling encouraged, I write back with my thoughts on possible reasons for the failure of the 2017 attempt to bring air pollution in as a theme. I had attended the session she is referring to. I remember how there had been more people on stage than in the audience. One of my suggestions is to have the air pollution session earlier in the conference instead of having it as a morning session on the final day like the last time (it had been at 9 a.m. on a Saturday), by which time, conference fatigue has already set in. I also suggest using star power to attract young folk to such a dry subject, preferably from the realms of Bollywood or cricket, or even a successful entrepreneur from the start-up scene. I counter that while we definitely needed solution-focused sessions, awareness sessions with medical doctors were equally important.

'The aim of getting TiE to raise this red flag at a corporate and start-up level is to generate interest among our young entrepreneurs and their financiers, not just to make them more aware, but to exhort and encourage them to find more solutions,' I write in my reply to Geetika's email and follow up with an earnest call.

Unfortunately, a few emails in we all come to the conclusion that we don't have enough time for the requisite preparations for the 2018 conference. Very regretfully, I abandon the plan. For the time being.

Unlike last year when the Airtel half marathon was scheduled a month after Diwali, this year the organizers have been smart enough to schedule it on 21 October, 17 days before Diwali, so the pollution is likely to be less of an issue. But by now, we've realized that there are several other runs scheduled and permitted during the pollution season in the capital – Airtel just happens to be the most high-profile.

From her overseas perch, Gita has started tracking such sporting events and emails some of the sponsors, pointing out the health harm of running in polluted air and asking them to be more responsible. She gets her information from websites like India Running Races and Universal Runners Marathon. We are shocked to find hospitals such as Jaypee Hospital and schools such as JBM Global School at the forefront of some of these runs. But more than others, one particular marathon is bothering the CFA team. French sporting goods company Decathlon has sponsored a 'fun run' and is promoting it when AQI is well over 200, whereas they have cancelled a marathon sponsored by them in San Francisco, due to wildfires that have polluted the air. Gita writes to Decathlon India asking why people are being treated differently and gets a polite but non-committal reply from Sylvain Deschamps, a company official. In the end, Decathlon goes ahead with its India run. MRTB tweets[8] about pollution racism,[9] and once again, talk of linking outdoor aerobic activity with AQI levels gains ground on all pollution groups. Responsible sports. Responsible luxury. Responsible travel. Like the carbon footprint, it seems we should also know what our pollution footprint is.

On 23 October 2018, the Supreme Court passes a very strong and balanced judgment on the use of fireworks. I unpack and explain it carefully in a piece I write for *Scroll*.[10]

'Air pollution scientists and doctors have emphasized that high episodic air pollution events (like one night of Diwali) set off higher all-cause mortality. They also act as triggers for those with pre-existing respiratory and cardiac ailments, the elderly and young, especially as the effects of the firecrackers remain in the air for up to one month after Diwali. It is in this context that the Supreme Court's judgment on Tuesday banning all high-emission fireworks...is very welcome. By stopping short of a blanket ban and permitting qualified "low-emission" or "green" firecrackers (of which there are none in the market at present, making this tantamount to a complete ban), the court has, in effect, upheld democratic principles while balancing them with the well-being and collective health of its citizens,' I state in the article.

The judgment bans not only the sale (both retail and online) but also the manufacture of such items. This is a happy by-product of the own goal scored by the firecracker manufacturers' association. The best part is that, for the first time, this is also a national ban, which means the court implicitly recognizes that air pollution is a national problem, affecting the entire country.

Equally important, the court has not associated the ban of fireworks to any particular festival – taking away the religion card that some lobbies used as a red herring to divert attention – thereby neatly avoiding the politicization of what is a national health emergency. The judgment makes a government agency (the Petroleum and Explosives Safety Organization) responsible for cracker-emission certification, which puts back the job of ensuring the safety of citizens in the hands of the government – or at least reminds it of its responsibility. Additionally, by making the same organization responsible for the disposal of all leftover stocks, the court has closed yet another loophole – that of responsible disposal.

Another important measure the Supreme Court has taken is to recognize that enforcement is key. By specifically naming the police station house officer responsible for any violations in his area, it has put some power back in the hands of vulnerable citizens. This means that the police will be held accountable for any inaction on reports of the sale of prohibited fireworks, their use or bursting in non-designated areas or times. This means that the station house officer can be hauled up for contempt of court, a jailable offence. Also, by talking about designated areas, the court has paved the way for community celebrations as opposed to individual ones.

This 'restricted' ban may be just one small step towards cleaning our toxic air but it is an important one. Some activists have labelled it 'limited'. However, if enforced strictly, this ruling not only has the potential for a greater and more far-reaching impact than the previous year's complete ban on cracker sales, but also the ability to quietly consolidate all gains made from it. For now, this is the best the Supreme Court can do. 'It has shown the way, and it is now up to the government, enforcement agencies, political parties, corporations and, most importantly, aware and vigilant citizens to take this forward,' the piece ends.

The following week is my mother's birthday, our first without her. I arrange to spend the day with my father and my siblings. We go to an organic fair together. 'Last year this time she had just finished packing for the hospital and was cutting a cake,' I remark, which sets us off, down memory lane. That's where our mother will live now. In our memories and hearts. When we hug each other goodbye, the distance between us seems to fade a bit. Maybe we are healing together, instead of healing apart, I think to myself.

It is only after I have gone the one year without her living presence – my birthday, her birthday, anniversary, Holi, every festival that she loved and sang at – that I will finally learn to accept her absence and gradually, her absence will become her presence. It will also teach me why conventionally, a mourning period in most cultures is usually one year – crossing each milestone without a loved one the first time is the toughest. It is the beginning of acceptance.

Ironically, her birthday falls exactly in the middle of the first-ever Global Conference on Air Pollution and Health, a three-day event in Geneva organized by the WHO, which Ravina and Dr Kumar attend.

The following week, on 4 November, the EPIC officially releases their AQLI tool. I am on a television panel with EPIC's executive director, Dr Kenneth Lee, and a pulmonologist. The statistics are shocking. According to their AQLI tool, by living in Delhi and breathing its air, we lose 10 years of our life. Other studies have a much lower number for India, but this one seems more granular and is detailed by region. All I can think is that if my parents hadn't settled down in Delhi, my mother may have had the chance to live a little longer – even though a rational part of me knows that there is no guarantee of that and that I can now never prove it. As many deniers say, it isn't as if her death certificate named air pollution as her killer.

Unknown to me, a courageous British mother, Rosamund Adoo-Kissi-Debrah, has submitted a 1,00,000 signature petition to reopen an inquest into her nine-year-old daughter Ella's death in London, asking for her death certificate to name air pollution as cause of death.[11]

Diwali this year is on 7 November, my first without my mother. Something extraordinary is happening in my neighbourhood this year: a very serious movement to go firecracker-free has taken off. The RWA has finally got involved, and many homes have got posters that declare the space cracker-free. But the best part is that my *ladi*-loving neighbour is finally converted. In fact, he is leading the way in convincing others in our neighbourhood. When I observe him smiling and telling some people how he used to light *ladis* and doesn't any more – because he has realized how uselessly polluting crackers are – I feel happy. One down. Millions to go. But it's a start.

Despite giving up on the plan to have an air pollution session at TiEcon, I still attend the conference. In one of the sessions, Kishore Biyani, CEO of the Future Group, is talking about how retail growth will drive overall growth in India. They are betting on the aspirations of India's aspirational class. Big growth numbers are being thrown around.

The excitement at the potential opportunities is palpable. I'm not an entrepreneur but even I can feel it. I've been whispering to the entrepreneur on my right, who makes CPAP machines to ease sleep apnoea. He tells me business is booming as he gestures to the podium.

'My God!' says the entrepreneur sitting on my left. 'I knew we were growing fast but didn't realize how fast. I didn't know the market was that big!'

I turn and ask him what he does. He makes leather products. He wants to grow his company quickly and sell it fast. Why the hurry, I ask. Well, he says, his wife and he want to have children. He needs to sell his company quickly so that they can leave the country. It's too polluted to bring up a child in India.

His aspiration is to sell consumer goods made through techniques that most likely add to local pollution – leather-making is traditionally a polluting industry – tap India's huge retail market to make his money, and then leave the country because he can't live in that pollution! Internally, I move from shock to outrage, and then I start laughing. He looks affronted and asks me why I'm laughing. I explain to him the irony of what he has just said. The young man looks struck and is silent for the rest of the session. It is clear he has never connected these dots.

After this conversation, I start thinking about how important it is for young Indians to understand the consequences of their actions first-hand and see the disconnect between growth and sustainability. Only then perhaps can they approach their own businesses and activities with greater responsibility. We are all complicit. And we are all victims. We need to break this vicious cycle.

In December 2018, the medical community is finally roused to action with the launch of Doctors For Clean Air (DFCA),[12] a nationwide network of senior doctors representing all states. DFCA is an initiative of Dr Kumar's Lung Care Foundation (LCF) and Health Care Without Harm,[13] an international non-profit which aims to become a community anchor for environmental health and justice. It represents more than 30,000 hospitals and health centres globally. Dr Kumar manages to get 12 leading national medical associations, representing over 1,50,000 specialist doctors, on board. 'This is the best thing that he could have done,' Dr Smith will tell me at one of our regular breakfast meetings in the months following this launch. 'Doctors highlighting the [health] ill effects of pollution and advocating for clean air will be powerful,' he says, and I couldn't agree more. Considering that doctors make more money from curing people from disease than preventing it, this sort of preventive initiative is not just heart-warming but also among the most effective ways awareness can grow across the country.

13

Breathing Here Is Injurious to Your Health

January 2019

For me, January used to be the month that held in its crisp chill the hope of a new year, the pageantry of Republic Day, my birthday. Now it also holds the date my mother breathed her last breath. The one-year anniversary, her *barsi*, of her passing away is coming up and I'm not sure I'm ready to face it. At least not in the grey dystopia of Delhi.

But first, I must attend a meeting on environmental issues that Shashi Tharoor has called on 3 January in the national capital. The Indian National Congress party, to which he belongs, has recently won state elections in Rajasthan, Madhya Pradesh and Chhattisgarh, which has made the political party hopeful about more wins. It wants to begin by creating a more inclusive manifesto. For many of us in various air pollution and environmental groups, this is a chance to embed clean air, water, forests and sustainable agendas in political manifestos. CFA has always been very clear that clean air needs to be a non-partisan issue across all political parties. Barun has measured PM2.5 levels of 617 outdoors and 460 indoors in Kolkata over this past Christmas, and Abhishek has measured 385 in Bikaner around the same time even as other pollution-aware people from cities like Varanasi, Nagpur and Chennai are sharing their PM2.5 numbers – all disturbingly high.

On the day, there are almost 40 people from different organizations who assemble at the office space tucked inside the newly restored, beautiful Sunder Nursery gardens, several of whom I recognize, including the intelligent and amiable Ashutosh Dikshit who heads the United Residents Joint Action (URJA). URJA networks 2,500 RWAs, trader associations, religious bodies and non-profits to help deliver last-mile governance. Ashutosh, who has also founded a research and advocacy group called The Citizens Alliance, understands air pollution thoroughly and is excellent at working collaboratively.

Dr Tharoor seems genuinely interested in the points that we raise, and more knowledgeable than I expected. And although it is pitch-dark by the time I leave and I can smell the smoky air even inside this green oasis, I feel hopeful. Romi Kapil Dev, an active RWA member gives me a ride back, and we discuss ways of mobilizing our neighbours to segregate garbage as a community. This year we have decided to focus on outreach and building communities, going beyond Delhi.

As part of our outreach, we meet the University of Chicago's EPIC team on 24 January – EPIC-India's executive director Dr Kenneth Lee and I have been in touch since November – and we agree to host their AQLI tool on the CFA home page. We decide to co-create awareness modules. At our board meeting the next day, we discuss whether we should increase our outreach, start fundraising, set up a secretariat, take the organization to the next level or play a more advisory role until we collect some money to scale our initiatives.

Meanwhile, an alumni from IIT Kanpur has written to CFA, inviting Anita and me to speak at a conference on 10 January.[1] The conference is titled 'Care for Air'[2] and organized by the Social Entrepreneurs and Enterprises, an initiative by the alumni group. I am unable to go to Kanpur but fortunately, Anita can make it and will speak about measurable, time-bound, real outcomes around solutions to pollution.

Over several phone calls, Jatin Vasandani, one of the organizers of the conference in the verdant IIT Kanpur campus, and I discuss its purpose and the other speakers. I'm curious about his unusual decision to pick air pollution as the theme for an alumni meet and ask him why.

'Well, because IIT-K has been on the forefront of air quality and climate research with an interdisciplinary Centre for Environmental Science and Engineering. Because the AQI was developed by an IIT-K team. Because the pollutants causing discolouration of the Taj Mahal were discovered by another IIT-K team. Because the latest work on quick cause apportionment was led by one of IIT-K's atmospheric scientists. Because a national aerosol facility is coming up in IIT-K, the first in India and among Asian universities,' he rattles off. 'But mainly,' he pauses, 'it is because Kanpur is the most polluted city in the world, and we want to change that.' He, along with the rest of the alumni, have managed to gather an impressive line-up. The speakers include atmospheric scientists such as Dr Sachchida Nand Tripathi, Dr Sagnik Dey and Dr Sumit Sharma. They have also managed to get officials of the Uttar Pradesh State Pollution Control Board and senior bureaucrats from the state and central Environment Ministry as well as Ronak Sutaria, an urban scientist who works with low-cost pollution monitors. It is networks of low-cost sensors such as his that have democratized pollution and made it visible to laypeople.

Jatin is struggling with the last-minute cancellation of one of the stars of the show, Ritesh Kumar Singh from the Environment Ministry. Mr Singh is an articulate joint secretary whose knowledge I've found impressive. He is one of the key officials coordinating an all-India comprehensive clean air plan. The NCAP[3] was first conceived and shared with state government stakeholders in March 2018 and comments on it from the public invited by May 2018. Some of us had found the initial draft weak, with no measurable goals, no timelines or legal mandates embedded in it. Based on feedback from different stakeholders over several consultations and meetings across states, the government had amended and redrafted it, and on 19 October, had passed the final draft unanimously, but still hadn't notified it. Activists have been waiting impatiently for an announcement. There are rumours that the central government plans to launch it on 10 January, and that Mr Singh's presence is needed in Delhi for that. In the end, Jatin manages to get Mr Singh to address the Kanpur gathering via Skype. A couple of hours later, the NCAP is publicly released. It is still deeply flawed. In June 2020, the Council on Energy, Environment and Water (CEEW) and Urban Emissions will jointly evaluate[4] the NCAP as weak, lacking a legal mandate, transboundary coordination, funding, clear, measurable targets and accountability – but at least we finally have a clean air policy and an acknowledgement of this gigantic problem.

'What his address made me – all of us – realize, was the extent of coordination between multiple governmental agencies that was required and the sheer enormity and complexity of this issue,' Jatin tells me later.

In planning and policy, a 'wicked' problem is one that is tough or impossible to solve because of incomplete, contradictory and changing requirements that are often difficult to recognize. Wicked problems have innumerable causes, are tough to describe and have no clear solution. Air pollution is thus best described as a wicked problem.[5] Which means it is going to be critical to collaborate with others in this area. The Clean Air Collective is growing exponentially, which is great. Our focus now turns to ensuring that it doesn't become another echo chamber of experts talking to each other.

Everyone should have this important information – in their local language. Making succinct videos highlighting the hidden negative health effects on people will be the most effective method. We discuss whether we can bridge the class–mass gap by involving the pollution-savvy Melba Pria, Mexico's ambassador to India, who has adopted the Indian CNG three-wheeler as her official vehicle and is commonly known as the 'ambassador with the autorickshaw'.[6,7] But a lack of volunteers and resources limits us. In February, I meet two young women at an air pollution talk who study at Delhi's Lady Shri Ram College (LSR). One of them reaches out to me in March. She is 20 and a part of Enactus, a global community of students 'committed to using the power of entrepreneurial action to make the world more sustainable'. After a few conversations with the students, CFA begins training a cohort of 25 young women from LSR's Enactus community in the hope that college students will make more dynamic ambassadors, becoming the active volunteers we so desperately need. We figure they have greater agency than high-school students who are caught up with school-leaving exams. They are also less dependent on parental support, we reason. CFA begins working with them on Barun's picturesque Paharpur Business Centre's refurbished green terrace where, he tells us, we are breathing Davos-quality air as we work, something I've heard him tell the press for years.[8]

I follow up with this group several more times from my home office, trying to get them to execute some of our ideas, including the Humans of Air Pollution media campaign. Coincidentally, students belonging to another youth-run, not-for-profit leadership development organization called AIESEC reach out to us through our website and we try and integrate them into our programme. We're also finally able to integrate the delhiair.org site with careforair.org. However, with so many newer, snazzier newsletters such as 'CarbonCopy' and 'Unearth', I'm beginning to wonder if it has outlived its utility, especially since Gen is only updating it sporadically. Perhaps it will have archival value.

Just three months ago, in December, our team of Barun, Manjali, Amrita and I had already trained another, much larger cohort of college-level students at the Fortune Institute of International Business (FIIB), and Gita has followed up by leading a full-fledged formal social internship programme. Her structured formats and teaching experience come in handy. The best part is that FIIB brings us in touch with several Hindi speakers. Perhaps we can now integrate all these college students as clean air ambassadors under one umbrella, graduating our school programme into a college movement. It is still March when I tweet a report by Dr David Boyd,[9] the incoming United Nations Special Rapporteur on human rights and the environment.[10] The report, on the right to a safe, clean, healthy and sustainable environment, says that air pollution is a violation of the basic human right to breathe clean air. Perhaps it is because of this tweet, in April, I receive an email inviting me to a virtual consultation on 15 May, on clean environment 'as a human right' with Dr Boyd.

At around the same time, I find short videos about air pollution online – exactly the sort I've been visualizing. The 50-second professionally made videos in Hindi, titled 'Pollution *ka kya plan hai*' form a series that highlights common pollution themes in an easy-to-understand format. I discover that the person behind these videos is Ashish Dhawan, a private equity professional who has set up an educational foundation called Central Square in 2012. I reach out to him and we meet at his office on 26 April.

Given how knowledgeable he is, I'm surprised to find that Ashish's pollution journey is just a few months old. It began accidentally when he started noticing how blue the skies are in China over the course of several business trips. He tells me that one of his business meetings has, coincidentally, been with the husband of the woman who made the independent documentary film *Under the Dome: Investigating China's Smog*,[11] a film that has been instrumental in transforming China's airscape. At the time, he didn't know what the film was about, nor did he have any in-depth knowledge about air pollution.

I've watched the moving 103-minute indie documentary, made by Chai Jing, a former China Central Television journalist, in which she talks about China's noxious air pollution and investigates its causes. She believes it caused her unborn baby's benign tumour. Although the baby survived, the self-funded documentary makes it clear that Chai Jing was deeply scarred by this and spent a year investigating China's smog. There is a scene in the film that evocatively documents how some Chinese children don't even know what blue skies look like. The film captures the voice of a six-year-old living in the polluted coal-mining province of Shanxi who says she has never seen stars or white clouds.

The investigative journalist backs her statements with data and science and squarely blames coal – and indirectly, China's development model, especially the monopoly of PetroChina – as one of the main reasons for its polluted air. She asks some tough questions about the politics and economics behind the smog. When it was uploaded on the internet on 28 February 2015, it gathered 100 million views in 48 hours.[12] 'Only in China would a documentary on air pollution garner more than 100 million views in less than 48 hours,' the BBC reported.[13] National Public Radio (NPR) put that number at 200 million.[14] It was subsequently translated into English by 'a group of passionate students and their friends' and is believed to be the film that compelled the Chinese government to take pollution seriously and reduce their coal usage. It is also believed that Chai Jing had the tacit approval of the Chinese government – its environment minister, Chen Jining had already watched the documentary and said he had phoned Chai Jing to thank her for her contribution.

The documentary and its coverage by the international media compels strong government action. I find so many similarities to India – Jing talks to a local environmental official so powerless to enforce the country's laws that he admits, 'I don't want to open my mouth because I'm afraid you'll see that I'm toothless.'

In the film, Chai travels to Los Angeles and London to learn how those cities cleaned up their air. She concludes that China can follow their example, and that its citizens should get involved. 'Ten years ago, I asked what that smell in the air was, and I got no answer,' she says. 'Now I know. It's the smell of money.'

Ashish knew none of this when he went to China on a business trip in the winter of 2018. What he did notice, however, was how the colour of the sky was bluer compared to his earlier trip the previous year. Curious, he tried to find out more and educated himself about air pollution. Over time, he met several Chinese air pollution scientists and experts who had worked on cleaning up China's filthy air and decided that he wanted to help reduce India's terrible pollution levels.

Ashish sees the challenge as one of low awareness and capacities. His view is that air pollution doesn't get the political focus it merits because politicians aren't convinced that this issue is important to citizens. He feels the government needs support to help implement measures to combat this menace.

He wants to approach the problem by inserting a supportive and well-resourced team to help government organizations and departments create value and make a meaningful difference. It is the same strategy he has used in his educational foundation. He has also realized that pollution needs to become more mainstream, that awareness needs to grow, and that to make any significant difference the executive and legislative branches of government need to be committed. He has created the videos that I find ahead of the upcoming Haryana elections in 2019 and Delhi elections in early 2020 with his own funds.

I suggest that perhaps CFA can collaborate with him. The sort of 'wicked' problem we're dealing with needs many people coming at it from different angles. Ashish invites me to a meeting with interested stakeholders to explore the next steps. Gopal and I attend on behalf of CFA. We walk in to hear other attendees, all clean air evangelists, talking enthusiastically and knowledgeably about air pollution and how to fight it. Surprisingly, many are senior members of the corporate world. I can't spot a specific collaborative opportunity immediately, but I love that the issue is finally getting so much traction among Indian decision makers. I would never have seen a room full of company CEOs and successful entrepreneurs and VCs talking about air pollution five years ago.

Less than a month later, on 11 May, I meet Ashish again. It is a brief meeting and he lets me know that they have decided to call themselves the Air Pollution Action Group (APAG) and have begun initial work.

They will address the problem through increased citizen engagement, policy research and implementation support to the government. By doing these three things in parallel, they will gather political will, a critical enabler, provide evidence on the impact of policies implemented so that those become more actionable and enforceable, and help plug capacity gaps through monitoring and evaluating initiatives implemented and upskilling.

After the meeting, when I switch my phone back on, I find 37 missed calls, almost all of them from my sister. It has to be about my father. I sit in my overheated parked car and with shaking fingers dial my sister's number. She picks up on the first ring.

By the time I reach the hospital emergency with my husband, the ambulance with my father inside it has just pulled up, an untidy crowd of people jostling around it. Through the chinks between the moving human bodies, I can see his white hair and broad forehead. His eyes are closed but going by the grimace of pain on his face, he appears to be conscious.

It turns out to be a gastrointestinal bleed caused by painkillers he has been taking for an ulcer in his mouth. They want to transfer him to the ICU, and I suddenly feel terrified at the thought that I may lose him. It isn't even 16 months since I lost my mother.

The next few days pass in a blur of hospital visits and long drives in the unrelenting May heat to the hospital, tests, reports, unmade decisions, queues outside doctors' rooms that remind me of my mother's stay in the same hospital. In the middle of all this, I remember the virtual meeting scheduled with Dr Boyd, which I'm able to join from the hospital parking lot.

It is after this meeting that I decide to file a petition requesting intervention by the UN on the right to breathe clean air. The virtual meeting with Dr Boyd has led to an epiphany of sorts. I've realized that it isn't just that the current government doesn't intend to clean the country's air, but that it is actively diverting massive funds from the green cess it collects away from clean energy policies. I knew this already from a July 2017 *Scroll* investigation, which had revealed that revenue raised by a tax on coal that was originally intended to support renewable energy was being spent on an unrelated policy[15] under the BJP's flagship goods and service tax regime. This had been covered by the international press too[16] and was based on official information. But now that a parliamentary committee on energy has pulled up the government on the diversion of the National Clean Energy and Environment Fund (NCEEF) to compensate states for GST losses,[17] and there is still no response, I feel there is no real hope.

'The coal cess collected from 2010–11 to 2017–18 amounts to ₹86,440.21 crore, out of which only ₹29,645.29 crore has actually been transferred to the NCEF [National Clean EnergyFund]. The amount financed from NCEF for projects is only ₹15,911.49 crore, or only about 18 per cent of the total amount collected as coal cess,' *The Hindu* reports. 'The committee feels that the fund should be used for its intended purpose, that is, to support clean energy initiatives and it should not be diverted to compensate GST losses. Diversion of this fund to unrelated activities reflects poorly on our commitment towards cleaner environment and shows government's apathy towards clean energy projects. Since it is levied on coal as that is a polluting fuel, the amount collected should be used to promote cleaner fuel,' the panel is quoted as saying.

What serves as the final trigger for me are the rumours I've recently been hearing that the government is planning to auction 40–50 new coal blocks and may even open these up to the private sector. I know once coal is mined from underground, it will never go back in, but find its way into our lungs. I'm losing hope in domestic protests. The last one was a public protest outside Paryavaran Bhavan on 7 December, more than a year ago, where we had shouted slogans against the extension of the deadline for thermal power plants to follow pollution norms. My mother was still alive, though the doctors had given up and we had brought her home. Reecha from Purpose had alerted me, texting me directly to come to the Environment Ministry office, figuring that I may not have heard of the protests.

'The ministry of forest and climate change passed a policy in 2015 to lower emissions from thermal power plants. The policy, if implemented, would cut down pollution by up to 30 per cent around the country and especially for northern India,' she had texted. 'The deadline for the norms to be implemented is tomorrow; however, not one power plant has implemented the standards which is essentially a filter the plants need to retrofit. The ministry of power has been lobbying against the policy. Now the deadline is being extended till 2020 for Delhi-NCR and 2022 for the rest of the country. This is unacceptable. We need the standard in place now if we are serious about lowering air pollution,' she had said. But it had made no difference. Later, in October 2019, I am alerted to a news article[18] that says that it was not just the power ministry lobbying to dilute thermal emission norms for state-owned power companies, but for two power companies belonging to Gautam Adani, the Gujarati industrialist known to have close ties with Prime Minister Narendra Modi. India's 246 coal-fired power plants provide 60 per cent of its total electricity, and most are inefficient and highly polluting. 'Yet coal is likely to dominate the country's energy mix for decades to come,' the *Financial Times* has calculated[19] in a detailed report.

It is definitely time to reach out for help from multilateral organizations like the UN.

I try and persuade others from the Clean Air Collective to petition with us. Several more organizations have joined this unbranded network and it is gaining momentum, but getting consensus, as I've learnt now, is next to impossible. After almost two months, on 6 July, CFA sends the petition to the United Nations Special Rapporteur on human rights and the environment. Giving the entire background as succinctly as possible, I end the petition saying:

> *We, the people, request the UN Human Rights Council to exert pressure on the Indian government to tackle pollution urgently as it is killing millions of us. More people die from breathing polluted air than due to war, terror, road accidents or any other disease in India. Those who aren't dying, are sickening, whether they know it or not. There are now measures that tell us how many years of our lives we are losing by breathing this polluted air. It is the enemy within and needs to be fought at a priority level. Being forced to breathe such toxic air is a human rights violation. Please help us by getting our decision makers, policymakers local, state and federal governments to clean our polluted air on an urgent basis.*

In those two months, I've also reached out to two disparate people on two continents whose journeys around air pollution, disease and death are inextricably linked. One lives in Shahdara, Delhi, and has survived pollution-triggered lung cancer by surgically removing more than half of his left lung, the other in Catford Bridge, London, where her daughter suffocated to death from air pollution.

—

On World Environment Day on 5 June, CFA collaborates with the University of Chicago for a training event with children from 15 schools and also begins some advocacy training. On 9 June, the Help Delhi Breathe campaign supported by the Clean Air Collective holds an exhibition under the graceful dome of Bikaner House near India Gate. On display are 60 unsettling images of how pollution affects people. Most studies that focus on air pollution talk about dying, but this exhibition speaks of people living with it across the country. It has stories from places as varied as Mumbai, Ennore near Chennai and Korba in Chhattisgarh. It has been collaboratively created and curated by activist and researcher Aruna Chandrasekhar and photojournalist Ishan Tankha.

This is the first initiative I've seen that attempts to make the issue personal by bringing out the human cost of air pollution. 'It is not just about getting out of our comfort zone. This is not a comfort zone; this is a war zone,' I overhear someone say at the exhibition. This event reignites hope in me.

We still have to ignite awareness in the corporate and business sectors, and connect the dots of their own actions to health harm. I resolve to get more focused on the TiEcon 2019 event in November. This time, I'm determined to remain in regular touch so that we don't run short of time.

The event also launches a song on pollution by Bollywood's Ankur Tewari called '*Dhuan Dhuan*', whose lyrics conjure up a visual memory of haze, dust and smoke. The young singer tells the audience that he was inspired to write it when he was passing by India Gate and saw the iconic monument vanish in front of his eyes in the polluted haze of Delhi. 'If something as permanent as a monument could vanish in front of my eyes, what chance does the human race have?' he says before he begins gently strumming his acoustic guitar to an elegiac melody. He has a mellifluous singing voice. My mother would have called him *sureela.*

In early July, I travel to London to meet Rosamund Adoo-Kissi-Debrah, who is fighting for children's health in London after her daughter Ella died of asthma triggered by air pollution. Rosamund and Ella lived near Catford Bridge by the busy South Circular Road. Ella died in 2013 after suffering from seizures for three years and making 27 visits to the hospital. She was not even 10 years old. An asthma and air pollution expert[20] in the UK linked her death to spikes in nitrogen dioxide and PM10 particulates that breached legal limits.[21] Five years later, in 2018,[22] with evidence of the health harm of air pollution growing, Rosamund petitioned the attorney general to get a fresh inquest into Ella's death and have air pollution listed as a reason for death on her death certificate. She got a major boost in 2019 when the UK's attorney general said that the high court should consider the application[23] and the mayor of London Sadiq Khan backed the call. This makes international headlines.

It is a fellow journalist Beth Gardiner's article in the *Guardian* which had alerted me to Ella's case. I first met Beth in New Delhi in 2015 when she was researching air pollution from ground zero for her book, *Choked*, which traces the impact of air pollution and the choices that governments and people have made that have caused dramatic impacts in the air we breathe.

The very first thing Rosamund tells me when we meet is that until the age of seven Ella was 'a perfectly healthy child' who walked to school every day. In reality, she was inhaling toxic diesel fumes as she did so, and that was what caused damage to her lungs, leading to her death. As we retrace Ella's path to school, I'm struck by how heavy the traffic is.

Rosamund is wearing a blue-striped shirt and black pants, and as we sit on a bench by the roadside near the location where she is planning to build a memorial park for Ella, I can't help but think of how Ella died of an asthma attack breathing these very fumes. A few feet away, people are sitting in cafes whose chairs are spilling out onto the pavement. Rosamund is quick to point out to me that there are no monitors close by, thus no way of knowing what the air quality is here.

She tells me that with the recent support from political circles and voices rising in support for her, she is hopeful of getting her daughter's death certificate to state air pollution as the cause of death. If Ella becomes the first person on this planet to have 'toxic air' recorded as the cause of her death, it will have far-reaching implications for human rights and unveil a silent killer. We talk of her plans to perhaps join local politics.[24] The Green Party is a good option for her as a clean air campaigner. She is also curious about the worldwide fight against air pollution, and I tell her about a recent class action lawsuit that the citizens of Jakarta are planning against their government as well as the petition by toddlers to ban firecrackers in India. I learn that she also met Dr Arvind Kumar a few months ago. 'Pollution is a chemical cause – but people die of diseases,' I remember Dr Kumar saying. 'However, pollution is the primary cause. It kills. All ages, all genders.'

That air pollution doesn't show up as a cause for death on death certificates anywhere is due to a technicality. 'If people that died from air pollution were marked with green spots, it would be very easy for everyone to understand. But when people's lives are shortened by air pollution, they die of the things that people die of anyway: respiratory diseases, heart disease, strokes,' says Dr Gary Fuller, an air pollution scientist and author of *The Invisible Killer*.

It is also this technicality that leads to it being politicized – in the UK as well, but more so in India. Instead of acknowledging the truth about air pollution affecting people's longevity, Dr Harsh Vardhan, the incumbent minister for health in 2018, adds to the controversy[25] by saying his benchmark for a medical 'emergency' is the Bhopal Gas Tragedy of 1984, once again proving how air pollution – a silent pandemic – can remain hidden in plain sight. The fact that he is an ENT surgeon doctor–politician makes this all the more uncomfortable.

The coronavirus pandemic has reframed the meaning of a public health emergency, but it doesn't alter the fact that air pollution kills many more than SARS-CoV-2 – just less dramatically. As an environmentalist in Los Angeles has told Beth Gardiner[26] so evocatively, 'If you see one person run over in the street, you'll never forget it but thousands dying from the effects of dirty air will never even faze you.'[27] Because, with air pollution, like the proverbial frog in the pot of gradually heating water, you die a little bit every day without even understanding what is happening to you.

London already has a mayor who has made clean air a priority. In April 2019, Sadiq Khan introduced tough vehicle emissions standards in central London to help reduce toxic air pollution and protect public health.[28] By doing this, Khan expects to reduce harmful road transport emissions in central London by an estimated 45 per cent in two years.[29] As someone who developed adult-onset asthma shortly before he was elected mayor in 2016,[30] he knows from personal experience that London's toxic air is damaging people's health. The central London Ultra Low Emission Zone (ULEZ) will operate 24 hours a day, seven days a week, 365 days a year. Research by King's College, London, has found that if these measures had not been implemented, London's air would not have come into compliance within legal limits for another 193 years. With the new measures, the analysis indicates that London's air will now reach legal limits in six years. The Environmental Research Group[31] at King's works closely with the mayor of London as the official air quality monitor.

I wish Delhi chief minister Kejriwal would create such zones, apply 'congestion charges' during peak hours, clean and improve public mobility and make private vehicles expensive instead of just imposing the ineffective odd-even road rationing scheme his government lapses into every time winter AQI goes off the charts. Internalizing costs of of pollution reduction measures has been shown to improve polluting behaviour.

When I'm sitting with Rosamund, I can't help noticing that this part of London looks crummier than central London where I've just come from after meeting Beth. Even without measuring, I know the pollution levels will be higher. But Khan has also addressed this inequity while pushing his ULEZ plan,[32] saying it will help the poorest Londoners most.

London is Beth's adopted city from where she has travelled to China, the US, Poland and Germany for a more global overview for her book. Talking to someone who has looked at air pollution through the same lens as me is energizing and helps me understand some issues from another angle. I tell her how counter-intuitive I find Delhi's odd-even road rationing scheme, 'National governments encourage car sales to increase GDP growth and profits. But they leave it to local authorities to keep those cars off the roads,' I complain. Jing's words that pollution smells of money have begun haunting me. I tell her how terribly skewed subsidies in India are, something I've recently learnt from a transportation researcher. Car owners are the most highly subsidized, when they should actually be paying parking and congestion charges. 'The government is indirectly subsidizing car owners instead of making ownership expensive and public transport cheaper – which is the only way to drive behavioural change,' I tell her. 'In India, we have roughly 30,000 buses for the entire country's population, while the city of Beijing alone has 25,000.'

Beth has her own learnings and grouses to share. The main one being that despite being caught,[33] car manufacturers are still selling vehicles whose nitrogen dioxide emissions are many times over the legal limit.[34] She feels strongly that they must be penalized for cheating. We discuss the Volkswagen cheating scandal that exposed rampant rule breaking and bending across the industry. Insisting that manufacturers make cleaner cars would be far more effective than policing where those cars can go, she says. London's ULEZs are good measures to begin with, and the best that a local government can do, but only the national government can enforce any radical change, she will write in an article.[35]

We agree that electric mobility, especially when electricity is generated by clean, renewable energy, is one of the quickest solutions. In India, this would entail that everything from public buses to the highly polluting two-wheelers runs on electricity generated by clean energy. But what the world really needs is fewer cars altogether. 'It's [fewer cars for mobility] a goal that's reachable if we reorganize the places we live to be denser, more pedestrian and bicycle-friendly and have public transportation and ride-sharing that is convenient and affordable,' Beth tells me. But no one is willing to pay the higher costs of clean air – even though its benefits are so clear. After this meeting, I catch the connecting train that will take me to Catford Bridge and Rosamund.

The same day, after I leave Rosamund, I also communicate with Simon Birkett, a clean air campaigner who sends me a copy of the Clean Air (Human Rights) Bill, a private member's bill that has been tabled in the UK Parliament to establish the right to breathe clean air, and requires the public authorities to achieve and maintain clean air and set and review limits for pollutants, as well as greatly enhances the powers of environmental agencies.

I find myself wishing that we had something similar in India. But pollution is a topic that has not entered the echelons of our Parliament as of yet.

A week after I meet Rosamund, I come across another family whose life has been upended and reframed by air pollution, this time in East Delhi. This is the family of Atul Kumar Jain, a non-smoker who was diagnosed with lung cancer at 39.

Atul lives with his wife and two sons in one of India's largest industrial hubs, at the intersection of three highways in East Delhi's Shahdara. It is as busy as London's South Circular Road, but couldn't be more starkly different. Both areas have high levels of pollution, but London has more nitrous oxides, and Shahdara more PM2.5. The consequences – disease, disability and death – are the same.

Shahdara, restless and pulsating, is less than 5 kilometres from the CPCB's Anand Vihar air-quality monitoring station. Anand Vihar records among the highest PM2.5 levels in all of Delhi. And in 2016, CSE has measured that ambient levels at breathing height are three times higher than those reported by the DPCC monitor.[36] My mother used to live within a 2-kilometre radius of that station.

Atul, a slim, sad-eyed man, has had more than half of his left lung removed, along with a large tumour that, despite its malignancy, showed no symptoms. I've met him before at the 'Breathless' exhibition. '*Mujhe Dilli main rehne ki sazaa mili hai. Yeh aur kissi ko na mile*,' Atul had started speaking on stage, before he broke down publicly. His young son, Pranav, spoke about his father's ordeal. Atul was silent. The poignancy of his words – and silences – has remained with me.

Atul ran a shop in Sadar Bazar when he was diagnosed in April 2017 – he has recently closed that business because he felt that the toxins he was breathing there contributed to his cancer. 'We have no family history of cancer, and we are all non-smokers,' he tells me.

I remember Dr Arvind Kumar's words: 'Technically, there are no non-smokers now in Delhi. Every child born in India is a smoker from day one. Pink lungs are now endangered.' What's worse is that as the entry point of dirty air, lungs are only the first organs to be affected. 'And you know what is worse? That *children* are the most affected. A child breathes from 26 to 30 times a minute. A newborn breathes nearly 50 times a minute. Can you imagine what quantities of toxins they are inhaling?' I hear him ask. 'It is a public health emergency. The parent of a child who knows this wants instant action. But policy-makers don't have the same kind of urgency and magnitude of response. India's Clean Air Act has existed for 30 years, but knowledge levels are still very low.'

In fact, seeing more black lungs in younger people – including newborns – over time as he operated is what has brought Dr Kumar out of the operation theatre and into the advocacy space. He is also the doctor who has operated on Atul Jain.

I navigate a warren of lanes to the Jain home. The entire area is a maze of criss-crossing streets and gullies looping dizzily around larger roads until they spill out directly into the highway. Google maps is unable to help me reach my destination, so Atul's older son Samyak guides me. Past tyre shops, plastic manufacturers, cement warehouses, doctor's clinics, property agents, builders and interior decorators, general hospitals, specialized nursing homes, ENT hospitals and more hospitals – so many hospitals. Despite being surrounded by so many hospitals, it took his wife, Pooja, six visits, an X-ray and a CT scan before Dr Belal Bin Asaf, consultant and vice chairman, thoracic surgery at Ganga Ram Hospital confirmed her worst fears. Because there were no symptoms, it was her persistence that saved his life, says Atul.

Pooja is petite, vivacious, with sparkling eyes set in a round face, an attractive cleft in her chin. She greets me at the entrance to their family home. She is the one who reminds Atul to show me the grisly photos of the extracted tumour, and introduces me to their young son, Pranav. Her exuberance is the perfect foil for Atul's soft-spoken demeanour. Pooja tells me how they came to know of Atul's actual diagnosis, repeating again how there were no visible symptoms, just her feeling that something was terribly wrong. She met Dr Belal Bin Asaf, the chest surgeon at Sir Ganga Ram Hospital, alone that evening. Dr Kumar was travelling.

'My husband didn't want to come inside the hospital, so I went alone while he waited outside,' recalls Pooja. Despite being prepared for the worst, she was felled by the news when she first heard the diagnosis. From her telling, it is clear Dr Belal was gentle when he broke the news to her.

As soon as I leave their home, I call Dr Belal. He remembers Atul's case and recalls meeting Pooja, even remembers the tears that immediately sprang to her eyes. It was 11 April 2017.

'She was taken aback,' he recalls, his gentle voice measured. 'At such a young age, to get such a diagnosis…' Years of experiencing such situations reflect in the weariness in his voice. 'What could I tell her? I told her it was good that it was detected early and that there was hope.' And there was.

Dr Kumar, with Dr Belal an integral part of his team, operated on Atul 11 days after his diagnosis.

'Of course, his cancer was due to air pollution,' Dr Kumar says. There is no doubt in his voice.

Dr Belal is more circumspect. 'Atul's cancer was most likely due to air pollution,' he says. 'There are some very definitive factors that lead me to say this. He was young, never smoked and lived in a very polluted place. But it is difficult to say that one specific person's cancer is due to one cause.' Public health researchers and epidemiologists would likely find Dr Belal's statement more accurate. From a public health perspective, causality needs an epidemiological approach at a population level, and individual cases can't be extrapolated to represent the entire population. This is more a matter of nuance and precision, something the scientific community values highly.

Atul recovers after surgery and when I meet him, he is a happy, if slightly sombre personality, still shadowed by the harrowing experience. But he is only one among many other cases Dr Kumar refers to. There are also those who weren't as fortunate as Atul.

Dr Kumar is among a handful of doctors who have been warning of a lung cancer epidemic in Delhi due to its toxic air. 'Air pollution is killing as many people as smoking does,' he has said on many occasions. 'In India, breathing kills.' His words may sound dramatic, but I already know so many people suffering from respiratory and lung diseases that I don't find anything he says an overstatement. The latest in my circle to be diagnosed with lung cancer is URJA's Ashutosh.

Doctors like Dr Kumar are at the front lines of public health and in a direct position to characterize and diagnose such illnesses. Their observations are critical red flags; we need their vigilance to alert us about any upcoming health epidemics. However, while it is important for doctors to call out poor air quality as alarming, it would be inaccurate to state that any individual case is 'proof' that air pollution is the cause of stage 4 lung cancer. Many factors contribute to developing this type of cancer. To establish actual causality of air pollution exposure with this type of cancer requires epidemiological analysis over far larger numbers of people in the entire population. We need to pool such data and conduct these studies on larger scales at the population level, a nuance that is difficult to balance.

What bothers me is that India has the researchers, expertise and capability to conduct the research, and yet no such research has been conducted. Findings from their analyses can influence our policymakers and healthcare system to respond to health harms associated with air pollution. Yet the focus of most conversations simply seems to be about fixing blame, not the problem. Perhaps networks such as Doctors for Clean Air (DFCA) will help bridge the gap between clinical and public health diagnoses. But until then we must continue to do all we can to drastically reduce and minimize our exposure immediately. That is the only way the needless suffering of families like Atul's can be avoided. I carry with me the image of his sombre face, his his family by his side, with me for months afterwards.

By the time I leave Shahdara, the sun is high in the sky. Cars, buses, trucks and Tempos are among every sort of vehicle I see on the roads. People want to live here, have babies here. I realize with a sudden shock that I'm in the heartland of aspirational India, the India every multinational wants to tap, every brand wants to access and every bottom line wants to reach. Despite early rains having washed away much of the grime, this heartland is covered in a light haze.

Unjustly, pollution affects the poor most. Dr Kumar has conducted lung-function tests on waste management workers in one of India's largest landfills, Bhalswa, and found their lungs to be irreversibly damaged, 'Marginalized communities suffer the most,' he said at a recent conference. Some of these poorest of the poor work in subhuman conditions such as in underground sewage drains and die from inhaling poisonous gases formed there.

August has been a wet month and the air has been cleaner. Chetan Bhattacharji joins CFA's governing board, a breath of fresh air himself. He is the managing editor of NDTV, and despite abandoning the idea of a parents' clean air force, is increasingly committed to clean air. I feel certain he can help improve our communications strategy. He begins creating a database of official information based on Parliament questions answered on air pollution. Later, as we start engaging more with Members of Parliament on this issue, he will be the one who will keep his eye on that ball, collating queries and ensuring that our legislators ask more questions on air pollution in Parliament. He also begins tweeting for CFA, helping boost our online engagement.

With the rains washing away PM2.5 and ensuring that the dust settles a bit, the Aam Aadmi Party is quick to take credit for the improvement in air quality with full-page advertisements in leading newspapers saying air quality in Delhi has improved by 25 per cent over the past four years. The minister for the environment, Prakash Javadekar, claims that the number of days with 'bad' air quality has come down by 33 per cent compared to 2016.[37] However, as a tweet by a clean air campaigner[38] highlights, the politicians fail to mention that there has not even been one 'good' air day throughout the previous year.

Spending public money to take credit for nature's clean-up job incites me to write an article in the *Wire*[39] questioning Mr Kejriwal's claims and asking him to show us the data – as presumably his claims are based on public data, collected with public funds. Within hours, I get a call from one of the editors, who says that the chief minister's office has responded and is sending a rebuttal. I am invited to write a second article based on the rebuttal but it never comes. Instead, I see the government highlighting a seven-point Parali Pradushan Action Plan that it had announced along with its claims of a 25 per cent fall in pollution to 'prepare ourselves for smog'. Sarath has already replied to Mr Kejriwal's seven-point pollution plan tweet[40] with an article he wrote for the *Wire* in 2016.[41] It is very telling that nothing has changed in three years.

By September, preparations for embedding an air pollution session at TiEcon are in full swing. Dr Laveesh Bhandari, an economist, data analyst and freshly minted environmentalist, has agreed to help me put the session together. I've known him for nearly 30 years, and he is also active with the URJA group of RWAs and knows Ashutosh well. Several emails, phone calls and meetings later, we manage to assemble a knowledge panel comprising Dr Randeep Guleria, now the director of AIIMS; Dr Kirk Smith, professor of global health at the University of Berkeley; Dr Ken Lee from the University of Chicago; Dr Navroz Dubash from the Centre for Policy Research; Dr Mukund Rajan from ECube; and Irfan Pathan, a young entrepreneur. Dr Smith is so happy with the fact that this event is outward-looking and not another echo chamber that he is willing to fly in to Delhi for this.

But the biggest challenge remains getting a celebrity to be a part of it. We need star power that will attract the crowds. Someone from the TiE team tries to get cricketer (and lung cancer survivor) Yuvraj Singh but fails. By October, our team is getting desperate. That is when a chance meeting with Shibani Thukral leads us to Bollywood star Dia Mirza. She is intelligent, articulate and environmentally conscious; she is also the UN Environment's goodwill ambassador for India. She is ideal for not only attracting young entrepreneurs, but also keeping them insightfully engaged. Someone from the TiE team has already tried to invite her but hadn't heard back. This time, with Shibani's good offices, with just a month to go, Dia agrees and we're ready to roll.

Preparations for TiEcon are in full swing. A couple of days before my mother's second birthday without her, I wake to the shocking news that Ashutosh has lost his battle with lung cancer. I feel devastated by his death. I only knew him as a fellow clean air campaigner but had been impressed by his knowledge and pragmatic cooperative skills. He worked tirelessly to improve local civic amenities, and clean air was a firm demand. I had been so hopeful that his strength and optimism would help him beat this. It feels too close – he was just four years older than me. I will miss him.

The stresses of the past few months added to the distress from the loss triggers in me a painful attack of shingles, just as the city's air quality, predictably, goes off the charts. Crop stubble burning has begun in Punjab, and the winds are bringing the smoke directly to Delhi into our lungs, and EPIC has chosen an appropriate time to launch its AQLI report in Hindi. The report states that pollution in the Indo-Gangetic plain (IGP) has increased by 72 per cent from 1998 to 2016, a region that is home to about 40 per cent of India's population.[42] The IGP region includes Delhi, Haryana, Punjab, Uttar Pradesh, Bihar and West Bengal, and with the report in Hindi, many more of those impacted will learn what is killing them and their loved ones so silently.

'Mom, your own oxygen mask first,' my children repeat to me, as I chafe that I can't participate in so many important clean air events coming up. It's that time of the year again. Oxygen mask is exactly what I need in this city, I think wryly as I call up my father to tell him to order an oxygen concentrator for the winter. Between air filters and the oxygen, he should survive another of Delhi's toxic winters.

Even as preparations for the large conference continue, an incident involving cricket comes as a telling reminder of how little the urgency that we feel about the air quality actually exists beyond the chambers we work in.

There is an India–Bangladesh match scheduled to be played in Delhi on 3 November 2019. Brikesh, who has banded together the rapidly growing Clean Air Collective, suggests we all jointly write to the Board of Cricket Control in India (BCCI) to move the match away from Delhi. The air quality is only expected to worsen by then. To make matters worse, the match is scheduled for the evening, when the falling temperatures keep the PM levels at the most inhalable height. In addition to the sportspeople on the field and off it, spectators too – especially the elderly and the very young – will be putting themselves at risk if they decide to attend (and we know they will). Sourav Ganguly has just been appointed the new president of the BCCI, which is encouraging since he has also been a professional cricket player and athlete. Our expectation is that he will be empathetic about the health hazard posed to the players and make a responsible decision. Ravina and I send the letter jointly from CFA and MRTB from the CFA email account.

In the letter[43] we say,

On 3 November 2019, India is scheduled to play against Bangladesh in a T20 match at the Feroz Shah Kotla ground at a time when pollution levels are expected to be between 'severe' and 'hazardous'. Indian doctors and health specialists in recent years have consistently advised us to protect ourselves, our children, elderly and vulnerable during this severely polluted season, and the Indian Medical Association has called this a public health emergency. It is now well understood that exposure to bad air even in the short-term impacts our day-to-day activities and performance. The only way to protect ourselves from these hazardous levels is by staying indoors, wearing masks and using air filters whenever particulate matter (PM) levels are high. Thousands of innocent spectators at the venue will be putting themselves at risk in order to watch the match.

Even worse, any outdoor aerobic activity raises the respiration rate of the human body, thus depositing even higher levels of toxins into our lungs and organs. This puts our sportspeople at even greater risk when they play outdoors. Any match played outdoors harms the health and the very lives of the players, and it is irresponsible to schedule sporting activities during times of such toxic air quality.

In the light of extreme pollution in Delhi, we would like to request you to consider shifting the venue for the first T20 outside of Delhi. *Making our cricketers play a physically demanding sport for three to four hours in Delhi's toxic air will end up doing more damage to our cricket team's health in the long run. We would also like to request you to consider setting up responsible sports protocols which take into consideration the AQI of venues and cities while scheduling cricket matches, be it domestic or international.*

We have been writing to government departments and corporates since 2015, asking that all outdoor aerobic activity for AQI levels of more than 250–300 be immediately suspended, without exception.

We also point out how a match held during similarly polluted conditions in December 2017 had resulted in players from the visiting Sri Lanka team complaining of nausea, with some even throwing up. The match had to be paused, resuming after a break.

Since the air quality is so obviously poor – the haze that is settling over Delhi is visible to the naked eye – we are hopeful our petition and the growing conversations in the media around poor air quality will pressurize the organizers to move the match out of Delhi into a less polluted location. But we get no response from the board.

The letter becomes a topic of discussion in print, broadcast and social media. Dia Mirza hears about it and reaches out to support the petition. She wants to add her name to the letter, which is not just gratifying but will also add much weight to our request. She also calls out the BCCI in a tweet.[44] When we speak on the phone, I realize she knows more about air pollution than I had assumed and is very keen to focus on constructive solutions. She wants to make a real difference. We agree to pick up the conversation during the TiEcon session, which is in two weeks.

Unfortunately, despite the media attention garnered by our plea, the match isn't moved out of Delhi, nor is the time changed to an earlier start. We feel defeated. However, a small win is that Ganguly publicly admits to the press at Eden Gardens in Kolkata that while it was 'too late' to reschedule the match this year, the BCCI will be more careful going forward and will take into account pollution levels before scheduling future matches.[45]

The AQI for 3 November had been predicted as being over 400 micrograms per cubic metre, but the actual level of PM2.5 on the day is above 600 micrograms per cubic metre. The period between 1 November and 11 November ends up being a continuous spell of hazardous air quality in the city and its surrounding areas. The entire city has begun to look like the film set of a dystopian movie. The outside air feels so smoky that I remain indoors, feeling trapped in the only two rooms in my home which have air purifiers.

Although I'm no longer part of the school PTA – my son has graduated – I hear of groups of parents going to the principal to ask for the same things that we had asked for – air purifiers, no outdoor sports, a late start, to give the sun a chance to burn off some of the pollution. Some angry parents are even demanding school closure.

Finally, the government orders closure of all schools, and the Aam Aadmi Party government – which in September had been claiming improvement in the air quality – distributes 5 million masks[46] among the city's residents. This makes international news,[47] with the BBC, ABC News, CNN and *Khaleej Times* running stories about the mass distribution of masks.

Through all this there is no acknowledgement of the problem from the central government. Meteorology is against us this year and PM levels remain high. People on all air pollution groups are getting increasingly restive. Agitated mothers from Delhi are spearheading a campaign called *Bachhon Ke Mann ki Baat* (The Inner Thoughts of Our Children), titled after the prime minister's monthly radio programme in order to get his attention. Children's Day is on 14 November and children start writing postcards to the government demanding clean air. Others are organizing protests at different locations, including outside of Delhi. With the frequency and desperation of these activities, it is clear that agitation around pollution is growing.

Despite being caught up in TiEcon prep, I too draft a letter to the prime minister requesting – no, begging – him to take leadership in the matter of cleaning the air that we, India's citizens, breathe. We need a bold and ambitious plan by a bold and ambitious person to tackle this problem. The letter also includes a request to reconstitute the EPCA, which has let Delhi become among the most polluted cities in the world.[48] The letter is signed by CFA, MRTB, URJA and the Clean Air Collective, and Anita uploads the letter. As I draft the letter for Anita to upload to the prime minister's portal, I feel a sense of déjà vu. We have been asking for the same thing for years. But our voices have remained unheard.

Respected Shri Narendra Modi, we say in our letter uploaded on the PM's portal on 3 November,

We, the people of India, request you to please take leadership to resolve the serious problem of air pollution and its related negative health impact in the whole country, but especially in the Indo-Gangetic plain and most specifically the capital Delhi, which is choking under a thick smog of lethal air. Today's AQI – even after a short drizzle of cleaning rains – remains around 632 in Delhi, according to the SAFAR monitors.

Instead of fixing the problem, every single political party remains intent on fixing the blame while Indians continue to die due to the terrible air. We need you, as representative of all Indian people, to rise above this petty politicking and make our health the first priority. Also, your political party is in power in most of the north Indian states and can improve enforcement of existing laws that will prevent open burning of every kind that is currently contributing maximally to poor air quality, especially through the malignant particulate matter that causes irreversible damage to our bodies.

Death certificates may never state air pollution as the cause of death. That is because air pollution isn't a disease, but it is a trigger for many diseases. You will already have the numbers. But for those of us inhaling these toxins, we know that each breath we take is killing us and our loved ones faster. Yet, we can't do anything about it and that makes us feel helpless, sad and angry.

Dr Randeep Guleria, the director of the country's top medical research institute, AIIMS, has already warned us that emergency admissions due to pollution have gone up by 15 to 20 per cent in Delhi, and are mostly people suffering from chest and respiratory ailments. But these aren't the only risks we face. Cardiovascular risks, heart attacks, strokes and other diseases also rise during times of episodic spikes like we are seeing now. Dr Guleria has also said that masks provide more reassurance rather than any real protection.

This problem of air pollution affects every single Indian, rich or poor, of all castes, religions, creed and across all state boundaries. No one apart from the prime minister of our country can take the lead to fix this issue.

The current members of the Supreme Court-mandated Environment Pollution

(Prevention and Control) Authority have failed in their duty to control pollution and levels have spiked sharply under their watch. We request these members of the EPCA be immediately removed, and dynamic, proactive members be installed, who will be able to bring pollution levels down with more urgency.

Our doctors have told us we are in a state of national health emergency. There is no time for reactive measures. We earnestly request you to save our children, our elderly, our most vulnerable who suffer the worst effects of pollution. Additionally, air pollution affects the poor far more than the rich. The poor cannot access expensive masks and purifiers and sometimes don't even have four walls to protect them from the toxic air. Air pollution is a social iniquity and goes against social justice. Delhi's chief minister calls his own city a gas chamber. Is air pollution not a violation of our basic human right to clean air?

Hoping for prompt and decisive action.

Jyoti Pande Lavakare & Gopal Sankaranarayanan- Care For Air,
Ravina Raj Kohli - My Right To Breathe
Atul Goyal - United Residents Joint Action
Brikesh Singh - Clean Air Collective

There is no response to the letter, not even an acknowledgement. But on 11 November, I see the verified BJP4India Twitter handle carry a dramatic two-minute video on Delhi's pollution levels.[49] Naturally, it is squarely blaming the Kejriwal government for the 'gas chamber' that Delhi has become. But for me, the exciting part is the BJP – the political party that is currently ruling at the centre as well as in several states and is headed by Prime Minister Modi – is finally officially acknowledging pollution as a problem. On 13 November 2019, Delhi is so polluted that the government shuts down schools again. The next day is Children's Day in India, and the children remain imprisoned in their homes.

When we will check the status of this letter on the portal two weeks later on 18 November, it will say 'closed'. PM2.5 levels in parts of north India that day will breach 20 times the WHO limits.

TiEcon finally arrives. It happens to be Children's Day. There have been some last-minute changes in the panel as well as in the date. Dr Arvind Kumar has replaced Dr Guleria, and Dr Smith is unable to make it for the session's changed date. The only thing the TiEcon secretariat hasn't agreed to is displaying at the conference venue the readings of low-cost monitors that measure the outside pollution at prominent locations in the city and other metros. They are concerned it will affect the turnout. I have a sudden epiphany on why it will never be in the interest of governments to make its people more aware. When the institution measuring pollution levels is also responsible – and accountable – for its removal or reduction, it will never be in its interest to spread awareness about this problem.

As I tuck in my sari pleats carefully before leaving for the Taj Palace, I can't stop going through a mental checklist. This is the first time I've attempted seeding difficult conversations on pollution within a demographic that is directly implicated in creating it. It is important for them to realize that they are as much victims of air pollution as they are offenders. We are all complicit.

I open the session to a hall that is completely full. The session is called 'Making Our Habitats Liveable'. 'For today's session,' I say, 'we will focus on the part of our habitat without which we can't even survive beyond three minutes…air. We can survive without food for three weeks, without water for three days, but without air, for less than three minutes.'

I look around and see that I seem to have got everyone's attention.

'A few years ago, we formed a platform called Care For Air,' I continue. 'Over the course of the years, I learnt air pollution was not just a Delhi problem. It is an all-India problem, though Delhi was the worst hit. That it was not just a winter problem, but a year-round problem, though winter was the worst. That it affected not just our lungs, but all of our organs, irreversibly, though our lungs are the worst hit. That it affects all of us, and though the rich are more aware, the poor suffer more of the harmful effects. It is a social inequity. But despite knowing so much about pollution, I couldn't prevent toxic air from seeping into my own mother's lungs, triggering lung cancer, which was diagnosed in

October 2017. I realized then that it's not enough to just know. We need solutions to what is now recognized as a national public health emergency. We are all victims and we are all complicit. And no one can fight this alone. This isn't a conflict between economic growth and environment. This is a fight to survive.'

I go on to emphasize the importance of sharing all this knowledge with people who can quickly understand the urgency of such a gigantic problem, problem-solvers who can innovate and invent to find solutions using technology and intelligence. In other words, the very audience I'm addressing. People are listening attentively, but I can sense from the murmurs and craned necks and ready camera phones that they are waiting for Dia Mirza to come up on stage.

Just before the session, I had walked around the conference venue encouraging young entrepreneurs to attend the air pollution session.

'That sounds interesting! When is that?' one young man had asked me, quickly leafing through his programme.

'The next session at the Durbar Hall.'

'Oh! The Dia Mirza session?'

Sigh. Yes. The 'Dia Mirza session'.

But that was the plan, wasn't it? To use celebrity power to ensure a large turnout.

The moment for Dia Mirza to take the stage arrives. But just before I start announcing her, I notice the organizers gesturing to me that she hasn't reached the hall yet. Slightly flustered, I move on to the keynote speaker, Mukund Rajan of ECube, a private equity company. Rajan has impeccable credentials as a genuine sustainability icon and his speech is crisp and to the point. It helps that he has the rock star charisma of his brother, former RBI governor Raghuram Rajan, and I suspect at least some of the young folk in the hall are there specifically to hear him.

'First, we are in the midst of an environmental crisis of emergency proportions,' Rajan begins. 'The statistics in India are stark. We account for 14 of the 15 worst cities in the world in terms of air quality according to WHO data... And when you factor in urbanization and lifestyle changes, the problems we face are going to worsen, dramatically,' he says.

The science and technology that will help us address the crisis is constantly improving, he continues, citing the problem of crop stubble burning – an important contributor to Delhi's current air pollution problem – and possible solutions for it as an example. He focuses on the notion of pricing, a very important one.

'Whether it is addressing the root cause of the water availability problem, or offering technology like the Happy Seeder and straw management solutions farmers might require, or providing subsidies to divert crop production, or paying compensation to keep farms fallow, there is a price to be paid for different solutions,' he says. 'The price can be justified when the costs of not acting are totalled up, including the healthcare and welfare costs and the lost productivity costs.'

Rajan says that a lot of very exciting research is going into developing new capital valuation techniques that will help us find equitable solutions. 'Forward-looking businesses are embracing the changes in the sustainability agenda,' he says. 'Companies are beginning to embrace the "circular economy", one where resources are circulated within the system releasing minimal waste into the biosphere. The leading companies are, in fact, placing sustainability at the heart of their business strategies. And those companies that have no intention of doing this, I am clear, will fade away,' he warns.

But all of this may not be enough, he says as he wraps up. He exhorts all thought leaders to help persuade the political system to 'create the appropriate governance structure for resolving the crisis we face'.

Fortunately, by the time his speech is done, Dia Mirza has arrived. I run up to the mike in relief. I can finally announce the person the crowd has been waiting for.

'To begin this journey, I'd like to invite up on stage our guest of honour, someone who doesn't just combine beauty with brains, but also with a heart…' I begin. The crowd is already applauding.

The session that follows goes exceedingly well. The hall is packed, every chair taken. Dia is persuasive, knowledgeable, charming. She speaks extempore, bringing in the unfortunate fact that pollution has imprisoned children indoors today, on Children's Day. Dr Kumar follows her – articulate, authoritative, precise, startling the audience without completely scaring them, bringing his operating theatre to the room. He shows pictures he has taken of the healthy, pink human lung, contrasted with the lung of a Delhi resident. I notice many people bring out their phones again and start clicking photos, looking unnerved. This is a good sign.

Dr Lee follows Dr Kumar's lead and talks about reduced life expectancy due to toxic air and how awareness about air pollution is still very, very low. 'Only when awareness increases will the demand for change increase,' he says. 'And only then will governments be able to gather the courage to take any real, significant steps.' Any steps to clean the air are bound to be unpopular, he concludes, because we have to pay for cleaning our air, and no one likes to pay.

All the speakers agree that we need to demand clean air from our politicians, across party lines, from our government, our courts and our prime minister.

'As citizens, we have to demand [that] our political parties tell us in their manifestos what they will do to solve [the] air pollution [problem], how and when,' chimes in Dr Dubash. He has the policy overview of this group and works in climate change at the Centre for Policy Research, and has also been appointed in a reconstituted EPCA, along with Dr Kumar.

'We need to develop a strategy for each source of pollution, because each source has its own characteristics, politics, mix of behavioural, regulatory and technical solutions,' he says, 'Technical solutions are important, but they need an enabling policy environment,' he adds. 'We need to be willing to bear the costs of change, either financially or by changing our behaviours or both – don't buy big diesel cars, use public transport and reduce waste creation.'

It is only when people across every strata of society understand the health effects of air pollution and start demanding clean air that this will become something that governments, political parties and courts will start taking strong action on. I know that even with our alliances, CFA is never going to be able to reach all of India's people across the various divides of languages and social classes. Especially with our limited resources. But that isn't a reason for not trying. It is better to have tried and failed than never have tried at all, I've always taught my children. Well, now it's time to practise what I preach.

On the Saturday following the TiEcon, there is a scheduled meeting of the parliamentary committee on pollution in Parliament House. Twenty-nine members are supposed to attend it, but only four show up. This reflects the importance our policymakers give to pollution. The media doesn't fail to note this, and several news programmes highlight it.

The next day there is a massive protest against air pollution at Leisure Valley Park in Gurugram, north India's 'millennium city', home to top corporates, both national and multinational, and about 8.7 lakh residents. Almost 3,000 people – most dressed in black – gather at Leisure Valley Park to raise their voices against the hazardous air they are forced to breathe. Strong winds have blown away the thick smog, and the bright sunny day is bound to have reminded the adults in the crowd what their city used to look like in winter in the days before the smog set in.

A local CEO speaks on behalf of NASSCOM Haryana, saying, 'Our people are unwell and our international clients are cancelling their trips to India. Instead of Gurgaon coming across as the "Millennium City of India", it is coming across as a dystopian apocalyptic city.' Some people are shouting in slogans in English, others singing against *pradooshan* in Hindi. What is different about this protest is that there are as many corporate executives as autorickshaw drivers, as many doctors as security guards, as many students from fancy private schools as government schools, as many teachers as street vendors, as many placards in English as in Hindi, as many women as men and as many senior citizens as schoolchildren.[50]

The next morning, Parliament's winter session begins. I wait to see if any pollution debates will come up in Parliament. By now, every legislator in Delhi should be able to smell, see and taste the worst of the pollution. I've heard that MP Gaurav Gogoi plans to move a private members' bill in this session itself, asking to amend the Clean Air Act of 1981, and a news story says this will also give the CPCB powers to prosecute polluters.[51] Gogoi has been one of the few legislators who has consistently brought up air pollution as a serious issue – as far back as in 2015, he attended Parliament sessions wearing a mask. Even though private members' bills aren't usually very effective, this is a good step and I hope he will make it focus on public health.

On 19 November, for the first time ever, the Lok Sabha specifically discusses pollution. I follow the five-hour discussion and am pleasantly surprised by how pollution-savvy and knowledgeable some of the MPs who speak are. The environment minister is supposed to reply to the debate – but he also serves as the information and broadcasting minister and has to leave to inaugurate an international film festival being held in Goa. The debate remains unfinished.

Two days later, the Rajya Sabha also debates the issue. But attendance is sparse and heavyweight leaders are absent. The biggest problem is that the prime minister is still not directly involved. It is clear that pollution still hasn't become important enough. It is time to fine-tune strategies. One single-point authority, a clean air CEO, becomes our next point of action. In other words, we need a sharp weapon (new Clean Air Act) and a bold, decisive wielder of that weapon (a Clean Air Boss) to fight air pollution effectively enough to have a positive health impact. I write an article for the *Quint* and NDTV titled 'Wanted: A Clean Air Boss'.[52]

'Every country that has cleaned up its polluted air has done so after reaching a tipping point,' I say in the article. That point has come after pollution has become undeniable and its health harm acknowledged, after people have realized that existing environmental laws have been bypassed by industries or lobbies with commercial agendas. Action is only possible after the implementation of new laws that serve public health over private commercial interest. 'Whether it is Mexico, Los Angeles, London or China, change has come after the tipping point is breached. India is at the cusp of that tipping point.'

For the first time, air pollution has made it to the national agenda.

With the debate in Parliament, however poorly attended, this important topic has finally reached the legislature. For years, dirty air was considered normal. Then, it was politicized. Hopefully, in the next round, India's toxic air will finally be cleaned up.

To be honest, with the amount of science, data and evidence backing the public health emergency India is currently facing caused by the levels of pollutants no human should have to breathe, this issue should not even have to be debated. Unfortunately, India's environment minister still seems to be unconvinced, telling Parliament on 6 December 2019 that no Indian study has shown a correlation between pollution and shortening of lifespan.[53] This is diplomatically but firmly refuted by the WHO's Dr Maria Neira[54,55,56] who, in a counter rebuttal, offers to facilitate access to the more than 70,000 scientific publications linking air pollution and health.

In 2015, the same minister in the same role had told Parliament that polluted air is responsible for morbidity and premature deaths.[57] At that time he had quoted a study co-authored by Josh[58] and reported by CSE's newsletter[59] which also said that 'the number of people who died every hour in Delhi because of air pollution has increased by three times in nearly 20 years. The current study also emphasizes that if no action is taken, these numbers could rise by 20 to 30 per cent.' Unexpectedly, the deaths were mostly from heart attacks and strokes, rather than from respiratory disorders. Now he is saying the opposite.

Any responsible government should have already been at work to find real solutions to this gigantic problem that is causing more disease, disability and death than war and terrorism. However, until now, it has only been the judiciary which has made any significant attempt at tackling it. It is now time that our legislature and executive jointly create the structure and mechanisms to solve this crippling problem. Instead of focusing on the politics of air pollution, it is time we looked at the bigger picture of how such a problem can be solved in a democracy like India.

It is only the central government that can bring together all the various entities with conflicting motives and differing agendas – the corporations, state departments, industries, sectors and individuals – to enforce regulations with significant and measurable impact on air quality. This is not to lessen the importance of private responsibility – air is a collective resource, essential for our very survival, and every resident at an individual level is responsible for keeping the air clean – but to emphasize the importance of public accountability.

India's current Air (Prevention and Control of Pollution) Act – all seven chapters and 54 sections of it – never once mentions public health. Clean air is fast becoming accepted as a fundamental human right – and rightly so. London's great smog had led to the UK's Clean Air Act 62 years ago. But in July 2018, the British Parliament introduced it as a human rights bill. The new legislation there aims to improve existing legislations and enshrines the human right to clean air in the country's laws. This is exactly what India's Clean Air Act should do.

As farm fires blaze on – they are now visible from outer space, CFA adviser Dr Pawan Gupta, a scientist with NASA, informs us – they add to the October Diwali cocktail, and air continues to worsen. The Supreme Court passes orders directing states to stop farmers from burning crops, and pulls up officials who aren't going after polluters. On 26 November, the court gives the Centre and the Delhi government 10 days to draw up a comprehensive plan to install 'smog towers' across the capital to deal with air pollution. These giant outdoor air filters will cost roughly ₹12 crore and Delhi will need several such towers, according to media reports.. However, every expert that I have ever spoken to has said that this strategy is suboptimal. None of us clean air campaigners are able to figure out why this myth never seems to die. We have even done myth-busting sessions about this during a recent CFA advocacy workshop. The thought of public money being wasted on what several experts have called a 'crackpot' solution is galling. We decide to immediately write an email and send it to the Supreme Court via their official email address, but get no acknowledgement. On 29 November, *Hindustan Times* carries our plea as a story[60] followed by the Press Trust of India (PTI), which is picked up by other newspapers.[61] We resend the letter via another email address. When there is still no response, Sarath helps us get this published as an open letter on 1 December in the *Wire*.[62]

In all versions of our plea we reiterate three main points:

- That India's leading air pollution scientists and researchers are unanimous in saying that outdoor air purifiers are inefficient to the point of being useless, and public money and scarce environmental resources should not be spent on these expensive and ineffective Band-Aid solutions. We point out that even the largest and most famous tower in Xi'an, China, has been unable to clean the air around it efficiently – their own team has admitted this at an international conference. Smog towers using physical filters may even add to pollution, we point out, when the dirty filters are disposed of and burnt in our already overflowing landfills.
- That such towers are inadvisable also because they give citizens a false sense of complacency and assurance, making them feel that they are getting healthier and there is improvement in the air quality, which is untrue. They are a red herring that gives false reassurance rather than actual protection, meant more for political mileage.
- That air pollution, specifically the most lethal particulate matter, PM2.5, can only be controlled by eliminating the emissions at all the known sources. Any other way is inefficient, ineffective and unscientific, and is only meant to buy time – which we are paying for with our breaths every day.

In the letter, Sarath also adds brief back-of-the-envelope calculations as data to prove exactly how ineffective the towers are. We clarify that it isn't that the technology doesn't work, just that it won't be effective outdoors. We even offer to send experts to make a presentation directly to the court. We give examples of other Indian cities which have experimented with smog towers – and failed – and point out how these are being used as dustbins.

We end by saying:

Please be assured that China and other countries haven't brought their pollution levels down by using smog towers. Rather, they have strengthened industrial emissions standards, phased out small and polluting factories and outdated industrial capacities, upgraded industrial boilers, promoted clean fuels, reducing usage of fossil fuels and strengthened vehicle emission standards. These measures have been implemented rapidly and enforced strictly – and that is what has led to the improvement, not smog towers... We request you to prevent public money from being wasted in such populist and ineffective strategies which aren't backed by science, data and evidence.

We hope the court take cognizance of this letter. Unfortunately, there is no response.

Then, without any warning, something happens that makes air pollution, masks, lung and cardiovascular health even more critical – not just in India, but in the world. Something that also ends up showing Indians what true blue skies and clear views look like, what clean air smells like. Something so intricately and delicately intertwined with air pollution that the two seem knitted together in a secret code, as research begins to unveil.[63,64,65]

14

Air Pollution in a Post-Corona World

It is a respiratory pandemic caused by a novel coronavirus, the SARS-CoV-2 virus causing Covid-19. As this unexpected, ruthless disease rips through the globe, wreaking havoc with lives and livelihoods, for the first time in years, my anxiety about health harm from air pollution is surpassed by a graver, more immediate concern. Even before I have read the first research paper on the connection between air pollution and this new disease, I *know* air pollution will make Covid-19 worse. I even tweet this intuitive connection before restarting research afresh.

One day, in an NPR podcast, I hear American pulmonologist Dr Nicholas Marks describe the lungs as 'these exquisite machines, containers of air that just kind of blow life-giving oxygen into the blood through a thin wall, a membrane'.

'What's so elegant about it is that that membrane is so thin and delicate,' Dr Marks explains. It is the thinness and suppleness of our lung walls that enables them to expand and contract and pass oxygen smoothly and makes breathing so effortless. I understand immediately what he means by the 'poetry of the lungs'.

Dr Marks says it is this membrane that he worries about when he first hears about Covid-19, because what Covid-19 does is inflame that membrane, making the gossamer-thin walls of the human lungs very thick. 'Suddenly, the lung gets really stiff. And instead of it being really easy to get enough oxygen in, now, it requires tremendous work to do it.'

Sometimes patients even need a ventilator to breathe for them, he says.

This is so similar to what I had seen happen to my mother in her final days. In her struggle to breathe – an involuntary, effortless activity I'd always taken for granted – I have seen that poetry turn into an elegy.

It's not just Covid that affects human lungs this way. Many respiratory diseases do – including those triggered by air pollution. The only difference is that some of those diseases may not be as immediately lethal as Covid-19 and, more importantly, they don't spread in bunched-up clusters, overwhelming doctors and hospitals at once. But their naturally flatter curve doesn't mean they kill fewer people. In fact, air pollution kills many more. Air pollution affects our lungs insidiously, indirectly, gradually. In fact, even when it doesn't actually trigger disease, air pollution ends up compromising and weakening the human lungs, making us more vulnerable to respiratory viruses like the SARS, MERS and now the novel coronavirus, the SARS-CoV-2, which causes Covid-19.

If Covid is a visible, viciously virulent, insanely infectious pandemic, killing swiftly and mercilessly, air pollution is its invisible, non-communicable evil twin, killing unhurriedly, under the radar, but equally pitilessly. It is a non-communicable disease (NCD) pandemic in slow-motion, matching – if not surpassing – the cataclysmic fury of SARS-CoV-2. Together, they convert a pandemic to a 'twindemic'.

Within weeks, research on the air pollution–Covid connections starts trickling in, with podcasts and broadcasts quickly amplifying everything related to this dangerous virus. There is a collective urgency in understanding this disease and finding solutions that I have never seen before. Very quickly the coronavirus pandemic reframes the very meaning of a public health emergency.

The *New York Times* is the first to report the new study[1] that shows the earliest clear link between long-term exposure to pollution and Covid-19 death rates, done by Harvard University's T.H. Chan School of Public Health. It shows that coronavirus patients in areas that had high levels of air pollution before the pandemic were more likely to die from the infection than patients in cleaner parts of the United States. 'An increase of 1 $\mu g/m^3$ in PM2.5 is associated with an 8 per cent increase in the Covid-19 death rate,' the cross-sectional Harvard report said.[2] 'Even a small increase in long-term exposure to PM2.5 leads to a large increase in Covid-19 death rate, with the magnitude of increase 20 times that observed for PM2.5 and all-cause mortality. The study results underscore the importance of continuing to enforce existing air pollution regulations to protect human health both during and after the Covid-19 crisis,' the report concludes. What is of greater concern for us in India is that the study was conducted in the US, where pollution is nowhere close to India's appallingly high levels.

Another paper[3] by Leonardo Setti of the University of Bologna and his colleagues from the universities of Bari, Milan and Trieste (first highlighted by the *Economist*[4]) indicates that reducing air pollution may reduce the rate of infection from the SARS-CoV-2. In this study, Dr Setti and his associates found themselves wondering why (even allowing for time lags caused by its arrival in different places on different dates) SARS-CoV-2 seemed to spread much faster in Italy's north – specifically in the wide plain that forms the valley of the Po – than in other parts of the country. Their hypothesis? That the catalyst was pollution – specifically, small airborne particles that might carry the virus on their surfaces. These are usually far more abundant in the Po Valley than elsewhere. In the paper, the researchers cited previous research that suggested that influenza viruses, respiratory syncytial viruses and measles viruses can all spread by hitching lifts on such microparticles. And they make a good case that, allowing for a 14-day delay caused by SARS-CoV-2's incubation period, the daily rates of new infections in the Po Valley correlate closely with the level of particulate pollution.

An alternative explanation for this correlation might be that, rather than carrying the virus themselves, airborne particles increase susceptibility to infection in those who encounter the pathogen by some other means. Either way, though, a reduction in airborne particle levels may be a second way, independent of reduced human contact, in which lockdowns will help stop the virus from spreading.

In addition to these studies, more research is emerging which proves that people living in highly polluted cities are likely to have compromised respiratory, cardiac and other systems, and are therefore more vulnerable to Covid-19's impact.

Evidence from older studies[5] conducted during the SARS outbreak in China also validates this. One study by researchers at the UCLA's School of Public Health[6] showed that patients with SARS were more than twice as likely to die from the disease if they came from areas of high pollution. The same seems true of Covid-19: the more dirty air you are exposed to, the sicker you are likely to get.[7]

In short, every day, emerging research shows new linkages between air pollution and respiratory viruses such as SARS-CoV-2, weaving them together in a denser, tighter web. Covid-19 is a new disease, but recent research already shows three direct interlinkages: 1. that people are more likely to contract respiratory diseases like Covid if they live in polluted areas (because high levels of pollution lower the body's natural defences against airborne viruses); 2. that Covid will affect people more severely if they suffer from pre-existing pollution-triggered diseases; and 3. that the current levels of air pollution that Covid patients are exposed to will add to the severity of the disease, leading to greater chances of hospitalization and death. A fourth interlinkage – that microparticulates act like tiny Ubers that SARS-CoV-2 viruses hitch a ride on to proliferate the spread of the disease – is still in the process of being validated.

In India, Public Health Foundation of India president Prof. Srinath Reddy tells BBC News,[8] 'If air pollution has already damaged the airways and lung tissue, there is reduced reserve to cope with the onslaught of coronavirus.' The same BBC report quotes Dr Maria Neira of the WHO as saying that countries with high pollution levels, many in Latin America, Africa and Asia, should ramp up their epidemic response preparations.

On 24 April 2020, the Centre for Research on Energy and Clean Air, registered in Finland, sums up existing research that validates these interlinkages in a compendium[9] even as fresh research continues to trickle in. Air pollution and Covid are interlinked in more ways than one, and the study of these connections remains dynamic – we are likely to discover even more as investigations pick up speed.

Essentially, all emerging research points to air pollution being 'one of the most important' contributors to Covid-19 deaths in four countries of Europe with nearly 80 per cent of Covid deaths in 66 administrative regions in France, Spain, Italy and Germany occurring in their most polluted regions.

Breathing is an involuntary, almost lyrical activity, critical to our very existence. Yet, as a race, we haven't cared much for what the air we breathe in contains. Chemical pollutants. Gaseous pollutants. Microparticulate solid pollutants. Even venomously high levels of these haven't worried us enough to push firmly for change. As long as we were only dying gradually from the effects of these pollutants, as long as no one has been able to prove direct causality, we haven't much cared. But now, with a microbiological pollutant like the novel coronavirus, there is finally an urgency. And with its connections to air pollution becoming so apparent, I'm hoping that our governments and people will finally act with the same exigency.

India has been among the first to impose an almost complete lockdown on its people, the process revealing a hitherto unseen coherence in execution and in the government's communication about Covid from wearing masks, to physical distancing and staying indoors.

The sheer scale of the lockdown proves that, if the government truly has intent, it is fully capable of reducing air pollution in India by a large margin. From the recorded audio messages about the SARS-CoV-2 spread that played on every mobile phone before the ringtone, to using technology and its enormous muscle to track and trace individuals all over the country, the Indian government demonstrates that it has every tool in place to communicate and manage this serious health issue. With similar intent it is capable of not just spreading awareness, but also lowering emissions at source, encouraging behavioural changes and penalizing polluters at both the individual and industry levels.

The effectiveness of the government's measures on the Covid-19 public health disaster is validated by a telephone survey by India's National Council of Applied Economic Research (NCAER) National Data Innovation Centre, which shows a high understanding of social distancing and support for the lockdown despite considerable hardships.[10] The government's use of science and evidence-backed information as the backbone, and mobile and data technology as tools to spread awareness in a targeted way, makes the lockdown more effective in India's model of democratic, decentralized governance.

But like most government plans executed quickly or without enough transparency, however well intentioned they may be (think demonetization), later events show that livelihoods have suffered much more than expected and millions have been pulled back into poverty. Even so, the point remains that India values human life. In the early days of Covid, when the US caseload (and deaths) is higher than India's, I see a tweet that stays with me. 'India seems to have sacrificed its economy to save lives. The US seems to have sacrificed lives to save its economy. That's strange, because we've always been told that human life is cheap in India and so precious in the US.'

Meanwhile, the lockdowns across geographical, political and social boundaries are creating another brighter, more aesthetic connection between Covid-19 and air pollution. A silver lining, if you will. We're suddenly seeing clear, blue skies, and breathing clean outdoor air, even in our densest cities and towns; experiencing hidden beauty – spectacular views which were always there, just shrouded in thick, unhealthy smog.

All at once, the air smells fresh, fragrant. Without micropollutants occluding its rays, sunlight dazzles. Birdsong is back. Rare bird sightings occur; dolphin tales abound. All creatures that had retreated due to the relentless advance of man's economic progress and greed are returning to habitats they were forced to abandon, as lockdowns cage humans, limiting their encroachments. Waterbodies are turning blue again, rippling clean, without chemicals frothing at their edges, reflecting cerulean skies. The night sky has turned magical, with faraway stars glittering gloriously.

Stopping the human race in its thoughtless tracks via the near-complete lockdowns has succeeded in lifting this malevolent shroud of polluted air. More specifically, in north India, just three weeks of lockdown has cleaned the air enough for people in Jalandhar to see the majestic snow-capped peaks of the Dhauladhar mountains for the first time in 30 years. On 4 April, the district recorded an AQI of 52 micrograms per cubic metre,[11] the best it has seen in the past decade, a Punjab Pollution Control Board official said. On 30 April, the dusty, mofussil town of Saharanpur in Uttar Pradesh's sugar and paper industry belt wakes up to the breathtaking sight of the snowy Himalayan peaks of the revered Gangotri glacier over 200 kilometres away as the AQI dipped below 50.[12] An entire generation that has grown up only hearing stories of such views from their elders can now see these views for themselves. Pictures of the Kanchenjunga peak also emerge from Siliguri, West Bengal on 1 May, as does an almost surreal photo of Mt Everest from Singhwahini village, 205 kilometres away in Bihar.

Not just the polluted Indo-Gangetic plain, but also across the country others post equally spectacular pictures and videos of clean lakes, chirping birds, clear, empty roads, postcard-blue skies, buzzing bees, bright-green spaces and sparkling rivers, a regenerating planet coming delightfully alive to nature's divine orchestra and harmonious colours.

Along with revealing nature's obscured beauty that shimmered beneath, the coronavirus-induced lockdown proves, to even the most vocal deniers and disbelievers, air pollution's man-made origins.

For me, my beautiful Delhi is back. *Hi,* I whisper to the blue sky on lockdown mornings as I lie in the garden where we have had so many CFA meetings on air pollution strategies, the clear sunlight making my eyes water. *I never thought I would see* you *again.*

Delhi's own pollution level on 22 March, when a day-long nationwide curfew was imposed by Prime Minister Narendra Modi (nicknamed Janta curfew in an official document), comes down by 44 per cent, compelling the CPCB to issue a 20-page report[13] that documents significantly reduced air pollution in at least 85 cities across India in the very first week of the nationwide lockdown beginning 24 March. The PTI reports that 92 cities with CPCB monitoring centres recorded minimal air pollution.[14] WhatsApp groups of clean air evangelists and activists tracking pollution trade PM2.5 numbers as low as 8 in some parts of Delhi, while some in Gurugram say their low-cost sensors have captured a 1, sending a virtual cheer through the groups. The US space agency NASA's satellite data shows that air pollution over northern India has plummeted to a 20-year low for this time in the year.[15]

That the air quality of major urban centres drops from near-apocalyptic levels before the pandemic to near-pristine in a matter of weeks, demonstrates another important fact: that pollution is reversible, and that such a reversal can, in fact, be effected very quickly.

This unintended silver lining of clean, breathable air comes attached to the dark cloud of the catastrophic economic, social and mental cost the lockdown has caused. People have been compelled to stay indoors; productivity has plummeted as factories shut and services freeze. There is an exodus of daily-wage migrant labour as they leave cities, even as families slide back into poverty. Supply chains falter as the Indian Railways, in an unprecedented move, for the first time in history, stops operations around the country. The massive impact on livelihoods and the global economy that these severe restrictions have brought about will likely take years to subside. The question, however, is: how do we retain the silver lining even after the Covid-inspired dark cloud rolls away? The only way to sustainably reduce emissions is not through painful lockdowns, but by putting the right energy- and climate-related policies in place.

For those who rarely step out without N-95 or N-99 masks to protect themselves from microparticulate pollution, the irony of finally being able to breathe clean outdoor air without a mask but being forced to stay indoors because of the very lockdown that has cleaned the air isn't lost. For those who promote wearing masks mainly to make the invisible problem of air pollution visible, the SARS-CoV-2 virus does what more than decades of campaigning has not been able to do. Face masks are suddenly ubiquitous. Assuming we will conquer this novel coronavirus before air pollution, it will be easier to encourage mask-wearing, I think to myself.

Importantly, what this lockdown also does is give air pollution researchers and data scientists an opportunity to monitor, record and parse how air pollution levels respond to a situation of almost complete stoppage of economic activity and what we can learn from this for the future.

'This is a model scientific experiment,' NASA scientist Robert Levy says about the lockdown and its effects on pollution in the same news report that notes lowest pollution levels in 20 years: 'We have a unique opportunity to learn how the atmosphere reacts to sharp and sudden reductions in emissions from certain sectors. This can help us separate how natural and human sources of aerosols affect the atmosphere.'

'The reductions we have seen correspond to the cessation of vehicular traffic, construction activity, industrial activity and brick kiln operations; but for the first time we also have an opportunity to study India's background levels of PM and other gases, and the influence of meteorological factors,' climate change media portal CarbonCopy quotes Dr Sagnik Dey, associate professor at the Centre for Atmospheric Sciences, IIT Delhi.[16]

Sarath, who runs three-day pollution forecasts via his Urban Emissions research group blog analyses measurements of individual pollutants that make up India's AQI on the first day of the extended period of the lockdown (15 April to 2 May 2020), to understand what caused these changes. Each of the pollutants has a unique story to tell, he writes[17] – the local PM2.5 levels prove that at least 70 per cent of pollution is locally generated, the dramatic fall in NO_2 reflecting that its main source is vehicular exhaust, its sharp fall in turn allowing ozone levels to rise, since NOx 'eats' ozone.

By May, I have begun seeing reports that say the cleaner air resulting from the lockdown may have saved more lives than the SARS-CoV-2 killed – and hypothesizing that if these low levels persist for a full year in India, it would save the lives of 6,50,000 people, lives that would have been lost due to air pollution's health effects.[18] Not just India,[19] but China[20] and Europe[21] are also reporting similar trends. In Delhi alone, the Centre for Research on Energy and Clean Air's (CREA)[22] data shows, between 1 January and 25 August 2020, the lives of around 4,600 people were saved due to lower pollution.[23] Any of those could have been my family or friends. Or me.

By September, when phase 5 of 'unlock' begins and AQI levels start rising, the *Economist* publishes[24] data collected by CREA that air pollution is returning to pre-Covid levels, a stark reminder that if we do nothing to capture these ephemeral gains, they will dissipate, leaving us right back where we started.

But more than the blue skies and spectacular views, more than a chance to prove that pollution is anthropogenic and reversible or conduct model scientific experiments on interlinkages between air pollution and Covid-19, what the lockdown has proven beyond the shadow of a doubt is that, if the government truly has intent, it is fully capable of reducing air pollution in India by a large margin. Chillingly, the reverse is equally true.

In its hurry to catch up on lost growth after the strict lockdowns, the government seem to have flattened the wrong curve. India has the second highest number of Covid cases in the world, and its quarterly GDP has contracted by 24 per cent.[25] In an attempt to kick-start the economy, the Modi government has announced a plan to auction off 41 Indian coal mines, opening a largely government-controlled sector to private investment for the first time ever. An environment ministry panel has also recommended an automatic extension[26] of forest clearance for government-owned mines, whose lease period got a 20-year extension.

'We can choose,' says Dr Kumar in a webinar, 'green growth or black lungs.'

As the government prepares a stimulus package to reinvigorate a stalled economy, it is clear to us that this is the time for all decision makers – legislative, corporate, elective, political executive – to reimagine and redefine a greener and more sustainable path towards economic growth. This is the time to course correct, to collectively grasp the opportunity of reprioritizing the sort of growth and progress that is truly important for our nation and its people, one that is in harmony with our environment, rectifying earlier mistakes.

'The big question is whether government stimulus measures lead to pollution levels rebounding above the levels before the crisis, like it happened after the 2008 financial crisis,'[27] says Lauri Myllyvirta, lead analyst at CREA. The report quoting him in the *Guardian* also says that signs from China, which is coming out of the other side of the coronavirus outbreak and where lockdowns are loosening up, are not positive. 'For the first four weeks after the Chinese New Year holiday in late January, when the coronavirus outbreak was at its worst, pollution levels fell by 25 per cent across the country. But since early March, levels of nitrogen dioxide pollution have begun to inch back up as the country gets back to work, with factories, businesses and power plants reopening and traffic returning… Indeed, the fear among environmentalists and residents is that, rather than attempting to maintain the low levels of pollution in the world's biggest capitals, when industry and cars kick back into action post-lockdown, the situation will go back to square one, and perhaps even worsen, as people and industry attempt to make up for the lost months,' it reports.

But thankfully, that may not be the only truth.

Europe, the UK, Japan and other countries are making a push for a greener revival. There are early opinion polls and pledges to dramatically reduce the footprint of cars by some of Europe's top city mayors. Public opinion in Britain appears to want a radical response to climate change, one implemented with the same urgency as that given to the fight against Covid-19. British research company Opinium polled 48 per cent of the public agreeing that the government should respond 'with the same urgency to climate change as it has [to] Covid-19.'[28] Already, Giuseppe Sala, the mayor of Milan, has led a call for stimulus spending to navigate a more sustainable path towards economic growth as hard-hit Italian cities recover from the blow of the Covid-19 pandemic.[29] 'If designed properly, using shared knowledge and expertise from cities across the globe, these stimulus packages can foster resilience within our economic and financial systems, while also creating truly sustainable means of protecting public health, reducing inequality, and preserving the global ecosystems we all depend on,' he said. Milan has also announced one of Europe's most ambitious schemes, reallocating street space from cars to cycling and walking, in response to the coronavirus crisis.[30]

Paris mayor Anne Hidalgo has been even more emphatic, vowing that returning to a Paris dominated by cars after lockdown ends on 11 May is 'out of the question'.[31] Hidalgo has been leading a radical overhaul of the city's mobility culture since taking office in 2014 and sounds even more determined to maintain her anti-pollution and anti-congestion measures even as cities rethink transportation policies to avoid Covid-19 transmission. Cycling activists from Germany to Peru are trying to use the moment to get more bike lanes or widen existing ones.[32] Japan has gone a step further, with its environment minister Shinjiro Koizumi reaffirming his country's allegiance to the United Nations' Paris agreement on climate change, promising a green recovery from the Covid pandemic with renewed focus on electric mobility and solar power. 'Now is the time to unite, to save lives, save the Paris agreement, and save our planet,' he said.[33]

This is exactly the sort of environmental priority that Indian leadership, local, state and central, ought to be aiming for.

Sadly, for us, the Indian government, in its zeal to revive the economy, is busy proposing watering down its own environmental norms.[34]

All organizations in the Clean Air Collective speak in one voice – India cannot, under any circumstance, roll back on existing environmental protective measures. We try and exhort civil society to speak out to ensure that the government does not use the pandemic as an excuse to relax hard-won rules and enforcements that lower emissions at source. Activists stand up against the government's proposal to amend its Environmental Impact Assessment (EIA) notification during the course of the lockdown, when it won't expose itself to adequate public scrutiny. At a time when we should be doing more to take care of the environment and strengthen environmental laws, the ministry of environment, forests and climate change releases a draft EIA Notification 2020 that weakens its more stringent 2006 rules. It is open for comments from citizens only for a very narrow window right in the midst of the biggest pandemic we're witnessing, when people's engagement with it may be enervated, inert. With all the opposition and noise around it, finally some heavyweight politicians get involved. Jairam Ramesh says it will destroy India's natural resources,[35] calls it 'deeply anti-democratic,'[36] and asks to stall old it until it has been thoroughly discussed.[37]

The EIA has far-reaching effects on India's forest and environment protection, and current proposals include shortening timelines for environmental clearances, increasing validity of mining and riverbed-related projects, and expanding the list of projects exempted from getting environmental clearances or no longer requiring public consultation. The notification also suggests doing away with individual environmental clearances for projects within industrial complexes, which will only lead to poorer compliance and adherence to environmental standards. It also makes no mention of individual accountability, which will inevitably increase the chances of environmental violations and degradation.

A year-long investigation by IndiaSpend has revealed how India is ripping apart its environment for business, and opening up wildlife sanctuaries and national parks to roads, railways, mines and industries by weakening its own regulations.[38] The report analyses data that shows India has approved over 270 projects in and around its most protected areas including biodiversity hotspots, in the six years since July 2014. 'At the same time, the Centre has watered down environmental safeguards, prompting stakeholders to warn that such interference not only imperils habitat and ecosystems, but also endangers public health,' the IndiaSpend analysis says.

The WHO has been warning for years that habitat destruction is changing the patterns of infectious diseases, including a growing number of zoonotic diseases like Covid-19. 'The chance of coming in contact with zoonotic diseases increases when humans enter biodiversity hotspots,' IndiaSpend warns.

Other more recent approvals too have been made in haste, disregarding environmental impact, like the April environmental clearances for infrastructure projects in 11 states that were hurried through via videoconferencing.[39]

Even the courts have proved complicit. The Supreme Court recently extended the deadline for selling leftover stock of cars with BS-4 engines, which are more polluting than vehicles equipped with the cleaner BS-6 engines and were to be phased out by 31 March 2020. The pandemic may have worsened the automobile sector's troubles in the midst of transitioning to stricter emission norms from 1 April this year, but that does does not warrant the relaxation of those norms.

Fears that this virus will make people perceive public transport as unsafe and cause a behavioural shift towards private vehicle ownership may counter falling demand to some extent, but the same fear will limit the demand for buses, trams and other public and shared mobility like Ubers. Ideally, the pandemic should serve as a point to embark on a path to cleaner urban transport, whether private or public, bicycles or electric cars. This is the time to choose an even faster transition to e-mobility and work out a plan to fund the reskilling of workers towards the manufacturing of electric vehicles (EVs).

At the same time, the government must accelerate the switch from thermal to renewable energy, especially as the latter continues to become relatively more economical. With the current demand for power at an all-time low, this is the best time to shut down old thermal power plants that do not meet emission standards. Experts believe shutting down such plants would vastly improve air quality. But the government's ongoing indecision has confounded activists and industry. Despite increasing evidence that coal continues to remain more expensive relative to renewables, the government continues to subsidize it. A report published by CarbonTracker[40] in mid-April states that 51 per cent of the country's coal power costs more to run than building new renewables and that almost a quarter of the planned 66-GW thermal power capacity will enter the market with negative cash flow.

Despite this, even until 2019, India subsidizes fossil fuels nine times more than renewable energy,[41] a report that maps the country's energy subsidies found. 'Renewable energy was given a subsidy of ₹9,930 crore in 2019. This is just 10 per cent of the subsidy fossil fuels get,' says Karthik Ganesan (fellow, CEEW) one of the co-authors of a study. 'Fossil fuels contribute significantly to air pollution and this happens without any penalty today. Taxing such emissions and using that to further the use of renewable energy would be crucial to support its roll-out. We could also spend less on subsidizing fossil fuels by targeting only those who absolutely need it – the poor and vulnerable, and let everyone else pay a market price,' he added. 'What would be a game changer is if renewable energy is given a leg up by taxing externalities (primarily particulate pollution) that result from the use of fossil fuels,' says Ganesan

Campaigners and environmentalists are becoming increasingly concerned about which way things will go. Will we slip back to old, polluting habits? Or will we be able to course correct, carve out a new normal where the air we breathe isn't taken for granted, and policies like the NCAP are implemented successfully even while the government partners with industry to bring the economy back on track. In fact, the Covid-19 pandemic demonstrates that the NCAP shouldn't just be seen as an environmental policy aimed at improving living conditions, but a mission of national importance aimed at improving public health and thus the overall productivity of the country.

In July 2020, the CPCB informs the Supreme Court in a virtual hearing that IIT Bombay has withdrawn from the smog tower project. The court threatens contempt against it[42] and directs the government again to install two smog towers in Delhi. By now, the cost of these towers is estimated at ₹18 crore each.

The move may be well intentioned but it is clear the court doesn't have the scientific expertise. The government has the expertise to create and implement a good air pollution policy, but doesn't have the intention, whereas the judiciary has the intention, but not the expertise to guide policy.

I go back to writing – this time it is a hard-hitting story for an international health publication quoting international and Indian experts criticizing this questionable technology.[43] At the same time, Gopal tries to intervene in the Supreme Court to present evidence that the smog towers are unscientific, but Chief Justice Arun Mishra dismisses the plea.[44]

I am appalled. By now, international papers have picked up this story.[45] For obvious reasons, none of the IIT scientists are willing to speak out publicly against smog towers – though privately, they agree that they won't work. But the fact that IIT Bombay withdrew from this farce is telling, and CFA files a PIL in October 2020. It is dismissed without even a hearing.

The level of desperation among some of us has become so high that we are considering unusual, outlandish options. Like suing polluters directly. Even China had allowed non-profits to sue polluters[46] at the peak of its pollution. Ravina has been trying to put together a class action suit or a personal compensation litigation in public interest. 'I want to make polluting industries accountable to people and public health. Yes, laws exist but they are very weak and compensation is low. There are many loopholes that favour industry, favour businesses over human life,' Ravina says. When I read about the US state of Delaware filing a lawsuit against 31 fossil fuel companies[47] in 2019 accusing them of misleading the public and seeking damages against harm caused by climate change to the environment, I immediately send her that link. This is a state government suing polluting companies!

The Delaware attorney general's argument is that these companies knew of the damage their activities were causing and they kept it hidden, and also actively stopped the spread of this knowledge. Due to this act of hiding information, the Delaware state government will need to spend huge amounts to replace property, threatened livelihoods and help with resettlement.

Actually, this argument isn't new. The Union of Concerned Scientists in 2016 had warned that major fossil fuel companies have known for decades that their products – oil, natural gas and coal – cause global warming, saying that their own scientists told them so more than 30 years ago.[48] Despite knowing this, these companies have deceived shareholders, politicians and the public about the facts and risks of global warming.

But what if the fossil fuel companies *belong* to the government? This is somewhat like the tobacco story, where big business was accused of hiding the negative impact of tobacco consumption. There are actually massive parallels between the tobacco and fossil fuel sectors with one major difference. The fossil fuel companies are far more powerful, far more integrated with the state, and governments across the world are highly dependent upon the tax revenues they generate; and therefore they will fight even harder against such lawsuits.

Devising policies that stimulate robust economic activity while also coordinating real action to clean India's air won't be easy. This sort of sustainable growth path will require coordination between and within all the states, as well as several levels and agencies of the government and civil society. It will require mindful economic restructuring and thinking out of the box, incorporating the ideas of fairness and restorative and regenerative justice. If there's one lesson that the response to the Covid-19 pandemic has left us with, it is that even the most extreme measures fall firmly within the realms of possibility if they can inspire both political will and public support. Political will bends to public demand – and, henceforth, a more aware public is more likely to demand better healthcare, which includes cleaner air and water, along with economic growth.

Covid-19 has brought with it an unprecedented threat to human existence and our lives, at once delicate as gossamer and strongly resilient. But it also presents an extraordinary opportunity, a chance to thrive, instead of merely survive. As we wait in this liminal bardo-like state between the earth's exhalation and inhalation, between the pre-corona and post-corona world, the past and the future, in collective limbo for a rebirth into a new normal, we have a chance for a fresh awakening, recalibrating to a better, fairer, more balanced world. Like the Zoom waiting room, our current bardo has forced us into contemplation, an invaluable gift, if we use it well, to listen to our inner voice.

The lockdown-caused blue skies have shown us that we may yet have another chance to repair the damage we have done to our environment. We must ensure that the growth path we choose this time is greener, fairer and more climate-friendly. It is imperative to choose sustainable development over pure economic growth. We cannot mortgage the future of our young. The young themselves should make the right choices, voting with their wallets as well as their ballots.

If we don't grasp this opportunity to reimagine growth, reset to a new normal, rebuild climate-smart, healthier and more equitable cities, and take a more sustainable path to growth, we will have lost our last chance to make amends with nature and will be forever doomed to suffer ill health and perhaps a final apocalypse, whether it is through nature's fury or through a more viciously virulent virus than SARS-CoV-2. And, this time, the poetry of our lungs will become its own final requiem.

At the core of my learning is that what India needs is a strong EPA-style authority. Shivam Vij, an Indian journalist, writes, 'Currently, there are many different organizations trying to combat air pollution with no top boss to marshal them all to achieve defined goals. There's NCAP and EPCA and GRAP and CPCB and MoEF and SPCBs and god knows how many other acronyms, each one failing more miserably than the other... [India] needs its own EPA,' he states unequivocally in the *Print*.[49]

What we have seen again and again, is that profits are booked privately, but the price is paid by all of us collectively. And the currency is our health. But disproportionately, the burden falls heaviest on those from the poorest demographic. This is directly validated in a long conversation I have with Santu, one of the workers at the Bhalswa landfill in 2019. Jay Prakash Chowdhury, better known as Santu, a former ragpicker, has grown up in the margins of garbage dumps. 'Air pollution has always been here,' he observes. 'But the talk around it has increased in the last two years.'

'Air pollution has settled deep in my lungs. My lungs are now made of pollution,' he says almost poetically. Santu should have been a politician or a theatre actor – so en pointe is his sense of timing and delivery. 'In 70 years, this country still doesn't have clean air, water, health or education,' he booms, his tiny frame growing with every sentence. 'People are dying. We only stop breathing one final time. But what about the millions of times you suffocate while trying to keep breathing? *Log mar rahe hain... Saans toh ek hi baar band hoti hai. Lekin joh ghut ghut ke jee rahe hain, unka kya hoga? Kuch toh karna hi padega,'* he says. It could be a line from a Bollywood film, except that it is real and it is true. And it is chilling.

'It is time,' says Ravina. 'This has gone on for too long. I'm not going to give up.'

These are voices of just two people, I think to myself. It is up to us to make them louder, amplify them until they are heard and acted upon. The team at CFA is committed to continue this fight person by person, letter by letter, question by Parliament question, even without a single rupee of funding. Although it sometimes looks like we're fighting a losing battle, every individual educated by our outreach is another individual who champions the cause for clean air. And if enough citizens wake up to the reality around them and begin to make changes – both in their habits and electorally – change is bound to happen in this country. Then, perhaps, we will see the day when the profits of clean air are shared by all of us as well.

Epilogue

The Road Ahead: Flight or Fight

I will never see my mother again, hug her, create an 'arty' bindi on her forehead, inhale her scent, comb and buff her thinning hair, hear her melodious voice practising her *taans* – except in my dreams. Then, over time, as my friend Anjali, who lost her beloved father to lung disease and was quietly shattered by it, says, I will be afraid of forgetting details. The sharpness of my memories of her still has the ability to hurt me, but underneath lurks the fear that once those edges soften, become blurry, there will be less and less to hold on to.

I know I'm not alone in mourning someone lost to a cause that can be linked directly to the foul air we breathe. Every day, I come across more and more people who are suffering from lung disease, cancers, fibrosis, strokes, cardiac disease and so many other diseases that are triggered by air pollution: friends whose mothers' lungs were found to have fluid, whose fathers suffered a cardiac arrest soon after Diwali, non-smoking neighbours who got a sudden, severe lung infection in the north Indian winter, elderly relatives who were admitted to hospital for a broken hip after a fall, but passed away from lung infection.

I never wanted to be an activist. I am not a pollution expert, scientist, public health researcher or epidemiologist. I never set out to be an environmentalist. I think of myself simply as a survivor, an aware, informed and vigilant resident of Delhi, who is trying to survive Delhi's poor air among its other urban challenges. All I want to do is to live a healthy, peaceful life in my city of birth and choice, but I'm being forced to fight for it.

Diwali used to be a time when I prepared my house for festivities and opened it up to friends and family. But now it is a time when I start worrying about the air quality and start shuttering my home to the outside air, duct-taping each window carefully in order to protect my family. That sinking feeling in my heart begins usually after Dussehra, just before the bright winter sunshine of my childhood withers to a dull, dystopian grey, when stepping out of the door makes my eyes water.

Every so often, I have a sudden memory of another sky, a clear, bright blue, of crisp winter mornings. Back then, I could enjoy the beauty of an orange-pink sunset without haze obscuring my view. Winters meant outdoor picnics with friends under cotton-ball skies, orange peels and peanuts, eating carrot halwa, sitting in dazzling sunshine enveloped by the intoxicating fragrance of flowers.

Now, I worry that I will grow old in the dim haze of grey Delhi winters, the winter of my own life overshadowed by the debris of diseases triggered by pollution, my few remaining friends suffering with me; those who can get away, forced to scatter. I know many others feel the same way – those who have known a different Delhi, who still have fleeting memories of that long-vanished sky.

Delhi's toxic pollution has become much more than an environmental problem for me. It is now an existential crisis that clings to me like a dull, aching sadness. I can't bear the thought of being pushed out of my city for a cleaner destination – and anyway, where would I even go, given that most of India is almost as polluted? Yet the thought of living and ageing in a dying city described as a gas chamber makes me anxious.

When I think back on these past years of grappling with air pollution, sometimes it feels like I've tried everything I could possibly think of. I've engaged with my community and founded, seeded and joined anti-pollution groups. We've tried to convert Delhi's frustrated communities into clean air advocates, urging and egging each other on when one of us loses steam. We have greater numbers now. More importantly, with growing awareness, each time one organization loses steam, others take up the baton. With the connection between air pollution and climate change becoming more evident, the two benefit from clear synergies.

Care For Air may have plateaued into an advisory group, but we continue to vigilantly flag issues, simplifying and amplifying the science behind air pollution. The members are still passionate and well intentioned but are finding it more and more challenging to give it the sort of time a problem of this magnitude needs. Every so often, I feel like giving up, but then I hear of other similar groups starting up, and I get motivated again to keep going. The latest to form are Warrior Moms (in September 2020) and the Bengal Clean Air Network (in October 2020).

Once you know how lethal air pollution is, you can never un-know it. The 25,000 breaths we take every single day remind me not to give up.

At the risk of repeating myself, here are some of the things I've learnt on this six-year journey as a layperson-turned-reluctant- activist.

1. Air pollution is an all-India problem at highly toxic levels. It is not just a Delhi/north Indian problem. It is not restricted to specific areas of the country, though weather and geographical conditions intensify it in the north. It is not just an urban problem. Pollution in rural areas in the Indo-Gangetic plain is as high as in some of the metros. Air has no geographic, political and socio-economic boundaries. Pollution levels in almost 98 per cent of India are above WHO guidelines.
2. Air pollution is a year-round problem in India. It is not a seasonal problem. The pollution levels remain over WHO limits for most of the year in most areas, though it is the worst in the winter, when pollutants get trapped by the cold air due to inversion. Sunshine and clear visibility doesn't necessarily mean air quality is excellent, although the reverse most likely means pollution is high.
3. Air pollution – especially PM2.5 – causes irreversible damage to the health of all humans – 70,000 scientific papers prove that. It is not a 'rich' or 'elite' people's problem. In fact, it harms the poor

disproportionately since their access to temporary protection such as masks and purifiers is limited, as is their access to quality healthcare and awareness. In fact, air pollution also affects non-human inhabitants of our planet. Studies on pollinating bees[1] as well as on stunted plant growth indicate its harmful effects.

4. Air pollution affects every organ of the body through inflammation and oxidative stress. It doesn't just harm our lungs and respiratory system, though as entry points, those are the first to be affected. It triggers cancers, strokes, heart attacks, obesity, infertility, diabetes, depression, Alzheimer's, autism and other cognitive disorders. Indian lungs and organs are no different from others, and we don't need specific Indian studies before taking action.
5. Some effects of pollution are short-term – such as allergies, asthma and respiratory distress – but most effects are chronic and irreversible, as toxic particles build up in the human body. The elderly and children are more affected. Children who have lived in polluted air have lower lung function, smaller lungs and irreversible lung damage, when compared to other children.
6. No one builds immunity to air pollution (otherwise, smokers would have the best immunity). On the contrary, pollution lowers the body's immunity due to the inflammation and oxidative stress it causes in the body.
7. Sharp episodic spikes in air pollution, however brief, cause lasting harm – especially to pregnant women, the elderly and children. Thus, episodic spikes during Diwali or due to cropstubble burning or any other brief exposure to severe air pollution can have a deep and long-lasting impact on the local ecosystem and public health.
8. Air pollution is a combination of pollutants and is caused by several factors. The worst effects come from the smallest particles, which are usually a result of some form of combustion. Different sources and sectors contribute to India's pollution load, and they differ in degrees depending on the area.
9. Since air pollution has many sources, the solutions too have to

be multifactorial, specific to each source and must target all sectors. Understanding sources and monitoring the air more extensively can help us direct policy to where exactly capacities and awareness need to be built. Combustion and construction are the two biggest contributors of PM2.5 and PM10.

10. Different pollutants harm human health in different ways. We need a bouquet of solutions that tackles every source of pollution. Air pollution policies, via their health impact, need to be embedded in every economic policy since they affect every part of the social and economic fabric. This includes fiscal policies since taxation and subsidies distort many costs and benefits.
11. It is best to target and limit emissions at source, rather than try to clean up polluted air. Thus, outdoor air purifiers such as smog towers and vacuum cleaners are inadequate and ineffective. They are a waste of public money. Lower emissions lead to lower pollution and lower exposure. To reduce emissions at source, we need to bring down our dependence on dirty fuels – fossil fuels such as coal and diesel – and move at a faster pace towards renewable energy like solar, wind, hydroelectric. This means we have to spend more on researching cleaner mobility options and move faster to electric mobility, cycling and pedestrianization.
12. Power, cement, steel, iron, coal and construction are, generally speaking, the most obviously polluting industries, but closer to Delhi, textiles, chemicals, brick kilns, metals and food processing industries have shown up as hidden delinquents. So it is for these that we need the cleanest technologies. We need technical solutions, such as cleaning up our cars and industries, as much as structural solutions, such as having proper monitoring, strong regulation and enforcement. A good place to begin is to make the polluters pay and use the cess collected to fund solutions.
13. To begin solving the problem, the first step is awareness and acknowledgement of the problem and the serious, irreversible health harm it causes. It is our collective obligation to spread science and

data-based knowledge about this.

14. Any amount – even the smallest amounts – of air pollution causes health harm.[2] The aim must be to reduce it to as close to zero as possible. Minimizing air pollution does minimize harm, but it is not a linear function. Ultimately, air pollution causes maximum harm at the initial levels. To put it another way, the first 10 cigarettes you smoke will cause maximum harm. After that, whether you smoke 20 or 40, the incremental harm will be less. This doesn't mean that we don't try to reduce from high levels to comparatively lower levels, but that we try and reduce to the lowest levels faster. We can't allow bad air to be normalized.
15. Air is a collective resource and we are all responsible for it. We are all victims and we are all perpetrators. Change begins at an individual level. However, as a collective 'public good', the government – both at state and central level – needs to lead the charge. Private responsibility goes hand in hand with public accountability, and public good must trump private profit. For all this, transparency precedes accountability. We can't allow bad air to be politicized.
16. We are in a national public health emergency. Even though the coronavirus pandemic has altered the meaning of public health emergencies, the health harm from pollution remains, and needs to be reframed. Because air pollution is a pandemic in slow motion, and we need urgent action from our government and leaders to arrest its increase.
17. Trees and plants are great providers of oxygen, and their roots hold down the soil, reducing ambient dust. Some varieties can also absorb volatile organic compounds and 'clean' the air, but in no case are they natural air filters that remove PM2.5 from the air. In fact, their own pores and stomata get blocked and choked by the PM particles, reducing their efficiency in producing oxygen.
18. The benefits of clean air outweigh the cost of cleaning it.[3] By causing illness and premature death, air pollution reduces the quality of life. By causing a loss of productive labour, it reduces incomes. By

stunting plant growth, it reduces agricultural productivity. Polluted cities are also less attractive to talented workers, which reduces the competitiveness of cities. One study estimates that air pollution cost India 8 per cent of its GDP, or $560 billion, in 2016 due to lost productivity, premature mortality and morbidity.

19. The biggest problem with AQI measurements is that air pollution levels haven't been attached to action plans. As a starting point, all outdoor aerobic activity should be linked with levels of air pollution. No sporting activity should be allowed in schools or organized for the public when PM2.5 levels are over 100.
20. Low-cost monitoring of pollutants has improved awareness and democratized it, even though it may not be as accurate as the government's expensive Continuous Air Monitoring Stations, which are few and far between. The difference between fixed and mobile sensors isn't significant,[4] which means we can get more localized data and greater understanding of sources. This information can then be used to target customized policy solutions towards the problem. They also help involve citizens in solving the problem.

Stepping back and looking at this holistically, I also realize that in the context of air pollution, there has been a colossal failure of governance, with every political party complicit. When the new Chief Justice S.A. Bobde appoints a a single-judge committee on 16 October 2020[5] to look into stubble burning, I point out the need for the entire government to play a part to see any real change in an essay for the *Wire*.[6] We cannot and should not allow that. Ultimately, it is the government's responsibility to provide clean air – a public, collective resource – to its people. It should really not be my job as an individual. It is my government's job. To make and enforce laws that reduce emissions at source, reduce exposure, encourage responsible sport, responsible luxury and responsible travel, use market economics, create and follow policies that move towards clean energy and clean mobility equitably. My job is to follow those rules and guidelines, segregate my garbage, cooperate with local agencies, reduce my air pollution footprint – and pay penalties when I don't or can't. My job is to pay my taxes. It is also to vote and invest mindfully in political parties and companies whose environmental footprint is small and green, thus voting not just with my ballot, but with my wallet.

But it is also my job to be aware, mindful and vigilant, to engage and assist with local government and non-governmental bodies. To hold my government (as well as the companies I invest in) accountable. That change begins from me. Lazy citizens make lazy governments and will get lazy governance. There are excellent organizations, both in the for- and not-for-profit sectors, that work in clean air. Researchers, air pollution and atmospheric scientists as well as energy mobility experts are happy to share their knowledge. We need innovative solutions, like Jhatkaa.org's digital tools that mobilized the public through relevant information and interactive maps that led to more accountability in Bengaluru[7] and reduced garbage burning. But equally, we need more action to apply existing solutions to scale.

Finally, India needs economic development, not just economic growth. Countries measure the latter through GDP – gross domestic product – which only counts national income or produce through one number. It is an artificial, complicated and abstract construct devised less than 80 years ago. The former is the real deal as it measures improvements in the quality of life and living standards – which include the measures of literacy, life expectancy and healthcare – and this should be our focus. The difference between the two is sustainability. If we end up fetishizing GDP numbers as a proxy for the nation's well-being, we will be doing ourselves a disservice. Economic indicators like the GDP disguise inequality and social disharmony. This number began as a tool to help policymakers measure a country's material output and was never meant to measure overall standards of living.

Recently, Mexico and China who struggled with poor air have made serious progress with significant reductions in air pollution. China imposed regional coal caps after Chinese people, particularly the urban middle classes, expressed increasing anger about the way pollution was impacting their health. The *Economist* explained exactly how China reduced PM2.5 levels by 54 per cent in just one year between 2016 and 2017.[8]

The top five learnings from China would be: first, a regional action plan and regional coordination mechanism involving Delhi and its adjoining states must be put in place. Second, the region needs time-bound, measurable targets to reduce pollution levels; without targets, action plans are meaningless. Third, the action plan should be an integrated one involving all pollutants and all key polluting sources. Fourth, concerted action rather than incremental change is the key to reducing pollution levels quickly. Lastly, without strict enforcement, all these measures will fail.

But, as Chai Jing has argued in her documentary, 'The strongest governments on earth cannot clean up pollution by themselves. They must rely on each ordinary person, like you and me, on our choices, and on our will.'

From an air pollution perspective, we are all offenders and we are all victims. We all use fuel and energy that isn't clean and generate waste that is burnt. In fact, India and some other developing countries are at a phase of development where they are dependent on much dirtier fuels. This is why the Indian population struggles with devastating levels of air pollution. In fact, it is commendable that we are beginning this journey towards clean air earlier than others. Because the human impact of air pollution is really horrific and remains under the radar. Especially since there are no data or metrics attached to it.

From an individual perspective, we must keep ourselves aware and make others aware by spreading science-backed information. We must consistently keep asking for clean air – from our legislators and the judiciary and through the media – and not stop until we get it. Further, we must be ready to pay for it. More and more organic and citizen movements and networks are needed to amplify the work of formal, funded organizations working in the area of clean air, clean energy and climate change. Data, science and awareness are the foundation, and acknowledgement, advocacy and action are the pillars to drive the change that we need.

Six years after I accidentally discovered this invisible killer swirling around and two years after I found it crouching in my own backyard, I find public discourse more open to conversations on air pollution. But until the narrative shifts to focus more sharply to air pollution as a health hazard, the urgency will be lost.

I will come to terms with the loss of my mother. I will also learn, again and again, that grief isn't a linear function, but comes in waves. I will learn that in the emotional landscape of loss, there is no map for our sorrow; we must create our own paths, and our personal journeys will bring us to our own peace. For some of us, these journeys could mean drowning oneself in work, for others, friends. For me, it has been leaning into the loss, trying to create some meaning out of it. So that others are warned.

Never forget India's omnipresent, invisible, toxic air pollution is sickening our children, killing us all – my mother, your mother – every day, everywhere. For every breath you take, remember that breathing here is injurious to your health. The road ahead lends two options: flight or fight. I hope you choose to fight.

Notes

Prologue: Never

1. 'Lung cancer kills more people but it is 100% preventable: Dr Arvind Kumar', YouTube, uploaded by ETHealthWorld, 27 July 2018.
2. 'Heart expert Naresh Trehan says curbing pollution only way out for Delhi', *India Today*, 11 December 2015.
3. 'Himachal lung shown pink, Delhi half black', YouTube, uploaded by NewsX, 10 December 2015.

Chapter 1: Forget

1. Michael Greenstone and Claire Qing Fan, 'Introducing the Air Quality Life Index: Twelve Facts about Particulate Air Pollution, Human Health and Global Policy', *AQLI*, November 2018.
2. 'How much longer would you live if you breathed clean air?', *Air Quality Life Index*, n.d.
3. 'Pollution Facts: Particulate air pollution is the single greatest threat to human health globally', *Air Quality Life Index*, n.d.
4. 'Kirk's Legacy: Clean Air for Everyone, Everywhere', *Collaborative Clean Air Policy Centre*.
5. Sourangsu Chowdhury, Zoe A. Chafe et. al, 'The Contribution of Household Fuels to Ambient Air Pollution in India: A Comparison of Recent Estimates', *Collaborative Clean Air Policy Centre*, CCAPC/2019/01, May 2019.

Chapter 3: Omnipresent

1. Jyoti Pande Lavakare, 'Organic Issue', *Chai Latte*, 15 October 2010.
2. Jyoti Pande Lavakare, 'Learning to be disaster-ready', *Business Standard*, 21 January 2013.

Chapter 4: Invisible

1. Heather Timmons, 'You Think the Air in Beijing Is Bad? Try New Delhi', *New York Times*, 31 January 2013.
2. DH News Service, 'Bengaluru hospitals see more heart disease patients due to pollution', *Deccan Herald*, 9 Dec 2017.

3. Reshma Ravishanker, 'Foul air causing early onset of heart disease', *Deccan Herald*, 16 Aug 2019.
4. Niranjan Kaggere, 'Air pollution is a factor in causing heart attack: Study', *Deccan Herald*, 8 February 2019.
5. Damian Carrington, 'Revealed: air pollution may be damaging 'every organ in the body', *Guardian*, 17 May 2019.
6. Tweet by Maria Neira, 6 December 2019, https://twitter.com/drmarianeira/status/1202972205811978240
7. Gardiner Harris and Benjamin Weiser, 'School in India ensnared in US diplomatic spat', *New York Times*, 15 January 2014.
8. Gardiner Harris, 'Beijing's bad air would be step up for smoggy Delhi', *New York Times*, 26 January 2014.
9. Samuel Kotis, 'Clearing the Air in New Delhi', American Foreign Service Association, September 2015.
10. Joshua Apte, 'Air Pollution in Indian Cities: Current Status and Prospects for a Cleaner Future', Lecture, 21 November 2014.

Chapter 5: Toxic

1. Gardiner Harris, 'Beijing's bad air would be step up for smoggy Delhi', *New York Times*, 26 January 2014.
2. Gardiner Harris, 'On bad air days in India, staying inside doesn't help', *New York Times*, 27 January 2014.
3. MyLinh Duong et al., 'Global differences in lung function by region (PURE): an international, community-based prospective study', *Lancet*, 10 September 2013.
4. 'Epidemiological Study on Effect of Air Pollution on Human Health (adults) in Delhi', Central Pollution Control Board, Ministry of Environment and Forests, Environmental health Series: EHS/1/2008, August 2008.
5. 'Study on ambient air quality, respiratory symptoms and lung function of children in Delhi', Central Pollution Control Board, 1 October 2012.
6. Aniruddha Ghosh and Pritha Chatterjee, 'Landmark study lies buried: How Delhi's poisonous air is damaging its children for life', *Indian Express*, 2 April 2015.
7. 'Is air pollution also making us depressed? Studies agree', *Times of India*, 4 November 2019.
8. Damian Carrington, 'Depression and suicide linked to air pollution in new global study', *Guardian*, 18 December 2019.
9. Zoë Schlanger, 'Legal levels of air pollution are killing the elderly', *Quartz*, 27 December 2017.

10. Santosh Harish and Pallavi Pant, 'What Does the Air Quality Index Really Show Us?', *Quint*, 15 November 2019.
11. Aastha Ahuja, 'Air Pollution: What Is Air Quality Index, How Is It Measured And Its Health Impact', NDTV, 18 December 2019.
12. Marilyn Miller, 'Kotis of Wellfleet lauded for "constructive dissent"', *Province Town*, 25 July 2015.
13. Samuel Kotis, 'Clearing the Air in New Delhi', American Foreign Service Association, September 2015.
14. 'National Air Quality Index (AQI) launched by the Environment Minister AQI is a huge initiative under "Swachh Bharat" AQI to act as "One Number-One Colour-One Description" to judge the Air Quality', *Business Standard*, 20 October 2014.
15. 'Choking India gets air quality index', *Economic Times*, 22 July 2015.
16. Janaki Lenin, 'India's air quality figures can't be trusted', *Guardian*, 20 October 2014.

Chapter 6: Air Pollution

1. 'Statements by President Obama and Prime Minister Modi of the Republic of India', The White House, 25 January 2015.
2. Natalie Pearson, 'Mr President, world's worst air is taking 6 hours off your life', *Bloomberg*, 26 January 2015.
3. David Spiegelhalter, 'Does air pollution kill 40,000 people each year in the UK?', Winton Centre for Risk and Evidence, Cambridge, 20 February 2017.
4. Committee on the Medical Effects of Air Pollutants, Government of UK, https://www.gov.uk.com
5. David Noble, 'As President Obama Visits India, US Embassy in Delhi Buys 1,800 Blueair Indoor Air Purifiers to Help Combat Impact Of Indian Capital's Severe Air Pollution', *Cision PR Web*, 24 January 2015.
6. 'Blueair Bags Major Order To Supply U.S. Embassy In Delhi, India, With 1,800 Air Purifiers', Blueair, 13 January 2015.
7. 'India Air Purifiers Market Revenue Set To Grow at 45% CAGR during 2013–18', *TechSci Research*, July 2015.
8. 'Death by Breath: A look at key studies on Delhi's pollution and how warnings were ignored', *Indian Express*, 8 April 2016.
9. Pritha Chatterjee and Aniruddha Ghosal, 'Seven years ago, everyone saw Delhi's air take a deadly U-turn but no one did a thing', *Indian Express*, 31 March 2015.
10. 'Delhi pollution: The studies no one acted on', *Indian Express*, 1 April 2015.
11. Aniruddha Ghosal, 'Death by breath: "You have to understand there are various

lobbies," says Sheila Dikshit', *Indian Express*, 3 April 2015.

12. 'PM Narendra Modi launches National Air Quality Index', *Economic Times*, 6 April 2015.
13. Simrin Sirur, 'Converting waste to energy is great, but also disastrous if done as here in Delhi', *Print*, 1 September 2019.
14. Jyoti Pande Lavakare, 'Ignoring Air Pollution Is Justice Denied', *Wire*, 7 December 2018.
15. Gardiner Harris, 'Holding Your Breath in India', *New York Times*, 31 May 2015.
16. Aniruddha Ghosal and Pritha Chatterjee, Landmark study lies buried: How Delhi's poisonous air is damaging its children for life', *Indian Express*, 2 April 2015.
17. Janaki Lenin, 'Why an opinion article on Delhi's air pollution upset many Indians', *Guardian*, 5 June 2015.
18. Tweet by Salil Tripathi, 4 June 2015, https://twitter.com/saliltripathi/status/
19. Bhasker Tripathi, 'Poor Lung Capacity In 8 Of 10 Delhi Children, Youth', *India Spend*, 8 February 2018.
20. Bindu Perappadan, 'Delhi kids have smaller lungs compared with children in US due to air pollution', 15 November 2017.
21. Seema Chowdhry, 'Clean air for our children', *Mint*, 7 November 2015.
22. Pratibha Sharma, 'Delhi's Air: Why Does No One Care About Unmanaged Waste?', *Economic and Political Weekly*, Vol. 52, Issue No. 50, 20 December 2017.
23. 'Ghazipur garbage dump almost as tall as Qutub Minar: Story behind Delhi's largest landfill site', *India Today*, 1 September 2018.
24. Phoebe Weston, 'India's "rubbish mountain" on course to grow taller than Taj Mahal', *Independent*, 4 June 2019.
25. 'Let's Do It! Estonia (2008) - country clean-up with 50,000 volunteers', YouTube, uploaded by World Cleanup Day, 29 March 2011.
26. 'Report of the Steering Committee on Air Pollution and Health Related Issues', Ministry of Health and Family Welfare, August 2015.
27. Jean Gough, 'Toxic air is harming our children with every breath that they take', UNICEF, 30 January 2019.
28. 'Air Pollution and Child Health: Prescribing Clean Air', World Health Organization, 2018.

Chapter 7: Is Sickening

1. Shuvabrata Chakraborty and Samir K Srivastava, 'A Novel Approach to Understanding Delhi's Complex Air Pollution Problem', *Economic and Political Weekly*, Vol. 54, Issue No. 36, 7 September 2019.

2. Nikhil Rampal, 'Odds against odd-even, scheme could not improve Delhi's air', *India Today*, 20 November 2019.
3. 'Sorry, Mr Kejriwal, but Delhi's air pollution rose 23% during second OddEven phase', *Firstpost*, 30 April 2016.
4. Bhasker Triathi, 'Odd-even may not cut Delhi air pollution. An expert from IIT explains why', *Business Standard*, 25 November 2019.
5. Carol Potera, 'Air Pollution: Asia's Two-Stroke Engine Dilemma', *Environmental Health Perspective*, 112(11): A613, August 2004.
6. 'Two- and Three-Wheelers in India', Innovative Transport Solutions (iTrans) Pvt. Ltd., June 2009.
7. Sanjay Dutta, '62% petrol used by two-wheelers, 27% by cars, survey shows', *Times of India*, 24 September 2013.
8. 'Two-wheelers consume over 62% petrol in India', *Policy Bazaar*, n.d.
9. 'Joshua Apte's Insights into New Delhi's Air Pollution', UC Berkley, 5 October 2011.
10. Julie Chao, 'Still a Lot to Learn About India's Deadly Air Pollution', Berkeley Lab, 11 August 2014.
11. Ruhie Kumar, 'Help Delhi Breathe and the people-powered movement to clean Delhi's air', *Mobilisation Lab*, 14 March 2018.
12. 'Haze over the Indo-Gangetic Plain', Earth Observatory NASA, 3 January 2016.
13. 'India had 14 out of world's 20 most polluted cities in terms of PM2.5 levels in 2016, says WHO', *The Hindu*, 2 May 2018.
14. Dhananjay Mahapatra, 'Will do our best to curb pollution, but not by playing havoc with economy: Supreme Court', *Times of India*, 22 January 2016.
15. Anumita Roychowdhury, 'Global Burden of Disease ranks air pollution as a top killer', *Down to Earth*, 17 August 2015.
16. Jyoti Pande Lavakare, 'Foul air blowing over India, not just in Delhi', *Hindustan Times*, 11 March 2016.
17. Rosheena Zehra, 'Airtel Delhi Half Marathon and Air Quality: Harmful Effects and Precautions', *Quint*, 23 October 2018.
18. 'Indian cities among world's most "unliveable" in Mercer Quality of Living Survey 2019', *Times Now*, 14 March 2019.
19. Central Pollution Control Board website, www.cpcb.nic.in
20. 'Push Factors', Globalization 101, 2017.
21. 'Hundreds Protest Over Delhi's Poor Air Quality at Jantar Mantar', NDTV, 6 November 2016.
22. 'Modi government spent over Rs 35 lakh on installing air purifiers in offices: Report', *Wion*, 20 March 2018.

Chapter 8: Our Children

1. 'Delhi's Air Pollution and Its Effects on Children's Health', *Yale Global Health Review*.
2. Bindu Perappadan, 'Delhi kids have smaller lungs compared with children in US due to air pollution', 15 November 2017.
3. Sunil K Chhabra, Rajeev Kumar and Vikas Mittal, 'Prediction Equations for Spirometry for Children from Northern India', *Indian Paediatrics*, Vol. 53(9):781–785, September 2016.
4. Ibid.
5. Pritha Chatterjee, 'Leave Delhi: That's what doctors are prescribing to patients with serious respiratory ailments', *Indian Express*, 2 April 2015.
6. Emma Walton, 'Tainted air: The link between pollution and Alzheimer's disease', *Biomedical Journal*, Vol. 41(3): 137–140, 25 July 2018.
7. Ruth Peters et al., 'Air Pollution and Dementia: A Systematic Review', *Pub Med*, Vol. 70(s1):S145-S163, 2019.
8. Naureen Ali and Adeel Khoja, 'Growing Evidence for the Impact of Air Pollution on Depression', *Oschner Journal*, Vol. 19(1): 4, 2019.
9. Ruopeng An et al., 'Impact of ambient air pollution on obesity: a systematic review', *Pub Med*, Vol. 42(6):1112-1126, June 2018.
10. Johana Sigaux et al., 'Air pollution as a determinant of rheumatoid arthritis', *Pub Med*, Vol. 86(1): 37–42, January 2019.
11. Alexandra White, Patrick Bradshaw and Ghassan Hamra, 'Air pollution and breast cancer: A review', *Pub Med*, Vol. 5(2): 92–100, June 2018.
12. 'Brick kilns sans zig-zag tech to shut after Sept 30', *Tribune*, July 2013.
13. Baishali Adak, 'French woman launches photo campaign to raise awareness for clean air in Delhi', *India Today*, 4 February 2016.
14. Ibid.
15. John Kania and Mark Kramer, 'Collective Impact', *Stanford Social Innovation Review*, 2011.
16. Ibid.

Chapter 9: Killing Us All

1. 'Supreme Court drops a bomb this Diwali: Apex court bans sale of firecrackers in Delhi-NCR till 1 November', *Firstpost*, 10 October 2017.
2. 'Supreme Court Reserves Verdict On Plea To Restore Ban On Firecracker Sale', NDTV, 6 October 2017.
3. Rohan Shah et al., Personal exposures to particulate matter <2.5 μm in mass

median aerodynamic diameter (PM2.5) pollution during the burning of six most commonly used firecrackers in India', *Lung India*, Vol. 36(4): 324–329, July 2019.

4. 'The Chemistry of Fireworks', Compound Chemistry, 30 December 2013.
5. Aastha Saxena, 'Delhi: Spike in emergency visits as air worsens, suggests AIIMS study', *Indian Express*, 5 November 2019.
6. '16 Delhi kids wrote a strong letter to the CM about the pollution and delivered it to his residence', *Better India*, 15 November 2016.
7. Delhi Pollution Control Committee, https://www.dpcc.delhigovt.nic.in/Order%206579-89.pdf
8. Ritwick Dutta, 'EPCA Was Specially Empowered to Deal With Air Pollution Crises. Is It Working?' *Wire*, 8 November 2018.
9. Ritwick Dutta, 'Do You Pollute the Air? Expect a Friendly Letter from the Authorities', 9 November 2018.
10. Ritwick Dutta, 'EPCA Was Specially Empowered to Deal With Air Pollution Crises. Is It Working?' *Wire*, 8 November 2018.
11. Interview with Vishnu Mathur, Director General, SIAM, 2 January 2012, https://micorporate.com/Bureau/Interviews/21/Vishnu-Mathur-Director-General-SIAM
12. Ritwick Dutta, 'Smog Towers: Delhi's Smog Is Here to Stay Because Air Pollution's Not the Crisis', *Wire*, 26 November 2019.
13. 'Special report on pollution hot spots in NCR with request for urgent directions to improve enforcement and pollution control', EPCA Report No. 106, 18 October 2019.
14. Saptarshi Dutta, 'Air pollution in Delhi: Indian medical association declares national health emergency', *Swachh India*, 10 November 2017.
15. 'Sharp decline in Delhi's air quality: Medical body declares public health emergency, says schools must be shut', *Firstpost*, 7 November 2017.
16. 'IMA declares "public health emergency state" in Delhi, wants Half Marathon cancelled', *Indian Express*, 7 November 2017.
17. 'Rashtriya Ekta Diwas live updates: PM Modi flags off Run for Unity on Sardar Vallabhbhai Patel's birth anniversary', *Financial Express*, 31 October 2017.
18. 'PM Narendra Modi Flags Off 'Run For Unity' On Sardar Vallabhbhai Patel's Birth Anniversary', NDTV, 31 October 2017.
19. Rosheena Zehra, 'Airtel Delhi Half Marathon and Air Quality: Harmful Effects and Precautions', *Quint*, 23 October 2018.
20. 'Avoid morning walks in Delhi to save your lungs, say doctors', *Times of India*, 3 November 2017.

21. 'Aujla gives talk on air pollution at WHO meet', *Tribune*, 30 October 2018.
22. 'Dr Arvind Kumar's Speech at WHO air pollution and health conference', YouTube, uploaded by Climate Trends, 31 October 2018.
23. 'Air pollution and lung cancer: testimony of a surgeon from New Delhi', YouTube, uploaded by World Health Organization (WHO), 12 November 2018.
24. '"Run for Unity" on Sardar Patel's 143rd birth anniversary', *Indian Express*, 31 October 2018.
25. 'On Sardar Patel's Birth Anniversary, Thousands "Run for Unity"', NDTV, 31 October 2018.
26. Tweet by Sunil Dahiya, 15 April 2019, https://twitter.com/Sunil_S_Dahiya/status/1117799170478202880
27. 'Delhi's Deadly Air', Al Jazeera, uploaded by Al Jazeera, 5 June 2019.
28. Vatsala Shrangi, 'Delhi records AQI of 41 – lowest since records kept', *Hindustan Times*, 1 September 2020.

Chapter 10: My Mother, Your Mother

1. Bharati Chaturvedi, 'Toxic mall', *Down to Earth*, 4 July 2015.
2. 'Local sources of pollution in UP, Haryana and Delhi primary reason for poor air quality: EPCA', *Economic Times*, 15 October 2019.
3. Bharati Chaturvedi, 'How Delhi's Security Guards Are Harming Themselves Most In Winter While Protecting Us', *Youth Ki Awaaz*, 4 December 2017.
4. 'Burning rubber', *Indian Environmental Portal*, 14 March 1995.
5. 'NGT bans tyre burning in the open, re-use of tyres as fuel', *Times of India*, 13 September 2014.
6. Mohit Sharma, 'Burning garbage may now attract Rs 1 lakh fine', *Hindustan Times*, 13 January 2016.
7. Tausif Alam, 'Pom Pom will pay you for your recyclable waste', *Your Story*, 6 January 2016.
8. 'Municipal Solid Waste Management Manual', Ministry of Urban Development, 2016.
9. '"We don't want electricity at the cost of lives": The Toxic Impact of Okhla's Waste to Energy Plant', *Bastion*, 12 December 2019.
10. 'Okhla waste to energy plant, Delhi, India', Environmental Justice Atlas, 12 April 2018.
11. 'Order of the National Green Tribunal regarding release of dioxin and furans by waste to energy plant at Okhla, Delhi, 09/10/2017', *Indian Environment Portal*, 9 October 2017.

12. Dharmesh Shah and Pratibha Sharma, 'Why the NGT Okhla Order Sets a Bad Precedent for Indian Environmental Jurisprudence', *Wire*, 16 February 2017.
13. https://ilsr.org/waste-incineration-renewable-energy/ Marie Donahue, 'Report: Waste Incineration: A Dirty Secret in How States Define Renewable Energy', Institute for Local Self-Reliance, 12 December 2018.
14. Ranjit Devraj and Swati Sambyal, 'How Delhi's waste-to-energy plants are way off the mark', *Down to Earth*, 20 January 2019.
15. E.J. Lopes, L.A. Okamura and C.I. Yamamoto, 'Formation of Dioxins and Furans During Municipal Solid Waste Gasification', *Brazilian Journal of Chemical Engineering*, Vol. 32, No. 01, pp. 87 - 97, January–March, 2015.
16. Jasjeev Gandhlok 'CPCB told to assess ecological damage from Okhla waste plant', *Times of India*, 1 October 2019.
17. 'Okhla waste to energy plant, Delhi, India', Environmental Justice Atlas, 12 April 2018.
18. Ranjit Devraj and Swati Sambyal, 'How Delhi's waste-to-energy plants are way off the mark', *Down to Earth*, 20 January 2019
19. '"We don't want electricity at the cost of lives": The Toxic Impact of Okhla's Waste to Energy Plant', *Bastion*, 12 December 2019.
20. Yamuna River Project website, www.yamunariverproject.org
21. Mapping Delhi Landfills – Yamuna River Project, www.yamunariverproject.org/mapping-delhi-landfills.html
22. AnkitYadav, 'Blame pollution? Delhi non-smoker gets lung cancer', *India Today*, 31 July 2019.

Chapter 11: Every Day, Everywhere

1. 'The Contribution of Household Fuels to Ambient Air Pollution in India – A Comparison of Recent Estimates', Collaborative Clean Air Policy Centre, 30 May 2019.
2. 'Report of the Steering Committee on Air Pollution and Health Related Issues', Ministry of Health and Family Welfare, August 2015.
3. 'Database on source apportionment studies for particulate matter in the air (PM10 and PM2.5)', World Health Organization, n.d.
4. 'India's polluted air killed 1.24 million in 2017: study', Al Jazeera, 6 December 2018.
5. Joanna Slater, 'Bad air kills more than a million Indians a year, study says', *Washington Post*, 7 December 2018.
6. 'Air quality guidelines – global update 2005', World Health Organization, n.d.
7. 'Report of the Steering Committee on Air Pollution and Health Related Issues', Ministry of Health and Family Welfare, August 2015.

8. Ibid.
9. Jyoti Pande Lavakare, 'PMUY yet to be acknowledged as efficient strategy to reduce air pollution', *Financial Express*, 21 August 2019.
10. Jayashree Nandi, 'Private lab to test for presence of dioxin in Okhla air', *Times of India*, 25 February 2014.
11. 'Special report on pollution hot spots in NCR with request for urgent directions to improve enforcement and pollution control', EPCA Report No. 106, 18 October 2019.
12. 'Govt advances BS-VI fuel roll out in Delhi to cut pollution', *Financial Express*, 16 November 2017.
13. Jyoti Pande Lavakare, 'Explained: Ban of BS-IV vehicles to raise air quality' *Financial Express*, 22 November 2018.
14. Amit Pandey, 'Vehicle scrappage policy could come by September end: Nitin Gadkari', *Mint*, 5 September 2020.
15. 'Amid lockdown, India switches to BS-VI emission norms', *The Hindu*, 2 April 2020.
16. Jennifer Hermes, 'How Traffic Jams Affect Air Quality', Environmental Leader, 5 January 2012.
17. Dianne Lugo, 'On Hot Days, Asphalt Can Release as Much Air Pollution as Cars', *Smithsonian Mag*, 9 September 2020
18. Proceedings of the National Academy of Sciences of the United States of America website, www.pnas.org
19. Jyoti Pande Lavakare, 'Ignoring Air Pollution Is Justice Denied', *Wire*, 7 December 2018.
20. 'Air quality not a class issue, but mass issue, says Shashi Tharoor', *Business Standard*, 9 September 2020.
21. 'Stubble Burning Caused 44% Of Delhi Pollution This Year: Pollution Board', NDTV, 14 November 2019.
22. 'The Punjab Preservation of Subsoil Water Act, 2009', Department of Legal and Legislative Affairs, Punjab, 28 April 2009.
23. Arvind Kumar, 'Law-aiding Monsanto is reason for Delhi's annual smoke season', *Sunday Guardian*, 30 December 2017.
24. 'Are GMOs killing off bees all over the world?', *DNA India*, 26 November 2013.
25. Arvind Kumar, 'Monsanto's profits, not Diwali, creating smoke in Delhi', *Sunday Guardian*, 3 November 2018.
26. Mike Listman, 'Alternatives to burning can increase Indian farmers' profits and cut pollution, new study shows', International Maize and Wheat Improvement Centre, 8 August 2019.

27. P. Shyamsundar et al., 'Fields on fire: Alternatives to crop residue burning in India', *Science*, Vol. 365, Issue 6453, pp. 536-538, 9 August 2019.
28. Mike Listman, 'Alternatives to burning can increase Indian farmers' profits and cut pollution, new study shows', International Maize and Wheat Improvement Centre, 8 August 2019.
29. Jyoti Pande Lavakare, 'Stubble Burning: What the government should do to control air pollution in Delhi', *Financial* Express, 29 October 2018.
30. Jyoti Pande Lavakare, 'Avoiding An "Airpocalypse" – Delhi Declares War on Air Pollution', Health Policy Watch, 7 October 2020.
31. Anna Molin, 'Ikea wants to make stuff from the stubble now being burnt in India', *Mint*, 15 November 2018.
32. 'IKEA contributes to reducing air pollution with FÖRÄNDRING, a collection based on rice straw', IKEA, 4 June 2019.
33. 'Change is in the air. Turning waste into products.', IKEA, n.d.

Chapter 12: Every Breath You Take

1. C. Rangarajan, 'Eminent Iconographer and Humanitarian Passes Away', *Cision PR Newswire*, 3 October 2016.
2. 'Ranjan Roy: The man who ran the network', *Times of India*, 11 March 2018.
3. Sukriti Dwivedi, '"Warrior Moms" Launch Nationwide Anti-Air Pollution Campaign Amid Covid', NDTV, 7 September 2020.
4. '"Warrior Moms": Mothers across India join hands to fight air pollution', *Indian Express*, 11 September 2020.
5. Vandana Ramnani, 'Tree cutting in South Delhi redevelopment project necessary to provide for underground parking for 70,000 vehicles: NBCC', *Money Control*, 25 June 2018.
6. 'Delhi HC stays cutting of trees after protests; LG refuses to take blame, NBCC to plant two lakh saplings', *Indian Express*, 25 June 2018.
7. 'Another brick oof the wall', *Centre for Science and Environment*, 25 August 2020.
8. Tweet by My Right To Breathe, 21 November 2018, https://twitter.com/MRTB_India/status/1065084118629781505
9. Tweet by My Right To Breathe, 22 November 2018, https://twitter.com/search?q=%23pollutionracism%20careforairindia&src=typed_query
10. Jyoti Pande Lavakare, 'Supreme Court's Diwali cracker order can have far-reaching impact on pollution if properly enforced', *Scroll*, 25 October 2018.
11. 'Inquest to determine if London air pollution caused child's death', *Guardian*, 17 December 2019.
12. Doctors for Clean Air website: www.doctorsforcleanair.org
13. Health Care Without Harm website, www.noharm.org

Chapter 13. Breathing Here Is Injurious to Your Health

1. 'Care for Air: Air Pollution' conference held at IIT Kanpur, 10 January 2019. www.aiitkblr.org
2. 'A Symposium by IIT Kanpur Alumni to Find Practical Solutions to Counter Growing Air Pollution', *Cision PR News*, 8 January 2019.
3. 'National Clean Air Programme', *Ministry of Environment, Forest & Climate Change*, 2019.
4. Tanushree Ganguly, L.S. Kurinji and Sarath Guttikunda, 'How Robust are Urban India's Air Plans?: An Assessment of 102 Cities', Council On Energy, Environment And Water, June 2020.
5. Jon Kolko, *Wicked Problems: Problems Worth Solving*, Austin Centre for Design, 2012.
6. Divya Kaushik, 'Melba Pria, former Mexican ambassador to India: I'll always be the ambassador with the autorickshaw', *Times of India*, June 2019.
7. Prabha Chandran, 'Meet H.E. Melba Pria, The Mexican Ambassador Who Rides in Style', *Huffington Post*, 15 July 2016.
8. 'In polluted Delhi, breathe 'Davos' air in this biz centre', Greentechlead, 22 January 2015.
9. David Richard Boyd website. www.davidrichardboyd.com
10. http://srenvironment.org/contact
11. 'Under the Dome (English subtitle, complete) by Chai Jing: Air pollution in China', YouTube, uploaded by Jiahua Guo, 8 March 2015.
12. Yuan Ren, 'Under the Dome: will this film be China's environmental awakening?', *Guardian*, 5 March 2015.
13. Celia Hatton, 'Under the Dome: The smog film taking China by storm', BBC, 2 March 2015.
14. Anthony Kuhn, 'The Anti-Pollution Documentary that's Taken China By Storm', *NPR*, 4 March 2015.
15. Kumar Shrivastava, 'India diverts Rs 56,700 crore from the fight against climate change to Goods and Service Tax regime', *Scroll*, 24 July 2017.
16. Megha Darby, 'India diverts $25 billion away from clean energy fund', *Climate Change News*, 24 July 2017.
17. Piyush Pandey, 'Panel pulls up govt. for diverting coal cess', *The Hindu*, 13 January 2019.
18. Dheeraj Mishra, 'Exclusive: Pollution Norms – That All Power Plants Except Adani's Were Complying With – Diluted', *Wire*, 3 October 2019.
19. Steve Bernard and Amy Kazim, 'Dirty air: how India became the most polluted country on earth', *Financial Times*, 11 December 2018.

20. Andrea Downey, 'First person to "die from air pollution" is girl, 9, who suffered asthma attack', *Sun*, 4 July 2018.
21. Ben Webster, 'Girl's death from asthma linked to car pollution', *Times*, 4 July 2018.
22. Jocelyn Cockburn, 'Mother of nine-year old girl Ella Kissi-Debrah delivers 100,000 signature petition to the attorney general to re-open inquest', Hodge Jones and Allen solicitors, 31 August 2018.
23. Stephen Moss, 'Invisible killer: how one girl's tragic death could change the air pollution story', *Guardian*, 22 September 2018.
24. Ross Lydall, 'Green candidate: toxic air killed my daughter, aged nine - now I'll fight election to beat it', *Evening Standard*, 24 January 2019.
25. Kundan Pandey, 'No Death Certificate Has Cause of Death as 'Pollution': Environment Minister Harsh Vardhan', *Down to Earth*, 6 May 2019.
26. Casper Henderson, 'Choked by Beth Gardiner review – the toxic truth about the air we breathe', *Guardian*, 3 April 2019.
27. Beth Gardiner, 'How Can We Stop the Air We Breathe from Slowly Poisoning Us?' *Lit Hub*, 19 April 2019.
28. Mayor of London, 'World's first 24 hour Ultra Low Emission Zone starts in London', 8 April 2019.
29. 'ULEZ: New pollution charge begins in London', BBC, 8 April 2019.
30. Georgina Stubbs, 'Sadiq Khan says London's pollution so bad it's given him asthma', *Independent*, 13 May 2016.
31. Environmental Research Group, Imperial College London. www.imperial.ac.uk/school-public-health/environmental-research-group/
32. Thomas Barrett, 'ULEZ set to benefit poorest Londoners most, according to research', *Air Quality News*, 10 January 2019.
33. Beth Gardiner, 'Dirty lies: how the car industry hid the truth about diesel emissions', *Guardian*, 22 March 2019.
34. Damian Carrington, '"Impossible-to-cheat" emissions tests show almost all new diesels still dirty', *Guardian*, 6 June 2018.
35. Beth Gardiner, 'It can't be left to Europe's cities to clean up noxious air', *Guardian*, 12 July 2019.
36. Anumita Roychowdhury, 'Exposure to pollutants higher than ambient pollution in Delhi's Anand Vihar: CSE', *Down to Earth*, 26 December 2016.
37. 'Delhi's 'bad air' days down by 33%, says Prakash Javadekar', *The Hindu*, 6 June 2019.
38. Tweet by Sunil Dahiya, 15 April 2019. https://twitter.com/sunil_s_dahiya/status/1117799170478202880?lang=en

39. Jyoti Pande Lavakare, 'Claim that Delhi Air Pollution Has Fallen by 25% Needs to be Taken with a Pinch of Salt', *Wire*, 15 September 2019.
40. Tweet by Arvind Kejriwal, 13 September 2019. https://twitter.com/ArvindKejriwal/status/1172469764540600320
41. Sarath Guttikunda, 'What it Means to Take the Long View on Air Pollution in Delhi', *Wire*, 7 November 2016.
42. Jayashree Nandi, 'People in North India may lose 7 years of life due to air pollution: Study', *Hindustan Times*, 31 October 2019.
43. 'Dear Sourav Ganguly, Delhi is Choking. Shift the T20 Match Venue', *Quint*, 29 October 2019.
44. 'Delhi pollution: Dia Mirza calls out BCCI for holding Ind vs Bangladesh T20 match despite severe AQI levels', *Hindustan Times*, 1 November 2019.
45. Shamik Chakrabarty, 'In the (bad) light of air pollution, Sourav Ganguly says scheduling needs to be 'practical' in the future', *Indian Express*, 1 November 2019.
46. Bilal Kuchay, '"Gas chamber": Pollution hits record high in New Delhi', AL Jazeera, 1 November 2019.
47. Guy Davies, '5 million masks distributed as "toxic" smog descends on Delhi during Diwali', ABC News, 1 November 2019.
48. Dutta, Ritwick, 'Twenty Years of EPCA: Lessons for the New EPCA', Legal Initiative for Forests and Environment, New Delhi, 2018.
49. Tweet by BJP, 11 November 2019. https://twitter.com/BJP4India/status/1193807021063069696?s=20
50. Niharika Lal, 'Sushant "Choke", Cyber "Huff", Aravalli "Biogas" Park: Climate protesters rename areas in Gurgaon', *Times of India*, 18 November, 2019.
51. Sweta Dutta, 'Congress MP Gaurav Gogoi labours over a new Clean Air (Amendment) Act to combat pollution, set to table it in winter session of Parliament', *Pune Mirror*, 17 September 2019.
52. Jyoti Pande Lavakare, 'Opinion: Wanted - A Clean Air Boss With Cabinet Rank To Tackle Pollution', NDTV, 21 November 2019.
53. Milan Sharma, 'Pollution does not shorten life in India: Environment minister Prakash Javadekar says stop fear psychosis', *India Today*, 6 December 2019.
54. Tweet by Dr Maria Neira, 6 December 2019. https://twitter.com/drmarianeira/status/1202972205811978240
55. Manka Behl, 'WHO contradicts Prakash Javadekar's views on pollution and lifespan', *Times of India*, 8 December 2019.
56. Tweet by Dr Maria Neira, 9 December 2019. https://twitter.com/DrMariaNeira/status/1204033642047123456

57. Anirvan Ghosh, '80 People Die In Delhi Everyday Due To Air Polliution, Says Environment Minister Prakash Javadekar', *Huffington Post*, 15 July 2016.
58. Joshua Apte et al., 'Addressing Global Mortality from Ambient PM2.5', *Pub Mud*, Vol. 49(13):8057-66, 7 July 2015.
59. Shirin Bithal, 'Delhi loses 80 lives to air pollution every day, says study', *Down to Earth*, 10 December 2018.
60. 'Experts write to SC against installation of smog towers', *Hindustan Times*, 29 November 2019.
61. 'Smog towers 'expensive', 'inefficient' to combat Delhi pollution: Experts in open letter to SC', *New Indian Express*, 30 November 2019.
62. Care For Air, 'An Open Letter to the Supreme Court of India Against Outdoor Air Purifiers', *Wire*, 1 December 2019.
63. Setti L et al., 'Position Paper Relazione circa l'effetto dell'inquinamento da particolato atmosferico e la diffusione di virus nella popolazione', SIMA - Società Italiana di Medicina Ambientale, 2020.
64. Yaron Ogen, 'Assessing nitrogen dioxide (NO2) levels as a contributing factor to coronavirus (COVID-19) fatality', *Science Direct*, 11 April 2020.
65. X Wu et al., 'Air pollution and COVID-19 mortality in the United States: Strengths and limitations of an ecological regression analysis', *Science advances*, Harvard University, 2020.

Chapter 14. Air Pollution in a Post-Corona World

1. Lisa Firedman, 'New Research Links Air Pollution to Higher Coronavirus Death Rates', *New York Times*, 7 April 2020
2. X Wu et al., 'Air pollution and COVID-19 mortality in the United States: Strengths and limitations of an ecological regression analysis', *Science advances*, Harvard University, 2020.
3. Setti L et al., 'Position Paper Relazione circa l'effetto dell'inquinamento da particolato atmosferico e la diffusione di virus nella popolazione', SIMA - Società Italiana di Medicina Ambientale, 2020.
4. 'Airborne particles may be assisting the spread of SARS-CoV-2', *Economist*, 26 March 2020.
5. Yan Cui etal., 'Air pollution and case fatality of SARS in the People's Republic of China: an ecologic study', *Environmental Health Journal*, Article number: 15, 2003.
6. University of California – Los Angeles, 'SARS Death Rate Doubles In Polluted Cities', *Science Daily*, 20 November 2003.
7. Neela Banerjee, 'Q&A: A Harvard Expert on Environment and Health Discusses

Possible Ties Between COVID and Climate', *Inside Climate News*, 12 March 2020.

8. Navin Khadka, 'Air pollution linked to raised Covid-19 death risk', BBC, 20 April 2020.
9. 'How air pollution worsens the COVID-19 pandemic', Centre for Research on Energy and Clean Air, 2020.
10. Sonalde Desai and Santanu Pramanik, 'Telephone survey shows high understanding of social distancing, support for lockdown', *Indian Express*, 20 April 2020.
11. Jatinder Mahal, 'Jalandhar air quality best in a decade, AQI recorded at 52', *Hindustan Times*, 5 April 2020.
12. 'Saharanpur wakes up to Himalayas, visible from town after 30 years as AQI dips below 50', *Times of India*, 30 April 2020.
13. Central Pollution Control Board, 'Impact of Janta Curfew and Lockdown on Air Quality', 31 March 2020.
14. 'India's 90 Cities Record Minimal Air Pollution Due To COVID-19 Lockdown', *Statesman*, 29 March 2020.
15. 'Air Pollution Levels in North India at "20-Year Low" Amid Lockdown: NASA', 29 April 2020.
16. 'Lockdown improves the view, but will it change the vision?', Carbon Copy, 15 April 2020.
17. Sarath Guttkunda, 'Data Analysis: How Has the Lockdown Changed the Pollution Over North India?', *Wire*, 15 April 2020.
18. Joe Wallen, 'India's cleaner lockdown air could save 650,000 lives', *Telegraph*, 11 May 2020.
19. 'Low pollution during lockdown may have saved 630 lives, $690 mn: Study', *Business Standard*, 17 July 2020.
20. Kabir Firaque, 'Cleaner China air saved more lives than Covid claimed, study finds', *Indian Express*, 16 May 2020.
21. Douglas Broom, '11,000 deaths avoided during lockdown in Europe – thanks to cleaner air', *World Economic Forum*, 11 May 2020.
22. Centre for Research on Energy and Clean Air website: www.energyandcleanair.org
23. Rosy Battaglia, 'Lower air pollution during coronavirus lockdowns saved 15,000 lives in 12 cities', *Life Gate*, 23 September 2020.
24. 'Air pollution is returning to pre-covid levels', *Economist*, 5 September 2020.
25. 'In charts: India's GDP shrinks more than other major economies, decline set in before pandemic', *Scroll*, 2 September 2020.

26. Jayashree Nandi, 'Covid-19: Environment ministry panel for automatic extension of forest clearance', *Hindustan Times*, 5 April 2020.
27. Hannah Ellis-Petersen et al., '"It's positively alpine!": Disbelief in big cities as air pollution falls', *Guardian*, 11 April 2020.
28. Jon Stone, 'Public want radical response to climate change with same urgency as coronavirus, poll finds', *Independent*, 16 April 2020.
29. Giuseppe Sala, 'Post virus, let's rebuild climate-smart, healthier and equitably', Thomas Reuters Foundation, 16 April 2020.
30. Laura Laker, 'Milan announces ambitious scheme to reduce car use after lockdown', *Guardian*, 21 April 2020.
31. Feargus O'Sullivan, 'Paris Has a Plan to Keep Cars Out After Lockdown', *Bloomberg*, 29 April 2020.
32. Aritz Parra, 'Cycle power: Bikes emerge as a post-lockdown commuter option', *AP news*, 3 May 2020.
33. Shinjiro Koizumi video: https://player.admiralcloud.com/?v=d49d44fd-93ad-4c9d-87aa-c37a711541f8
34. Jay Mazoomdar, 'Explained: Reading the draft Environment Impact Assessment norms, and finding the red flags', *Indian Express*, 10 August 2020.
35. Mitali Mukherjee, 'Jairam Ramesh on Draft EIA 2020: "It Will Destroy India's Natural Resources"', *Wire*, 17 August 2020.
36. 'Draft EIA notification "deeply anti-democratic": Jairam Ramesh', *Indian Express*, 19 August 2020.
37. 'Put on hold draft EIA till it is discussed, Jairam urges Javadekar', *The Hindu*, 10 August 2020.
38. Tish Sanghera and Disha Shetty, 'India Is Ripping Apart Its Environment For Business', *Article 14*, 2 May 2020.
39. Jacob Koshy, 'Apex wildlife panel holds virtual conference, clears infra projects', *The Hindu*, 8 April 2020.
40. 'Countries to risk over $600 billion on dirty coal power post Covid-19 pandemic: Carbon Tracker', *Carbon Copy*, 9 April 2020.
41. Vibhuti Garg et al., 'Mapping India's Energy Subsidies 2020', Council on Energy, Environment and Water, April 2020.
42. 'Experimental smog tower: Supreme Court warns IIT-Bombay of contempt action', *The Hindu*, 29 July 2020.
43. Jyoti Pande Lavakare, 'Indian Clean Air Advocates Slam Supreme Court Order Pushing Questionable "Smog Tower" Technology', *Health Policy Watch*, 5 August 2020.
44. 'Work on setting up of Delhi 'smog tower' has begun, SC told', *Statesman*, 17 October 2020.

45. Amrit Dhillon, 'In India, can New Delhi's smog towers reduce pollution? Experts say they're more hot air than clean air', *South China Morning Post*, 16 August 2020.
46. 'China encourages environmental groups to sue polluters', *Guardian*, 7 January 2015.
47. Ellen Bardash, 'Delaware AG Jennings Sues 31 Fossil Fuel Companies in State Court Over Damages from Climate Change', *Law*, 10 September 2020.
48. 'Holding Major Fossil Fuel Companies Accountable for Nearly 40 Years of Climate Deception and Harm', Union of Concerned Scientists, 22 March 2016.
49. Shivam Vij, 'India needs a Clean Air Act and an autonomous new body to enforce it', *Print*, 6 November 2019.

Epilogue: The Road Ahead – Flight Or Fight

1. Geetha G. Thimmegowda et al., 'A field-based quantitative analysis of sublethal effects of air pollution on pollinators', *PNAS*, 25 August 2020.
2. Richard Burnett t al., 'An Integrated Risk Function for Estimating the Global Burden of Disease Attributable to Ambient Fine Particulate Matter Exposure', *Environmental Health Perspectives*, 1 April 2014.
3. 'India takes steps to curb air pollution', World Health Organization, bulletin 94:487-488, 2016.
4. Joshua Apte, 'Scalable multi-pollution exposure assessment using routine mobile monitoring platforms', Health Effects Institute, 2019.
5. Krishnadas Rajagopal, 'Former Supreme Court judge Madan Lokur, aided by students, to save Delhi-NCR', *The Hindu*, 16 October 2020.
6. Jyoti Pande Lavakare, 'Not just a committee – we need the whole govt to address stubble-burning', *Wire*, 19 October 2020.
7. Raj Macchan, 'On Jhatkaa citizens talk garbage and more', *Civil Society*, 12 September 2020.
8. J.P., 'How China cut it's air pollution', *Economist*, 25 January 2018.

Further References

Thank you for reading this book. For those of you who know just enough and already want to drive action, I'm sure you will find your own niche, your personal path on your journey as a clean air campaigner, a climate change activist or just a vigilant, aware resident. Pick your strength and begin from there. A good place to begin is your social media – whether it is WhatsApp, Facebook, LinkedIn, Telegram, Instagram or one of the newer platforms. But that doesn't mean you only take a virtual stance. Talk about the health harm of air pollution with your friends, your family, most importantly, your children and your elders. Discuss things about air pollution that shocked or surprised you in this book with them. What is the difference between immunity and endurance in the context of pollution? Are masks a solution or just a temporary mitigation measure? All research tells us outdoor aerobic exercise is beneficial for health – but what if we exercise outside in high levels of pollution? We know pranayamas and breathing exercises help improve lung function – but doesn't doing these traditionally, outdoors under a neem tree harm rather then help?

Once Covid-19 is behind us (inshallah!) make air pollution a topic of conversations at all gatherings, and not just in the winter months. Don't stop talking or writing about it in your WhatsApp groups.

And remember, even if you're unable to take significant action, you can just start with segregating and composting your garbage, buying less, reducing, reusing, recycling, carpooling, taking public transport, cycling, walking more and just being aware and informed.

At the very least, you will be able to spot the red herrings when those with loud voices tell you they are spending your money on installing outdoor smog towers to clean the air. Question them and remain vigilant about this collective resource that is essential for our very life. There are different types of campaigners and here is a quick guide to find out where you fit.

For others who prefer a deeper dive, apart from careforair.org, here is a resource list that you can use as a take-off point. It is by no means exhaustive (remember those 70,000 papers linking air pollution to human health?) but will serve as a beginning for those who want more information. This list will also be up on careforair.org and will be updated regularly.

I'd like to do a crash course on air pollution. Where do I go?

1. 'Air pollution: Causes and impacts', *EdX*. www.edx.org
2. 'Air pollution, facts and information', *National Geographic*. www.nationalgeographic.com
3. 'Air Pollution: A Global Threat to our Health', *Coursera*. www.coursera.org
4. Moms Clean Air Force. www.momscleanairforce.org

I like reading books. What books can I read to learn more about air pollution?

1. Beth Gardiner, *Choked: Life and Breath in the Age of Air Pollution*, University of Chicago Press, 2019.

2. Gary Fuller, *The Invisible Killer: The Rising Global Threat of Air Pollution – and How We Can Fight Back*, Melville House, 2019.
3. Siddharth Singh, *The Great Smog of India*, Penguin Viking, 2018.
4. Mansoor Khan, *The Third Curve: The End of Growth as We Know It*, 2013.
5. Ramachandra Guha, *How Much Should a Person Consume?: Thinking through the Environment*, Hachette India, 2010.
6. Kamal Meattle and Barun Aggarwal, *How to Grow Fresh Air: India's Top Experts Teach You How to Beat Air Pollution*, Juggernaut, 2018.
7. Doug Brugge, *Particles in the Air: The Deadliest Pollutant Is the One You Breathe Every Day*, Springer, 2018.
8. Richard C.J. Somerville, *The Forgiving Air: Understanding Environmental Change*, American Meteorological Society, 2008.
9. Dean Spears, *Air: Pollution, Climate Change and India's Choice Between Policy and Pretence*, HarperCollins India, 2019.
10. Tim Smedley, *Clearing the Air: The Beginning and the End of Air Pollution*, Bloomsbury Sigma, 2019.

I'm not into books but podcasts will do. Are there any out there?

1. Third Pod from the Sun. https://thirdpodfromthesun.com/2019/06/24/centennial-e7-night-of-the-killer-smog/
2. Atmospheric Tales. https://atmospherictales.com/
3. MIT Energy Initiative. http://energy.mit.edu/podcast/energy-economics-and-air-pollution/
4. Peak Planet, hosted by Karthik Ganesan. https://www.ceew.in/news/podcast-peak-planet
5. Earth Matters podcast from The Bigger Picture. Episode on India's Air Pollution: https://bfm.com.my/podcast/the-bigger-picture/earth-matters/india-air-pollution
6. Political Climate politicalclimatepodcast.com/how-to-listen

I want to access data on air quality and health. Where do I go?

1. Open access data on air quality from around the world is available on *OpenAQ*: https://openaq.org/.
2. Open access data on long-term trends of air pollution and health for countries around the world is available on *State of Global Air*: https://www.stateofglobalair.org/
3. Air quality data on *Resource Watch*: www.resourcewatch.org
4. Urban Emissions: www.urbanemissions.info

5. WHO Global Ambient Air Quality Database: https://www.who.int/airpollution/data/cities/en/
6. Global Air Quality Forecasts from CAMS: www.windy.com

Resources for air quality monitoring in India

1. 'Report of the Steering Committee on Air Pollution and Health Related Issues', *Ministry of Health and Family Welfare*, August 2015.
2. 'National Clean Air Programme', *Ministry of Environment, Forest & Climate Change*, 2019. http://moef.gov.in/wp-content/uploads/2019/05/NCAP_Report.pdf
3. Centre for Science and Environment has a detailed air pollution section. https://www.cseindia.org/page/air-pollution
4. Urban Emissions for India-specific air quality data and forecasts: https://urbanemissions.info/
5. IndiaAQ Hub. A digital knowledge hub on air pollution in India: https://indiaaq.blog/
6. Policy briefs and op-eds from Collaborative Clean Air Policy Centre: https://ccapc.org.in/
7. Centre for Policy Research's air pollution seminar series: https://www.cprindia.org/projects/clearing-air-air-quality-regulation-and-governance-india and op-ed series: https://www.cprindia.org/news/clearing-air-op-ed-series-india%E2%80%99s-air-pollution-crisis
8. Air Quality monitoring and forecasting by ISRO: https://airquality.iirs.gov.in/

I use Twitter and would like to follow accounts that talk about air quality in India. Who do I follow?

@CareforAirIndia
@LetMeBreathe_In (also on Instagram)
@airqualityindia (also on Instagram)
@carboncopyinfo
@LungCareFoundation
@UrbanEmissions
@DrMariaNeira
@IQAir
@IITMPune
@m_parrington
@somagnik

@pawanpgupta
@myrighttobreathe
@warriormoms

Other resources

1. 'The Weight of Numbers: Air Pollution and PM2.5', *Undark*. https://undark.org/breathtaking/
2. To read about the health effects of air pollution:
   2.1. 'Health effects of air pollution', *State of Global Air*, 2019. https://www.stateofglobalair.org/sites/default/files/soga_2019_health_effects_factsheet.pdf
   2.2. 'Revealed: air pollution may be damaging "every organ in the body"' by Damian Carrington, *Guardian*, 17 May 2019. https://www.theguardian.com/environment/ng-interactive/2019/may/17/air-pollution-may-be-damaging-every-organ-and-cell-in-the-body-finds-global-review
   2.3. Collaborative on Health and the Environment, 2019: https://www.healthandenvironment.org/environmental-health/environmental-risks/global-environment/air-quality
3. Learn to decode what Air Quality Index means and check the AQI in your city:
   3.1. 'What Does the Air Quality Index Really Show Us?'by Santosh Harish and Pallavi Pant, *Quint*, 15 November 2019. https://fit.thequint.com/health-news/explaining-air-quality-index
   3.2. Central Pollution Control Board website. https://app.cpcbccr.com/AQI_India/
4. 'What can individuals do to reduce personal health risks from air pollution?' by Robert Laumbach, Qingyu Meng, and Howard Kipen, *Journal of Thoracic Disease*, 2015. https://www.ncbi.nlm.nih.gov/pmc/articles/PMC4311076/
5. 'Fighting for Clean Air Around the Globe', *OpenAQ*, 2018. https://files.wri.org/s3fs-public/fighting-clean-air-around-globe.pdf. This provides a perspective into what shapes the fight for clean air.
6. C40 Knowledge Hub resources on air quality: www.c40knowledgehub.org
7. What can cities do to address air pollution?
   'Accelerating City Progress on Clean Air: Innovation and Action Guide', *Vital Strategies*, 2020.www.vitalstrategies.org
8. I hear we need more air pollution monitoring but I have a lot of questions. Go to the 'Air Pollution Monitoring 101' page on UrbanEmissions.info for answers.
9. I hear we need good source apportionment data but I'm not sure I know what that means.

Go to the 'Primer on Pollution Source Apportionment' page on UrbanEmissions.info to learn about source apportionment.

10. NASA Worldview – Near Realtime Satellite Data Access: www.worldview.earthdata.nasa.gov
11. 'Addressing Global Mortality from Ambient PM2.5' by Joshua Apte et.al., *Environmental Science and Technology*, 2015. www.pubs.acs.org
12. 'Delhi's Air Pollution and Its Effects on Children's Health', *Yale Global Health Review*.
13. 'Government indifference over air pollution crisis in Delhi', *The Lancet Planetary Health*, 1 December 2017.
14. 'Air pollution retards lung growth in Delhi children; studies point to health emergency', *Down to Earth*, 15 November 2017.

Videos, podcasts and infographics

1. 'Smog War – Polish Air Pollution Documentary', YouTube, uploaded by Ramsey United, 12 September 2019, https://www.youtube.com/watch?v=Xs70ewSdEjE
   Following the historically smoggy winter of 2016–17, Michał Konopa, a Warsaw-based father of an asthmatic child, decides to make a film about the complex world of Polish smog during the winter 'burning season' of 2017–18.
2. 'Dying to breathe: Mongolia's polluted air', YouTube, uploaded by Unreported World, 29 April 2018, https://www.youtube.com/watch?v=kUNuHxrd7Y0
3. 'Fleeing climate change – the real environmental disaster', YouTube, uploaded by DW Documentary, 1 May 2019, https://www.youtube.com/watch?v=cl4Uv9_7KJE
4. WHO Breathe Life, https://breathelife2030.org/resources/#video-infographic-library
5. 'Under the Dome (English subtitle, complete) by Chai Jing: Air pollution in China', YouTube, uploaded by Jiahua Guo, 8 March 2015, https://www.youtube.com/watch?v=V5bHb3ljjbc
6. Miscellaneous infographics from Urban Emissions, available at https://urbanemissions.info/resources/infographs/
7. 'Delhi's Deadly Air', Al Jazeera, 5 June 2019, https://www.aljazeera.com/programmes/peopleandpower/2019/05/delhi-deadly-air-190529055623225.html
8. 'Joel Kaufman: "Air Pollution and Cardiovascular Disease: Research and Implications"', YouTube, uploaded by University of Washington School of Public Health, 20 August 2012, https://www.youtube.com/watch?v=t1t4tj9sRq8

9. 'Air pollution and lung cancer: testimony of a surgeon from New Delhi', YouTube, uploaded by World Health Organization (WHO), 12 November 2018, https://www.youtube.com/watch?v=TWP5gMyIw1k
10. 'Why is air pollution a problem?', YouTube, uploaded by British Heart Foundation, 2 March 2017, https://www.youtube.com/watch?v=vYSAPwQwMTk
11. 'Talks@ATREE - Pallavi Pant' on the Air Pollution Narrative in India: Delhi and Beyond, YouTube, uploaded by ATREE Bangalore, 6 August 2018, https://www.youtube.com/watch?v=5Vp7vMxEY1w
12. *An Inconvenient Truth* (2006) and *An Inconvenient Sequel: Truth To Power* (2017), films about former United States Vice President Al Gore's campaign to educate people about global warming.
14. A list of films on air pollution is available at: https://www.greenfilmfest.org/airpollution2019
15. 'Checking Air Quality from Space', YouTube, uploaded by Pawan Gupta, 29 October 2019, https://www.youtube.com/watch?v=jpyLuGkTw2o&feature=youtu.be
16. 'ScienceCasts: Monitoring Air Quality', YouTue, uploaded by ScienceAtNASA, 27 June 2016, https://www.youtube.com/watch?v=qkY5oFQD2cc

Information brochures

1. 'Air Quality and Health', *European Respiratory Society*. https://www.ersnet.org/pdf/publications/air-quality-ENG.pdf
2. American Lung Association has a wealth of resources on air pollution and human health https://www.lung.org/clean-air

Newsletters

1. Carbon Brief's Newsletters: www.carbonbrief.org
2. The UNEARTH Bulletin: www.indicus.org
3. Carbon Copy Newsletter: https://carboncopy.info/
4. Air Pollution News Digest by Clean Air Collective

Apps to check air pollution levels in India

1. Plume Air Report
2. Air Quality: Real time AQI
3. SAFAR
4. IQAir
5. Sh**t! I Smoke
6. PurpleAir

Websites to aid learning

1. World Health Organization: https://www.who.int/health-topics/air-pollution#tab=tab_1
2. Down to Earth Available: https://www.downtoearth.org.in/
3. SatAQ: https://sataq.net/
4. SAFAR: http://safar.tropmet.res.in/
5. Urban Emissions Info.: http://www.urbanemissions.info/
6. Council On Energy, Environment And Water: www.ceew.in
7. Air Pollution Action Group: https://a-pag.org/
8. Vital Strategies: https://www.vitalstrategies.org/programs/air-pollution-and-health/

What organizations can I volunteer at or help out at?

Here is a loose list of organizations that have banded under the umbrella of 'Clean Air Collective', and are growing every day, just in case you would like to join or donate to any of them after your own due diligence. Depending on our volunteer strength, this list will also be up on careforair.org and will be updated regularly.

- Air Pollution Action Group
- AirPollution.io
- Bengal Clean Air Network (Bengal-CAN)
- Blue Sky Analytics
- Care for Air
- CAG (Citizen Consumer and Civic Action Group)
- CEEW (Council on Energy Environment and Water)
- Carbon Copy/Climate Trends
- Chakr Innovation Pvt. Ltd.
- Chintan
- Clean Air Asia
- Clean Air Fund
- Centre for Chronic Disease Control
- CSE (Centre for Science and Environment)
- CPR (Center for Policy Research)
- CSTEP (Centre for Study of Science, Technology and Policy)
- Centre for Environment Education
- CEED (Center for Environment and Energy Development)
- CREA (Centre for Research on Energy and Clean Air)
- Conservation Action Trust
- Doctors for Clean Air
- EarthDay org
- Energy Policy Institute at the University of Chicago (EPIC India)
- Envecologic
- Gati Foundation
- Greenpeace
- Green Planet Society

- Haiyya
- HEAL
- Help Delhi Breathe
- Health Care Without Harm
- IndiaAQ Hub
- India Climate Collaborative
- Indicus Foundation
- Indian Institute of Public Health
- Indraprastha Institute of Information Technology
- Integrated Research and Action for Development (IRADe)
- Jhatkaa.org
- Jorro Networks
- Kolkata Clean Air
- Legal Initiative for Forest and Environment
- Let India Breathe
- #MRTB (My Right to Breathe)
- NRDC (Natural Resources Defense Council)
- New Delhi Nature Society
- National Coalition on Inclusive and Sustainable Urbanisation (NCISU)
- Parisar
- Peoples Resource Centre / National Alliance of People's Movements
- Pi Green innovations Pvt ltd
- Public Health Foundation of India
- Purpose
- Respirer Living Sciences/ UrbanSciences
- Rocky Mountain Institute
- Saahas
- Sensing Local
- Shakti Sustainable Energy Foundation
- Swechha
- SwitchON Foundation
- The Climate Group
- The Nature Conservancy
- The Regulatory Assistance Project
- United Way Delhi
- URJA (United Residents Joint Action)
- UrbanEmissions.in
- Urban Voices.in
- Vanashakti
- Warrior Moms
- Watawaran
- WWF India
- WRI
- YLAC (Young Leaders for Active Citizenship)
- 3MinLive